"I don't mind whe

Her eyes widened, as if she were surprised by her own words.

He was touched by the admission. "A woman should enjoy her man's kiss, not merely allow it." With her face bathed in the soft light of the moon streaking in through the window, she looked vulnerable.

"I'm not sure I know how to enjoy." Her words were brutally honest. "C-could you…"

He leaned closer, enclosing her with his body. "What would you like, *piccola*?"

"A kiss. Like it's supposed to be," she whispered.

Her words betrayed that, for her, kissing had never been a pleasure. One day soon, he'd find out who had abused her, but for tonight, he would kiss her as an innocent was meant to be kissed—with tenderness and just a stroke of passion.

Just enough to tantalise.

The Seduction Request
by Michelle Celmer

৩ᗰ৩

Realising that Matt had gone awfully quiet, she glanced up and caught him staring at the front of her shirt.

Again. All through dinner he'd been looking at her, undressing her with his eyes.

"They're breasts, Matt. I'm sure you've seen plenty, so mine shouldn't be all that fascinating."

He had the decency to look apologetic. "Sorry, I just can't get used to the way you look now."

"*Different,* right?"

"Good, Em. You look *really* good."

She narrowed her eyes at him. "Let's be clear on something, Conway. Friendship is one thing but I am not, under any circumstances, going to sleep with you again."

Something hot and dangerous sparked in his eyes and her knees instantly went mushy. "That sounds like a challenge, Emily. And you know how much I love a challenge."

Available in December 2005 from Silhouette Desire

The Fierce and Tender Sheikh
by Alexandra Sellers
&
Daring the Dynamic Sheikh
by Kristi Gold

ᎦᎠᏇ

Branded
&
Caught in the Crossfire
by Annette Broadrick

ᎦᎠᏇ

Awaken to Pleasure
by Nalini Singh
&
The Seduction Request
by Michelle Celmer

ᎦᎠᏇ

Never Naughty Enough
by Jill Monroe
&
Warm & Willing
by Kate Hoffmann

Awaken to Pleasure
NALINI SINGH

The Seduction Request
MICHELLE CELMER

SILHOUETTE®
Desire™

DID YOU PURCHASE THIS BOOK WITHOUT A COVER?
If you did, you should be aware it is **stolen property** as it was
reported *unsold and destroyed* by a retailer. Neither the author nor
the publisher has received any payment for this book.

*All the characters in this book have no existence outside the
imagination of the author, and have no relation whatsoever to anyone
bearing the same name or names. They are not even distantly inspired
by any individual known or unknown to the author, and all the
incidents are pure invention.*

*All Rights Reserved including the right of reproduction in whole or in
part in any form. This edition is published by arrangement with
Harlequin Enterprises II B.V. The text of this publication or any part
thereof may not be reproduced or transmitted in any form or by any
means, electronic or mechanical, including photocopying, recording,
storage in an information retrieval system, or otherwise, without
the written permission of the publisher.*

*This book is sold subject to the condition that it shall not, by way of
trade or otherwise, be lent, resold, hired out or otherwise circulated
without the prior consent of the publisher in any form of binding or cover
other than that in which it is published and without a similar condition
including this condition being imposed on the subsequent purchaser.*

*Silhouette, Silhouette Desire and Colophon
are registered trademarks of Harlequin Books S.A.,
used under licence.*

*First published in Great Britain 2005
Silhouette Books, Eton House, 18-24 Paradise Road,
Richmond, Surrey TW9 1SR*

The publisher acknowledges the copyright holders of the
individual works as follows:

Awaken to Pleasure © Nalini Singh 2004
The Seduction Request © Michelle Celmer 2004

ISBN 0 373 60222 7

51-1205

*Printed and bound in Spain
by Litografia Rosés S.A., Barcelona*

AWAKEN TO PLEASURE
by
Nalini Singh

NALINI SINGH

has always wanted to be a writer. Along the way to her dream, she obtained degrees in both the arts and law (because being a starving writer didn't appeal). After a short stint as a lawyer, she sold her first book, and from that point, there was no going back. Now an escapee from the corporate world, she is looking forward to a lifetime of writing, interspersed with as much travel as possible. Currently residing in Japan, Nalini loves to hear from readers. You can contact her via the following e-mail address: nalini@nalinisingh.com; or by writing to her c/o Silhouette Books, 233 Broadway, Suite 1001, New York, NY 10279, USA.

To Diane Dietz, editor extraordinaire, and the team at Silhouette Desire—thanks for taking a chance on me.

One

Rain slashed against the windscreen of Jackson's car with fierce intensity. Aware of the dangers inherent in the dark winter's night, he kept the speed of his powerful car well under control, watching out for reckless pedestrians.

However, in sharp contrast to the usual Friday night crowds, there was an almost deserted air about the brightly lit centre of Auckland. He knew it was illusionary. The revelers were there but hidden in soundproofed, weatherproofed basements and upstairs rooms, full of pumping music that drowned out the driving rain. He'd passed one such room on his way out of his studio office. It had been the site of a wrap party for a murder drama.

A reed-thin blonde had caught him leaving the building and invited him to join in. Her eyes had been frank with invitation for a much more private party. Unfortunately for her ambition, he didn't play those kinds of games, and ever since Bonnie, blondes held about as much appeal as arsenic.

After the day he'd had, all he wanted was some cognac and a hot bath. Taylor looked like she could do with both. The poor baby was standing outside in the icy rain, waiting for a bus, her face pinched with cold. She could probably do with a hot man in bed as well but…

Taylor?

Standing in the pouring rain under a barely glowing street-light, shivering and blue?

"Dio!" He screeched to a stop and then backed up, thanking God for the lack of traffic. As soon as he reached her, he leaned across and threw open the passenger door. "Get the hell in!" The weather obliged, but Taylor didn't.

The sodden woman outside made a face, as if debating whether to take his less than warm offer. Needle-sharp rain continued to pelt her, hard and certainly painful, even through the thick wool of her pantsuit. "The bus is supposed to come any m-m-m-minute."

Her chattering teeth enraged Jackson. For a second, he thought he saw fear in those big eyes of hers but it had to have been a trick of the light. He'd never met a woman less afraid of him than this bedraggled creature. "Get in here right now, Taylor."

She looked like she was going to be obstinate, but then the universe took pity on him. It started to hail. With a tiny shriek that was undeniably feminine, she scrambled into the car and pulled the door shut. Her trembling hands immediately went to the warm air circulating from the ventilation shafts.

He turned up the heat before pulling away from the curb to make a right turn instead of going left. Taylor lived on the opposite side of the city from him. Outside, the night had become immeasurably darker, but the hailstorm petered away after a short but brutal reign.

"I'm wet…your car…" Taylor began, through lips that were blue with cold.

He was furious with her. "It'll dry." A plume of water from a passing motorist momentarily blanketed the windscreen in sleet. He slowed to a crawl until the vehicle had passed, taking the chance to send a glare Taylor's way. "What the hell were you doing catching a bus at this time of night?" His voice was a lacerating whip. How dare she put herself in such a vulnerable position?

"None of your b-b-business." The sound of chattering teeth destroyed her attempt at a haughty dismissal.

"Taylor," he warned, in a tone that he only used when his temper was on the thinnest edge, as she very well knew.

"You're not my boss anymore, so don't *Taylor* me." His passenger's unrepentant stubbornness was a living being in the air around them.

Jackson was used to being obeyed, especially by pretty young women. Everyone loved the man who could get them onto the silver screen, though he remembered vividly that Taylor harbored no such ambition. He also recalled the steely spine beneath that beautiful exterior. Aware that the more he demanded, the more obstinate she'd become, he tried a calmer approach. "I'm being a Good Samaritan. Humor me."

She didn't say anything for a while but he figured that was because she was thawing out. When she finally spoke, what she revealed made his blood boil. All thoughts of calming down were consigned to the deepest hell.

"My ride wanted more than I did. I left." Out of the corner of his eye, he could see her huddling into the seat. The small sign of vulnerability tore at him. All of his protective instincts awoke fully armed.

"Did he hurt you?" His hands had turned into claws on the steering wheel.

A pause. "No."

"Taylor."

"Don't Taylor me!" she cried again, but her voice broke at the end—another uncharacteristic sign of weakness. "He was a bozo." She sniffed. "I thought he was someone I could trust. We were at a party on the Shore thrown by Dracena Medical—the place where I've been temping for the past three months. My contract ended yesterday, but they invited me to the party anyway. When it began to break up, one of the project directors offered a few of us a ride home. I didn't realize that I was going to be the last one left in the car until it was too late." She was babbling, betraying her fear even as she tried to convince him of the lightness of the matter.

"I'd never have gone with him otherwise. I thought I'd get dropped off first because the others live farther out, but apparently, they'd all decided to get off in the city and go dancing. He didn't tell me that. I still thought it would be okay until…well, as soon as the others left, he started talking about…s-spending the night with me."

Jackson became quietly murderous at the evidence of this man's predetermination to get her alone. "Did he hurt you?" he repeated, knowing that she'd told him the truth about why she'd accepted the ride. He'd long ago learned of her wariness around most men.

She mumbled something under her breath.

"Did. He. Hurt. You?" He was ruthless, aware that her emotional state made her susceptible to questioning. Freed from the constraints which had forced him to keep his distance in the past, he would protect her with every breath in his body. "Answer me."

"He ripped my shirtsleeve when I was leaving the car. And he's got my purse. No big deal," she muttered.

A wave of red rose in front of his eyes. "Name?" Taylor had always touched the deepest, most primitive part of him. Tonight, that part was beyond furious.

"Jackson, I…" She sounded hesitant.

"Name?" The night outside wasn't as dark as his thoughts about the man who'd dared to assault her.

"Why?" The question was far more confident, his stubborn, temperamental Taylor rising back from the upsetting experience.

He gave her an imminently reasonable answer. "How else are you going to get your purse back?"

"You're, um…not going to mess him up are you?"

"What do you think I am—some sort of mobster?" He was well aware that he looked like one. Big, dark and thickly muscled. Half of that was genetics. Being part Italian and part Viking tended to do that to a man. The other half was nightmares. Exercise took his mind off them. Add his black hair and eyes and he could easily pass for one of the mafioso.

"Maybe." She didn't sound timid, as one should while conversing with a mobster.

"I'll just pick up your purse. No problem," he lied. This creep was going to have major problems.

"Promise you won't hurt him first."

"Why?" The thought that this might've been just a lovers' quarrel rocked him. Pain squeezed his gut at the idea of her wrapped in another man's arms. Blinded and numbed by the horrifying revelation after Bonnie's death more than a year ago, had he left his pursuit of Taylor too late?

"Because I don't want you in trouble."

The relief he felt at her response should have shocked him. "Tell me his name."

"Promise first or I won't say." She folded her arms. The smell of wet wool rose into the air.

He swore under his breath, well aware that she was mule-headed enough to do exactly that. "I promise not to touch him," he gritted out.

Deprived of his preferred form of revenge, he accepted that the man could be taught a lesson in another way. He knew a few men whom he could count on to do what was right, and one of them was a detective in sex crimes.

There was silence from the recalcitrant woman in the passenger seat, as if she was debating whether or not to trust his promise. At last, she sighed. "Donald Carson."

He nodded, absurdly pleased that his word was good enough for her. "Are you warm yet?" He was beginning to overheat, but she'd been soaking. She needed to get out of those wet clothes but he wasn't going to make that insane suggestion. Being alone with a naked Taylor was not the best of ideas. Especially when the primitive side of his nature was blazing with the need to brand her with his mark.

"Getting there." Her voice was soft, unintentionally stoking the hunger inside of him.

Desire burned through the anger, turning his voice rough. "There is a picnic blanket in the back seat." He was aware that the cadence of his speech was changing, as his long-dormant instincts awoke. It was a habit that betrayed too much, and he made a concerted effort to rein it in.

He heard her move. "It's still in the plastic wrap."

"It was part of a gift. I threw it back there months ago." Rain pounded the windscreen as he drove out into a particularly unsheltered part of the road. "You still live in New Lynn?" He named a suburb about thirty minutes out of New Zealand's biggest city, under normal circumstances.

"Uh-huh." Her voice was muffled.

When he chanced a quick glance, he saw that only her bright little face remained uncovered by the woolen blanket. With long black hair beginning to curl in the heat, and thickly lashed blue eyes smudged with tiredness, she looked like a bedraggled and bad-tempered kitten.

And he wanted to scoop her up into his lap and kiss and cuddle her until she melted for him.

His reaction to Taylor went against all of the vows he'd

made after he'd found out the terrible revenge Bonnie had taken on him for leaving her. Standing over his estranged wife's grave, he'd sworn to never again let a woman close enough to wound him so terribly. At that moment, while his heart felt like it had been ripped from his chest to lie torn and bleeding on the crying earth, such a vow had been easy to make.

However, around Taylor, that pain-fueled promise held about as much weight as air. She'd affected him in an inescapable way since the minute he'd first seen her standing in his office doorway. Married at the time, he'd convinced himself that he liked Taylor because she was a good kid and a hard worker. Now, there was no Bonnie, and he'd seen Taylor with her blouse stuck to breasts that were definitely those of a woman.

"Where's your brother?" He tried to lead his mind down less inflammatory paths, but all the while he was thinking that maybe it was time he gave his instincts what they'd always craved. A long, slow taste of sweet little Taylor.

"Nick's on a wilderness camp with his class, in Riverhead forest, just out of the city."

That explained why she was out so late, as she organized her life around Nick's needs. He'd only met her brother twice, once during a barbeque for employees' families and again when he'd unexpectedly needed Taylor to come into work on a Saturday and she hadn't been able to find a sitter. However, Taylor's daily reports—glowing updates more like a mother would give of her firstborn, than a sister of her brother—had made him feel like he knew the boy intimately.

"You're still temping with the same agency?"

"Yes."

"I've asked for you when I needed a temp." Each time, the hapless replacement had had to bear the brunt of his unreasonable temper at her absence.

"Oh." She turned a little toward him. "I didn't know." A pause. "I don't work in the film industry anymore."

"Why not film?" Had she been avoiding him, he thought with a flare of anger that was rooted in possessiveness that he'd never consciously acknowledged. Until now.

"It's not the kind of environment I want to be in."

Stopping at a red light, he faced her. "Environment?"

She shrugged, her cheeks a little pink. "Excess, glamour, money, money, money."

He'd always known that she'd fight against coming into his world. "What about art?"

"What about it?" she scoffed.

He smiled and accelerated with care when the light turned green. "Poor Taylor. Disillusioned so young."

"Don't patronize me." The order was sharp.

She'd been the only one of his secretaries who'd given him backchat. He'd offered her a permanent position after her contract ended, but she'd been adamant in her desire to leave. He'd wanted her more than he'd craved anything in his life, but honor had forced him to let her go, before he stole both her youth and her innocence. Yet, he'd kept waiting for her to walk back through the door. The memory made his voice curt. "Sorry."

"No, you're not."

He shrugged. "What can I say? For a kid, you're very cynical." At thirty-two, he was only eight years her senior, but in his heart, he was decades too old.

Taylor's temper started to simmer. Why did Jackson always treat her like a child? "I'm not a kid!" Her feelings around him were definitely those of an adult.

His big body tended to do things to her insides that scared her, because she had no idea what to do to feed those wild, hot feelings. With her history, she could never, ever allow

NALINI SINGH

herself to love a man, but the minute she'd met Jackson Santorini, she'd learned that she couldn't stop herself from lust-
ing after this particular male.

A deep chuckle heated both her cheeks *and* her temper.
"Next to me, you're a baby."

"Crap." She was so furious that she could barely get the
single word out.

"Crap?" He was laughing at her again, in that superior
masculine way of his that made her want to scream.

"Age makes no difference to the person you become
once you're an adult." She needed him to accept her as a
woman, though she shied away from the implications of
that need.

"Of course it does." His response was infuriatingly calm.
"More experience, more life lived."

"More years doesn't necessarily mean more experience!"

His sardonic look dared her to prove it.

She did, goaded beyond endurance. "I'm bringing up a
child. Can you say the same?"

"No." His response was so cold that the inside of the car
suddenly felt like a freezer.

It was clear that she'd offended him deeply with her care-
less words. Not for the first time, she wondered if his child-
less marriage had been his choice. "I'm sorry," she said
quietly, "I shouldn't have said that."

"It's true." An emotionless response.

She bit her lip, debating whether to continue. "Yes. But
so soon after Bonnie's death…I shouldn't have said it. I
wasn't thinking."

It was her own emotional anguish over the possibility of
losing custody of Nick to her stepfather, Lance, that had
made her so reckless. Even tonight's desperate attempt to forget her fears for a few hours had ended in a nightmare. Except for being picked up by Jackson, her day had been sheer

hell. And now, she'd made him angry. Somehow, that was the worst feeling of all.

"It's been twelve months since Bonnie overdosed." Jackson knew his voice was hard, but so had been surviving the losses a year ago. "You know our marriage was finished long before then. Hell, the whole world knew."

They'd been married, but not to each other. He'd had his work and for a brief glittering moment of pure happiness, Taylor's smile. Bonnie had had drugs. They hadn't even slept together for over two years, except for that one fateful time four months before her death.

She'd been so lovely that day, a shimmering memory of the girl he'd wed, before news of her father's death had stolen her joy. He'd long since learned that that girl had been a mirage, but when she'd turned to him for comfort, he hadn't been able to deny her. Not when grief had ripped apart the mask of sophistication that had become her face.

And they'd created a child.

Whom Bonnie had murdered when she'd taken her life with a cocktail of drugs. If she hadn't, he might have been a parent, too, able to refute Taylor's claim. He could still feel the knives that had sliced through his soul when the autopsy had revealed her to be pregnant. Further tests had proven that the child had been his flesh and blood.

But, even that incredible grief hadn't compared to his rage at discovering that Bonnie had known of the tiny life growing inside of her. She'd known that his child was in her womb when she'd taken her final lover, and she'd known that his child was in her womb when she'd ingested the fatal drug cocktail.

At that moment of understanding, hate had spread through his body like a virus, decimating his ability to feel tender emotions.

Two

"**S**he could be nice sometimes," Taylor said, betraying the soft heart behind that tough exterior.

"When she wasn't drugged to the gills." He knew too much about the kind of pain "nice" Bonnie could inflict.

"I wonder why she did all those things."

He knew she was talking about the drugs and that final affair, unearthed by the press and gleefully announced to the world. What would she say if he told her that Bonnie's famous lover had been the last in a string of men?

He'd stopped touching Bonnie as soon as he'd discovered the infidelities. His love for her had died long before. After a lonely, barren childhood, her joyful charm had drawn him, only to teach him an even deeper sense of isolation. They hadn't shared a bed again, except for that day four months before her death. After hours spent at work in Taylor's company, aching for things he had no right to demand, his defenses had been at an all-time low. Seeing Bonnie smile after

weeks of depression, he'd desperately wanted to believe that
they could salvage their marriage.

As the forgotten child of an impulsive celebrity union,
he'd promised himself that he would not repeat the cycle of
divorce and remarriage that characterized his parents, and
which had already spread to his three younger half siblings.
Even the youngest, Valetta, had a broken marriage under her
belt.

Driven by that promise, he'd kept trying to glue together
his and Bonnie's shattered relationship. He'd even let Taylor go without a single touch, stifling the hungry need her
presence always aroused.

But even his most precious vows had a breaking point—
he hated Bonnie for teaching him that lesson. The final straw
had come the day she'd flaunted her faithlessness, meeting
her newest lover in a place haunted by the paparazzi. That
humiliating betrayal had forever severed any remaining loyalty he'd had toward the girl he'd married, and he'd immediately filed for divorce.

He still remembered her reaction.

"Oh please," she'd mocked, cocktail in hand. It had been
barely 10:00 a.m. "As if you've been faithful."

The tragedy was, he had. The only infidelity he could be
accused of was of the mind. In his bleakest moments, he
hadn't been able to stop thinking about Taylor, but he
would've never touched her while a wedding band encircled
his finger. *Never.* She deserved better than that.

After he'd walked out on Bonnie, a cautious hope had
taken root in his heart. Once the divorce was final, he'd intended to seek out Taylor and see if someone so young and
untouched could find something to love in him.

Then all of his dreams had crumbled to dust. Bonnie's
death hadn't shocked him; she'd been trying to kill herself
for years. It was discovering the murder of his child that had

destroyed his hope. He'd been bleeding too badly to do anything but merely function.

Taylor's voice broke into the nightmarish memories. "I mean, Bonnie had beauty, talent, wealth and you. What was missing in her life?"

Jackson's heart slammed hard into his rib cage at her befuddled tone. "Maybe I'm not such a prize."

"I know you're incredibly loyal and generous. Your protectiveness might annoy your wife but she'd know it sprang from deep caring. That would make it bearable."

Her naive belief in his goodness rocked him to the deepest recesses of his misbegotten soul. "I wish you were a reporter." They'd savaged him after Bonnie's last affair, taken his humiliation and broadcast it to the world. Jackson Santorini's private pain sold a lot of papers.

When Bonnie had overdosed, they'd turned on him again, like a pack of wild dogs, vicious and unfeeling. But, they'd done such a good job the first time around, he couldn't give them any more rage or any more anguish.

"Plus, you're gorgeous." Taylor wondered what she was doing. Her words were true. What was also true was that she could never deliver on the promise implied in the flirtatious tone. And even if she could have, she was nowhere near Jackson's league. The man was linked with superstar actresses whose beauty shone from the silver screen and glittered on red carpets.

Just last week, she'd read an article where a titian-haired actress had stated that the reclusive head of Santorini Studios was her dream man. Though the megastar couldn't understand why such an important man chose to live in so small a country, it made him all the more interesting to her. All the more desirable.

"I don't think anyone would describe me as gorgeous." Jackson's response was dry. "But thank you."

She scowled. "You're not pretty, not like the actors. There's nothing soft about you. Your face is strong, interesting...gorgeous." She wasn't going to back down. Just like the world-famous actress, dark-eyed, dark-haired Jackson Santorini was her dream man.

Some people might say that he was a little too muscular, but on Jackson, the bulk looked good. Very, *very* good. She wanted to reach over and squeeze one of those taut arm muscles to see if there was any give at all. Then she wanted to bite down on that firm, golden flesh.

And therein lay her problem.

Jackson had been the best employer she'd ever had. The most demanding but also the most appreciative. A permanent job with him would've been perfect...if she hadn't stupidly gone and fallen in lust with her married boss.

Until she'd met him, she'd thought of lust as something frightening and dirty. Given her childhood, she knew that was understandable. But, the moment she'd seen Jackson Santorini in the flesh, it had hit her like a thunderbolt. She'd been flabbergasted, having no idea what to do about the heat that pooled in her stomach like high-octane fuel whenever he so much as glanced at her.

Even more disturbing were the other emotions that had crept in while she wasn't guarding her back. Dangerous emotions like trust. And hope.

Not that she'd ever followed up on the attraction. Touching another woman's husband was an unbreakable taboo. Even if her morals hadn't stopped her, practicality would have—she'd seen firsthand what happened to discarded mistresses. But she hadn't been able to stop fantasizing about her sexy Italian boss, even as she adamantly refused to open the door to any other feeling.

When the media storm had broken over Bonnie's lover, she'd wanted to slap the other woman for throwing away a man of Jackson's worth. Though she'd had no right, she'd ached to go to him, and try and soothe his unbearable pain. How *dare* that woman hurt Jackson where he was most vulnerable—in that proud heart of his?

It had been over a year since their last meeting but her feelings hadn't changed. Even her upsetting experience at Donald's hands couldn't alter that, because she trusted Jackson on a gut level. She'd never felt safe with a man until he'd started bullying her with his protectiveness, walking her to her car and more than once following her home late at night to ensure that she arrived safely. And he'd *never* made any demands in return.

The truth was, her sexy ex-boss still made her burn.

Jackson was stunned by Taylor's little speech. Nobody had ever called him gorgeous, not even starlets who thought he might be influenced by flattery. That was a lie too big even for them. And yet he knew that the woman in the passenger seat did not tell lies. Who else but Taylor would've dared to inform him that he looked like he was strung out on cocaine when he'd dragged himself into the office one Monday after fighting with Bonnie all weekend?

The question was, what was he going to do with the knowledge that she considered him gorgeous? At that moment, his attention was caught by flashing red lights up ahead. "Looks like there might have been an accident."

"I hope no one was hurt." Taylor leaned forward, blanket clutched tight. When he glanced at her, he saw that heat had given her face a soft pink glow that was at once enchanting and innocently seductive.

"Let's see." Reaching the poncho-clad cop standing in the middle of the street, he wound down the window. Sharp drops of rain immediately assaulted his face. "What's the problem, officer?"

The young man leaned down. His eyes flicked to Taylor and then back to Jackson. "There's been a three-car crash up ahead. Pretty messy. We're detouring people up though there." He pointed to an upward-sloping street on his right, the route marked with orange safety cones.

Jackson nodded. "Was anyone badly injured?"

"No fatalities." His relief was clear. "Drive safely." Moving back, he let them pass.

After turning up the small incline, Jackson said, "Look, you need to dry out and with this detour and the weather, we won't reach your place for at least another hour." Water sloshed around the tires as he came to a level section of the road. "You can spend the night at my place—the drive will only take twenty minutes."

"I can't do that!" she cried.

"Why?" It angered him that she didn't trust him, when he'd never given her reason not to. Okay, so maybe he'd yelled at her once or twice while she'd been his secretary, but she'd yelled right back and they'd got along fine.

Once again, she surprised him. "Because paparazzi stalk you. They're probably hiding in the bushes by the door. I don't want to be famous." She sounded determined.

He shook his head at her amazing mind. "If there is a paparazzo there tonight, *piccola,* I swear I'll beat him up for you." The endearment slipped out without thought. "Of course, he's probably already drowned."

A laugh escaped her. "Well, if you promise."

Traffic being much lighter on this side of the city, they reached his eight-month-old Mission Bay home in less time than he'd anticipated. Pressing an electronic key, he drove the car through the security gates. About fifty meters up the drive he pushed another button to raise the garage door before driving in. It shut behind them, enclosing them in a dry haven lit with a strong white bulb. The sound of rain on hard surfaces was muted to a soft lullaby, lending an unexpected intimacy to the air.

"Don't you think garages should have bleary yellow lights?" Taylor stretched out to pop her door open.

He let her lighten the mood, giving her space. For now. "You think something's wrong with my ambience?" Stepping out, he found her standing beside her door like some sort of disheveled fairy wrapped in tartan.

She wrinkled her nose at him. "When I'm no longer in danger of turning into an icicle, I'll tell you."

Biting back his first real smile for a year, he led her out of the garage, through the converted basement which he used as a gym, and up to the first floor of his home. "Bathroom's upstairs on the right." He pointed to the stairs leading up from the living room. "There should be fresh towels on the rails. I think the cleaning service came today. I'll find you a robe and throw it through."

"Don't peek." She started to struggle up the stairs, trying not to trip on the blanket she refused to release, an empress giving an order to a lowly servant.

Shaking his head at her impudence, he dropped his keys on a table in the living area and walked into his study.

Ignoring the blinking message light on his phone, he placed a call to the Auckland Police Station. As usual, Detective Cole McKenna was pulling the graveyard shift. After Jackson explained the matter to one of the few men he trusted implicitly, Cole swore creatively under his breath.

"Your lady doesn't want to press charges?"

Jackson thought about Taylor's attempts to brush off the entire incident. "I'd like to take care of it without pulling her into something messy."

"Yeah, that's what I figured. I need a diversion from paperwork anyway. Let's see—Donald Carson, Project Director at Dracena Medical." He tapped some keys. "Got him. I think 3:00 a.m. sounds like a good time for a visit."

Jackson itched to face Carson himself but he'd made a promise and if he saw the man, he'd surely break it. "Thanks."

"I'll swing by your place and drop off your Taylor's purse when I'm heading off shift, just after six."

Yes, Jackson thought, she was *his*. "I don't want Taylor to start thinking I'm about to get arrested so leave the black and white at the station," he joked, trying not to let his frustration at being unable to act himself seep into his tone.

Cole chuckled, seeing through him. "Lady must be something special if you're trying to behave."

They hung up on that note. His tension easing now that he'd done something about the man who'd dared to hurt Taylor, he quickly played back his messages. All four were from very smart people, including his mother, wanting something.

The demanding note in his mother's voice wasn't unusual. A rising star when she'd inconveniently fallen pregnant with Jackson to Anthony Santorini, her husband at the time, Liz Carlyle had had neither the time nor the inclination to raise her son. She'd saved that for his half brother Carlton, born almost ten years later.

As for Anthony, the celebrated director's paternal instincts had finally kicked in nine years after Jackson's birth, when he'd sired Mario closely followed by Valetta, with wife number three.

However, now that Jackson was a success, both Liz and Anthony preferred to forget that the closest they'd ever come to parenting him was writing checks for boarding schools and nannies. Neither had any compunction against using family ties to solicit his help. Frowning, he noted the details of the messages before erasing them. He'd take care of their requests later.

After he took care of Taylor.

Heading upstairs, he passed the closed door of his admittedly huge bathroom and entered his bedroom, knowing he had an unused robe someplace. Except when he reached the closet, he picked out his favorite.

The instant she shut the bathroom door, Taylor dropped the blanket and started removing her damp clothes, pausing only to place her cell phone in a safe spot. Clipped to the waistband of her pants, it hadn't disappeared with Donald. The small change in her pockets clinked as she dropped her pants to the floor—forgotten from an earlier purchase, the money would have been just enough for the bus.

She noted the sunken spa to the left but headed straight toward the shower. Encased in glass, it had an enormous amount of space, the fixtures steel and glass. Obviously, it had been custom-built for someone much bigger than her.

Immediately, her brain bombarded her with images of Jackson's muscled bulk in the shower, his arms bulging with strength as he did things to her in the watery enclosure that were surely not anatomically possible.

"Even if they were, you're such a coward that you'd run a mile if he tried."

With a self-mocking laugh that was tinged with a trace of disappointment, she stripped and stood in the centre of the cubicle, under the three showerheads. The spray hit her so high that she was in danger of drowning. She reached up and tried to tilt them down but they wouldn't budge. Giving up, she stood shivering on the tiles outside. Jackson's firm knock came a minute later. Cracking open the door, she peeked around it.

"You should be getting warmed up. I told you I'd throw it in." He scowled, all male annoyance and faintly menacing good looks.

And yet she trusted him. He had a rock-solid integrity that
defied her to put him in the same unflattering category as the
rest of his sex. A thought nudged at the back of her mind but
she pushed it aside. Her stepfather's attempt at wresting custody of Nick from her was *her* problem and despite his kindness, Jackson wouldn't want to know about it. After all,
she'd just been his temporary secretary.

She grabbed the robe, hiding behind the door. "Wait."
Snuggling into the garment, which smelt reassuringly of
Jackson and devoured her entire body, she tugged the door
fully open. "I need you to set the showerheads lower. I feel
like I'm standing under Niagara Falls."

Shaking his head, he walked into the humid room.
"They're electronic." He showed her a control panel on the
outside wall of the shower. "See?"

Taylor flicked her gaze up from her appreciative view of
his backside. The man was muscled *everywhere*. She
couldn't help but wonder what it would be like to run her
hands all over that beautiful golden skin. "How was I supposed to know your house was gadgety?" Grateful that she
sounded normal, she made a face at him. "Okay, fix them
anyway now that you're here."

Giving her one of his rare but extremely lethal grins, he
did as ordered. "Enough, shortie?"

Nurtured by the warmth of that smile, something woke in
her heart, something that wasn't lust. Used to protecting herself from emotions that promised joy but could just as well
lead to incredible suffering, she tried to ignore it. "Thanks,
Mr. Mobster." She could barely wait to luxuriate in the heat.
"I need to thaw now. Shoo."

He left with another grin that seared her nerves. Disgusted
at both her physical and unexpected emotional susceptibility to a man so far out of her reach, she shucked off the robe
and stepped into the shower.

* * *

Jackson stood outside the bathroom, trying to relearn to breathe. It wasn't easy when erotic visions of Taylor in black lace dominated his thoughts. His lovely guest had apparently started stripping at the door and not stopped 'til she'd reached the shower. Ignoring the trail of feminine clothes, ending in a pair of black lace panties, had been a forced lesson in self-control. Especially when he noticed that the bra matched.

He hadn't thought that Taylor would be the black lace type. Showed how much he knew. Groaning, he leaned on the wall with both hands and dropped his head against the white paint. His shoulders were rigid with tension, his jaw set as he wrestled with instinct.

"I will not seduce Taylor," he repeated over and over, and knew he was lying. Having her encased in his robe wasn't enough. He wanted her encased in him, while her body sheathed his in hot, wet welcome.

Poor, sweet Taylor would probably run a mile if she discovered what he was thinking. Bundled up in his white robe, she'd looked even smaller than usual. Though she wasn't a petite woman, next to his bulk she appeared fragile. His biceps bulged as he tensed his body, trying to tame the desire rippling through him, hot and voracious. Its talons tore at his control, hungering for heat and abandon and sheer, unadulterated pleasure.

Taylor had definitely awakened the sleeping tiger within him. The question was, did she have any interest in satiating it? Well…she *had* called him gorgeous. Despite his frustrated desire, he smiled, remembering the first time he'd seen her.

He'd looked up from drafting changes to a contract, expecting to find a mature woman in his office doorway. The agency knew his requirements. He didn't want some young would-be starlet trying to impress him with her "charms"— he wanted superb typing skills not mediocre acting skills.

The woman in the doorway had had dark hair pulled back into a severe bun, lush lips softened only by gloss and lovely blue eyes. He'd detected a trace of challenge in those too-blue eyes, as if his reputation didn't scare her. She'd been dressed in a knee-length skirt and fitted jacket, both in solid navy, looking every inch the executive assistant.

He'd wanted to groan in despair. It would've taken a blind man not to notice that she was stunning. He'd known from experience that if he gave her the slightest encouragement, she'd pull out some undoubtedly beautiful hair from that bun, undo the buttons on her jacket and sashay over.

"I need this dictation typed yesterday," he'd growled, throwing her a tape.

She'd caught it and left, without commenting on his brusqueness. Dismissing her from his mind, he'd started to race through another piece of work, aware that without a competent secretary, his day was likely to end sometime in the wee hours of the morning.

Less than half an hour later, she'd walked back in. Handing him several typed sheets, she'd picked up his handwritten edits to the contract and returned to her workstation. Wondering at her confidence, he'd turned his eyes to what she'd given him and just about died of shock.

Stalking out, he'd stood over her desk. "Name?"

"Taylor Reid." Her response had been cool.

"Do you want to be a movie star?"

Blue, blue eyes had widened. "Good God, no."

He'd grinned at that disgusted statement. It had been the first time that she'd made him smile. "Fine. Good work. Do I have you for the next three months?"

"Yes."

His delight in having found an extremely efficient secretary hidden beneath the form of a beautiful woman had been borne out. By the end of her first week, she'd organized his office, caught up on the backlog of filing and yelled at him when he'd raised his voice to her.

And somewhere along the way, he'd found himself coming to work just to hear her tart responses to his questions, and bask in her sunny smile. They'd never crossed any line, never even touched, but in his heart he'd known that he wanted to claim her as his woman. Only his promise to himself that he'd be faithful, unlike his philandering father and womanizing half brothers, had kept him from taking her. Or perhaps it had been the fact that Taylor had seen him as honorable and he'd wanted to live up to her expectations.

Now, there were no barriers to what he wanted to do with sweet, sexy Taylor, and his body was demanding he make up for almost three years of abstinence, broken only by that one, bittersweet afternoon with Bonnie. After her death, he'd had plenty of offers and no trouble refusing them all. He'd thought his emotional centre had died with his child, taking with it his need for a woman's soft touch. But his reaction to Taylor told him that his body hadn't shut down, it had merely gone into hibernation, waiting for the one woman who could bring him back to life.

Taylor.

The shower shut off. Shaking his head, he pushed off the wall and headed down the stairs to the kitchen. After her assault tonight, Taylor would hardly be reassured if she found him waiting for her outside the bathroom, blatantly aroused and more than ready to peel off her single layer of clothing. He didn't know if he could control himself around skin pink from heat, body naked and touchable under the robe. *His* robe.

Then, minutes later, she walked into the kitchen, wrapped in that damn robe. "Is that coffee I smell?"

He'd kicked off his shoes in the living room and saw that she was barefoot, too. "You'll get cold on the tiles. I'll find you some socks." He didn't even to try to fight his protective instincts toward her.

She came to stand next to him, holding out a hand for the cup of coffee he held. "Coffee first."

"This is…mine," he finished, as she stole the cup and took a big gulp. He watched her swallow, heard her sigh in appreciation and felt all sorts of things harden in his body. Her fresh, womanly scent made him want to strip her down to her glowing skin and crush her body under his, while his hands stroked and kneaded. Frowning, he backed off a couple of steps. "How are you feeling?"

"Better." She turned, cradling the cup in her palms. "Donald didn't really scare me—I guess I just felt betrayed." Disappointment edged her tone.

He understood. "You're safe here."

Her smile was glorious. "I know. I trust you."

Dio! he thought. No way in hell could he seduce her now. "I'll get you those socks."

"Don't worry about it. Let's go in the living room instead." She put down the now empty cup. "Are you coming?"

Bemused, he followed her into the spacious room. A small music system was arranged in wall brackets on the left, while a large sofa upholstered in blue sat against the opposite wall. However, the main feature was the floor-to-ceiling window immediately in front. Stretching from one end of the room to the other, it looked out over the sea to the dormant island volcano of Rangitoto. Tonight, the weather obscured most of the view, allowing only a glimpse of crashing breakers.

"It's so open." She walked across the plush dove-grey carpet to spread her palm against the glass.

He came to stand beside her. "It's reflective. No one can see inside, even if they get into the grounds."

Next to him, Taylor's profile was clean and pure. The curling hair around her face looked like it would be incredibly soft to the touch. The urge to reach out and test his theory was so strong that he shoved his hands into his pants pockets and clenched them tight.

"Your home's very tidy."

To him, it looked barren. "I don't live with a kid."

She smiled fondly. "He is a tad messy but I suppose muddy sneakers come with little boys."

"I'm surprised you let him go on the camp."

Her eyes moved from contemplating the turbulent sea to fix on his face. "What's that supposed to mean?"

He raised a brow. "You're very protective of Nick."

"I'm his only family." Her defensiveness was clear. "I can be protective if I want."

He left the topic for now, aware how touchy she was about her brother. He'd tried to broach the subject with her while she'd worked for him, but she'd frozen him out. At the time, he'd been frustrated at having to accept that he didn't have any rights over her brother...or over her.

Yet.

He wouldn't touch her tonight, because he'd promised her safety and he would never renege on that assurance. But, after tonight, all bets were off, because he wanted rights over Taylor. All sorts of rights.

Three

"One of the spare rooms is made up. It's to the right of the upstairs bathroom. My bedroom's across the hall if you need anything." Jackson's tone was businesslike.

Taylor knew a dismissal when she heard one. "Yes, boss." She looked from the tumultuous weather outside to the powerful man standing next to her. He could be just as dangerous as the storm winds.

"I certainly never heard that when you were working for me." His words were light but the look in his eyes was intensity itself, hot and possessive.

She knew what that look meant and had from a very early age. She just didn't want to deal with it. Heart thudding, she said an abrupt, "Good night," and left.

There was no lock on the bedroom door but she didn't worry. Jackson would never assault her. That didn't mean he didn't want her. In the past, when life had threatened to become too bleak or lonely, she'd hugged the awareness of his desire to her, safe in the knowledge that nothing would ever come of it. She wasn't that kind of woman.

And Jackson wasn't that kind of man. His personal code was stronger than lust or passion. He wouldn't have broken his wedding vows no matter what Bonnie had done. But now his wife was gone and he'd acknowledged the smoldering fire between them, if only with his dark eyes.

Confused by her warring emotions, Taylor started to get ready for bed and then realized she had nothing to sleep in. About to search the closet in the room, she heard a heavy tread outside her door. A curt knock followed.

Opening the door, she found Jackson holding out a white shirt. "Thought you might need this." His voice was low and that banked fire in his gaze wasn't apparent.

Her heart turned over. "Thanks." Just as she took the shirt, her cell phone, which she'd dropped into the pocket of her robe, rang. Immediately, worry shot through her. "That might be Nick. Hold on."

Unfortunately, it was her stepfather, Lance Hegerty, on the line. "Where are you, Taylor? No one's answering at your place. Where's my son?"

She knew he'd said the last deliberately—a cruel reminder that Nick was only her half brother. No matter that she'd raised him, in the eyes of the law she had less of a right to Nick than Lance, his biological father.

"Why are you calling? It's late." Her voice threatened to tremble. She crushed the shirt in her hand.

"You haven't responded yet."

She knew her face was losing its color. Turning her back to Jackson, she said, "I have two more weeks." A bare fourteen days before time expired to file legal papers in opposition to his claim for sole custody.

His laugh was cruel. "We can do it easy or we can do it hard but I'll win. Remember that and don't forget your place, brat—you're nothing but a rich man's castoff. My *son* deserves better than a life with you."

She hung up, hand shaking. Lance could reduce her to tears with a few well-chosen barbs, but she prided herself on never breaking down where he could see or hear her.

"Who was that?" Jackson demanded.

She could almost feel the heat of his big body against her back. The urge to tell him was overwhelming, but remnants of the fear generated by the call held her back. Jackson was a rich and powerful man, too. He might take Lance's side. Bewildered and a little lost, she could barely think. All she knew was that she couldn't let that monster take Nick. Suddenly, panic hit her. What if Lance took him by force? She had to call the camp and warn them!

When she turned to face Jackson, the clean, male scent of him taunted her with promises of safety. "Someone I don't want to talk to," she admitted, trying not to let him see the panic riding her.

"Do you want me to deal with it?"

She shook her head. "No. I think I'd like to go to sleep." Her words were blunt, her inner resources depleted by the force of her apprehension.

Though his dark eyes narrowed, he left, his shoulders almost filling the doorway. Despite the horrible feeling in the pit of her stomach, the urge to touch those shoulders made her throat dry. Big, strong Jackson seemed like the safest port in the storm of her life.

Trembling, she closed her door and immediately called Nick's camp counselor. After waking her from a deep sleep, she made the poor woman do a bed check on her brother and then swear that she'd ensure that no one but Taylor was allowed to pick him up, during or after camp. She wanted to go get him right now, but Nick had been so excited about the camp, she couldn't bear to cut it short.

Calmer now that she knew he was safe, she got out of the robe and into the shirt. It came almost to her knees and she had to fold back the cuffs several times before her hands poked through the sleeves. But, for some reason she didn't want to face, it comforted her to be wearing Jackson's shirt. She crawled into bed, craving sleep.

Instead, fear hammered at her temples, creating an excruciating headache. Whimpering in pain, she sat up, aware that her suffering was stress induced. She needed to release some of the pressure by asking for help—by asking Jackson? Out of the grip of the illogical terror that had bewildered her after the call, she knew that her fears that he'd take Lance's side were groundless. Jackson Santorini might be dictatorial and dominating, but unlike her tormentor, he had honor.

Life had forced her to be strong, but this time there were so many burdens on her that she felt as if she would collapse. Despite that, her heart rebelled against asking Jackson. She remembered how his family ignored him, except when they needed his help. Becoming another burden chafed, but she'd do anything to protect Nick. Including asking the help of a man who made her wish for impossible things.

Afraid that her courage would desert her if she delayed, she jumped out of bed. It was only when she was standing before Jackson's bedroom door that she remembered her only clothing was his shirt. Her knuckles had hit the wood by then and it was too late. The door swung open before she could retreat. Jackson stood in front of her, wearing a pair of white boxer shorts.

Captivated by the view, she lost her train of thought. His thickly muscled wall of a chest, covered with a sprinkling of black hair, was only the start. Ropes of muscle ran across his shoulders and arms, and his abdomen was ridged in a way that told her he carried no excess flesh. His thighs looked like tree trunks. She'd been right—the man was muscled *everywhere*.

He shifted and she jerked her head up, aware that she'd been staring. But, how could any red-blooded woman resist indulging herself with such a prime example of masculinity? Especially a woman who'd been shown time and time again that this masculine power would never be turned against her. She expected to see amusement in those dark eyes, but something else awaited her.

Desire.

Hot, rippling desire.

Scorching desire.

She was familiar with desire—Jackson inspired dreams of such erotic power they left her drenched in sweat. But she was even more familiar with desire in men's eyes. After she'd turned fourteen, her mother's boyfriends had looked at her with eyes hot with wanting. Then there had been that…she didn't like to think about that much. It still made her feel dirty and used.

"*Cara.*" Jackson's husky whisper sent shivers racing through her, but she couldn't move away.

He tipped up her face with a finger under her chin and then bent down to press his lips gently against hers. Instinctive defense mechanisms kicked into place and she stood still, not fighting but not responding either. Frustration gnawed at her stomach as she realized that despite her age and knowledge of Jackson, childhood terrors still had a stranglehold over her.

He broke the kiss. "My apologies. I did not realize that you did not accept my kiss."

So formal, she thought, so icy, when his lips had been warm and soft. She felt suddenly bereft but knew it was her own fault—the fruit of cowardice. "I accepted."

He braced his right hand on the doorjamb, his face expressionless in a way she hated. "Like a statue. I won't touch you again if that is what you prefer."

That option didn't sound good to her. Nibbling on her lower lip, she looked down at the lush grey carpet and then back up. "I don't deal well with men wanting me." While she didn't trust Jackson's desire, she trusted his intellect. He would never judge her for her fear, not when he'd been hurt so much by others. "I…had some bad experiences when I was younger." She hadn't meant to admit that much but couldn't bring herself to regret the confidence.

Jackson's protective instincts were jolted awake. "Who?" he demanded, his tone barely above a growl. Closing the distance between them, he put one hand on her hip. He'd expected her to recoil but to his pleased shock, one fine-boned hand fluttered to rest on his bare chest. Heat engulfed his body but he ruthlessly caged the fire, aware of the fragility of her faith in his goodness.

"I don't want to talk about that right now." Her answer didn't satisfy him, but then she said, "I wanted to talk to you about the phone call."

He was placated by that evidence of her trust. For this night, it was enough. "Who was on the other end?"

"Why didn't you press for more information before?"

"I figured I had no right to know." Her face was so solemn, so lovely in the frame of midnight-dark hair. He loved Taylor's thick, curling mane. Dreams of the silky strands spread over his arm as she slept beside him had tormented him since their first meeting. "Do I?"

Taylor knew what he was really asking. "I don't know if I'm ready to let you into my world."

He was silent for a moment. "Why?"

"You're…" How could she admit that she was scared of what he made her feel, what he made her ache for?

"You trust me, don't you?"

The answer came easily because he'd always been far more than just her boss, no matter what she'd tried to convince herself. "I'm here." And she wouldn't be if she didn't trust him on a deep, unshakable level.

That trust was rooted in the knowledge that he'd never co-erce her to do anything against her will. Jackson was a pro-tector. And she needed his protection from Lance. More importantly, *Nick* needed his protection. "Nick is the most precious part of my world," she whispered, making a deci-sion.

"I know."

"He's returning from camp in a couple of days," she told him. "Do you want to come pick him up with me?"

"Yes."

Taylor felt something change in their relationship at that moment. With her invitation, she'd accepted Jackson's claim over her and made a claim of her own. But did she have any right to him when her whole being was wracked with fear over Lance's threats to take her brother away?

"You only ever speak of Nick." One big hand stroked her hair. Instead of fear at the intimacy, she felt a shy sense of pleasure because this was annoyingly protective Jackson. "Do you have no other family?"

"Not in truth."

"Tell me what that means, *piccola*." It was a masculine demand disguised as a request.

Taylor found that she wanted to tell him. He'd never been given any privacy with his life and it seemed only fair that he should know something of her as well. And the truth was, she needed to tell someone and aside from Jackson, who was there?

The first words took time, but he didn't hurry her. Stand-ing in the hallway with her toes digging into the carpet and Jackson's heat surrounding her, she'd never felt safer. He might want her, but he would *never* force her—she'd stake her life on that. "My mother brought us up, well, she brought me up anyway. She died when Nick was six." Keeping her voice steady was an effort. "I was twenty and her death wasn't a surprise. She was an alcoholic."

To her shock, right then, Jackson picked her up and walked into his bedroom. The only light came from the full moon outside. She remained absolutely silent as he pulled a blanket off the bed and then sat down in a window seat similar to others about the house. He slung the blanket around her shoulders and held her in his lap like she belonged to him, while he leaned against the wall. She sat up but his body surrounded her. Protected her.

"Why am I telling you?" she asked, wondering how it was that she felt so safe with him. And whether she should be frightened at the reason behind the feeling.

"Because you obviously need to talk. Did that phone call have anything do with your brother?"

"How…" She gasped at his perception.

"It terrified you. You only react like that when Nick's hurt."

Her nod was jerky. "It was Nick's father, Lance."

"Your father?"

Her blood seemed to turn ice-cold. Taking a deep breath, she told Jackson the reason why Lance cared nothing if he destroyed her. "He's not my father."

Jackson looked down at the flat sound of Taylor's voice. "What?" The urge to wrap her up in his arms and press her against his chest was almost irresistible. He fought the urge because he needed to see her face.

"My mother, Helena, was pregnant by another man when she married Lance." She stared fixedly at the dark square of the bedroom doorway. "My biological father was already married. He didn't want his mistress after she became pregnant and refused to get rid of me. She was destitute."

"That wasn't your fault." He was shocked at the self-recrimination in her tone.

"Lance *never* let her forget," she continued. "Almost every week, he'd say something to remind her that I wasn't his, that he'd taken her in when she was 'knocked up.' He didn't even give me his name."

Jackson felt his hands curl into fists but forced himself to remain silent, aware that she needed to talk. It humbled him that she trusted him enough to share something so painful. He'd had no choice when his secrets had been ripped from him and used to sell newspapers, but he knew just how much courage it took to deliberately entrust another person with such private pain.

"And she never stopped reminding me that it was because of me that she was stuck with a man who beat her when he was bored, and…and used her." Her slim shoulder shifted as she took a deep breath that hitched. "While I was growing up, Lance used to disappear without explanation for weeks, and then return like nothing had happened.

"My mother used to wait for him, as if he'd come back and rescue us from poverty. Then one time, he didn't come back. They divorced when Nick was barely two." She stopped speaking, staring down at her hands.

Jackson wanted to strangle her parents. Instead, he gave in to the urge to touch her and closed one of his hands over hers, not certain that she'd tolerate any further contact while mired in the past.

Her eyes were confused when she finally turned to look at him. "Why did she love him for such a long time? Why did she? We both knew he had other women. Was she that grateful that he took her in when she was pregnant?"

Jackson could imagine her mother's befuddlement at this child of hers who was so without deceit, a child who wouldn't allow her to forget grim reality in useless illusions. "She sounds like a woman who lost her way."

"Yes." Poignant sadness colored that acknowledgement.

"Where does Nick's father fit in?"

Fear clouded her gaze. "Lance didn't return for him after

our mother died. Even before her death, I was the one who took care of Nick. But now he's back."

Encouraged by her lack of resistance to their linked fingers, he reached out with his free hand and stroked her hair off her face, shifting his body closer to hers at the same time. "What exactly does he want?"

"Nick." Pain devastated the pure blue of her eyes to a dull shade. "I'll fight him 'til I have nothing left, but I'm afraid. He's Nick's father. I'm only his half sister." She leaned just a little into his stroking hand.

He was pleased that she saw him as a source of strength. "You've raised him."

"You don't understand. Lance isn't some riffraff—he's rich. He always was, though he never gave us a cent. I suppose he married my mother because she was so very beautiful and he wanted her. But, then, he threw her away. He didn't care about Nick then." Desperation was apparent in her too-fast speech.

"He told me that he'd remarried and had a stable home for his son. I think he only wants Nick because he can't have children with his new wife." She was shaking, as if with rage. "I can't let that happen! Lance will hurt him. I saw him hit Nick when he was a baby!" Releasing his hand, she clutched at his forearm. "I saw him!"

Gently disengaging her fingers, he took a chance and wrapped his arms around her. After a momentary hesitation, she softened. "You must not worry so, *piccola*. I am here." Her pain tore at him. "How rich?"

"He's a partner at Hegerty Williams. He's the Hegerty." She named a prominent law firm. "He knows judges and psychiatrists. He said he'd have me declared unfit if I didn't give him Nick, and that he's convinced judges who are friends of his that I have a bad lifestyle.

"I've tried to fight it but all my motions to the court keep getting denied and his accepted. I've fought every way I can but I don't know how much longer I can stall him. I'm so scared. I can't lose Nick. *I can't.*"

Jackson felt his instincts growl in warning. How dare anyone threaten this woman? This strong, beautiful woman, who, unbeknownst to anyone, belonged to Jackson Santorini. He pulled back and tilted her face up with a finger under her chin, his anger intensifying when he saw that her eyes were shiny with tears she refused to shed.

"Do you trust me, Taylor?" If she didn't, he was damn well going to teach her to, even if he had to cuddle her in his lap all night long.

She nodded. "Yes." Then she scowled. "I don't think I should've admitted that."

He was pleased with her despite her dark expression. "Then believe me when I say I'll help you."

"I'm sorry to ask this of you. I know how people always want things from you. I don't want to be like them!" Her frustration was clear.

"I know you don't think like that." He'd always had to fight her pride to give her the smallest consideration. Stroking the cool smoothness of her cheek, he said, "Come now, *piccola*. Where is my little tigress?"

Her full lips curved upward in a rueful smile. "I think she's in hibernation."

"That's more like the Taylor I know." Without stopping to think, he pressed a hard kiss to her lips, withdrawing the instant he remembered what he'd done. "My apologies again…" His gut twisted at the thought that he might've broken her fledgling trust in him.

Her fingers on his mouth stopped him. "I…I don't mind when you touch me." Her eyes widened, as if she was surprised by her own words.

He was touched by the admission. "A woman should

enjoy her man's kiss, baby, not merely allow it." With her face bathed in the soft light of the moon streaking in through the window, she looked indefinably vulnerable.

"I'm not sure I know how to enjoy." Her words were brutally honest. "C-could…you…"

He leaned closer, enclosing her with his body. "What would you like, *piccola?*"

"A kiss. Like it's supposed to be," she whispered.

Her words betrayed that for her, kissing had never been a pleasure. One day soon, he'd find out who had abused her, but for tonight, he would kiss her as an innocent was meant to be kissed—with tenderness and just a stroke of passion. Just enough to tantalize.

While Taylor's heart pounded so hard that she could feel every beat in her throat, Jackson moved one big hand to cradle her head and lowered his mouth to hers. Braced for pressure, all she felt was a teasing graze of lips on lips that left her with no idea how to react.

"Just feel." He grazed her lips again but this time, lingered over the caress. "It feels good doesn't it?"

She nodded, throat dry. There was no pain, no force, nothing but the male scent of Jackson and the burning heat of his almost naked body. Her hands were on his beautiful skin and she could feel the raw power barely contained beneath the surface. Despite the blatant evidence of male muscle, she let her lashes flutter shut. If he'd wanted to hurt her, he could've done so long before this moment. All those nights working alone with him, she'd never once felt less than safe. His old-fashioned sense of chivalry had even stopped him from inviting himself in for coffee when he'd followed her home.

"Then just feel. Sweet, sweet, Taylor." His hand tipped her head back and he dropped a single kiss on her neck. She whimpered in surprise.

"Relax for me, *bellissima*," he cajoled, as his lips touched hers again, hot but undemanding. "Feel."

Seduced by that deep voice, she did as he asked. She just felt. Felt the soft-hard duality of his lips, felt the tenderness with which he was coaxing her to open her mouth for him, felt the shudder that ripped through him when she did. Yet, he didn't invade her mouth. Instead, he teased her with feather-light strokes of his tongue across her lips. As each slow lick built her desire, he whispered hot promises to her in Italian, his voice darkly smoky, teasing, tempting but not delivering.

At last, she gave a frustrated little moan and pressed closer, her hands clenching in his hair to hold him to her. Only then did he touch tongue to tongue, a quick foray that didn't remind her of the forceful kisses that had hurt and shamed her as a girl, because he invited rather than took. Curious, heart thudding, she followed. His arms tightened around her, chest muscles tensing as her breasts were crushed between them, barely covered by the shirt. Beneath her bottom, she could feel the hard ridge of his erection. Panic tried to rise but failed, because despite his obvious arousal, his touch remained heartbreakingly gentle.

Their lips parted with a silky wet sound, deeply intimate in the semidarkness of the room. The man holding her nipped at her full lower lip with his teeth. "You taste like you belong to me."

Instead of inciting fear, his possessiveness heated her blood. "I like touching you. Kissing you." She was talking with her lips on his, her hands deep in his hair. The pure, sensual pleasure she derived from touching him enthralled her.

"Good." There was a very satisfied glint in his eye, and the thumb he ran across the lip he'd bitten was nothing less than proprietary. When he pressed her down against his chest, she sighed and gave in.

Remnants of the passion that he'd aroused in her unawakened body glowed like embers, keeping her warm and relaxed. A new kind of trust took root in her heart, a woman's trust, a sexual trust, which dared her to take what her sexy ex-boss was offering and not look back to a young girl's easily bruised sensuality.

"Are you awake, *cara?*"

"Yes."

A pause. "Do you wish to tell me why you have such fear of men's desires?"

"I promise I will, but not tonight." She couldn't bear to taint the sweetness of that kiss, the almost unbearable tenderness of it, with such horrible memories.

"You must sleep then." He stood, with her in his arms.

At her door, he set her on her feet. She put a hand on his arm as he turned away. "Thank you for your help."

Something dark shaded through his eyes. "I do not want your gratitude, Taylor."

Somehow, she knew it wasn't rejection but a question. "It wasn't gratitude. It was trust." It took courage to confess that. Before she'd met Jackson Santorini, she'd never trusted a male in the prime of his life.

He touched her hair again, a softer curve to his unsmiling mouth. "Go to sleep, *piccola*. I will find a way to help you and your brother."

It was a measure of her trust that she slept the night through, without nightmares. Truth to tell, it scared her a little, this faith she had in Jackson. A woman could be fooled into love with something as powerful as trust to lead her astray. And her love was the one thing that Taylor would never entrust to any man.

Not even Jackson.

Four

The next morning, Jackson drove Taylor home.

Prior to starting the trip, he'd astounded her by producing her purse. Cole had dropped it off early that morning, while Jackson had been working out. His friend had also indicated that Donald Carson was now so terrified of being labeled a sexual offender by the police, it was a sure thing that he'd never assault a woman ever again.

Because the sleep-deprived detective hadn't stuck around, Jackson had had to explain to Taylor that he hadn't left her in the night and done away with Carson. He knew his tone had been edgy, his instincts still raw from being unable to go after the bastard himself. He had a feeling Taylor had seen that all too clearly, because she hadn't pressed him for anything other than Cole's name on the drive to her apartment.

Now, while she changed, he made several calls to his legal people. An idea was brewing in his gut, but he wanted to be certain he was right. As he'd told her the night before, he didn't want her gratitude. Neither his heart, nor his pride, would ever settle for such a paltry emotion from this strong woman.

He was the child of a broken marriage, reared by nannies and the survivor of a loveless union. It was enough loneliness for a lifetime. This time, he needed a woman capable of endless loyalty and utter devotion. Taylor was the only woman he wanted and he hungered for *everything* she had. He would fight for it, but he wouldn't steal it. Not when she'd gifted him with her trust.

At Jackson's request, Taylor packed an overnight bag and accompanied him home after changing into clean clothes. Exhausted from weeks of trying to fight Lance, she couldn't resist leaning on him.

"I have to go to a meeting. Wait for me. We'll talk when I come back," Jackson said after brunch.

She fought her natural instinct to probe, aware that she'd already asked too much. "When will you be back?"

"As soon as I can." He touched his lips to hers in a light caress. "Stop bristling. I need to talk to some people who won't appreciate an audience."

She scowled at his perception. "Don't be too long."

"Try and relax. You might want to think about whether you want to work as my secretary again."

After he left, she did just that, quickly deciding to accept. After all, there was no longer any need for her to hide her desire for her sexy Italian boss.

Jackson didn't return until it was almost dinnertime.

"Did you find out anything?" she asked.

"I am following something through."

She could see fatigue in his eyes and decided not to push

for more information before he ate. Her heart, always fascinated by this man, became a little more his at the quiet way
he was helping her. Several calls interrupted their meal but
finally when there was silence she made some coffee and
took it into the living room.

She handed him a cup. "Here you go."

"Thanks." Curiously remote, he walked over to stand facing the window, his gaze on the darkness outside.

Shunning the couch, she perched on the third step of the
stairs leading up to the bedrooms, her eyes on Jackson. He
was such a big man, she thought, with wide shoulders and
powerful arms. He'd shoved up the sleeves of his black
sweater to bare thick forearms dusted with dark hair.

In the muted light of the room, his skin looked dusky but
she knew it was warm golden brown, evidence of his Italian
heritage. Jackson was a vibrant presence, powerful even
when standing still. Silhouetted against the dark, he looked
isolated and she couldn't bear to see him so alone. She knew
what it was like to be separate, to not belong.

"What're you thinking?" she whispered.

He turned to face her, leaning one shoulder against the
glass. "What would you say to marrying me?"

"Marry you?" Her hands clamped around her coffee cup.

"Yes." Cool and calm, Jackson's eyes gave her no indication of the tenor of his offer.

"Why?" He was her dream man, but in her life dreams had
a nasty way of turning into nightmares.

"I've talked to several lawyers and a judge I know. As
Nick's biological father, Lance has strong rights."

She felt the bottom drop out of her stomach. "No!"

"But," he continued, "to retain custody, you can argue
abandonment and show the court your ability to provide a
good home. Unfortunately, having a husband will count, especially since Nick will need a male role model."

Confusion and hope warred within her. "But what's in it for you?" He was a powerful, handsome man. Why would he want to tie himself to a nobody like her?

"I want a wife—I've always known the value of family and loyalty, and I know you, too, understand those things. I need a hostess who I know will be exemplary. If Nick is still basically the same boy I met, we'll get along fine." He paused and then added, "Because of your love for Nick, I also don't have to worry about word of our arrangement ever being splashed across the tabloids, should we part ways."

And what about me? Taylor wanted to ask, despite the selfishness of such a question. Jackson's proposal seemed so cold and calculated, disregarding the emotional links already tying them together.

Before she could answer, he said, "You'd have the security and stability you want for Nick. I promise you that whatever it takes, Lance won't touch him. I can tie this up legally for years, if that's what it takes." The hardness in his tone underlined each word.

"But dragging Nick through that type of case…"

He put down his coffee cup before answering. "That's a worst-case scenario. My gut says it won't happen. Lance's reputation is built on professionalism and discretion. He won't want his dirty laundry aired in public."

"But he's already filed a lawsuit against me." She squeezed her cup, trying to warm suddenly cold hands.

"He saw you as powerless. Family court operates a lot behind closed doors and he was probably counting on that. But once I get involved, he'll know that the media will sniff out every single detail, including the way he left Nick." His conviction made her want to believe.

"What happens if we marry?" Being married to Jackson Santorini was almost impossible for her mind to comprehend. She'd barely been able to handle a kiss and now this?

"No judge is going to pick Hegerty's side over mine, no matter how deep they are in each other's pockets." There was a harsh edge to his voice that reminded her of some old-world mobster, at once terrifying and magnificent. "At worst, we'd get a fair hearing. I'm not going to lie to you, if that's what happens, it's likely Lance will be granted partial custody at least."

She respected him for not sugarcoating the truth. The worst-case scenario was still better than the certain failure that she'd been facing until now. "And at best?"

"At best, Hegerty will withdraw. In fact, I'm betting on it. He doesn't sound like a man who picks on those strong enough to fight back." His lip curled in disgust.

"I'd do anything for Nick." She found her way with those words. "Are you sure it'll work?" For Nick, she'd even chance marrying the one man who threatened to batter down the painstakingly wrought walls around her heart.

"Yes. I protect those who belong to me." The statement was without compromise. "Nick would have every advantage."

"So long as we're together," she blurted out. "Your family's track record isn't so good." She *would not* put Nick through the pain of gaining a father, only to have that father walk away. Her own experience at Lance's hands had taught her that sometimes it was better to never have a father at all. "And what if we divorce before he's eighteen? Lance might try again."

He nodded, those dark eyes going even more opaque. "I'm willing to make a commitment to a certain number of years together. I was with Bonnie for six."

"But not happy."

"No." A bald truth.

"Why chance that again?" Despite her concern for Nick, she remembered the deep sorrow she'd sometimes glimpsed in Jackson's eyes. That hidden pain had only deepened since their last meeting.

Something terrible had happened. Something worse than Bonnie's affair, her suicide and the ensuing media frenzy. Whatever it was, it had wounded him terribly. She couldn't bear to cause him more pain. Worry for Nick and Jackson collided. How could she buy one's joy with the other's unhappiness? She couldn't. Both her men deserved better.

And so did she.

"I hardly think you'll take up drugs and spiral into depression. You care too much for Nick." He spoke of their marriage as if it were only a business arrangement. As if the tender kiss last night had never happened. Perhaps that powerful moment of trust had meant nothing to him, used as he must be to far wilder displays of passion.

"As for Nick having every advantage, I'll set up a trust fund for him, to be his whether we're together or not." He walked over to stand at the foot of the stairs, looking down at her from his considerable height.

She narrowed her eyes, worry about his reasons for the proposal, and confusion over her own feelings, momentarily overridden by irritation. He'd better not offer her money as well or she'd scratch out his eyes. She had no pride where Nick was concerned but for herself, she had plenty.

"I'd make sure you were taken care of," he began, his hand on the banister.

"Stop right there." Putting down her cup, she stood up on the second step, level with his face. "The only reason I'm considering this crazy idea is because it will help me keep my brother. I don't want your money!" In her anger, she didn't stop to consider why he'd offer to sweeten the deal, when she was the one without options.

"I'd be asking you not to work while you were my wife, even though I'd lose the best secretary I ever had."

"Why not?" She put her hands on her hips. This reasonable man was not the passionate, wild creature she knew. Where was her Jackson?

"More than half my business is done via social events. Bonnie alienated a large number of people we need to woo back. You'd be working, but in a way that the outside world would never appreciate." He continued in that calm and practical way, stoking her simmering temper.

"If we separated, it would be difficult for you to get back into the workforce. It's only fair that I give you something to tide you over. You'd never use Nick's trust fund and it would hurt him if you were without resources."

"You really know how to hit the jugular don't you?" Her tone was sharp.

"It's a skill." His voice was uninflected but she knew that she'd hurt him.

Why had she done that? Was it because she was afraid of what he made her feel? She'd vowed to never love a man as much as her mother had, because she knew that in some ways, she was the same as Helena. They both loved with a passion that could be destructive if it wasn't returned.

Her mother had loved the man she'd had an affair with, and she'd ended up loving Lance, too. Her suffering when they'd both thrown her aside like used tissues had been fatal. Taylor never intended to be in that position—never would she allow herself to be that vulnerable. Except sometimes, Jackson made that ultimate weakness seem tempting.

Unable to bear his hurt, she reached out to touch his cheek, rough with five o'clock shadow. "I'm sorry."

"There's nothing to be sorry for." He didn't move away from her touch, but neither did he show any reaction.

She pushed her hand into his thick hair while he stood there, letting her do whatever she wanted. "Don't you ever get angry, Jackson? Flat-out mad?"

"No." He looked into her eyes, completely cold.

"No, you just go icy," she whispered. He'd yelled at her in the office but that had been over little things. When it really mattered, he simply shut down. She wondered if he felt too much and had to feel nothing at all to survive. Her heart hurt for him. "Well, guess what?"

He raised a brow at her snappish tone.

"If you marry me, you have to live with a temper."

"I face tantrums all the time in my line of work."

"Tantrums?" Leaning across, she put her other hand in his hair. She trusted him to not let her fall from her precarious position. He didn't let her down. Big, warm male hands clasped her waist tight. "Don't you ever say I have tantrums, Jackson Santorini, or I'll show you angry."

"You wanted to know if I could handle temper." Despite her deliberate provocation, his tone remained even.

"Okay." Until this moment, she hadn't realized the depth of his pain. Just who was Jackson Santorini behind his guise of powerful producer? "How do you deal with the tempers in the business?"

He gave her a humorless smile. "You know we talk money and if the demands are unreasonable, we get hard-nosed. Or, we send in people to soothe their famous nerves."

She stifled a laugh. "So, how's that going to work for me, Mr. Big Shot Producer-Guy?"

For a second, he looked dumbstruck. Then he said, "Guess I'll have to learn to soothe your nerves."

"Nerves!" she cried, before glimpsing the tiny spark of humor in his eyes. Relief at finally getting through to him made her giddy. "Ooooh. You make me so mad."

The hands on her waist tightened. He lifted her up without visible effort and set her on her feet in front of him. "How mad?"

"Sooooo mad." She had to tilt her head back to look up

at him. The position made her vividly aware of his size and power. He was so hot and alive. So male that it made the woman in her whimper for things she knew nothing about.

The moment stretched and she saw desire begin to warm those Italian-dark eyes. Involuntarily, fear shivered through her. His tenderness last night hadn't been enough to destroy scars she'd carried since childhood. He removed his hands, his face tensing, all angles and harsh shadows.

"If we marry, I won't force anything on you." He paused, as if making a decision. "But, I do wish for something from this marriage."

"What?" At last, she thought, a reason behind this improbable proposal.

"A baby." His eyes were fathomless. "If we can beat your fear and have sex, I don't want you using protection."

Taylor was momentarily silenced, stunned by the request. Despite the newly awakened desire between them, why would he ask this of her, a woman who could barely allow him a kiss? Maybe he didn't understand the extent of her fear. She would marry him to keep Nick but she wouldn't trick him. He had to know that her problems ran deep.

"I may never be able to give you what you want. Are you willing to never father a child?" She had to make him understand that this wasn't something that would pass easily. It might never pass. Even if they managed to overcome her fear of intimacy, having children terrified her for a much more painful reason. After witnessing her mother's despair, she wasn't sure if she could ever make herself that vulnerable to a man. Even a man like Jackson.

At that moment, Jackson felt dark, nameless emotions rock his soul. Taylor was asking him to make a choice— her or a child. It was a choice that he'd made easily standing over Bonnie's grave, but applied to this honest blue-eyed woman, it seemed terribly wrong. "You are right, I am not." The words were torn out of him. "How about we give ourselves a year? If there is no child, then we will part."

It hurt him to say that, going against all of his vows that he would not have marriage after short marriage like the rest of his family. But he'd buried one child who'd never had a chance to be born. He needed to replace that memory with one of a healthy *bambino*. The problem was, in his imagination, all his children had Taylor's blue eyes. How could he possibly walk away from her if she didn't allow him to touch her? And yet, how could he not?

Taylor's next question was subdued, as if she hadn't expected the time limit. "And Nick?"

"I think we can fix things so that Lance has no chance, even if we're not together." He looked at her and said bluntly, "Tell me the reason behind your fear of sex."

Taylor put her hands on his hard chest, dismayed at her disappointment. She should've been celebrating a husband who only wanted a child from her, not love. Or had she cherished some hidden dream of a far more romantic proposal? If she had, it had been a girlish fancy. A bargain like this was far safer. Romance and love died but Jackson Santorini would never renege on an agreement.

"It's not you. Please know that," she said, at last.

His scowl made him look more like a mobster than ever. "Was it someone your mother brought home?" His voice had dropped an octave into the deep and menacing range. He put his hands around her waist again, and this time the warmth and weight of them calmed her.

She swallowed. "It was a maintenance man." Her voice shook as she revealed something she'd never told anyone. There was more, much more, but she didn't have the courage to tell him the whole truth at once.

"What did he do?" Jackson's voice rasped and the hands

on her hips pulled her closer, as if he couldn't stop the protective movement. She went, glad to be near his warmth.

"I...developed around fourteen. That was when he started staring at me. I didn't know what that look meant then, hadn't learned." It mattered that Jackson understand, that he didn't look at her with those icy eyes when she couldn't respond beyond the most innocent caresses, because she cared what he thought of her. "He followed me to the laundry room. I thought he was going to fix a broken machine." Even now, she could feel her fear when she'd finally realized that he was just standing there in the corner, watching her, eyes slimy.

"When I tried to go up the stairs after I loaded the machine...he stalked me until I starting backing up. I dropped the basket and tried to get away but he—he grabbed me and pushed me hard against a linen closet down there." Tears streaked down her face and she was that terrified young girl again. "I was so scared. He said he could understand my fear. He'd teach me not to be afraid. He'd make me like it. And you know what made it worse?"

"Tell me, *piccola.*" One big hand was stroking her hair, while the other was pressed flat on her lower back.

"I kind of had a crush on him before that. He was a university student working part-time. Good-looking. Smart." She pressed her cheek against Jackson's chest, wrapping her arms around his waist. "I didn't think he'd be vicious like Lance was to my mother. God, I was a fool." She took a gasping breath and admitted the most horrible part of it. "It was my first kiss. He split the inside of my lip. The bruises on my arms and back didn't fade for weeks."

"*Taylor.*" Jackson's voice was gruff, giving her permission to end this if it hurt too much.

She couldn't stop now. "He was pressed up against me and I could feel him...being aroused. I fought but he was too strong. I thought he'd keep hurting me but then someone came down the stairs. He'd forgotten to lock the door."

"You had a chance to escape?"

"Yes." She'd thanked God over and over while she'd thrown up in the bathroom.

"Did he touch you again?" The quiet rage in Jackson's voice somehow soothed her.

She shook her head against him, unwilling to lose the steady sound of his heartbeat. "He watched me but I stopped going anywhere in the building by myself. I encouraged the children in the other apartments to tag along everywhere. Gra—the maintenance guy couldn't risk offending their families by scaring them off. Some of their parents wouldn't have thought twice about taking care of him."

"Grant? Grant who?" Jackson demanded.

"I won't let you get in trouble." She set her jaw.

"I promise you I won't. But I need to do something—you didn't let me have Donald." There was such ferocious anger in his request that she worried about him.

"No!"

"*Cara mia,* please."

She bit her lip, undone by the softly spoken endearment. Sometimes she forgot that Jackson's father was Italian, but right now, she could very well believe that this man came from a land that believed in vengeance and an eye for an eye. "I can't prove it."

"You don't need to prove it to me other than by your words and I am the only one who matters." He was holding her so close, so very close, but she wasn't afraid. There was just some part of her that refused to place him in the same category as other men. Did that make her a fool, or was she being given a precious chance to fight the lessons of the past and seize something glorious?

"Grant Layton." It was too hard to resist the temptation to tell the one man who'd ever cared about her.

"Thank you, *piccola*. Thank you." His embrace tightened, his potent masculinity surrounding her.

Close contact didn't scare her. It was only when anything sexual happened that she was that fourteen-year-old again, backed up against the door of the cupboard, with the handle digging into her back. Her mind had been black with fear and betrayal as the object of her teenage crush had destroyed her innocence before it had a chance to blossom. But perhaps her childhood heart might've recovered from that, if something worse hadn't happened.

Jackson's hand moved up and down her spine, soothing strokes that relaxed her. "Thank you for telling me."

"You had to know," she whispered. "I won't steal your happiness to find my own. I'd run with Nick before I'd do that." He deserved better than a woman so damaged she'd resigned herself to a lifetime of loneliness.

"You're traumatized." He kept stroking her. "We can get you counseling if you want."

She started shaking her head before he could finish. "The thought of exposing my thoughts for a stranger to pick through…no. I'd rather trust you with my secrets."

He was silent for a long time and she thought that she'd asked too much of this man who guarded his emotions so carefully. He'd offered her a pragmatic bargain. There had been no mention of gentler, softer feelings.

"I am honored." His heart thudded under her cheek. "But, I might not be the best choice. I want you."

"Will you force me?"

"Never."

"In my heart, I've always known that."

Jackson was stunned by that calm acceptance of his promise when he was starting to see that Taylor had experienced only fear and violence from the men in her life. She hadn't said anything to indicate further abuse, but if the young maintenance man had noticed her developing beauty, what had other, older men noticed? And what had they done to his sweet Taylor? He stifled his questions for the moment, aware that she was emotionally wrung out. "How?" he asked instead.

A pause, then, "You might hurt me with indifference and coldness but you'd never physically abuse me."

He winced at her honest response. "I'm not indifferent to you." But he was a cold man. He'd had to become one to survive his solitary childhood and then Bonnie. The last blow had been the loss of his child.

He needed Taylor's fire as his anchor against the coldness swallowing him alive, needed her to be the candle in the darkness that brought him back home. And though he'd never let her know, he needed her love. Because he did, he fought for her. "I will always be there for you, but I know of a therapist who specializes in sexual trauma." He'd made it his business to find out that information earlier today.

Taylor tensed. "I don't know…"

"Can you try, *cara?* She might help you in ways I have no knowledge of." His need to encourage her spirit overcame his desire to *be* her strength. Faced with her pain, his first instinct would be to reassure and shield, possibly thwarting her recovery. The therapist would be far tougher, forcing Taylor to use the courage that had let her successfully raise a child, to heal herself.

This time, it was her hand that stroked his spine. "I'll try…we can learn together."

What was she offering to teach him? He didn't care. He'd take whatever she could give him. It was a disturbing thought.

Five

Taylor awoke in Jackson's guest bedroom on Sunday morning, wearing his big white shirt. Rain beat overhead, a rough lullaby that signaled the return of the storm. Warm and comfortable, she had no desire to rise.

A sharp knock on her door made her scowl. "Come in."

Jackson pushed the door open and stood in the doorway, clad all in black. "We have to talk."

She yawned and pulled out one hand from her cocoon to pat at the bedspread. "Sit."

There was an inferno in his caressing gaze. "*Cara mia,* I am only a man."

Her heart thundered. "Please?" Why was she making him do this? Was she testing his promise that he wouldn't force her to do things that terrified her?

Sighing, he came and sat beside her. "Happy?"

"Maybe," she teased. "Where's my engagement ring,

Jackson Santorini?" She was trying to be lighthearted, for what right did she have to demand anything?

To her surprise, he reached into his pocket and pulled out a finely made gold ring with tiny shards of diamond embedded in the beautiful scrollwork. Despite its simplicity, she knew it was no ordinary ring. Her hand trembled as he slid it onto her ring finger, under the rain-drenched sunlight falling through the skylight.

"Jackson, this is so lovely." Her voice was barely a whisper as, sitting up, she stared at the ancient gold.

His smile was slow. "The ring was my paternal grandmother's. Her name was Gia and she was married to my grandfather Josef for over fifty years."

Her eyes smarted with tears. No one had ever given her something so precious, so from the heart.

"Why are you crying?"

"I'm not." She rubbed at her eyes with her free hand.

"Piccola." He reached out and pulled her from the blankets and onto his lap, pressing her cheek against his chest. Instead of fear at the intimacy, she felt a fierce sense of belonging. "Why do you cry like this?"

The sudden change in the cadence of his voice startled her. "You sound so Italian."

"I *am* Italian." He stroked her hair in that way of his. She'd never imagined that such a big man could be so incredibly tender. "Have you stopped crying?"

"Yes." She kept her head against his chest. "Thank you for the ring." She wanted to ask if Bonnie had ever worn it but couldn't find the courage. After all, despite the hurt that his first wife had caused him, he'd loved her when they'd married. It hadn't been just a bargain.

"The ring has been sitting in a vault for ten years. You will bring it to the light once more."

The words made her heart swell. Maybe it was selfish, but

she wanted a part of him that Bonnie hadn't seen and hurt.
She didn't know the details of what they'd done to each
other, but she knew that the results had devastated the man
holding her so very carefully. The feel of his hard body made
her want to luxuriate in him, but the slight tension in his muscles reminded her that this wasn't fair.

She moved off his lap. "I'll meet you downstairs for
breakfast—I'll cook."

"I'll look forward to it." He rose at once, and with a pang
in her heart, she knew that he'd been waiting for the moment
when she'd set him free.

Twenty minutes later, she watched Jackson pick up a fork
and use the edge to cut the corner off a pancake. She watched
his lips as he forked in the bite, and somewhere along the way
her desire to know if he enjoyed her cooking was overcome
by the urge to taste his lips. To try and see if she could come
out of sexual deep freeze.

"Good."

The short accolade snapped her out of her sudden, sensual need to explore the man she was going to marry.
Quickly, she choked down some of her own breakfast.

"We'll marry within the week," Jackson said after she'd
taken a few bites, his tone matter-of-fact.

Her mouth felt fuzzy with nervous tension, but she managed to ask, "Won't a sudden marriage look odd?"

He raised a brow. "We've been secretly seeing each other
for months, not wishing to be dogged by paparazzi."

"Clever."

He acknowledged the compliment with a wry smile.
"Valetta did something like that when she decided she was
ready for marriage. That lasted about six months—a record
even in my family."

"How is your sister anyway?"

"I don't know. Haven't seen her for months."

"Don't you care?" She couldn't hide her disapproval.

"My family is not close like you and Nick." His clipped response didn't encourage further conversation on that topic. Strung taut as she was, she didn't have the inclination to pursue it today. "I believe we can be married by Tuesday."

"Tuesday." She put down her fork. "Registry?" A twinge of pain arrowed through her heart. Despite the nature of their bargain, she didn't want this marriage to start out so very practically, devoid of any hint of hope.

"Only if that is what you wish."

"What do you mean?" She looked up, wondering at the change in Jackson's speech rhythms. As usual, it had happened without warning. At first, she'd thought it was caused by strong emotion, but that couldn't be true, because he was very calm. Whatever it was, the more Italian he sounded, the worse her self-control became.

"There is an isolated farmstead about an hour out by helicopter. It is often used as a wedding venue. I've checked and we can have it for Tuesday if we want."

"But it's Sunday today! We couldn't organize everything by then…could we?" Hope blossomed.

His beautifully shaped lips gentled into a smile. "If we could, do you want the farmhouse?"

"Of course. I'd like to invite some friends."

In the next few hours, Taylor learned about the power of money and charisma. Shops opened just for them, caterers called in relief staff, florists ordered shipments of flowers in special air packages and a couturier flew in from a weekend retreat to show her his wedding collection.

"Come in, come in." The little artiste waved them through to his upstairs showroom.

Flustered, she looked up at the darkly beautiful man who was her companion. "Jackson?"

"Hmm." He bent his head a little, hand on her lower back. She'd always guessed that he was a possessive man and he'd let her see that side of him today. No one who met her was in any doubt that she was now Santorini's woman.

Taylor felt ambivalent about the claiming. Part of her was delighted. But, another part of her, the lost, lonely, abandoned girl, was terrified. Yes, he was claiming her now but there was a time limit on their relationship. If she didn't give him what he wanted, he'd abandon her, just like everyone else. The brutal truth was that this was nothing more than a business deal.

Faced with the couturier, she was lost. "What am I supposed to do?" she asked Jackson, her voice a whisper. She had never been a rich girl, in spite of Lance's wealth. He'd never treated them to any luxury, and had begrudged them every penny he did spare.

Jackson's hand curved over her hip, blatantly proprietary. "You're a very valued customer. Take only what appeals." The caress in his voice touched her deep within, even though she tried to remain unmoved. How could she hope to resist the one man who'd never let her down?

"But he came all this way for us."

"He knows I'll remember that when we need a wedding dress for one of the new movies in the works. Don't worry, *cara,* he will get his payment."

Bolstered by his confidence, she started to look through the many beautiful creations brought out for her inspection. Jackson spent a lot of time on his mobile phone, checking on security details for their wedding. It was while he was standing by the window, phone to his ear, that she found the dress she wanted.

"How very lovely." She picked up the smooth satin-silk fabric, which looked like it had been embedded with pearls crushed to the consistency of the finest white sand. The dress had a cowl neck which would drape softly over her breasts, before the sleek material swept gracefully down her body. The bias cut ensured it would hug her curves and swish gently around her ankles.

"I'd like to try this on." She glanced over her shoulder to ensure Jackson wasn't looking her way. "I don't want him to see it before the wedding."

The little man was delighted to help in her conspiracy. "Use the back fitting room and if you like it, I'll box it up out of his sight."

It was a perfect fit, as if it had been made with her in mind. The couturier gave her a shimmering gossamer veil to go with the dress, and even found a pair of shoes. Jackson simply raised a brow at her secretiveness but paid for the purchase with a gold card.

"It's costing you a lot," she said, in the car.

"It's my choice, Taylor. It's my wedding, too."

That didn't make her feel much better. "I don't understand," she burst out, raw from the evidence of his wealth and her lack of it. "What do *you* get out of this? There are so many women out there who wouldn't hesitate to bear you a child." Women who weren't flawed, she thought. Women he wouldn't have to rid himself of after a year.

"I get you and I get Nick, two people whose loyalty will be mine without question. In this business, loyalty like that is priceless." His tone was forceful. "And, I may get to father a baby, who I *know* will have a good mother—there aren't many women whom I'd trust with that responsibility."

Jackson could see that Taylor wasn't convinced, but he knew that she wouldn't protest. Not when Nick's future was at stake. He barely understood his own need, need which had been hidden for so long that it was starving for a taste of her. He just knew that he had a chance to make Taylor his and he was taking it.

She saw herself as without passion, damaged. He saw in her the promise of a magnificent woman. He wasn't a saint and he wanted her. But neither was he a brutal man who would force compliance. That didn't mean he wouldn't try to find the sensual woman in Taylor, the one who made him feel things he hadn't felt for so long he'd thought them dead.

It had pained him to admit that the ache to father a child was so great he would give her up if she couldn't bring herself to bear his touch. Yet, it was the truth. He'd never wanted much in his life, but he wanted to hold his child in his arms. How could someone as innocent as Taylor understand his need to find redemption by creating a life where Bonnie had destroyed it?

Taylor spent that night at home. She rose at seven the next day and was ready an hour later to go and pick up Nick, who would be dropped off at the school with the other children. Jackson was on her doorstep just after eight.

The sight of him rattled her. She'd just spent hours dreaming of him and none of the dreams had been comfortable. It was as if her own mind was taunting her with what *could* be. "I don't know if you should come," she finally said. "I know I invited you but it might be too sudden." Her worry was genuine but she also needed time alone to sort out her tumultuous feelings.

"He has to know. And we have to see how he reacts to me." Taking the bag she'd packed in anticipation of spending the night before the wedding at his house, Jackson touched her on her lower back, a subtle pressure that reminded her she now belonged to him.

Her feelings of confusion intensified but she didn't move away, because while Jackson might be the most disturbing thing in her life, he was also the safest. "I don't want him to know why we're marrying." She couldn't bear it if Nick thought she was sacrificing something for him, because she wasn't.

"I agree."

As they drove to the school, Jackson said, "Don't worry. He's met me before so it won't be a total surprise." The fleeting touch on her cheek was unexpected but welcome.

Dutifully chaperoned by his camp counselor, her brother was waiting for them by the gate. When the sleek black Mercedes stopped in front of him, she saw his eyes widen. She stepped out and felt Jackson follow. While she went to hug Nick, after thanking the counselor, he picked up her brother's bags and dumped them in the trunk.

After a quick hug that apparently embarrassed him from the speed with which he pulled away, Nick looked up at the man beside her. "Hi, Jackson."

"Nick."

Nick was a smart boy. He looked from her to Jackson. "What?" Speculation turned his blue eyes sky-bright.

Taylor didn't want to tell him right now but realized that she didn't really have a choice. "What would you say if I told you that…me and Jackson…"

Nick started to grin. "Are you gonna marry my sister?"

Her jaw dropped. "How did you know that?"

The boy shrugged. "I dunno. 'Cause Jackson likes you?"

Flustered, she looked at Jackson, who just said, "Smart kid. Jump in the car—we'll talk on the way."

Nick scrambled in, already asking his first question. "Are we going to live with you?"

"Yes," Jackson answered.

A short silence. "Will I always stay with you?"

Taylor frowned, not understanding. But Jackson evidently did. Stopping the car at the side of the street, he looked over his shoulder. "Yes. I went to boarding school and I would never send a child of mine there."

"But, I'm not yours."

Taylor's heart clenched at that quiet statement. Her instinct was to reassure him but she remained silent, aware that

something important was happening between the solemn
ten-year-old and the charismatic man in the driver's seat.

"You are now." There was no arguing with Jackson's decisive statement. He turned and restarted the car.

Nick was quiet for a long time. Then he said, "Will I have
my own room like I do now?"

"Sure. You can't sleep with us, after all." Jackson grinned
in the rearview mirror. "You can have one of the two big first
floor bedrooms. We'll be on the second floor."

Meanwhile, Taylor's stomach went into freefall. He'd said
"us." Did he expect her to have sex with him from the start
in spite of everything? The idea of being with him wasn't ab-
horrent, had never been so. It was the fact that she knew she'd
freeze up and he'd hate her for it.

Once at the apartment, she sent Nick off to pack enough
fresh clothes to see him through to the wedding.

Jackson came to stand in front of her. "Something's both-
ering you." His body language conveyed that he wasn't moving until she confided in him.

She swallowed and decided to be blunt. "Are we going to
be sharing a bedroom?"

His mouth thinned. "I won't go back on my word, Taylor. You may not have noticed, but my bedroom is part of a
suite. It's internally connected to a smaller bedroom. You can
use that. Nick will never know."

"I hadn't considered what he'd think if we were in separate bedrooms." She was flustered, used to providing everything for her brother's happiness.

Jackson took her hand in his, his dark gaze trapping hers.
"You can't think of everything. Learn to depend on me a little. We males like to be needed."

"I'm depending on you a great deal."

The strong lines of his face were suddenly sharper. "Do
not just depend on me as someone powerful, but also as a

man. As your husband. You are now in my care." His rough declaration made her eyes widen in surprise.

"Taylor! I don't have a suit for your wedding." Nick barreled out of his room. Worry stamped his face.

Jackson reached out and tousled his jet-black hair. "I've ordered you a tux. If you're ready, let's head home."

Nick's smile strengthened Taylor's resolve. She'd do anything for her brother. And, she thought, a little shocked, she'd do anything to keep a smile on Jackson's face, too. She *would not* hurt him by withholding herself—he understood her fear but it was a rejection all the same, telling him that she didn't trust him. If she couldn't trust her body with Jackson, who could she trust?

It was a startling insight.

That day was a whirlwind of activity. With Nick tagging along quietly, Taylor went to work with Jackson, helping him organize matters so that the studios could temporarily function without him at the helm. After lunch, she left to meet Maggie, the therapist she'd agreed to see. To her surprise, she found herself comfortable with the older woman who welcomed her into her office.

When she returned to the studios, Jackson simply asked, "So?"

"I like her. It might work."

Giving her a smile, Jackson went back to work and after checking on Nick, she continued to assist him. They'd agreed to leave town for a few days on the pretext of a honeymoon, so that Lance would have no room to ask awkward questions about their marriage. As Nick was now on vacation, it was decided that he'd spend the time out on a farm, with a friend of his who'd moved out of the city.

"I want to take him with us, but I know we have to give the impression of being on a honeymoon," Taylor said, late that night. She was pacing in front of the sofa, while Jackson stood by the window, back to the night, cognac in hand. The amber liquid sparkled through the crystal snifter, momentarily catching her gaze. "I've missed him so much. I don't know if they'll take care of him out on the farm."

"You're overprotective." Jackson's quiet declaration stopped her midpace.

Shocked, she clenched her fists. Her temper ignited. "What would *you* know about bringing up a child?"

She thought pain flickered over the rugged beauty of his face but his tone was calm. "I was a boy at one stage."

"And you think that gives you the right to tell me how to raise Nick?" Just because he was helping her keep her brother didn't mean he could dictate to her.

"No. What gives me the right is that I can see he's unhappy and that he'll never say anything to you, because he loves you too much."

An arrow to her heart would have done less damage. "Unhappy?" she whispered.

"He's been getting bullied for being a sissy."

"How do you know? He just got back from camp."

"He told me while you were having a bath—he couldn't hide it after I saw the bruise on his leg."

"What!" she cried, fighting the urge to wake Nick and check up on him. "Who? I'll kill them."

"That's just the problem."

"Why didn't he tell me? What's the problem?" She couldn't bear to think of her sweet baby brother being bullied. Why hadn't he trusted her with this? Why had he told Jackson, whom he hardly knew?

"You're always sticking up for him. Even at school."

"You wouldn't know, but that's what elder siblings do." Her hurt made her cruel. "You don't even know where your sister is at the moment."

Jackson didn't blink but she knew him well enough to know that her barb had found its target. The skin over his cheekbones tightened and he looked away from her and over the water vista out the window. The night was peaceful and the water moved in gentle symphony, but inside, she felt like she was crashing and burning. His hurt pained her.

"I'm sorry," she whispered, meaning it.

"It doesn't matter." He shrugged, shoulders taut under the blue shirt. Jackson Santorini, she remembered, was used to being hurt. His wife had torn into his pride and the world had lapped up his suffering. She even knew that his family never contacted him except to complain or ask for something. No wonder he didn't keep in touch. It had only been her own feelings of inadequacy at having let her brother down that had made her strike out.

She wanted to kick herself. "Yes, it does." Walking over, she touched her hand to his back and rested her head against his thickly muscled arm. "I hurt you. And I despise myself for it, for taking out my frustration on you."

He put his drink on the windowsill and slipped his arm around her. "You know something?"

Relieved that he wasn't holding a grudge, she said, "What?"

"I think you're the first person I've ever met who really means they're sorry when they say so."

And she knew she was forgiven. "I do. So don't be angry. I know what your family's like, and I don't blame you for keeping them at a distance. It just makes me crazy to know that Nick's being hurt."

"I showed him some moves."

Her brows furrowed. "Moves?"

"Self-defense."

She bit her lip. Nick had kept something else from her. Once, he'd shared every new experience. "And?"

"He's a natural."

"But he's not very physical."

"He's never had a chance to be." He hugged her tight, as if aware that this was hurting her. "Trust him, Taylor. He's an extraordinary boy."

She heard the affection in his tone and knew that he meant it. "I hate it when he's hurting. I hate it!"

"I know, *cara mia.*" The endearment made her want to reach up and kiss him. "Let me help."

Her instincts rebelled. She was used to looking out for Nick on her own. But, though it was a painful concession, she acknowledged that over the past year, his needs had changed in a way she couldn't fulfill. He was starving for a male role model. She'd considered enrolling him in a youth group of some sort, but here was a strong, independent male, offering to look after her baby.

Jackson knew he was asking a lot. He wasn't exactly a prize. What the hell did he know about children? A sharp pain stabbed him. Damn Bonnie for stealing his chance to learn. Taylor's drawn out silence seemed to signal rejection. His pride told him to withdraw the offer, but the memory of the joy on Nick's face when he'd paid attention to him pricked his paternal instincts into fighting mode.

"Look," he began.

"Hush." Taylor held up a slim hand. "This is important. I have to think."

He didn't know whether to be flattered or insulted. People usually didn't gainsay him, much less reject his help. Then again, in most cases, it wasn't a little boy's happiness on the line.

"Yes."

His heart clenched at that decisive sound. "Yes?"

"You'll be good for him. It pains me to know that I can't

give him everything he needs but I can handle that. I had to think about it because if I make the wrong decision, Nick's heart could break. I trust you to never hurt him."

It would be so easy to promise. "At times, I'm likely to do that without meaning to."

"That's okay. Even I slip up." Her candor was followed by a nod. "Just don't ever do it on purpose." There was a pregnant pause. "If we part ways after a year…will you promise to stay in touch with him?"

"Yes." The boy was now one of Jackson's people, just like Taylor. For the first time, he had the startling realization that even if they never had a child, he might not be able to walk away from this woman.

His woman.

Six

"Then I have no arguments," Taylor stated.

He sucked in a breath. "That's a lot of trust."

"I know."

They stood there for a long time before Jackson spoke. "What about you?"

"What about me?" Her voice was wary.

"Trusting me."

She was silent for a long while. "It's hard."

He made himself ask. "Why?"

"It's hard to forget."

"Nick's father?" Taylor was a sensitive woman. From what she'd told him, he knew that though she hadn't been able to comprehend why her mother loved that bastard, she'd understood Helena's pain at Lance's indifference. It would've twisted her impression of what marriage was about. What love was about. Not that he was any closer to the answer, Jackson thought bitterly.

"My mother loved two men. They both left her." It was a harsh explanation. "I don't know if I'll ever be able to forget that lesson."

"You are telling me that you do not believe you will ever love a man?" he forced himself to ask.

The answer was a whisper. "Yes…I'm sorry."

"There is no need for an apology, *piccola*." Anger burned in him for the hurts of her past, hurts that he could not undo, but he didn't allow her to see that. "We are equals. I know even less of love than you."

She gave him a shaky smile. "Equals, huh? Are you going to remember that after we're married?"

"If I do not, you will remind me. So, you do not trust men because of what two of our sex did to your mother?"

"Yes…and because of what the others did…to me."

Jackson's heart slammed into his chest at that lost, broken sound. He'd guessed that her sexual fears were rooted in events beyond her assault at the hands of Grant Layton, but having it confirmed was an unwelcome shock. Fury erupted inside him. Used to being calm and in control, he knew that if any man had hurt his Taylor, he'd rip them limb from limb and suffer no pangs of conscience.

He'd forgotten to tell her that while he wasn't a mobster, back in Italy a branch of the Santorini line was very deeply enmeshed with the mafioso. He could well understand why. Violence and rage roared beneath the surface of his composed front, demanding vengeance. His woman should never have been touched by anyone.

Moving the forgotten glass to a nearby table, he turned and sat down on the window seat. Holding Taylor's cold hands, he tugged her between his spread legs. Her eyes were bruised against her pale skin but she held his gaze.

"Tell me about the others." His voice was harsh, a demand

that she submit to his care. He was so angry for her that he couldn't be the civilized man she needed.

Her head jerked up. Whatever she saw on his face made her eyes widen. "No. No. Nothing like that, Jackson."

To reassure her, he forced his anger below the surface. "Tell me then."

Her hands became fists. Then she made a tiny movement that gave away her need to be held. He held out his arms and she fit her wonderfully giving body against him; sitting in his lap with her knees drawn up, feet flat on the window seat beside his thigh and arms tight around his torso. Fierce protectiveness shot through him. He'd never known that he could feel this much. When she began to speak, he tried to remain calm for her sake, even though her words provoked his most primitive instincts.

"I think…after a while, my mother lost hope, or lost the hope that she'd managed to nurture. At first, when Lance didn't come home for weeks, she'd wait for him." She nestled herself impossibly closer.

"It was as if while he was out of her sight, she'd convince herself that this time, it'd be different. But, it *never* was." Her hands dug into his back. "And one day, I don't think she could fool herself any longer. I'll always wonder why they didn't divorce earlier. He was barely around long enough for Nick to be conceived."

Jackson wanted to hurt Lance for being the cause of the pain he could hear in Taylor's voice. Only the fact that he was Nick's father was keeping him safe. "Why do you think she lost hope?" His voice sounded ragged to him but she didn't seem to notice that he was riding on the thinnest edge of self-control.

"She didn't wait for him anymore. At first, I thought that was a good thing." She took a gasping breath. "Then she started bringing the men home."

He felt his jaw lock. "Where were you?"

"She locked us in our room in the apartment."

"Us?"

"Nick was a baby. I used to take care of him—I didn't trust her not to hurt him by doing something wrong."

Jackson squeezed his eyes shut to blink back tears. Loyal didn't begin to describe Taylor. She was ferociously protective of those she considered her own. Now he understood why she was so determined to keep Nick safe.

"Sometimes, she'd make me come out and say hello to the men. She'd be drunk and not like my mother at all. It was horrible."

He froze. "You said nothing happened."

"I…nothing really bad…" She took a long, deep breath, as if the memories were choking her.

He resisted the urge to order her to tell him everything. "What *did* happen?"

"Their eyes used to crawl over me." She shivered. "I wanted to throw up. But I could cope with that. Then the men she brought home started to hurt her."

Jackson's jaw was clenched so tight that his whole face ached, while his mind became quietly, dangerously, angry. She'd always made him feel protective of her sunny innocence. Now he saw that she'd been hiding very real wounds beneath that smile, and he adored her even more.

"They'd…hurt her," she repeated, as if she couldn't bear to elaborate. "I couldn't stop them. I had to protect Nick because she certainly didn't. I think she hated him." Fierce blue eyes met his when he glanced down. "It wasn't his fault that his father was a horrible human being."

"Of course not."

As if reassured, she put her head back against his chest. "Once, I got scared by the violence and I called the police. They came and took that man away."

Hairs rose on the back of his neck. He knew that her story couldn't have had a happy ending. "What happened?"

"My mother was grateful. She said she'd picked a real mean one. He got locked up and that was okay."

"But?"

"But he got out in a couple of months and he followed me home from school. I didn't know he was behind me until I was crossing a park along the way—I was rushing to get home to Nick. He jumped out from behind a tree and dragged me into the bushes. His hand was on my mouth. I couldn't breathe or scream." Her voice shook.

"He pinned me against the tree, out of sight of the path, one hand on my mouth, the other around my hands. Then he let my mouth free but before I could scream, he gripped my throat. I thought he was going to choke me to death."

Jackson knew she was crying silently and there wasn't anything he could do but hold her. No wonder she couldn't bear a sexual touch. She'd been bruised again and again, at the very time that her developing sexuality would have been at its most vulnerable.

"He started whispering about what he'd like to do to a ripe young thing like me. All the things he said…they were sick and disgusting." Her hand clenched on Jackson's shirt. "He groped my…breasts while I tried to get him to break his chokehold."

"You got away?" He needed to know that because if she hadn't, he couldn't do anything about the pain she'd suffered. He was a man used to taking control but this time, there was nothing he could do. His sweet Taylor had been brutalized by a man who'd had no right to be near someone so pure and in-nocent.

"He stopped touching me and started to undo his pants. His grip loosened for just an instant, but it was enough. I kneed him in the groin and took off."

Thank God she was a fighter. "Did he come after you?"

"Yes, but when I was at school they started this program in my neighborhood. People who were usually at home and were judged good people by the community were asked to have their letterboxes painted bright yellow. That meant they were safe houses."

He remembered hearing something about a similar campaign. "You found one?"

"I knew there was one just around the corner. By the time he caught up, I was halfway up the drive. For a while, I thought he'd follow me but then the door opened and Mrs. Willis took me in." Taylor smiled at the memory.

Mrs. Willis had been the only good thing to come out of that day. The kindly widow had made her stay and drink several cups of tea until she'd stopped sobbing. "She rang the police. The man was hanging around nearby—probably thought he'd get me when I left." She could still remember the bone-crunching, nerve-flaying fear she'd felt that day.

"Did he stay locked up this time?" Jackson's body was taut against hers.

She found herself trying to comfort *him*. "For a lot longer. I think he got hurt in jail. He never came back."

He didn't back off under her soothing but his tone gentled. "Was he the only one?"

"Yes. But the whole time, I kept thinking that one day it could just as well be Nick taking the brunt of some man's anger." The blinding fear had been a mother's for her child. "From then on, when our mother went out, I left with Nick and spent the night at Mrs. Willis's house."

"You care for this woman."

Her nod was sharp. "She treats me like a daughter."

"Do you keep in touch with her?"

"Yes. But, her health isn't so good anymore." Her voice was less than a whisper. Unlike her mother, this Mrs. Willis meant a lot to her. "I worry. That neighborhood isn't the greatest but she refuses to move."

Jackson marveled at her. She'd told him of a terrifying experience, one that she must've been constantly afraid would be repeated, and all she was worried about was an old woman's health. He would ensure that her savior received the best care, because he was in Mrs. Willis's debt for saving her from unbearable suffering.

"Taylor?"

She looked up, lingering traces of memory turning her blue eyes cloudy. "Yes?"

"Thank you for telling me." For trusting me, he thought, with bittersweet joy.

Her smile was forced. "You needed to know." She swallowed and he could see that she was gathering the courage to say something. He waited. When it came, it was so unexpected that he just stared.

"Did you just ask me if I was going to keep a mistress?" he repeated, dumbfounded.

She sat up in his lap, arms folded. "What's so silly about that? I won't be providing…what you need and you're a man." Her tone was belligerent.

He tried to tell himself that she knew only one kind of man and it wasn't personal. He shouldn't feel so hurt because she could be so blasé about giving him to another woman. If she ever touched another man, that man wouldn't live to regret his mistake. And Taylor? He might just handcuff her to his bed forever.

"I can control myself. I don't feel the need to have sex with complete strangers and that's what it would be." He made no attempt to hide the growling edge to his voice.

"I've put my foot in it, haven't I? You're angry."

Her honesty made his lips curve. "I hardly think it'll be the last time." Tipping her chin up, he said, "Tell me one

thing. Do you find me personally disgusting or repulsive?"
He knew that his big body could be considered brutish and
after hearing what she'd been through, he was surprised at
the amount of trust she'd already shown him.

She immediately shook her head. "Of course not! I told
you, you're gorgeous. And…I like the way you kiss me."

"Then, we will try, *piccola.*" He moved the hand on her
back, subtly coaxing her awareness of him.

"Try?" It was a whisper but he could hear the faintest trace
of intrigue.

"What could it hurt?" Even as he spoke, he realized that
it might shatter his heart. It would be worth it if Taylor looked
at him with passion in those vibrant eyes.

She lowered her head, uncertain. "What if I can't?"

"I'll turn into a monk." He didn't bring up their one-year
agreement.

There was wariness in her eyes, but she let him hold her.
And the next day, she married him, in a ceremony that was
quietly beautiful, just like her.

Dressed in a gown that kissed every womanly curve with
a lover's tenderness, her wild black hair tumbling down her
back, and her blue eyes fixed on him alone, she was his
every dream come true. When he slid the plain gold wedding
band onto her finger, she beamed at him and something deep
within him started to whisper in hope.

He would rather have spent his life alone than have a
string of meaningless marriages like his parents, or a replay
of the deceitful and hurtful first marriage he'd barely survived. Some kinds of loneliness were worse than others.
But, with Taylor smiling at him like that, he believed that,
this time, it would be different.

It would be forever.

Understanding at last just how deeply she lived in his

heart, he decided that the one-year time limit on their marriage was totally unacceptable. The thought of her in another man's arms, even unwillingly, had almost killed him—he would never let her go by choice. Unless his bride repudiated him, he was in this for life. He'd let her know that when she was feeling a little less overwhelmed by the speed at which he'd pushed for their union.

Perhaps, with this woman who made his heart awaken and body rejoice, he might find a way out of the darkness of his past and into the sunshine of her smile.

It was his wedding night.

The location was an exclusive resort on an island off the coast of Fiji. It was his wedding night and he was all alone in his bed, while his sexy new bride slept across the hall, in the other room of this luxurious seaside cabin. An erotic fantasy involving black lace and soft white skin had been tormenting him for the past hour.

Desperate, he went down to the floor and began doing push-ups, clad only in white boxer shorts. Exhaustion might allow him to catch a few hours sleep.

The gentle knock came when he was on his fiftieth push-up and more aroused than he'd thought humanly possible. Groaning at his pretty little wife's timing, he growled, "Come." The single word sent a cascade of sensual imagery flooding through his mind. He could imagine teasing Taylor to that final edge and then ordering her to "come."

The door opened and the enticing scent of woman whispered over him. *Dio!* A hundred more, he decided grimly and kept going. His peripheral vision showed small feminine feet, toes painted bright pink, padding closer. The edge of an eyelet lace nightgown fluttered around her ankles.

He wanted to reach out a hand, grab onto one slim ankle

and lick his way up his wife's gorgeous legs. His *wife*. She belonged to him and he wanted to stake his claim.

"What're you doing?"

Grunt. "Exercising."

"It's almost midnight." She didn't sound disapproving. He frowned. She seemed...fascinated. But, by what?

"I like it." He pushed down, feeling his biceps start to burn.

"I can see that." Feminine interest laced her tone.

He almost jerked to a standstill but something forced him to continue. To his surprise, he saw her move around to sit on the edge of his bed. Her pretty little feet were flat on the floor, inches away from him.

"Can I stay and talk?"

She wanted to talk? "Sure."

He waited for her to say something but she remained silent. He didn't dare break the moment. He had Taylor in his bedroom and at ease with him. That was a huge step. He just wished he knew what the hell she was thinking.

Taylor was mesmerized by the rhythmic bunch and release of Jackson's muscles. Her cheeks flushed. She waved a hand in front of her face to cool herself down. The man was *built*. All strong lines and corded muscle that she wanted to sink her teeth into. Her sleeveless, Victorian-inspired gown was suddenly too hot. She undid the top two buttons. His back muscles had her fascinated but his arms rated a mention. And those powerful thighs...

She shook her head. What was she doing? Why was she alone with Jackson, with him almost naked? Big and gloriously naked. Why was she feeling hot and needy, when no man had ever been able to touch the sexual core of her?

Because she was lonely.

And it was her wedding night.

And she'd missed him.

And, she'd wondered if he'd really meant it when he'd said that they could try. Wondered if the courage her therapist had kept saying she had, in their long-distance phone call tonight, was real, and not a figment of her imagination.

Now, she wondered if this aggressively male creature in front of her would be patient. She wondered if he'd be tender. Most of all, she wondered if a wife who'd been married for convenience was allowed to stroke her husband's beautiful body without consequences.

Have the courage to fight for him, she ordered herself. He's never hurt you. And…he never will.

Mouth dry, heart in her throat, she reached out and ran a single finger down the bunched muscles of his back when he rose on his arms. Smooth, hot skin and rippling strength. She shivered.

Jackson froze and just about stopped breathing. "What are you doing?"

Silence. Had he blown it?

"T-touching you."

The slight hesitation got him back on even ground. "I'm sweaty." Why the hell had he said that? That wasn't how you seduced a woman.

"I don't mind," came the very quick response.

He lowered himself to the varnished wooden floor, not caring about dust or the comfort of his heavily aroused body. Resting his head on his arms, he silently gave her permission and wondered what she'd do.

After a pause that seemed to last forever, she knelt beside him, the fine material of her nightgown fluttering against his heated skin. He could feel the soft warmth of her, hear the whisper of her breath, almost smell her desire. The wait had his instincts tugging at the reins, fighting for the freedom to devour her.

Then she touched him.

Hesitant, exploratory strokes that tipped him into sweet insanity. When he remained quiescent under her, she put her hands flat on his back and stroked harder. Kneaded. Played. He could imagine those hands on other parts of his anatomy, all soft heat and soft pain. He wanted to tell her to use her mouth on him, to nibble and caress and kiss. Sweat beaded across his brow when he felt her straddle him, her gown resting atop his back and thighs.

"Am I too heavy?" An intimate question.

"No." His voice was raw.

"Jackson?" She halted her eager exploration. "I'm hurting you. I'll go."

"Don't!" This *was* torture, but of a kind no hot-blooded man would resist. "Stay, *piccola*."

To his relief, she settled against him again, her hands continuing to stroke and squeeze. Her teeth scraped at the bunched muscles of his upper arm and the sexy warmth of her generous breasts pressed against his back. "You're so strong." Warm breath whispered over his arm. "So wonderfully sexy. I want to just…" With a groan, she laid an open-mouthed kiss on his upper back, before suckling the spot. Her tongue soothed even as it stroked the inferno burning up his body from the inside out.

He wondered if a man could die of unadulterated sexual pleasure. Then she was scattering teasing, nibbling kisses across his shoulders and he decided he didn't care. Her small hands were everywhere, tracing firm muscle and hot skin, shaping and learning. And caressing.

He'd never been petted like this. Bonnie had preferred heat and speed, not interested in this kind of erotic love play. Before her, the women he'd attracted had wanted hard, rough sex—what his strong, muscular body represented to them. He'd thought he hadn't minded but now found that he'd minded very much. He liked the way Taylor was exploring him, as if she was delighted with him, as if she'd been saving up all her fantasies just for him.

Wiggling down his body, she grazed her teeth over the taut skin of his lower back. Everything was taut, Jackson thought, as she skipped over his buttocks and rested near his knees. Her fingernails grazed the backs of his thighs.

"Dio!" He jerked up so hard that he almost threw her to the floor.

"Jackson?" Those fingers had frozen on his thighs. "Did I do something wrong?"

He took a deep breath. "Only when you stopped."

A second later, she was running those damnably gentle hands up the backs of his legs. "I love the way you feel against my skin—so rough, so different from me. Your body heats me up from the inside out. Sometimes...I just...I just want to rub myself up against you. Naked."

That halting confession shattered what was left of his mind. For the first time in his life, Jackson Santorini became a totally sensate being, focused only on the feel of the woman who held him in her sweet hands, who found his body delicious and seemed to want to spend hours at her pleasure.

Seven

Taylor woke up feeling so fine. She grinned when she remembered why. Poor Jackson. Wonderful, lovely, beautiful Jackson. He'd let her touch him as much as she wanted, let her squeeze and caress and bite and taste. And he hadn't moved throughout it. He'd been on the floor when she'd left. Her delectable husband might still be there.

A masculine knock on her door put an end to that silly illusion. Remnants of fear infiltrated her heart. Would he expect what any man would, after his wife had pretty much treated him as her property the night before?

"Come in." She sat up, sheets pulled up to her chin.

He was dressed in blue jeans and a white T-shirt, his hair damp, as if he'd just showered. His T-shirt was loose, but did nothing to hide the definition of the upper arms she'd lavished such attention on, only hours before. She finally found the courage to meet his gaze, fearing she'd see the red haze of desire. All that met her was a coolness she'd rarely seen when he spoke to her.

"We need to discuss some things."

"Okay." It was a shock to find that she hated her husband's expression. She'd rather see dangerous passion than this nothingness. "Are you angry with me?"

He shook his head in a sharp negative. "Come down when you're ready."

"Tell me what's wrong. And don't pretend it's nothing." She glared at him.

"*Taylor.*"

"I told you, don't Taylor me. Tell me why you're brooding!" Frustrated, she punched the pillow by her side.

He blew out a breath between clenched teeth and then stalked to the bed, dark eyes glittering. Leaning over her, he put his hands flat on either side of her hips. "I am not angry," he repeated. "I am also not a saint. You're dressed like an invitation and you spent last night with your pretty little hands all over me. I didn't mind. Feel free to do it again any time you please. But," he paused for breath, "I can't be in this bedroom and talk with you as if we're just friends, so let me deal with it. Don't push."

Mouth dry at the quietly powerful confession, she said, "I won't apologize for last night."

"I didn't ask you to." A tiny spark of humor appeared in his eyes. "I'm not an idiot."

Memories of tactile pleasure had her heart racing. "Can I really do it again?"

He groaned and went to push off the bed. She wrapped her arms around his neck, caught in the tantalizing grip of a sensual world she'd never imagined could exist for her. Without warning, his entire face went taut.

"Let go, Taylor. My control is so close to the edge that you don't want to continue."

She released him, convinced by the dark passion she saw prowling behind the civilized mirage of his eyes.

When she came downstairs, Jackson was sitting at the table on the verandah, waiting for her. Breakfast had been delivered while she was upstairs.

Taking a seat, she asked, "What are those?" when he lifted a document from the pile at his elbow.

"Legal papers." He raised his head and those dark eyes wouldn't let her glance away. "I want to adopt Nick."

She put down the melon wedge she'd chosen. "Why?"

"I'm certain that Hegerty will back off on his custody application. But, if we manage to do this, it'll be almost impossible for him to come after Nick later on."

"Is that the only reason you want to adopt Nick?"

"Is it not enough?" Nothing in his tone gave her a hint of his emotions.

She shook her head. "It will mean something to Nick. He's never really had a father and I don't think he could bear the hurt if you adopted him and then forgot him." As a child, she'd experienced that brutal truth over and over.

"You'd share him that much with me?" The quickly masked hope in Jackson's eyes was unexpected. Then she remembered his desire for a baby. Maybe, in spite of her recent courage, she might never give him a child who was his flesh and blood, but she could give him this.

"Of course," she said, softly. "He needs you but it'll only work if you can go the distance, even if we part. If you adopt him, you'll have to be his father. *Forever.*"

"Yes." It was an answer so strong that she didn't need to hear any more. Nick's heart was safe with Jackson. Right now, she didn't want to think about her own.

"Can I authorize the adoption?"

He nodded. "To a point. You're a legal guardian."

She picked up the melon wedge. "Mrs. Willis suggested that Mom make me a testamentary guardian in her will."

"Under the law, it's likely that we can dispense with Hegerty's consent since he abandoned Nick. But, we have to consider the possibility that it might be needed in case the court refuses to make a finding of neglect."

Her head jerked up. "He won't give consent."

Jackson's smile was without humor. "Somehow, I think I can talk him around if it comes to that."

She believed him. No one could stand in Jackson's way once he was set on a course. While she ate, he made a quick call that set the new train of legal proceedings in motion. Afterward, he sat opposite her, not eating, just looking out to the blue, blue sea with eyes that seemed to be lost in memories. She couldn't bear his withdrawal. Standing, she walked around behind him and bent down to hug his neck.

He looked up, one hand on her arm. "Hey." Surprise was evident in his Italian-dark eyes.

"Don't." It was wrenched out of her.

"Don't?"

"Don't go away from me," she ordered. "Please, Jackson." A softer plea.

Her mother had shut her out. Neither her biological father nor her stepfather had ever truly acknowledged her existence. Nick saw her, but today she realized it wasn't enough. She needed this beautiful man to see her, too.

Jackson tugged at her hands until she came around to stand in front of him. He pulled her into his lap. "I'm right here, *cara*." His attention was focused wholly on her.

Touched by his unexpected tenderness, her smile came from the heart. "Where did you go?"

"It is not something to speak of this bright day."

She touched his jaw in a firm gesture. "Yes, it is."

A hint of amusement softened his stern expression. "Bossy little madam."

"*Your* bossy little madam," she said boldly, testing her wings, seeing how far her very dominant husband would let her go, learning how much she would have to fight to ensure he didn't become a despot.

His smile widened. Leaning over, he pressed a hard kiss to her lips. "Yes. *Mine.* Don't ever forget it."

She was startled by her enjoyment of the fleeting pressure. "Don't you get ideas about being possessive."

"Too late." The look in his eyes was dark fire, slumbering heat. And suddenly, she remembered the feel of his skin against her mouth. The hands she'd put on his shoulders clenched as desire flooded her bloodstream.

His eyes took in her flushed cheeks. "You look at me like you want me."

"I do," she acknowledged. "Will you kiss me again?" Her fingers stroked the vulnerable skin of his nape.

The look he gave her was pure male heat. "My body is for your pleasure, *mia moglie.*"

Fire rippled through her as he tipped her head down with a gentle grip on her chin and tasted her—slow and thorough, as if he had all the time in the world. He played with the seam of her lips and bit down on the lower one, suckling it into his mouth but never entering hers.

She wrapped her arms around his neck and parted her lips, greedy for the pleasure she knew he could lavish. Chuckling at her eagerness, he accepted the invitation with male enthusiasm that made her head spin. She moaned at the sensation of his tongue inside her mouth, flirting with hers. Desperate to deepen the kiss to a higher level of intimacy, she dared the slightest touch in return.

He broke off the kiss with a gasp. "*Piccola,* you will kill your poor husband." Dark eyes glittered.

Then before she could protest, he took her lips in a kiss that was undeniably intimate, unquestionably possessive and incredibly tender. He tasted and licked and nibbled like a man who knew his woman's every desire, the quick jabbing of his tongue inside her mouth letting her know that while he'd wait for her passion, he wasn't averse to persuading her. She wasn't averse to being persuaded.

Waves of heat and almost painful desire rode her body, inciting her to cling to his male bulk, silently asking for more. In response, he gave her such a rawly sensual kiss that had she been standing, her knees would have buckled.

This time, when the kiss broke, she lay her head down on his chest, breathing hard, trying to find her feet again. Maybe, her mind whispered, if this felt so good, the rest would be even better? Fighting to find something less inflammatory to break the tension, she recalled his earlier preoccupation. "I haven't forgotten you know." She sat up.

"What?" His tone was very male, pitched to send her sensitized nerve endings skittering.

Struggling against her reaction, she realized that she was stroking the bunched muscles under the edge of his sleeve. Because she adored touching him, she didn't stop. "That you didn't answer my question about what it was that took you so far away from me."

"Taylor." He said her name as he always did when annoyed with her, a bit exasperated, a little stubborn.

"Where?" she repeated, determined to find out what was haunting him. This marriage would only work if he trusted her as she was being forced to trust him.

He looked at her for a long moment. "Your speaking of Nick reminded me of my own childhood."

"What was it like, being the child of a director and an actress?" His parents were both winners of awards at Cannes and the Oscars. His half sister, Valetta, looked to be following in their illustrious footsteps, while his two half brothers, Mario and Carlton, were having a somewhat rockier road to fame on the silver screen.

"Lonely." The honesty was raw. "I was the only child from their brief union, nine years older than Mario. My parents were very young when I was born. My half siblings are strangers to me. My mother kept Carlton after her marriage to his father, her third husband, broke up, and my father decided to build Mario and Valetta's mother a home next to his. I grew up with nannies and then boarding schools—aside from my name, all they ever gave me was the best care money could buy. Nothing more. Nothing less."

There was, she realized, no self-pity or anger in his tone at the injustice of being emotionally abandoned by his parents. Jackson Santorini's past had shaped a strong man, a man who would not easily break.

"I began boarding school at age five," he continued. "I saw my mother twice that year."

"And your father?" Taylor asked, hurting at the intense loneliness she heard behind the calm words. Despite everything, she'd never really been alone. Helena had not been the best of mothers but she'd never abandoned her children, and sometimes she'd even helped Taylor through the things a girl needed her mother for. Then there had been Nick to love and he'd loved her back.

"Once that year." His mouth quirked. "To introduce me to Amber or was it Mandy? Another big-breasted blonde. They get younger with each wife."

"They sound like absolutely terrible parents," she declared, without thinking that it might not be politic.

He stared at her for a moment and then started to chuckle. "I guess they are."

"Sorry." She was abashed by her rude words.

"No, you're right." He kissed her neck, as if he was tasting her. His lips were soft, his breath hot. "I was determined to never be like them."

"And you're not!" Snapped out of the sensual fog he could spin so easily, she sat up, scowling at the self-disgust she heard in his tone.

"I am my father's son." Jackson acknowledged the awful truth. "I may have inherited his frailties."

Taylor rolled her eyes. "Don't be silly."

"I once married a young blonde."

"You and the blonde both happened to be the same age at the time. Your father tends to go for the cradle." Her quick response was accompanied by a dry smile.

"I can't promise you loyalty." He didn't trust himself, not when his father's philandering genes ran in his veins. He'd never once cheated on Bonnie, but who knew when the badness would kick in.

"You're not a dog."

He scowled at her. "Stop being flippant." He knew how hurt she'd been at being abandoned by Lance, and yet he couldn't help himself from telling her the truth, needing her to accept him despite his flaws. It was an impossible situation because once she knew the truth, she would never trust him with the love he wanted. The love he needed.

One eyebrow rose. "Why not? You're being overdramatic. Must come from working in the movies."

"Taylor." Nobody else ever reduced him to growling.

"That doesn't work anymore," she said, gleefully.

"It never did." He was undone by her irreverence. "Don't you want to know the truth?"

"I know all I need to know. You'll care for me and you'll care for Nick while we're yours and afterward, you'll make sure that we have what we need." Her words were practical, her tone even. Implicit was an acceptance that this marriage would end in a year. He wanted to shake her out of her blithe assurance that she could walk away from him, force her to accept his claim. "That's more than anyone's ever done for me. It's enough."

It wasn't enough for him. He should have been glad at finding such a sensible woman. Yet he kept thinking that he was being shortchanged, if he accepted that this was all Taylor had to give him. Taylor, who had so much spirit and courage and hope. Taylor, who he'd thought would lead him out of the darkness into which he'd tumbled after years of cold loneliness.

He supposed he deserved it. After all, a practical arrangement was all he'd asked for and she'd promised to deliver—Nick's safety in exchange for a baby. His eyes narrowed. He had a year to make Taylor pregnant. Once he had her carrying his child, he'd teach her to trust him with her love, even if it took a lifetime. Poor Taylor. She had no idea who she'd struck a bargain with.

"I think we have to at least show up at this party," he told Taylor later that day. They'd spent most of the previous hours working on legal documents, taking only a short break to explore the nearby coral reef. The excursion had been worth making time for, if only to see the wonder on Taylor's face as they snorkeled through the reef's colorful and fearless inhabitants.

Though he was aware that after their return Taylor had spent time on the phone with her therapist, Maggie, he hadn't asked her about it. It was enough that she'd found someone who was able to help her. "It's being hosted by the resort owners." Knowing them was the reason he'd been able to get a spot on the exclusive paparazzi-free island on such short notice.

Scowling, Taylor said, "No, we're not going."

He was so used to her sunny nature that he was momentarily stunned by the determined denial. "Why not?"

He heard her gritting her teeth. "I was poor, Jackson. I

won't know how to fit in there. It'd be different starting out in our home because it would be *my* territory."

Her response astounded him. She was usually so self-contained and confident that occasionally he wished she'd show a little more need for him, but he'd never wanted her so vulnerable that she was hurting.

"You've worked in the industry…" he began, at a loss. And yet, the primitive part of him was exulting that she'd forgotten herself enough to share her fears with him.

"As a secretary!" Her eyes glittered. "They'll look down on me."

He walked across the verandah and clamped his hands on her shoulders. "*Cara mia,* I would never let them hurt you."

She bit her lip. He knew about her lack of trust in men and their promises, and could even understand it, but it still hurt when she didn't immediately believe in him.

"I won't let the vultures near you." He wanted to show her the tenderness she needed, but his voice came out rough, almost a command that she trust him.

To his surprise, she reacted favorably. Her back straightened and she threw him a glare for daring to give her an order. "I don't have anything to wear."

"We can go shopping in the resort boutiques. Whatever you wear, you'll knock 'em dead."

Her smile was brilliant, far more like the woman he was used to. "Thank you. You're a kind man."

When she pecked him on the cheek, he grit his teeth against the urge to haul her to the floor and indulge his starving senses. *Kind?* If he'd been a kind man, he'd have tried harder to think of a way to help her without marrying her. The truth was, when the idea had come, he hadn't looked any further, because he'd wanted sweet Taylor for his very own. And he would fight to keep her.

Santorini men weren't known for their sharing nature.

* * *

Taylor found a long, electric-blue gown in a shimmering fabric that was light enough for the tropical weather, but had a shine to it that meant it would do for an evening gown. It had no sleeves, and the soft curves of material at the neckline emphasized her breasts. The only things holding up the flimsy creation were two small diamante clasps on the shoulders. Up to that point, the dress was lovely. It was the fact that it had practically no back that had her biting her lip in indecision.

Looking over her shoulder into the dressing room mirror, she found the curved line of her spine framed in blue. She knew that if she went out in this dress, her husband's big hand was going to be on her bare skin for long periods of the night. She'd always known that Jackson would be very, very possessive about his woman. So, he would touch her in public, make his claim, make certain no one had any doubts about the fact that she belonged to him.

She shivered at the image, the tiny hairs on her body standing up. The thought of Jackson's hands on her didn't scare her, but it had taken Maggie to make her realize the depth of trust she had in him.

"What are you afraid of?" Maggie had asked earlier that day, deep into the long-distance session.

She'd remembered being pushed against the door in the basement, of the hand over her mouth in that park. "Pain, humiliation…of having my trust broken again."

"Oh, so Jackson hurts you? Debases you?"

"No! How dare you say that?" she'd yelled, furious.

"If I'm so wrong," Maggie had paused, "then what are you really afraid of?"

It had taken her long minutes to answer. "My own cowardice. What if I can't be what he needs?"

"What if you can? Take one step and find out."

* * *

One step. Like having Jackson's hands all over her. It was a distinctly tantalizing image after the way she'd run her own hands all over *him* and received such pleasure.

Her eyes widened as she slipped out of the dress. In the mirror, her breasts were almost quivering with desire. Oh, yes, the thought of having her husband's hands all over her wasn't a reason against buying this dress.

The party wasn't as harrowing as she'd feared. Though she'd worked hard to climb out from under Lance's shadow, sometimes his barbs about her worth returned to haunt her. But, it appeared that her panic had been for naught. True to his word, Jackson was by her side throughout the night and once it became clear that she was very much *his,* people treated her with a sort of cautious pleasantness.

Taylor had to hide her smile. She'd never inspired fear in anyone, but her dark and very Italian husband certainly did. She approved. In this world, he needed every advantage. It was enough for his wife to know that he wasn't a man who would hurt those he'd sworn to protect. No one else needed to be aware of his tenderness.

The only sour point came toward the end of the evening. A buxom blonde sidled up to Jackson, as if Taylor weren't held firmly by his side, his big hand flat on her lower back. As she'd guessed, he hadn't stopped touching her for more than a few seconds at a time. On occasion, he'd move his thumb in an idle movement and her breath would catch while the bottom fell out of her stomach.

The heat of him was enticing enough but when he moved his hand…she wanted to beg him to move a little lower. Oh yes, having Jackson's hands all over her was becoming more and more intriguing. Especially if he touched her whole body the way he'd touched her back tonight. No pain, extreme possessiveness and a hot, wanting look in his eyes.

She had the feeling that if she'd been an ordinary woman with no hang-ups, they'd have either arrived at the party very late or not at all. The minute she'd walked out of her room, his face had tensed and he'd growled at her to get her "little butt back in there" and change out of that "excuse for a dress."

Of course she hadn't, but with any other woman she knew Jackson would've probably won the fight by the simple expedient of tearing off the dress, and keeping her in bed until it was too late to make an appearance. The primitive desire that had glittered in his eyes when he first saw her had been an explicit indication of exactly what he wanted to do to her. If they did end up making love, she'd have to watch his tendency to take over her life and she had no illusions that he wouldn't try.

That was the man he was, difficult to handle, almost impossible to fight, but perhaps, she thought with feminine insight, he could be coaxed, gentled. And if he did allow her to tame him, even just a little, didn't that mean she had some power in the marriage? Being with him was very definitely a partnership—he expected her to match him.

Trusting Jackson with her body became an even more attractive option when she understood the dynamic of their relationship, so attractive that she was involved in a heated daydream about her big husband and her naked body, when the top-heavy blonde sashayed over.

"Jackson Santorini! I thought it was you." The twit made the mistake of laying a hand on Jackson's sleeve.

Eyes narrowed, Taylor reached out and brushed the woman's hand off. "Oops. I think *my* husband had some…dirt, on his sleeve. You really should watch that, darling." She glanced up at him, a warning in her eyes.

He was trying not to grin. "Thank you, *mia moglie*."

The sensual glint in his eye told her that he was pleased at her little show of jealousy. She didn't care. Forget anything she'd ever said about allowing him a mistress. If he touched another woman, she'd gut them both.

"Do I know you?" Jackson hugged Taylor to his side, soothing her with his obvious display of ownership.

A spark of anger appeared in the blonde's eyes. "Belle Bouvier. We met at the Vanderbilt party last spring."

"Apologies, Belle. You look a little different."

"Oh." The twit dimpled, apparently forgiving him. "I remember! I'd dyed my hair black! Can you imagine?"

"Well, I did see you when it was black."

Taylor could tell that he was fighting the urge to burst out laughing. "Hello, Belle. I'm Taylor."

"Nice to meet you." The poisonous look in her eyes said otherwise. "I just wanted to congratulate Jackson."

"For what?" Jackson asked.

"My sources tell me that you've just been voted *Glitter* magazine's sexiest bachelor of the year."

"No longer a bachelor." He looked down at Taylor, who was fuming. "Thank you, Belle, but you'll have to excuse me. I believe our hostess is signaling us."

As they walked, Taylor muttered, "Bouvier, my foot."

Jackson snickered, hugging her to him. It appeared that while Taylor could talk about him keeping a mistress, reality was another matter. He had a possessive little wife on his hands. Life had just become a lot more interesting.

"Stage name, I would guess." He moved his hand on the smooth skin of her back, coaxing her back into a good mood. Not that he minded the reason for her temper. He was confident enough of his masculinity to enjoy being considered her personal property.

She made a little feminine noise but before she could respond to his physical cajoling, a man slithered to a stop in front of them. Henry Carey. Jackson detested the man. It seemed their night for meeting unwelcome acquaintances.

"Santorini."

"Carey." He hugged Taylor closer to him. She complied, a sleek, giving woman who fitted her body to his.

"Congratulations on your marriage."

"Word travels fast."

"You know how it is." Henry smirked and turned to Taylor. "So, it must be…interesting, being married to a man of your husband's size…and strength."

The insinuation was clear. The papers had had a field day after Bonnie's suicide, using Jackson's face and image to hint at violence and pain. He usually ignored Henry, finding him pitiful, but tonight his pride rebelled against Taylor hearing the lies about him. If she heard them often enough, maybe she'd start to believe, maybe she'd start to fear him. He could bear anything but that. About to move toward Carey, he was stopped by his wife, who stepped protectively in front of him.

"Why you *odious little man,*" Taylor said, her voice hard but low. "My husband is a better man than you'll ever be, you weedy, pompous creature. I bet you don't even know what to do with a woman…when you can get some female drunk enough to co-operate."

Jackson couldn't believe Taylor was defending him and insulting Henry, and doing it well. The other man wasn't used to trading barbs with a smart woman who didn't consider herself bound by the rules of their impolite society, which deemed that nothing must ever be said with blunt force, only covertly implied.

"How dare you…" Henry began, mouth pinched.

"Oh, go away." She flicked her hand in a dismissive gesture. "You annoy me. And if I ever hear you say anything against my husband, I'll tell everyone exactly how you got the funding for your last miserable picture."

Henry's face paled. "How do you know?"

Jackson was fascinated. Absolutely and utterly. He stood behind his wife, one hand curved around her body to lie on her stomach, not interfering. Delighted amazement kept him from taking over. No one had ever stood up for him. Not a single person. He was stunned at the feeling that spread through him at seeing Taylor's protectiveness.

She raised a brow. "You really should be more discreet. Now, leave." It was a regal order.

Henry left, looking at Taylor with more fear in his eyes than he'd ever shown Jackson.

"*Piccola?*"

"Yes." She was scowling at Henry's retreating back, her arms folded like some avenging warrior-goddess.

"What do you know?"

"Secretaries hear everything. I keep in touch with my friends in the movie business. Let's just say that Henry participated in a casting couch…,in reverse."

"But, who'd want Henry?" He was flabbergasted.

"Exactly what I said."

Eight

Jackson had just started unbuttoning the formal black shirt he'd worn to the party, having eschewed any kind of jacket because of the heat, when Taylor wandered in from across the hall. She had her face scrunched up in concentration and her hands on the clasp of her necklace.

"Darling, can you…" She turned her back to him and swept aside her hair to bare her nape, creamy white against the electric blue of the dress.

He walked over, hands aching to touch her. "Darling," she'd called him, like they were a normal couple. Tonight had been an education, exposing both Taylor's possessiveness and her protectiveness. But, the fact was, they weren't a normal couple and despite those delightful revelations, he was strung taut with desire for his sweet, sexy wife.

He undid the clasp without speaking, afraid he'd give away his frustration if he opened his mouth. Her damn dress was a husband's nightmare. He'd had to have a hand on her throughout the evening to warn off the predators. A lot of the men had had a look in their eyes that said they were just waiting until he was distracted, before they pounced. He hadn't being distracted by anything other than the feel of his wife's sleek body under his palm. She'd seemed perfectly happy to let him stake his claim so publicly, not that he'd given her much choice.

Or ever would.

When the necklace fell into Taylor's hand, she didn't turn and leave, but bent her head to look at something in the chain that had caught her interest. This time, he couldn't resist the urge. Leaning over, he put his hands lightly on her hips and pressed his lips to her nape.

A gasp of surprise. "Jackson?"

"Yes." Since she hadn't moved, he kissed her again, his hands pressing a little more firmly. Lord but she was soft. The urge to pull her tight against his straining arousal was almost irresistible.

"What are you doing?"

"Pleasuring you…and me." Another kiss. His hands itched to rise up and cradle her breasts. He kept them still on her hips by force of will alone.

"Sexual pleasure?" It was barely a whisper.

His gut clenched with guilt. He drew back. "I am sorry, *piccola,* I should not have pushed. A kiss doesn't mean permission to ask for more."

She didn't look at him but shook her head. "Push."

He froze. "Taylor?"

"I'm tired of being afraid. I want to know what the fuss is all about." It was such a Taylor-like answer that he had no trouble believing her. "And I meant what I said to that odious creature. You're a good man. You'd never hurt me so I have no excuse for fear. Show me."

He bit back a grin, passion tempered by tenderness at her bravado. "Are you sure?"

She sent him a scowling look over her shoulder. "Yes." She reached out and threw the necklace onto a small table in one corner of his room. "Jackson, what if I can't…finish this? What if I freeze?"

"Baby, the finish line can be wherever you want. It can end with a kiss or with me inside you. Your choice." He put his hands back on her hips. Aware that he could feast on her forever if he did this right, he caged his rampant desire. Tonight, he'd be the tender lover she needed, not the marauder he was.

"Just keep pushing until I say stop." Her words were flippant but her tone nervous.

He adored her. "I'm at your command." A sudden thought gave him pause. "*Cara,* are you protected?" He didn't expect her to be. After all, she was a virgin. And, he'd ordered her not to guard against pregnancy.

"I know what we agreed, Jackson, but I don't think I could handle being pregnant with everything else that's happening. We need to use something." She sounded worried but resolute.

He kissed her neck again. "Okay, *piccola.* One step at a time." Though his Italian soul rebelled against his wife protecting herself from his seed, the civilized man knew that she was too fragile right now. First he'd seduce her until all worry left her. Then he'd make love to her so often that *nothing* would protect her. And then, he'd gently love her as she grew big with his child.

A sigh of relief from his beautiful wife. "Thank you. If…we manage to do this, I'll organize a prescription for birth control when we return home. Have you…?"

"Yes." Despite his autocratic demands, he'd brought protection, wise enough to know that he couldn't push her too far, too soon. "I am healthy, *mia moglie*." He'd had himself tested after he'd discovered Bonnie's infidelities, his pride in shreds. "After you are on birth control, I want to be skin to skin with you." The image of Taylor's body enclosing his in passionate heat momentarily blinded him with need, obliterating any painful memories.

Her neck flushed. "Yes. What…" He felt her swallow. "What does *mia moglie* mean?"

"My wife." He didn't bother to hide his simmering satisfaction at that fact.

He'd been gently stroking her hips the entire time they'd been talking. Now, he tugged her backward just a little, until their bodies touched along her entire length. He sucked in a breath at the lush feel of her against his erection. She didn't demur at the intimacy, so he moved one hand to lie flat on her stomach, while the other ran up the smooth skin of her arm. She gasped but let him do as he would. Jackson wondered if she'd be a passive lover. The thought didn't appeal. Taylor's fire was one of the reasons he found her so sexually compelling.

"Jackson?" Her tone was pure female temptation.

"Yes?" His voice was becoming hoarse as desire took a stranglehold on him.

"Can I touch you, too?" Fingers settled hesitantly on his arm, as gentle as butterfly wings.

"Anywhere," he managed to answer, his body taut with memories of her stroking the night before.

"Oh, good." A sigh of relief. "You've probably noticed that I can't control myself around your body."

He couldn't help it. Chuckling, he hugged her around her middle and buried his face against her warm neck, breathing in the tart scent that was indisputably Taylor.

"What's so funny?" Leaning back into him, she clasped slim hands over the hand he had on her stomach.

"I was thinking that I am the same where you are concerned, *piccola.*" He kissed his way up her throat. She tasted like woman. Soft, delectable, welcoming woman. Her body melted for him, accommodating the hard angles of his own body with such sweetness that he was undone.

"Jackson," she murmured, when he moved to the other side of her neck, pushing her hair aside. Her voice was slumberous, pleasured, as sultry as the tropical night.

"Mmm?" He placed both palms flat against her stomach, accustoming her to the feel of him. Taylor wasn't petite—her head reached his shoulder, but she had a feminine build that made her very vulnerable to his obvious strength. His shoulders were twice the width of hers. If Bonnie had called him brutish before he'd really started pumping weights, what would Taylor think?

A hint of worry stirred but he fought it. Taylor wasn't Bonnie. She would never deliberately hurt him with cruel barbs. But, given her experience with the more brutal members of his sex, he wondered if she might find his body too big and bulky when he wasn't lying down on the floor, as he'd been when she'd touched him. Possessive, demanding and adoring as he was, rejection from her might kill him.

Taylor interrupted his shadowy musings. "You know how you have your shirt half unbuttoned?"

"Yes." He nibbled on her. She shivered and angled her head to give him easier access. He smiled and sucked her skin into his mouth.

Breathily, she asked, "Can I undo it all the way?"

It took a few moments for the soft question to penetrate his dazed brain. "When?"

"Now?" Not so confident a response.

He knew he could seduce her to a point where his body wouldn't matter. But she might wake with disgust in her eyes, and he couldn't bear that. He turned her in his arms, preparing himself to accept any reaction. She immediately started unbuttoning his shirt. Relieved more than he wanted to acknowledge at her continued fascination with his body, he kissed whatever part of her he could reach.

Until she pushed at him.

He moved back a step. Another push on his chest, small hands warm on his skin. Another step back. Sable lashes lifted and dark blue eyes met his. He wondered what she was doing. Then the bed hit the back of his legs.

"Sit." An order made palatable by her smile of anticipation, as if she couldn't wait to touch him.

He sat and was glad he'd obeyed when she moved into the V of his legs. Unable to resist temptation, he placed his hands on her back, just above her sweetly curved bottom. A sexy smile flirting with her lips, she ran her fingers down the sides of his face to his neck. Her gaze lowered. She licked her lips. His erection grew to impossible proportions. Bending, she pushed the now open shirt off his shoulders, fingers lingering on his skin as if she were indulging her sense of touch. Her breasts were so close that it was torture for him to remain still.

"Move your hands." A husky command. "Please, Jackson. I'm trying to be brave because I have to know if I can beat this fear, but…well, maybe I'm not so very brave."

He was hers. Completely. How could any man deny helping this woman find her way through the world of the most intimate sensuality?

He obeyed and helped her get rid of his shirt. When he would've returned his hands to their former position, she shook her head and stepped back. Nervous courage and determination were stamped on her features. Facing him, their gazes locked in an intimate embrace that went far beyond the sexual, she reached up and released the diamante clasps on each shoulder.

Breath lost, Jackson watched the material slither to her feet. Stepping out of the pool of shimmering blue, she returned to him. Dressed only in black lace-topped stockings that reached midthigh, lacy black panties and a garter belt, Taylor Santorini had a body that drove her husband insane with lust and hunger. He fixed his gaze on her face, knowing that if he looked at her bare breasts he'd devour her.

"Jackson?" She was back between his legs. When he looked up, she sat down on one thigh, arm around his neck and legs primly together between his own legs, the backs of her knees and calves touching his leg on one side.

"Yes?" One of his hands was resting flat on her lower back. Now, he placed the other on her knee.

"You have to take over now." Her big eyes were solemn. "I don't know what to do."

He didn't answer her in words, didn't think he could speak. Instead, holding that gaze, woman and girl combined, he leaned down and pressed his lips to hers. Her mouth opened for him at once and she invited him in. He knew she liked kissing, so he kissed her with tender heat, teasing and inviting and tantalizing.

He began to move the hand on her back, while he slid the other one to her thigh, just above the lace of her stocking. Almost at once, her body began to stiffen. While Taylor trusted him, she'd been afraid for too long to give in without fear. He remembered the look in her eyes as she'd stripped so sensuously for him, and wondered about the best way to seduce his wife. Utterly and completely. Until she was whimpering. And cajoling. And demanding.

When he drew back, her gaze fixed warily on him. "What comes next?"

"Whatever you like," he whispered, moving his thumb along the top edge of her stocking.

She sat up in his lap, both arms around his neck, breasts

grazing his chest. It took every ounce of self-control he had not to lower his head and suck a nipple into his mouth. He could almost *feel* the succulent flesh against his tongue, almost taste the uniqueness that was her. "I don't have any practical experience. I thought you'd like to be in charge this time around."

So serious, so solemn, like she was learning a lesson in school, Taylor's very innocence gave him the reins he needed to leash his escalating hunger. As a young man, he'd had very earthy appetites. He'd forcibly caged that part of his psyche for years, but when he'd seen Taylor on that rainy night, it had shattered the chains and stretched awake. It had been gaining in power over the past week and tonight, he knew it would storm him. Before that happened, he needed to have her trust. Otherwise, he thought darkly, the strength of his passion could devastate her.

"I'm afraid of hurting you," he admitted. He ran the hand on her thigh up her side. Her skin was so smooth and silky that he just wanted to lay her down and indulge himself in her body. Tugging her hand off his shoulder, he pressed his palm against hers. "I'm so much bigger than you." Their differences were graphically illustrated by the way his hand dwarfed hers.

Eyes wide, she stared and then carefully intertwined her fingers through his. Pulling their clasped hands to her lips, she kissed his knuckles one by one, her lips velvety on his skin. The tenderness of the caress shook him. Biting sensual need was overlaid with a painfully soft emotion. No woman had ever touched him like that. As if she was afraid of hurting *him*.

"Cara." He released her hand and returned his to her curvy hip. "I want to give you only pleasure. Tell me what would pleasure you, my little wife."

"I'm not little." She glared and pushed her hands into his hair. "Well, only next to you."

"I'm the only one who matters." He kissed her once more, loving the taste of her. "What do you like? This?" He moved his thumb on her thigh again.

"Yes." It was a whisper against his lips.

"This?" He reluctantly left her lips to press kisses along the tops of her breasts. He was careful to use only his mouth to caress her, aware that she had come to associate male hands on her breasts with pain.

"Oh, yes. Can you…"

He raised his head, the barbarian maleness within him scenting victory within his grasp. "Yes, *piccola?*"

Blushing, she shook her head. "No, it's okay."

"Tell me. I don't want to be a brute." He deliberately played up his helplessness. He was floundering, not wanting to scare her, but he also knew that for some reason he would never understand, his little wife was insanely protective of him.

"You're not!" She frowned at him, fingers digging into his flesh. "Don't you ever let anyone call you that."

He bit back his smile to nibble at her lips. "Tell me then. What would you like?"

She looked down and then back up. Her cheeks were pink. Dressed in strips of delicate black lace, she was sexy innocence personified. "I just wondered…"

"Yes." He cradled her nearer, pressing her against the heat of his body. The pressure of her full breasts on his chest pushed him one step closer to insanity.

She snuggled impossibly closer. "You know how I like to touch you?"

Did he know? He'd never been as aroused as he'd been last night. "Yes." It came out a rough growl.

"Um…I thought since you liked it so much and I liked doing it…I thought it might work in reverse."

Crazed with desire, it took him a few seconds to understand. He buried his face in her hair, trying to relearn to breathe. The scent of her twined around him, turning up the heat several degrees. He burned. For her.

"No?" A faint whisper. "You wouldn't like that?"

Raising his head, he kissed her hard. "Like it? I feel like all my Christmases have come at once."

Her lips parted in surprise. "Why?"

He smiled, finding his footing again. "Because you're going to let me touch you." He stroked his hands to clasp her waist. "Kiss you." He pressed his lips against her jaw. "Fondle you." He ran one hand boldly to her breast and closed over it very, very gently, shocking a gasp out of her. "And do anything else I please." Grinning, he kicked off his shoes, then put her on the bed, lying down beside her, propped up on one elbow. "Can I touch you anywhere?"

Wide-eyed, she nodded. "It only seems fair."

Chuckling, he put one hand on her stomach. "Do you like everything I've done so far?"

Her immediate nod made him grin.

"What did you like best?" He leaned close, giving her the intimacy she needed to make her sensual requests.

She swallowed but said, "Your hands on me."

He fought off a shudder. "In that case…" Moving the hand on her stomach, he brought it to her garter belt. "Can I take this off?"

"I can…" she began to offer, reaching between their bodies. Her knuckles brushed his abdomen and he had to bite back the demand that she move lower.

"I want to." After a little fumbling, he flicked open the catches holding the entire contraption together. Pulling it off her, he threw it aside. Now, his pretty little wife was dressed only in barely there panties and lace-topped black stockings.

He saw her swallow. Her eyes fluttered shut. It was just

as well that she wasn't looking, because he was sure that the lust in his eyes would've scared his sexy Taylor. His teeth-gritting control after she'd first stripped had flown out the window with the garter belt.

He'd known that she had lush breasts, just right for his big hands, but he'd never thought that they'd be so delicate, traced with blue veins and translucent skin. He could spend hours adoring those breasts, topped with coral-colored nipples that peaked for him when he touched them with the tip of one finger.

"Oh!" Taylor's body arched and her eyes opened.

Looking up, he held her gaze as he closed a hand over her left breast. It was time she learned to associate pleasure with this particular man's hands on her. Because he intended to have them there on a regular basis.

Her body went taut. Her heartbeat accelerated.

"Breathe," he instructed.

"I can't, not when you're doing that!" She sucked in a breath, giving lie to her declaration. "That feels…good." Her surprised words trailed off into a moan as he began to massage her sensitive flesh. "Jackson, please don't stop."

He had to bite back a smile of satisfaction at the little victory. "Try and make me." He played with her breasts until a sheen of perspiration covered her body, a fine layer that made her skin shimmer. He thanked God that she hadn't thought to ask for the lights to be turned off. The sight of her long-limbed, luscious body coming to life for him was indescribable. Her nipples were very sensitive—a touch and she whimpered, a rub and she gasped, a squeeze and her entire body went taut.

When she was moaning, needy without knowing what she searched for, he leaned down and took one pouting nipple into his mouth and suckled. Hard. Her body shuddered. Against her, he smiled in satisfaction and moved to her neglected breast. He wasn't going to be merciful and let her rest. Not when he could feel his own need trying to buck the reins. Another wave of shudders rippled through her. Her hands clutched at his body, desperately trying to find an anchor.

Using his teeth to hold it for a moment, he finally released her nipple, sending tiny shock waves through her limp body. While she was half-dazed, he got rid of the rest of his clothing and took care of protection. She'd barely risen through the pleasure-fog when he rejoined her.

There was no fear in her eyes, nothing but surprised joy and welcome. For him. Certain of her acquiescence, he ran his hand down her stomach to the satin and lace protecting her core. Wet heat met his cupping hand. The wild hunger in him came within sniffing distance of freedom. He pressed his fingers against her, pushing her toward another precipice. Blue eyes, almost blind with desire, opened.

"Jackson…" She sounded lost.

He moved over her, careful not to scare her with his weight, but she relaxed at the touch of his body. Arms around him, she parted her legs. The trust implicit in the action shook him. Sliding one hand under her neck, he tangled his fingers in her hair and lifted her head for a kiss that was lusty and wild and erotic. She reciprocated stroke for stroke, meeting his demands and making her own, her breasts pressing against the crisp hair on his chest. With his other hand, he continued to stroke her through her panties, assuaging the need he'd aroused.

Possessive need roared through him when she squirmed under him. She was *his*. No other man had ever touched her like he was touching her. And, he vowed, no other man ever would. A year be damned. Child or not, Taylor Santorini was *never* going to be allowed to leave her husband.

* * *

The sensation of Jackson's crisp, black hair against her breasts rendered Taylor almost insensate with bliss. All these years, she'd associated shame with her breasts. After tonight, if she survived, she'd think only of the pure heat in Jackson's eyes as he'd indulged himself. After his attentive loving, her flesh was incredibly tender. Hardly knowing what she was doing, she rubbed herself against him and heard him groan, deep inside. The hand between her legs was removed.

She ripped her lips from his and said, "No! Come back!" and surprised herself with her own boldness. Twenty-four years of sexual starvation had made her voracious. And Jackson's tenderness had made her daring. The joy she felt was overwhelming.

He growled at her as if he was almost over the edge, and kissed her again. When she felt close to mindless, he pushed her down into the pillow and she felt his big hand slipping under one side of her panties. She was puzzled by the action for only a second because by then he'd ripped the fragile material from her body. Then he did as she'd asked and cupped her again. Except this time there was no barrier between her most sensitive place and his big, possessive hand. Or his fingers.

She writhed against him, loving the weight of him on her. When he nudged at her with his hips, she wrapped her legs around his waist. Hot male skin sizzled against the tingling skin of her upper thighs. He was naked. Opening dazed eyes, she said, "When?"

He didn't answer, intent on kissing the side of her neck while his fingers stroked and rubbed and did everything to make her lose her fragile control on reality. She dug her fingers into his arms and tried to tug him up.

Dark eyes slammed into hers when he rose. "You want

something?" His voice was edgy, dangerous. If he hadn't been hers, she might've been scared. Except he *was* hers and the rough desire in his voice made her feel exquisitely, utterly sexy.

"You." Against her thigh, she could feel the hard heat of him. For her. Jackson Santorini desired *her.* "I want you."

"You're not ready." He dipped his head to kiss her breast-bone, his tongue stroking a line up to her neck.

Goose bumps broke out over her body. "What?" She tangled her hands in his hair. "I am."

"I'm too big. You have to be wetter."

She swallowed. Then his finger started rubbing a very, very, very pleasurable spot between her legs, and she stopped wondering just how big her big husband was. All she could think was, please don't let him stop. He didn't. He kept going until she was whimpering, limp and aching with need.

"Please," she begged. "Oh, please, Jackson."

He was without mercy. "I have to make you ready, *piccola.* There will be only pleasure for you this night. Absolute pleasure." He pushed one finger deep into her. Her body clenched around him, trying to capture his power. "Feel the strength of what is between us. Give me your satisfaction." Demanding eyes met hers.

She tried to say that she had no more pleasure left to give, when he carefully slid another finger into her. A scream was torn from her as tiny, exquisitely erotic quakes shook her body from the inside out. Even as she rode the storm, she could feel him gently but insistently spreading his fingers within her, an intimate invasion that sent flames racing through her bloodstream, marking her as Santorini's woman.

"Why?" It was all she could trust herself to say, her gaze locked with his in an intimacy so deep, it took the sexual connection to another level.

"I'm stretching you, my little *wife.*" There was an emphasis on that last word, an edge in his voice that could only be described as dominant. "You must take one more before you will be ready." It was a sensual dare.

Pulling his head down, she kissed him, taking a sharp bite out of his lower lip in retaliation. He chuckled hoarsely against her and she felt him slide that third finger, oh-so-slowly, inside her. Unable to stop, she clenched around him, her body strung taut in expectation. This time, she wasn't going over alone.

"Now!" she ordered. "Right now, Jackson Santorini!"

His eyes flashed at the order but there was a curve to his mouth. "My pleasure, Mrs. Santorini." He withdrew his fingers and rose above her, arms braced on either side of her head. Then he ran one hand down her side to cup her buttock and hold her in place, while his thighs kept her parted legs open for him. Without further prelude, he thrust into her in a single powerful stroke.

She screamed and bucked at the invasion.

"Hush. The pain will pass." It was a low-voiced command, almost a growl. "It was better all at once."

The sheer maleness of the comment snapped her out of her sudden shock. She hadn't expected it to hurt so much. Catching her breath, she glared at the sexy man holding her prisoner. "Easy for you to say. Big, my eye! You're enormous!"

She couldn't believe he started to grin through the strain on his face. "Wait 'til I am really aroused, little one." It was clear that he was teasing her with that emphasis on "little."

"Ha, ha." In an effort to settle him more comfortably inside her, she wiggled.

His eyes squeezed shut.

She froze. "Jackson? Am I hurting you?"

He sounded like he was struggling to breathe. "You're torturing me." He opened his eyes. "Do you suppose you're ready for me to move?" The rough amusement in his tone made her sigh in relief.

His chest was as delicious as ever. The wide expanse of hot male skin had quickly distracted her from the sharp pain. It was the feeling of complete and utter penetration that took some getting used to. "Can you go slow?"

He looked at her like she was mad. *"Dio!* After I die in this bed, please tell the church that I am a candidate for sainthood." Despite his obvious arousal, he did move slowly, making her sensitive inner tissues feel almost too much. Under her hands, his back muscles moved in an erotic symphony. Fire began to ripple through her.

Two slow, deep strokes later, he stopped. "I can't."

"Can't?" she cried, desperate. "You have to! It feels wonderful." The sensation of his big body moving inside her was the best thing she'd ever experienced.

He glanced down at her with that dark male look that had always scared her. Except on him, it made her want to pet and soothe. And give.

"I. Can't. Go. Slow." He was enunciating his words very carefully, as if he'd forgotten how to speak English. The Italian in him was very much apparent, all smoky heat and possessive hunger.

Wrapping her arms and legs tight around him, she whispered, "Then go fast." Her trust in him was absolute.

"Taylor." His eyes went darker than night at her consent and she could almost see his control snap. "Hold on, *mia moglie e bellissima.*"

Clasping her hard against him, he surged into her and then there was only passionate fury. Her husband's body drove deeper and deeper until she felt indelibly marked. Forever branded. Her skin tightened over her entire body as he stroked her closer to a shattering crescendo so magnificent that her mind could barely comprehend the sensory overload.

Then every muscle in her body seemed to stiffen and barely a second later, explode. She screamed as hot, hard sexual pleasure short-circuited every nerve she possessed, shocking her into ecstasy so powerful that she felt singed. Her only anchor was her husband, big and powerful and hers.

Hers.

Nine

Jackson roused at six the next morning to find Taylor crushed under him. He lifted himself off at once.

"Whatchya doin'?" A sleepy Taylor raised her arms above her head and stretched. Her breasts rubbed against his chest, plump and inviting.

"I was squashing you." He laid his hand on her rib cage, indulging in the feel of her sleep-warmed skin, like liquid satin under his palm.

"Um." Lazy blue eyes blinked at him. She raised her hands and squeezed his biceps. "You're kinda heavy but I didn't mind. It's nice. Like a sexy blanket." Then she tried to span one muscular upper arm with her small hands, without success. "You're so…" She just sighed.

His throat turned dry. "I wasn't hurting you?"

She leaned up and ran her teeth along the muscles she seemed fascinated with. "What?"

"Never mind. Go right ahead." He let her push him onto his back, more than ready for her soft caresses.

To his surprise, she suddenly sat up wide-awake. "Am I being selfish? I should be thinking about my brother."

"We've done all we can for the moment." He reached up to touch her cheek. "Enjoy yourself. It might be tough for a while once the paparazzi descend."

Her scowl was ferocious. "If they hurt you again, I swear I'll kill someone."

He pulled her down to sprawl on top of him. "Thank you." His heart was so used to cynicism that he could barely understand this new emotion shouldering its way in.

"You're welcome." She made a solemn face, then leaned up on her elbows and kissed his jaw. "Jackson?"

"Yes, *piccola?*" He felt such tenderness for her that he spoke to her as he never did to another human being.

"Thank you for last night."

She was thanking him for the most sensual experience of his life? "I'm the grateful one here, Taylor. I've only one word to describe you. Hot."

"Really?" She propped herself up on his chest with her forearms. "I'm hot?" Her wildly tousled hair caressed his skin while her smile brought sunshine into the room.

"Yes." He chuckled at her delight. "I forgot to give you something last night."

"What?"

"It's over there, in the drawer." He hadn't wanted to give her the intimate gift until she'd accepted him as a lover, but hadn't been able to stop himself from buying it.

She wiggled off his body and walked over, holding a sheet to her front. Grinning, he feasted on the back view instead. "This big box?" She pulled out a flat box, her long hair curling just above her bottom, drawing his eye to her perfect shape.

"Yes." Hot was an understatement. She was giving him third-degree burns with that body of hers.

He sat up when she came to kneel beside him on the bed. Tearing off the paper, she bared the name of a well-known lingerie designer. "Ooooooh." Eyes wide, she pulled off the lid to expose several pieces of lacey silk underwear. Picking up a tiny pair of panties, she gave him an arch look. "Is this a present for me or you?"

He kissed a nipple, biting back a smile. "Both."

She dropped the silky creation back into the box and pushed her hands through his hair, her smile bright. "I think I'm okay now, Jackson. I'm not afraid anymore."

He looked up into her blue eyes. "Perhaps you accept that you are safe with me in bed, but what about the fears in here?" He touched her heart.

She looked troubled. "Just being able to make love isn't enough, is it?"

"No, but it's a fine place to start." He tumbled her below him, vowing to teach her to entrust him with her love. For now, he'd work on obtaining her complete trust in bed, because despite her belief that she wasn't afraid anymore, flickers of fear still shadowed her eyes, her wounds too deep to be healed by one night of loving.

To her everlasting shock, Taylor found that she liked sex with Jackson. There was no painful groping, no horrible kissing, no embarrassment. It was just bliss. Two days of indulging her new addiction hadn't in any way lessened her ardor. Though it worried her that Jackson was holding back so as not to scare her, that worry wasn't enough to dim her delight at having overcome her fear of intimacy.

Keeping her end of their bargain was no longer an issue...physically. But, what about the emotional scars? Jackson had alluded to her decision never to love, but he had no way of knowing that she feared having a child even more than simply loving. If her mother hadn't been pregnant with her, she might've been less vulnerable to a man like Lance. And, if Helena hadn't had Nick to link her to Lance, she might not have descended into despair at his desertion.

But, she thought with sudden insight, she wasn't Helena and Jackson was unlike any other man she knew. Lance had never wanted her because she was another man's child. Well, so was Nick. Yet, Jackson's treatment of him had been nothing short of paternal.

But what about her? Was she strong enough, secure enough to give Jackson what he wanted? The truth was, she didn't know. He was the only man she could ever imagine being with, but a part of her didn't believe that he'd never leave her and condemn her to the emotional hell Helena had endured. Perhaps time would prove her fears to be groundless. But, the clock was running against her. If she wasn't pregnant within twelve months, she'd lose her husband. Yet, a year wasn't very long when she'd had twenty-four years to nurture her beliefs about marriage, children and a woman's dependence on a man.

Jackson walked out of the shower while she was sitting on the bed. Immediately, she pushed her anxiety aside. For this week out of time, she'd given herself permission to indulge. There would be more than enough time to face reality when they returned home.

Towel hitched around his lean waist, he shoved a hand through his wet hair. Instead of heading to the wardrobe, he stood in the centre of the bedroom, scowl on his face.

My, but he was sexy, she thought, her face heating. So rawly masculine that it made her feel ultimately female. She might like sex but she was new at it. Her husband's thickly muscled body made her want to squeeze and stroke and just plain old touch! She bit her lower lip as heat pooled in her stomach and spread throughout her body, fingers of flame that enticed and urged.

"What're you thinking?" she asked softly, shifting to kneel on the bed. Her frivolous and decadently short white nightie, part of Jackson's gift, brushed her upper thighs. The tiny hairs on her bare arms rose in anticipation.

"Hmm?" He walked over to stand in front of her kneeling form. "The call this morning was about our newest picture. Britnee Case is demanding another million."

She raised a brow. "That girl's not worth it."

He nodded. "But she's the only one David wants."

"Hmm." She ran a finger up his washboard stomach, still slightly damp. "Can you replace David?"

He slid his hands through her unbound hair. In the heat, she would've preferred to put it up, but she was well aware that her husband liked to play with it. And she wanted to please her husband, the way he pleased her.

Deep inside, she was afraid that he found her wanting. He always had to hang onto his control because, despite everything, she wasn't quite able to make love without fear yet. Groundless fear. He would never hurt her—she just had to remember that and she'd be fine.

"No, he's too valuable," he said. "The last movie he directed is the hot favorite for several Golden Globes. Even more important," he admitted wryly, "his films make money."

Something floated up from her subconscious. "David's proud of his rep as a straight arrow. Drop a few hints that if you meet Britnee's demands, it might look like you were doing favors for the director's lover. He'll either talk Britnee around or get another actress."

"Lover?" His voice was becoming husky.

Screwing up her courage, she licked his stomach. Impossibly, the muscles tightened even more. "Uh-huh. A little birdie told me."

"Taylor, you're an excellent source of information and you haven't even been in the business for a year." His hand fisted in her hair, a heavy weight that told her he liked what she was doing.

Used to the way he played with her hair, she found the gesture possessive but nonthreatening. "I kept in touch with the staff I met while working for you." Her real objective had been to keep track of him, but gossip of all sorts had flowed to her. She'd be useful to him in that way as she had no intention of letting those contacts lapse. "Is using that kind of stuff unethical?"

"Not when she's blackmailing us with the location shoot scheduled to start in three days."

"Umm." Just to see if she could, she tried to take a bite out of his firm stomach. There wasn't enough excess flesh to do so.

He tugged at her hair. When she glanced up, he said, "Only if you want to, *piccola.* I am in no hurry."

She was shocked that he understood her fears. "I want to be the woman you need."

"You are. Everything about you pleases me."

The simple statement rebuilt her confidence and the look in his eyes reignited her desire. "How much do you exercise to stay like this?" She kissed her way halfway up his chest, relieved to be allowed to just touch his body, without expectations or demands.

He tugged her head up with the hand clenched in her hair, dark eyes indulgent in a way that she'd only ever seen in bed. When he looked at her like that, she wanted to lay herself down for his delectation.

"I always kept fit but after Bonnie began to cheat, I did it obsessively. Better than becoming an alcoholic." His smile was tight.

Bonnie, she thought with an inward flare of anger, had a lot to answer for. "And now?"

"Habit. Once a day or at least once every two. Why?"

"Can I watch?" she found herself asking, admitting to a secret fantasy that was at once exciting and scandalous.

"Watch?" He was aroused under the towel. In fact, she had no idea how the soft white fabric was staying in place.

"You, working out. Do you wear a T-shirt?" She saw him swallow. Her heartbeat accelerated.

"Sometimes. Do you want me to?" Rough and dangerous, his tone told her that she'd be well loved tonight.

If she wanted to be loved.

His hunger for her was a heady aphrodisiac that made her fight her fears. "No. I want to see you sweat."

He groaned. "Taylor, I hope you're trying to seduce me because if you're not, we're in big trouble."

She laughed and stood up on the bed, which made her a little taller than him. "Am I any good?"

A slow smile broke across that dark face. "You're better than good." His hands rested on her barely covered bottom, moving in slow circles. "How about you pay up?" A far more serious question lingered in his eyes.

"Promise, first." She pressed close, a silent answer to his unasked question. This play was more than okay. It was delicious and tempting and wicked.

"Promise what?" He seemed distracted by her breasts.

"That I can watch." The heavy sensuality on his face made her want to give him the delight he gave her in bed, made her want to be bold and sexy and wild. She'd never know whether she had it in her if she didn't try.

He shuddered. "Promise. Now, down woman."

Taylor slithered out of his arms and down his body before Jackson could catch her, a look in her eyes that seared him from the inside out.

"No." She pushed at his abdomen when he would've followed her onto the bed. "I want to…" Leaving the sentence unfinished, she knelt before him again, running her hands over his hips. The towel fell to the floor.

Taylor's gasp made his entire body go taut. Her captivated expression destroyed any will he had to press her down onto the bed and just take her. He'd been afraid that the way she was rushing her exploration of sensuality would backfire into fear, but the look in her eyes was one of dazed discovery. His tough little Taylor was more than up to the challenge of facing her demons.

"Does it hurt?"

"No." His voice sounded strangled to him. "Yes." He contradicted himself. "It hurts good."

"Oh." She looked up, all big blue eyes, and he thought that maybe she was out of her depth.

"*Cara,* let me…" he began. It was enough that she'd come this far. More than enough. He wanted to adore that body of hers and tell her without words just how much it meant to him that she was able to be so free with him.

Then she smiled, a soft woman smile that let him know she was perfectly happy to muddle her way through this…if he'd let her. Stunned, he stood there and let her.

Her gaze returned to that part of his body which declared his hunger. Reaching out, she clasped his erection in one slim hand, the action almost nervous. Jackson could feel his shoulder muscles screaming as he forced his body to remain still instead of thrusting as instinct dictated. He didn't want to scare her and lose this precious moment of complete trust.

"Jackson?"

"Yeah?" he groaned.

"How hard can I squeeze?" The concern in her tone pulled him back from the beckoning edge. Though they'd made love countless times, he'd always been the one in control. This was a first for them. Holding her gaze, he reached down and clasped his hand around hers and squeezed.

"Harder…" He removed his hand and let her do it herself. With every stroke, her confidence seemed to build. "Harder… yes, *piccola*. Yes, just like that…"

With his peripheral vision, he saw her head bend, saw her lips part and closed his eyes. Next time he'd watch, next time he'd savor the indescribable intimacy. This time, he just wanted to survive. Then her hot, wet mouth settled on him and his mind blanked for an instant, before consciousness punched through him with such power and strength, he felt as if he were drowning in the influx of raw sensation.

Somehow, he managed to let her kiss and caress him for at least a minute before he hauled her head away. "Enough." He wanted to penetrate her deep and hard.

"No." She scowled at him and went back to what she'd been doing, her hands clasping the backs of his thighs. He was so surprised at the unexpected sensual defiance that he didn't pull her away. Then it was too late. Shocking pleasure rocked his body. He clenched his hands in her hair, closed his eyes and wondered if his sweet little wife had expected what she got.

He collapsed afterward, sprawling across the bed on his front, Taylor by his side. He was aware that she was stroking him, like he was some great big cat. He lay there and enjoyed the experience, glad that his loss of control hadn't revived her fear. When he finally managed to rouse himself, he turned his head and muttered, "Sorry."

She lowered her head until her lips brushed his. "I am an intelligent woman you know. I knew what was…coming."

"Did you…" he croaked.

She swallowed very deliberately. "What do you think?" There was mischief in her eyes and just a tinge of shyness. But, no doubt, his baby was coming out of her shell.

His eyes went wide. "*Dio!* I've created a monster." Utterly delighted with her, he glanced at her little-nothing nightie. "Why aren't you naked?"

"Should I take it off?" she asked, a blush heating up her cheeks.

He just raised a brow at the silly question.

Sitting up on her knees, she grabbed the fluttering hem and pulled the nightie off, leaving her clad only in a pair of tiny lace panties. He recognized them.

"You're wearing my present." Reaching out, he touched her between her legs. The material was damp. White-hot heat radiated from her core. She remained in her kneeling position, legs spread, letting him lazily explore.

"When are you going to give me another present?"

Despite her continued blush, the cheeky question was so sensually playful, he could hardly believe it was asked by the same woman who'd feared a simple kiss. "What do you want, *bellissima?*"

Her eyes were wide and her breathing hitched. "Use your imagination, you're pretty good at it."

Smiling smugly, he sped up his finger strokes, aware that despite her open desire, she continued to hold back part of herself. But each time they loved, that fear-inspired reserve lessened. Soon, soon he'd have everything.

"Um…oh…more, please, please more."

He gave her more, wanting to satisfy her because she'd satisfied him so very well. A while later, when she was squirming, he pressed hard against the throbbing nubbin between her legs, then withdrew before she could crest.

"Jackson!" Her glare was pure heat, her shyness lost under the pleasure and frustration.

He chuckled, enjoying her feminine rage. "You are so sexy. Come down here so I can kiss you."

"Lazy." But, she started to move down. While she was doing so, he rolled over onto his back. Putting his hand on her shapely little bottom, he said, "Straddle my chest."

Frowning at the order, she asked, "Why?"

"Do it and I'll show you."

Curious, she followed the instruction. "Now what?"

"Move up a little."

Her eyes wide, she obeyed. And stopped. He told her to keep going. She did. And then, hardly breathing, she moved that final inch. Chuckling at her scandalized expression, he shifted aside the gusset of her panties and returned the favor she'd done him. With interest.

"Jackson..." she began to protest and he thought that he'd gone too far for her.

He licked one long, slow lick.

She shuddered and clutched at the headboard.

"Wet and hot," he murmured, satisfied that she'd let him have his way. "Just the way I like my wife."

She was whimpering with his first kiss and sobbing with his second. By the time he began the third, her body had started to ripple with waves of pleasure.

They spent their last afternoon in Fiji at the beach. Taylor lathered herself with sunscreen and coaxed Jackson to let her smooth the cream over him, too. His body was vital in the sunshine, all golden muscle and strength against her fingertips.

"How about a swim?" He looked over his shoulder to where she knelt behind him.

Putting down the sunscreen, she thought over their earlier exertions. "Not after that hike you talked me into this morning." Her complaint was without heat because seeing the tropically forested upper regions of the island had been worth the trek. "I'll float, you swim.

Chuckling, he rose to his feet and tugged her up. "Sexy," he murmured, a teasing gleam in his eye.

Taylor knew very well that her modestly cut one piece bathing suit was no such thing. "Studly," she responded tongue in cheek, glancing at his board shorts.

Only his sudden smile gave her a hint of what he was about to do. Laughing, she tried to dodge him but he scooped her up in his arms and ran deep into the water before throwing her giggling body in. She came up still smiling and drenched from head to toe. Scraping her hair off her face, she took one look at him standing there laughing at her and narrowed her eyes. Using both hands, she splashed a huge wave of water onto him.

Dripping, he grinned. "Is that a declaration of war, *piccola?*"

In response, she splashed him again. Giving a mock roar, he lunged after her. The ensuing water fight was the most fun that Taylor had had in years. She laughed so much that her stomach hurt and when Jackson declared himself the victor, she was too exhausted to dispute it.

Dragging herself from the water, she collapsed on the fine white sand and sunbathed while her far too energetic husband struck out for a longer swim. As she watched his strong body cut through the water, she realized that she'd never been as happy as she was at that moment. Simple joy suffused her entire body, as if particles of happiness were trapped in the tropical sunshine which gilded her skin.

This was a memory she'd always cherish, she thought with a drowsy smile, setting down to wait for her husband in the joyful sunshine.

Coming back to real life the next day was a shock for Taylor. Especially since the first thing she saw was a large envelope from Lance's firm. Jackson peered over her shoulder as she picked it up from the pile of mail collected by their security people. Heart in her throat, she walked over to the big living room window.

Jackson came to stand behind her, hands on her waist. "It's postmarked a week and a half ago."

"It's been forwarded from my apartment." She tore it open and pulled out a letter and attached legal documents. "He's filed for a priority date for the custody hearing…oh my God, he's really claiming that I'm an unfit guardian and Nick's in danger!" Panic started to gather in her body.

Jackson took the papers from her, one arm still around her waist. "Idiot." The single short and derisive comment calmed her at once. After a quick scan of the documents, he gave them to her to hold. Without further discussion, he picked up the phone and punched in Lance's number.

"Mr. Hegerty, it's Jackson Santorini." A pause. "I'm fine. My *wife* isn't doing so well. It seems you've filed a suit for custody of her brother." A longer pause.

Taylor stood wide-eyed, wondering what was happening. Jackson sounded very calm and collected but there was something faintly dangerous about his tone.

"I understand, Mr. Hegerty, but I take my wife's unhappiness very seriously. Do you understand?" Now she knew what it was about his voice that disturbed her. He sounded *exactly* like a mobster—a cool, slick, dangerous mobster. Then he said, "My family doesn't take it too well either. Santorinis look after their own."

She just about collapsed at that ominous tone.

"Yes, you think that over. Call me within the next three days or we'll take measures of our own." He hung up.

"Your family? I thought you didn't really see them?" She needed a moment to ground herself before she found out what was happening with Nick.

He gave her a narrow-eyed look. "Italians have big extended families. When I turned eighteen and was free to make my own choices, I went to live in Italy with my paternal grandparents and uncles, who had always kept in touch with me. They are my true *famiglia*. In fact, they are already pestering me to bring you and Nicolas for a visit."

"And they'd be...unhappy if I was?" She swallowed. "They're not...um..." How did she ask if they were part of the criminal underworld without offending her new husband?

It looked like Jackson was smiling faintly. "I might've forgotten to mention that some of them aren't exactly upstanding citizens." He released her.

She sat down on the window seat. "I...see. What did Lance say?" She could only deal with one thing at a time. Her husband's underworld relatives would have to wait.

"He blustered, but I know the lawsuit will disappear soon. Then, if necessary, he will consent to the adoption."

"You sound very confident."

"I am. We've already got legal motions in progress if he doesn't. Worse comes to worst, we'll just tie him in legal knots for years." He touched her cheek. "Don't worry, Taylor. I'll keep my part of the bargain." His eyes turned almost black. "Come, I need to claim you again."

It was such an old-world way of speaking, such a masculine statement that she couldn't fight it, her body going soft and welcoming at the rich darkness of his tone. Something about his words disturbed her, though it was hard to hold the thought when he took her into his arms. Yes, they'd made a bargain, but that wasn't the only reason she'd married him. Then he decided to take her against the wall and all she could concentrate was on his big body, hot and hard and demanding.

The next morning felt like the true start of her new life. Nick had arrived home about an hour after their return, and was now on his way to school. She'd bitten her lip and let Jackson lead him away, because it was clear that Nick needed her husband to claim him publicly.

"Be good, *cara.* Call me if you need anything." Before

leaving, Jackson had kissed her with lazy thoroughness, mimicking the far more erotic kiss with which he'd woken her this morning.

For the first time, she was alone in her new home. She took the opportunity to call Maggie and schedule another session before thinking over the rest of her day.

Jackson had suggested she organize a small dinner party. Though their marriage was already public knowledge, politics dictated that certain people be told in a more private manner. In addition, in a couple of months, they would spend a week in Los Angeles, socializing with those who lived in the heart of the moviemaking world.

Having kept her ear to the ground, she had no problem preparing a list of invitees. By eleven, she had the wheels rolling and was beginning to feel a little more settled. This was work, she realized. Very delicate work.

Jackson needed these people to be willing to cooperate with him. Bonnie had antagonized a large number of them and the fallout had hit the beautiful man Taylor had married. When the papers had ripped into him, not many in the business had come forward to defend him, still smarting from their brushes with his wife, and the coldness Jackson had cultivated to survive her.

By the end of the day, she was wearing a satisfied smile, sure of her ability to be the partner Jackson needed. Flush with newfound confidence, she was waiting impatiently at the top of the driveway when her men arrived home—her brother had stayed late to try out for soccer.

"So?" she asked Nick as soon as he got out of the car.

He smiled slowly. "They want me to be goalie. The coach said I had quick hands."

Excited for him, she hugged his thin frame. "Well done. Now get in there and shower, you muddy hooligan."

After he'd run off, she turned to Jackson. "I'm glad you

talked me into letting him try out." When Nick had asked her to sign the permission slip, her instinct had been to refuse. What if he was hurt? Then she'd glanced at Jackson and the look in his eyes had made her change her mind.

"I'm glad I talked you into marrying me."

The unexpected response made her very pleased with her Italian husband. She smiled, stood on her tiptoes, and leisurely kissed him. He deserved it.

A flashbulb went off.

Ten

Startled, she jerked back. Jackson immediately shielded her with his body. But, before he could speak, she made a judgment call and moved around him. Though she hadn't wanted to be in his world, she now was and had to learn to deal with the repercussions.

"Hello." She smiled at the defiant man in front of them, wondering how he'd evaded the fence alarms. "Are you going to use that kissing picture?"

"Yes." He held his camera protectively, obviously aware that he was trespassing.

"I'd rather you didn't." Because paparazzi weren't known for their kindness, she asked, "How about a deal?" *Feeling* her husband's rising temper, she surreptitiously dug her elbow into his rock-hard stomach.

"What're you offering then?" The photographer's accent was distinctly British.

"We cooperate with you for photos and give you a quote. It would be an exclusive on our marriage."

He looked at Jackson. "Good deal if you stick to it."

"You have to surrender that whole roll of film."

"Don't you trust me?"

"Not as far as I can throw you," she said cheerfully.

He handed her the film, a wary look in his eye. "Do you want your husband looking like a murderer in the pics?"

"Give us a moment." She turned and forced Jackson to come with her until they were out of earshot.

He looked furious. "What the hell are you doing bargaining with that vulture?"

She could see hurt in his eyes. These people had turned his pain into a spectator sport and here she was, consorting with them. She touched his arm. "Whether we cooperate or not, they'll get pictures. This way, we have some control over the first impression people have of us."

"Manipulate the media? Dangerous game." Yet, there was a spark of interest in his enigmatic eyes.

"The truth is, your status in the business means we have to exist in the limelight at times. We can fight the press and lose, or we can use them to our advantage."

"What do you suggest I do?"

The fact that he was taking her lead made her glow. Unbidden, she recalled her conclusion that her wild husband could be gentled, if not fought. She leaned up and straightened the collar of his black shirt. "You look gorgeous—tall, dark and dangerous. Just act as you'd do if you didn't want to eat a photographer for breakfast."

She thought he might have smiled. "Right."

Reaching up, she unclipped her barrette and let her hair fall over her long-sleeved blue top. "Come on."

They posed with Jackson wrapping his arms around her from behind. The photographer started snapping away.

She stopped him at shot ten. "Enough."

"Have you got any photos of Nick?" Jackson asked. Her heart jerked in panic. She hadn't even thought of that.

The photographer's eyes shifted. "Yes."

"If you use them, the deal is off."

"People want to know." It was a halfhearted attempt to justify himself.

"Anyone who uses Nick will find their life being made very difficult." Jackson's icy calm emphasized the threat. "You know how this works. I can't stop you invading my life, but his is off-limits."

The man sighed but Taylor thought that he was happy enough. He yielded another roll of film. Ten minutes later, he had his quotes and was gone. Jackson immediately rang his security company and ordered them to check the fence alarms *now!* Then he hauled a surprised Taylor to him and proceeded to kiss her senseless.

After Nick went to bed that night, Taylor tracked down her husband. He was in his study, staring at the front page of an old newspaper. She recognized it at once.

Furious, she snatched the paper from him. "Why are you hurting yourself like this?" This piece of gutter journalism had blamed him for Bonnie's death, implying that domestic violence had caused her suicidal depression. Eyes narrowed, she scanned the room and found other newspaper clippings in an open file box on his desk.

"Sometimes I wonder if I could've stopped her."

Grabbing the file box, she walked over to the shredder in the corner and started feeding in paper. "This is what I think of that ridiculous suggestion." She was so angry, her hands shook. God, she hated Bonnie. That woman had hurt Jackson so much that he'd probably never trust another woman enough to love her. Not that she wanted the complications of love...or did she? Did she want everything Jackson Santorini's heart was capable of feeling? Could she cope with such passion?

"Taylor, you don't know—"

"Did you put drugs in her hands? Did you find her a lover to cheat with?" Her words were clipped. Inwardly, she was cursing the photographer who'd resurrected the past with his mere presence.

His mouth firmed. "Don't go there."

She finished shredding and swiveled around to face him, throwing the empty box aside. "Why not? Let's have this out, right here, right now."

"Why?" He'd never sounded more intimidating.

"See me? *I'm* your wife now, not Bonnie!" She slapped her hand against her chest. "And I don't do secrets."

"What do you want to know?" Dressed in black, arms folded, he looked exactly what he was—a big, strong Italian male unused to taking orders from his wife.

A male who'd been betrayed by one wife.

Their friendship had eased her way but Taylor knew that she couldn't expect total trust until she'd earned it. But she refused to be the only one in this marriage who was starting to feel in over her head.

"Stop acting like an enforcer for your *famiglia* and giving me a crick in my neck. Sit down." She walked around the desk and patted the back of his leather chair, expecting him to balk on principle.

To her complete surprise, he obeyed. "Satisfied?" There was an edge to his voice. For some reason of his own, he was letting her dictate to him, but it obviously chafed.

"No. This is better." Fighting his ability to distance himself, she perched on his lap, relieved when his arm encircled her waist. "Why are you angry?" She hated the way anger made him cold, hadn't realized until now just how dependent she'd become on the attention he lavished on her.

"You're imagining it." He sounded irritated.

Jackson wondered why he was allowing her to see his aggravation. He had no intention of revealing that he'd found her practical response to the media a blow to his emotions. He'd made this bargain with her and she was definitely keeping up her end of it. It was his problem that he hungered for more from his wife than practicality and logic. Damn this sudden vulnerability!

"Are you going to tell me?"

"No."

After a tense moment of utter silence, she looked up and shoved at his shoulders. He held her tight, shocked at the blazing anger in her blue eyes.

"Then keep your secrets, I don't care!" Too late, he remembered his little wife's big temper. "All I wanted to do was protect you and this is what I get in return!"

Protect him?

"A big, brooding man who doesn't appreciate me. Who doesn't care that I'm just trying to keep the vultures happy so they don't peck at him! Who gets mad at me for no reason!" She opened her mouth to continue and unable to think of how else to stop her tirade, he kissed her.

She refused to cooperate, wrenching her head away. "No. Don't you kiss me when I'm angry, Jackson Santorini! You're not seducing me out of being annoyed with you!"

Jackson was stunned speechless. No one had ever accused him of using sex to control. Then again, no one had ever wanted him with the passionate hunger of his wife. *"Cara mia."* He was appeased by her confession of protectiveness. "I did not know that was why you did it."

"Why else would I have done it? I was so worried for you, I didn't even think about Nick."

"You had no reason to imagine they would sink low enough to exploit a child."

"They're bottom-feeders." She folded her arms across her chest. "I couldn't let them turn us into something sordid. Our kiss would've had a hideous headline."

"I understand."

"We're not sordid." It was as if she were daring him to disagree. "We're special."

His heartbeat accelerated. "Yes."

"So don't you get angry at me for protecting us."

"I will not."

She glared at him for another minute. Then she leaned over and hugged him hard. "I'm not Bonnie so don't you ever think of me in the same breath as her. Understand?"

He nodded. This spitfire was definitely nothing like his first wife. "Apologies, *mia moglie.*"

"You know what you do to me when you sound so Italian," she accused, eyes softening already.

He knew. "What do I do to you, *cara?*" He kissed the pulse in her neck, warmed by the fire of her temper. She didn't love him but she was protective of him. It wasn't the devotion his primal soul hungered for, but it was a start. Santorini men were nothing if not determined.

She drew back. "What did she do to you?"

There was no question who she was talking about. "You know. Everyone knows." And that humiliation still hurt.

She shook her head. "There was something the papers didn't find out, something terrible. Tell me about it."

The memory turned his voice harsh. "If I don't?"

"I can't make you." She touched his cheek with a hand that was soft and so tender, he ached. "But, I want this marriage of ours to work, and to do that, I need to know who you are. I need to understand you."

What could it hurt? Jackson thought. "Bonnie was pregnant with our baby when she overdosed and she knew it."

Taylor's eyes brimmed with tears. "That *bitch.*"

The short, sharp expletive shocked him less than the deep anger in her. Taylor had a mother's instincts. "Yes," he agreed, "that's what she became at the end."

"I won't give you platitudes—I can't imagine your grief. But," she said, eyes bright with unshed tears, "let me hold you tonight. Let me show you tenderness. I know it isn't very macho, but I think you have hurts that need to be healed and I need to try and heal them."

He was stunned at the quiet power of her. "Ah, *piccola,* when I am with you, I almost believe that there is true goodness in the world."

When she rose and tugged on his hand, he let her lead him out. And he let her stroke and kiss and make love to him with such feminine sweetness that he was lost. When she curled up beside him to sleep, her arms hugged him tight, keeping her promise to hold him through the night.

Despite her care, he lay awake through the dark hours of twilight, thunderstruck by the riot of emotion in his soul. With her unexpected tenderness, Taylor Santorini had demolished the blockade guarding her husband's heart.

He belonged to her completely.

After his experience at Bonnie's hands, it wasn't a weakness he welcomed, but he was no coward. He accepted the powerful feeling and swore to do everything in his power to teach his wife to love him back, because damn it, there was no reason for her not to trust him with everything in her.

As usual, the papers were delivered to their home in the morning. Taylor was up and about, while Jackson was in the shower. Nick was still asleep. Anxious to save her husband any unnecessary pain, she flicked through the pile until she found the tabloid carrying their photos.

For a long time, she just stood there, stunned at the image.

She'd expected Jackson to look annoyed, in spite of her instructions. At best, she'd thought he'd attempt neutrality. Instead, the photographer had caught him as he'd glanced down at her, and there was something in his dark gaze that took her breath away.

"What's that?" Still in his pajamas, Nick walked out of his room and hugged her middle. "Cool. Jackson likes you a lot, huh?" He was looking up at her, seeking reassurance.

Reaching out, she stroked his hair. "I think that maybe he does." She wanted to believe it was real, that expression of intense protective care, but more than likely, her own terrifying hunger for his passionate heart was leading her to imagine things.

"What're you two looking at?" Jackson, dressed in slate-grey slacks and a white shirt, unbuttoned at the neck, came to stand behind her. By unspoken agreement, neither of them referred to the powerful intimacy of the night he'd spent in her arms.

His willingness to let her hold him had shaken all of Taylor's beliefs about men, about him. For such a dominant man to accept her need to care…it had revealed a sensitivity to her emotions that forced her to confront some harsh truths. Jackson had trusted her despite the betrayals he'd suffered in the past. Did she have the courage to do the same? Or would she always be a coward, unable to commit to anything?

She saw him ruffle Nick's hair and he hugged her from behind before playfully biting her neck. "Morning, wife."

Forcing the uncomfortable thoughts from her mind, she said, "Morning, husband."

He reached out with one hand and shifted the paper so he could read the article. "Well, there's nothing too objectionable in it."

Nick had wandered off to get ready for school, so Taylor

indulged herself. "Did you notice it describes me as your *beautiful* new wife?" She peered over her shoulder, taking the same light tone as him. Surely he would've said something if the picture had revealed what she'd thought it had. Disappointment hit her hard, shocking her with the strength of her desire for his love.

Smoldering dark eyes met hers as he turned her around. "Just as well he doesn't know of your temper."

She made a face at him and got herself thoroughly kissed for her trouble, his hands slipping under her thick terry-cloth robe to touch skin.

"I have a meeting," he rasped against her lips. A minute later, "Maybe, I can postpone it." He nuzzled her.

"Hush." Her body was already itchy for him and he was only making it worse. "Do you want coffee?"

He grinned. "I want you." He reached up to cup her breasts, teasing the tips with the pads of his fingers.

She swallowed at the gleam in his eye and tried to concentrate on his mouth rather than his clever hands. But, looking at his lips only made her want to haul him down to her for a scorching kiss. He removed his hands from her robe just when she was about to start whimpering.

"Coffee!" She shoved a cup into his hands to stop him from doing further mischief.

After breakfast, Taylor waved off her men and spent the majority of the day on the final organization for the dinner party. That accomplished, she got on the phone with her network of secretaries and other administration staff, inviting them to a very different kind of party.

"A party at Jackson Santorini's?" one of them whispered, "Are you sure he'll want the riffraff around?"

She rolled her eyes. "He married one of us, you dolt."

"Yeah, but you were always classier than average. I'll be at your barbecue with bells on. See you in a week."

"Bye, Tina."

After hanging up, a hint of disquiet infiltrated her mind. She'd thought she had carte blanche with Jackson's home but maybe he *would* mind. Nothing in their bargain said that she had the rights an indulged and loved wife would have. Feeling uneasy for the first time, she rang him.

"*Cara?*"

That warm tone put her at ease. "Jackson, I'm inviting several of my friends, including studio people, to a barbecue, a few days after the dinner party." There was no response. "Is that all right?"

"They are your friends?"

She wondered at the odd note in his voice. "Yes."

"Then they are welcome in our home." He sighed. "The secretaries aren't going to lynch me are they?"

So, that was the problem, she thought in relief. "No, I'll protect you."

"Don't ever stop, *piccola*." The request was quiet but her heart thundered. Had she imagined the incredible tenderness in that deep voice?

"I won't," she promised. "Have you heard from Lance?"

"Nothing definite but it looks like he's withdrawing his pleadings. If anything happens, I'll let you know."

After they hung up, she spent a long time wondering at the indefinable vulnerability she'd heard in his tone.

Jackson sat at his desk wrestling with a strange mix of emotions. Part of it was an irrational jealousy that these people had Taylor's affection and friendship, without paying for it. He'd made the decision to bargain for her and he'd made a very good bargain. She was a protective, affectionate and sexy wife. It was his problem that he'd been hoping for something more, something that had eluded his family forever, something he'd never touched.

What would his wife say if she realized that big, tough Jackson Santorini would lay his heart at her feet, if she would only give her trust and love into his keeping? If she would only let him banish the shadows in her eyes that told him she still expected him to walk away from her.

He snorted, crushing the starving creature inside him. His wife was far too practical to think about love in relation to their marriage. All her love was bound up with her brother, and she'd told him point-blank that she didn't trust anyone else enough to love them. Other men might have begrudged Nick her affection, but Jackson couldn't, not when he'd been a child whom no one had loved. He wouldn't wish that utter loneliness on anyone.

Until he'd met Taylor, he'd thought that love between a man and a woman was a fool's dream. Maybe, despite his recent resolution to make her feel the passion he did, he'd been right all along. Look at his parents and siblings. They fell in love every other month and all they got for their trouble were divorces littering the world.

He had a family filled with joy, and he had to concentrate on nurturing it rather than trying to get his wife to give him something she wasn't capable of. Nick's loyalty was his without question, but he needed to fully bind Taylor to him. She'd never divorce him if a child was involved, so he had to make her pregnant as soon as possible. His desire for a baby now came second to his desire to keep Taylor. There was no way in hell he could lose her. He would never survive the loss.

Late that night, Taylor sat at her vanity, her back to Jackson. He was stretched out on the bed, dressed only in his boxers, watching her prepare for bed. Arms folded behind his head, he looked every inch the proprietary male. Though she was wearing an ankle-length silk nightgown, his hot gaze made her feel as if she were in the sheerest slip.

"What are you thinking so hard?" she asked, meeting his intense gaze in the mirror.

"Lance has completely withdrawn his proceedings. It was confirmed at 5:00 p.m. I've also managed to convince him of the wisdom of consenting to Nick's adoption." He lifted a cynical brow. "Money talks very loudly to Lance Hegerty."

Joy made her giddy. "Oh, Jackson! Thank you!"

She put her brush down and turned to face him, intending to run into his arms. But, when she looked at him, she was startled to see that his expression had become even more intense. "What is it?" For something to do, she started plaiting her hair, uncertain how to handle her husband when he looked so unapproachable.

"There aren't any more worries." His eyes went darker than she would've believed possible. "I don't want you going on birth control."

She froze. "I…why can't we wait?" Just today, she'd put a note in her diary to contact the doctor.

"I'm not going to force you into it. What would be the point?" He sounded calm but she could almost see his tension in the taut muscles of his upper arms. "But, tell me one thing—do you *ever* want to have my child?"

"I…I haven't really had a chance to think about it," she lied, panicked.

If she had Jackson's baby, she would become ultimately vulnerable to him, connected in a way that would make escape impossible. Her powerful, possessive husband would *never* give up the right to watch his child grow day by day, and neither would she. Even worse, the experience of creating a life would bind their emotions together with such strength that she wouldn't be able to fight falling in love with him. And loving a man terrified her.

"When do you want to have a child?"

"Soon." Jackson's Italian-dark eyes met hers. "The child will have a trust fund, too. Have a think about it."

"I...I will." Stomach in knots, she walked out of the bedroom and into the ensuite bathroom, where she began washing her face. She should have picked something harder. The simple act gave her too much time to think.

A baby.

It had been part of their bargain. He had a right to expect it after he'd delivered his side of their agreement, yet he wasn't pressuring her. Of course, there was a time limit on his patience. And if he saw that she had no intention of trying to get pregnant, would he dissolve their marriage before the year was up? She clenched her fists on the edge of the sink, unable to bear the thought.

But, a baby?

Years ago, she hadn't even allowed herself to dream of it when she'd realized what it meant. Reliance. Complete and utter trust in a man. Desolation and anguish if that trust was betrayed. Her hands shook as she dried her face. She'd never trusted any man enough to chance that kind of pain. Could she trust Jackson? He understood her need for a safety net—he'd offered their child a trust fund.

A bribe.

It hit her with the force of a roundhouse punch to the jaw. She sat down on the small stool by the handbasin, face white. Her husband was trying to bribe her for a baby. Just like he'd bribed her to be his wife. That time, the bribe had been Nick's safety. This time, it was security for the child they would create between them.

He'd bribed her into going to that party in Fiji, and though the gift of seductive lingerie had come after the lovemaking, he'd bribed her for sex, too. Maybe that's not how he'd consciously thought of it, but the pattern of behavior was becoming clear. Today, an exquisite diamond necklace had been delivered to her from an exclusive jeweler—a present for the dinner party.

Suddenly, she understood the depth of hurts her silent husband carried. Jackson didn't expect anyone to give him a gift without a price attached, or care for him without being paid, without compensation. She'd been so selfish and he'd let her, not expecting anything more. His childhood had been spent with people who demanded recompense for the slightest expression of care—baby-sitters, nannies and boarding schools. Tears pricked at her eyes. Stupid man. How dare he do this to her?

Taking deep breaths, she began to think, remembering her earlier thoughts of courage and cowardice. Yes, she would be incredibly vulnerable if she had Jackson's baby, but, he was the only man with whom she could even consider such an act of trust. What was the alternative? Never to know the joy of nurturing a child in her womb, never to hold a little human being who was part of her, never to give Nick the happiness of playing the role of a big brother, and more importantly, never to give her husband the baby he needed to erase the pain of Bonnie's selfish choice.

Despite his own concerns, she knew that he wouldn't cheat on her. He'd been faithful to Bonnie and he'd had all the reason in the world to take a lover. He would never abuse her, having too much self-control. And, if the worst happened and they separated, he had too much honor to leave her to survive on her own.

She frowned. If their marriage didn't last, they'd both be to blame. But, she had no intention of ever giving up the hope she'd found in his arms. A small light flared inside her heart. Jackson, too, wanted a lifetime commitment, unlike the rest of his family. He would stick by her, unless she gave him a reason to leave. And she would never give him such a reason.

Jackson Santorini belonged to her.

Eleven

Jackson lay there in the semidarkness of the bedroom, having dimmed the light after Taylor slipped away. The woman he'd shown such tenderness and care was hiding from him…as if he was the monster Bonnie had accused him of being. Pain threatened to rip apart his heart.

Their bargain had been clear. A child within a year or they would separate. But he would never let her go. Even if it meant accepting that he would never father a child, because the awful truth was, his wife didn't want to give him that gift. He had no right to berate her but damn it, he wanted to. He adored her, would cherish their child as he cherished Nick, but it was apparent that she didn't feel the hunger he did to create another soul out of their feelings for each other.

In the dark, he knew his smile was cynical. As far as Taylor was concerned, they had nothing more than a bargain. Unfortunately for her, he was too much like his grandfather

Josef. He'd made his choice, and his heart was too passionate to accept anything less than everything from his wife. He would fight for Taylor until she had no choice but to trust him. Santorini men could be adoring husbands but they could also be merciless hunters.

The door to the bathroom opened. He blinked and pushed his pain and resolve to the background. It did no good to let anyone see your vulnerabilities. He'd made that mistake with Bonnie and she'd used the knowledge to rip him to tiny pieces, before he'd stopped letting her matter.

Taylor came to sit beside him on the bed, placing one hand on his bare chest. "I have to tell you something."

"I know," he began, wanting the pain over with as quickly as possible.

"Please listen." In the soft light, her face looked so young that his heart clenched.

He lifted a hand and touched her cheek, unable to stop the action. This small woman could hurt him far more than Bonnie ever had. "Tell me, *piccola*."

She held his hand when it dropped, clasping it between both of hers. "I'm afraid to have a child. Not physically afraid. Afraid of the vulnerability it creates."

"Because of your mother." He understood at once.

She nodded. "I've been afraid for so long—I can't forget what her life ended up like, all because she trusted a man with her body and her heart. I can't forget. I just can't and the fear is so strong, sometimes it chokes me."

He was pulled in two directions. Protecting Taylor and protecting his dreams. There was only one real choice and he made it with brutal swiftness. "It is all right, *cara*. We have Nick." She'd already given him a son to teach and love. It would have to be enough.

She shook her head, tears glimmering in her eyes. "No, it's not all right! I don't like being afraid, Jackson. I hate that feeling of being strangled. I am *not* Helena and you're not Lance. We're stronger than them."

"Yes." He was astonished by her ability to see the truth through her pain. Her strength of will had never been clearer, so her next question humbled him.

"You taught me to make love without fear. Will you teach me to have a child without fear?"

He was so stunned that he couldn't speak for a long time. "How do I do that, little one?"

"By holding me, by being there whenever I need you, by never leaving me to flounder, by being there, just being there." Her hand was clenched around his.

Opening his arms, Jackson invited her in. When she came, he snuggled her face-to-face. His heart was painfully tight in his chest. "I'll always be there, *cara*. Always."

"Don't ever leave me or our children, Jackson." A single tear trailed down her face. She dashed it away.

For the first time he understood the depth of pain that she'd suffered at being abandoned, not only by her biological father, but also by the man who'd married her mother. His little wife had experienced as much loneliness as the rich boy sent to boarding school at age five.

"On my family's name, I promise you, Taylor Santorini, that as long as I draw breath, I will never leave you or our children. Remember who I am, *piccola*—an incredibly possessive tyrant where you are concerned."

She gave him a shaky smile. "I believe that."

He wiped away her tears, awed by the evidence of her trust in him. When he'd believed that she was rejecting having his child, he hadn't understood the courage it would take for his wife to fight the lessons of the past and take that step. And yet she was, for him. *For him.*

"Hold me, Jackson. Hold me," she whispered, allowing him to see a need whose potency he'd barely suspected.

He held her all night and kissed her when she turned to him, warming her with his constant presence. He would never leave her to sink or swim. Never.

Taylor didn't think of herself as a needy woman, but she needed Jackson. The wonderful thing was, he was always there. Like now. He hugged her before their dinner party, three days after she'd agreed to have his child.

"You look ravishing, Mrs. Santorini," he said, planting kisses on her neck. "Do you think our guests will notice if we're late?" Hands moved possessively over her body.

She laughed. "You're looking far too gorgeous, yourself. Make sure the blondes don't touch you." She was only half joking. Around him, she felt positively feral.

His amusement at her possessiveness was overlaid with a hint of approval. "Cross my heart." A glint of mischief lightened his dark eyes.

"What?"

"I want to thank you for last night, *bellissima*. Your mouth is so…"

She clapped her hand over his mouth. "Behave!" Her attempt to sound stern failed miserably, memories of their loving turning her tone husky. She hadn't yet conquered all her fears, but each night, she became stronger. Strong enough for the man she'd married. "You're a menace." He smiled knowingly against her hand, and licked her palm with his tongue. Giggling, she pulled away. "Jackson!"

"Nick was raring to go when I dropped him off tonight. I think he considers spending the weekend at his friend's house more exciting than hanging around with us."

"I think you're much more fun." She rubbed her body against his in deliberate provocation. Having the power to arouse her sexy husband was an addictive feeling.

Jackson kissed her, his eyes gleaming with a masculine

warning that told her she'd have to pay for her teasing. "Let's go, Mrs. Santorini. I suppose we have to show up at our own dinner party."

Wanting to create an intimate atmosphere, Taylor had had the dinner party catered but limited the number of serving staff to two. The neatly dressed men had arrived an hour previously and were now standing in readiness for the arrival of the guests. Prior to dinner, one would tend the small bar set up in a corner of the living room, while his partner was to circulate with the hors d'oeuvres.

"Thank you. Everything looks lovely," Taylor said to them both, after sampling one of their offerings. "Your firm has surpassed my expectations."

They beamed.

Just then the doorbell chimed and Jackson's voice sounded in her ear. "Showtime."

Linking her arm with his, she took a deep breath and let him lead her to the door. Their security firm was controlling entry onto the property, so once the guests passed through the gates, they were able to drive right up to the house. When that door opened, some very powerful people were going to walk into her house.

Jackson paused in front of the door and turned to say very quietly, "Together."

Startled out of her nervousness, she glanced at him, only then realizing that this had to be hard for him, too. Some of these wary people had once been close friends. A slow smile bloomed in Taylor's heart as she understood that he'd let her know that deliberately, welcoming her support to negotiate what could be a difficult evening and offering her his.

Sliding her hand down his arm, she entangled the fingers of her right hand with those of his left. "Together."

At first, the guests were on their guard, watching her as

if they expected Bonnie's ghost to possess her. But she noticed that they relaxed within minutes, warming in the glow of her husband's attention. Always charismatic, today, with a smile flirting with his lips, he was devastating.

"I've never seen him smile, I swear," Temple Givens, one of the hottest scriptwriters around, said. "Have you given him some happy pills?" She laughed and took a sip of an award-winning chardonnay produced in Gisborne.

Taylor liked the slender redhead and since Temple had already invited her to lunch in a few days' time, she knew the feeling was mutual. "He doesn't need them. Teasing me is enough." She was aware that Jackson, standing a foot away, could hear her.

He turned from his conversation to throw her a grin. "What drug could compare to you, Mrs. Santorini?"

Temple gasped, the other guests laughed, and that set the mood for the party. People seemed fascinated by their relationship. She just shrugged and acted like herself. This was her home, no matter who these big shots were. The fact that they were invited to several events by their departing guests was a sure sign that she'd done well.

"A roaring success, sweet little wife," Jackson whispered in her ear, as they got ready for bed. He'd undressed at the speed of light and come to hold her around her middle, chest to her back and chin on her shoulder. He often took that position and she loved the tiny intimacy. Just like she loved everything with Jackson. Already nervy because of her decision to try and conceive, she was unwilling to consider what that meant. Instead, she concentrated on the physical fire he could arouse in her.

"Thank you, honey." She smiled in delight. "I think we're going to be hot together."

He cuddled her closer. "*Cara,* we burn up together." And then he proceeded to ignite the passion between them.

* * *

The next day, she received several thank-you calls regarding the dinner party. Gifts started arriving, too—belated wedding presents.

"We made some friends," she told Jackson that night. Clad only in a pair of black sports shorts with stripes of white on the sides, he was prowling around their bedroom, while she sat in bed. Needless to say, with her husband's body on display, the book in her hand was going unread.

"It's all your doing." He bowed to her like some old-world courtier. "You are so lovely, they couldn't resist your charm, *mia moglie e bellissima.*"

She threw a pillow at him. "I'm already your wife, you big Italian stud. You don't need to seduce me." Her susceptibility to him should've worried her but she reveled in the intensity of their passion. In her ability to match him. Each time they made love, he lost a little more control and she conquered another piece of fear.

Catching the pillow, he grinned. The naughty light in his eyes warned her that he had something up his sleeve. "In that case, I'm going to do weights."

Taylor's head jerked up. Against her short and barely decent white nightie, her nipples peaked.

He chucked the pillow back onto the bed, saying, "You can watch," before he left the room.

She swallowed.

To Jackson's surprise, Taylor didn't come after him. Maybe, he thought, she was getting over her delight in his body. Scowling, he began to exercise. Some time later, he heard the door to the workout room being shut. Turning, he found Taylor sitting on the last step leading down into the converted basement, a jug of ice water beside her and a full glass in her hand.

His whole body went taut. "Is that for me?" he said, watching her roll the glass against her cheek.

"No. It's all for me. Now, exercise."

He'd never performed like this for any woman. But, then again, no woman had ever needed to cool herself down in his presence. Damn, but he enjoyed her reaction to him. Pleased with his little wife, he indulged her, doing arm curls with weights that made his biceps bulge.

Taylor moaned.

"Want to come over?" he invited.

She shook her head and lifted the glass to her lips. Her short nightie rode up as she spread her thighs without noticing. After draining the glass, she said, "Will you do some push-ups?"

"For you, *bellissima,* anything." He put down the weights and with his body right in front of her, began to do as she'd asked, keeping his spine and legs in perfect alignment. He wondered if he could persuade her to kiss him all over, as she'd done last night. Though he'd never admit it, he had a weakness for the gentleness of his wife's caresses. After fifty repetitions, he got up. "Enough?"

"Not hardly." She'd opened all three buttons at the top of her nightie and one hand rested in the opening. "But I think I'm getting heatstroke."

He walked over to the bottom of the steps. "Maybe we should start slow. We can work up to chin-ups," he teased.

She put down the glass and stood up, blue eyes hazy with passion. Her small hands ran up his chest in a gesture that was as proprietary as it was adoring. "Maybe I could…assist you to work out."

He wanted to groan at the images that inspired. "You're not dressed for it. Here, let me help." Moving her hands aside, he pulled the nightie over her head and threw it to the floor. "Now, you're dressed right."

"I'm naked," she whispered, a sexy sparkle in her eye. Before his eyes, she'd blossomed into her sultry sensuality, until tonight, he could read no hint of reticence or fear in her. "Don't I need a sports bra?"

"You're right. Come here." He pulled her along until she was standing in front of the machine he used for his lats. It had a black leather bench that he could sit on while pulling down on the T-shaped handle, which was connected to weights at the back of the machine.

First, he removed all the weights but one. Then, moving around, he sat down on the bench…after taking off his shorts. "Now, straddle me. Face away from me."

Eyes wide, she did as he bid. He held her up by the waist when she realized that the bench and his body were too wide for her feet to touch the floor. "I don't think this'll work," she complained, clearly disappointed.

"Sure it will." Grinning, he lowered her onto his thrusting erection. Starved as he was, the sight of her heart-shaped bottom coming down on him made him want to savage her. But he'd been saving up this particular fantasy since his wedding night. Because she looked so goddamn sexy taking him in, he brought her halfway and then lifted her up, only to slide her down again.

"Oh, Jackson…" Her words faded off into a groan as he oh, so slowly lowered her onto him a third time. She was so tight, he always took the greatest care not to hurt her. Except sometimes, like tonight, she took matters into her own hands and pushed down. "Oh!"

Leaving her impaled, he gritted his teeth and pointed to the T-shaped handle near her head. "Put your hands on either side of the bar."

"What? Why?" She wiggled on him.

He tightened his grip and made her stop. "Do it," he commanded, unable to restrain the dominant part of himself.

Then again, his wife didn't seem to mind the way he loved her. He'd never had a lover more suited to his temperament and sexuality. In bed, she could be a demanding tyrant or a sweetly submissive witch, but whatever mood took her, she was always with him to the end. "We're working out, remember?"

Arching her back just a little, she put one hand on either side of the horizontal bar. Once she was in position, he sat up fully and pulled her snug against him, cupping her breasts and squeezing just because he could.

"Now you have a sports bra." She gasped and let go of the bar. "Keep holding on. And pull down."

"Why?"

"I think it's time you did all the work." He wondered if she realized that the mirror on the left wall afforded him a very interesting view.

It took her a moment to gather the strength to pull the bar down. She could only bring it as far as her upper chest. "Now what?"

"Release the weights but control their descent."

As he'd guessed, she wasn't strong enough to perform that part of the maneuver easily. And with her feet hanging off the floor, she had no traction. She almost rose off him, her inner muscles reluctantly releasing him, as she tried not to clank the weights.

"Oh!" Understanding his intent, she pulled again and slid lusciously down his body.

He kneaded her breasts with his hands, loving the feel of her skin, loving the way she fit him like the most exquisite glove, as if she'd been made just for his most extreme pleasure. His wife. Only his.

"I like this." She sounded breathless.

He groaned. "Why are we torturing ourselves?"

"Because it feels gooood." She slid half off him.

"I was going to lay you down and just thrust the first time, after all your teasing." He squeezed a nipple with his fingertips, taking advantage of her sensitivity.

"Me!" She let the weights go and put her hands over his where they rested on her breasts. "I'll show you teasing." And she did something with her inner muscles that just about brought him to climax.

"Where did you learn to do that?" His voice was hoarse as he fought the urge to pour his seed into her.

"Secret." She was smiling smugly at him, looking over her shoulder. "I think I could do with some thrusting now. It's probably good for making a baby."

He couldn't believe she'd said that. Just like he couldn't help himself from holding on to her hips and taking over. There was a lot of thrusting. Hard. He went deep and then deeper. His desire had gone over the edge into madness by this stage and it wasn't deep enough. When he pulled her off his body, she protested. "Jackson, get back!" There wasn't even a shadow of fear in her.

He nipped the side of her neck. "I want you spread out on your back."

In less than ten seconds, he had her arranged as his imagination demanded, lush and ready for his pleasure; creamy skin touched with pink, against soft black leather. The word sexy didn't begin to do her justice. With his hands under her calves, he lifted her long legs high, spreading her thighs wide. His original intent had been to put her in a position where he could indulge his need to thrust deep, but now that he had her where he wanted, temptation beckoned in the silky wet folds of her body. How could any man resist such a delicious feminine invitation?

Sinking to his knees in front of her, he pulled her bottom to the edge of the leather bench. Continuing to hold her legs high in the air with his hands, he spread her thighs farther apart. Musky heat and the scent of feminine arousal rushed over him like a powerful drug.

"No!" She tried to pull away. "I won't survive."

"Be still, wife. I want to indulge my hunger for you." Slow and deep, his first stroke down her parted flesh made her scream.

"I'm going to kill you!" Her whole body quivered as he stroked again. "Oh…oh! Jackson!"

Using his strength to tilt her body a little more, he thrust his tongue into her, tasting her, marking her, branding her. Again and again and again. She thrashed and writhed but her body was a fountain for him, giving him the taste he craved— the flavor of her passion for him.

"Again!" He thrust his tongue into her after she went over the first cliff, forcing her to the second precipice. "For me. Come, *cara*. For your husband." She didn't disappoint him, her spine arching as she trembled in a release that made her skin ripple.

His own body roared with triumph at her shuddering orgasm. But it wasn't enough. Not yet. Rising above her, he put his hands under her thighs and pulled her further from the bench, until her entire bottom was off the leather. Her body was on an angle that made his entry deeper than he'd believed possible.

She screamed as he slid into her and he felt her internal walls contract again and again as pleasure ripped through her, without mercy. Pulling out, he thrust deeper, clasping her buttocks in his palms. Forced to remain in position by his body, her legs ran up his chest to point at the ceiling. Her breasts moved as she rode the wave of ecstasy, but it was the sound of her calling his name over and over that finally destroyed any control he might've had. He surrendered to the rampaging heat inside him and thrust so deep, he thought he'd touched her heart.

* * *

Sometime afterward, Taylor propped herself on his chest and said, "I have one question."

Under his back, the exercise mat was cool. "Hmm." He was idly stroking her bottom.

"Did you think this was a one-shot thing? If you did, you'd better invest in some heavy-duty locks because I intend to watch at every opportunity." Her warning was delivered in a tone usually reserved for serious matters.

He thought it over. "You can watch so long as I get post-workout sex."

She nodded. "Fair enough."

"Lots of sex."

"You get that anyway."

"What did you mean about making a baby?" He didn't want to get his hopes up, not when she had been so honest about her fears.

"Pretty self-explanatory don'cha think?" She began kissing his chest.

"Taylor." He fisted a hand in her unbound hair and forced her head up.

"I'm fertile and unprotected," she said simply.

A kind of hesitant wonder lit his face. He touched her cheek. "A baby?"

"Yup." Taylor felt the impact of that smile deep inside. Tonight for the first time, Jackson had totally let go of passion's reins and she'd never felt more powerful as a woman. Yet, the unexpected tenderness of his smile threatened to shatter her.

"Are you sure it's not too soon? I know I have been arrogant in my demands but I can wait."

She felt her heart jump. "You're the only man I can imagine taking this risk with. And now is the time to take that risk, while I have the strength to fight the fear." While she was still floating high on the success of conquering her sexual demons. "Who knows what could happen in the future? I don't want to let this chance go by."

He hugged her tight. "Thank you, *cara mia.*" After a while, he freed her from his almost bruising embrace.

"We haven't made a baby yet."

"Yes, we have." He touched her stomach. "Our child is growing inside you right now."

"What? Are you in contact with all your little soldiers?" She laughed. "Has one breached the castle walls?"

"Wait…" He curved one hand around his ear. "I've just received a transmission. Castle walls have been breached. Our *bambina* is on the way." He smiled at her and it was a smile of such pure delight that her heart was shocked into a sort of frozen wonder.

"It might be a *bambino,*" she whispered, amazed that she was going to have a child with this magnificent man. What a terrible and wonderful gift, she thought.

He chuckled. "Have you been studying Italian, *mia moglie?*"

"I have no idea what you mean, *mio marito.*" She put the same possessive emphasis on the word *husband* that he'd put on *wife*.

His delighted laughter gave her hope. Yes, having a baby terrified her, but so had making love. With Jackson, anything was possible.

Twelve

A month later, she told Jackson he'd been right. To her shock, they'd made a baby on the first go. Standing in front of him, while he sat in his armchair, she couldn't miss the joy that lit his dark eyes from deep within.

"A baby," he whispered, his voice rough. Shaking visibly, he put his hands on her waist and looked up at her. "*Nostro bambina* is inside of you?"

"Our baby is definitely inside me. I did *six* of those home pregnancy tests." She was touched in the most secret part of her heart that he trusted her enough to show her his vulnerability. Jackson Santorini's reputation did not allow for eyes glazed with elation at the announcement that he was about to become a father.

"Come sit with me, *piccola*."

With a woman's instinct, Taylor knew that this was the closest her very masculine husband would ever come to asking to be held. Going into his arms, she embraced him while he digested the news, her heart overflowing with tenderness so great, she was afraid what it meant.

Like Jackson, Nick couldn't contain his happiness when he was told the news. "Really, a baby? Cool!" He made a face. "I won't miss anything when I go to the soccer camp?"

Taylor had to stifle a grin. "No, honey. You've got almost eight months to look forward to."

He glanced from her to Jackson. "Are you…I mean…"

She frowned but Jackson apparently knew what was causing her brother's anxious expression. Tousling Nick's hair, he said, "The adoption papers have been lodged. You are my eldest son, Nicolas. Make me proud."

"I will." Nick hugged a startled but happy Jackson.

Tears pricked her eyes at the way her husband had accepted her brother, so hungry for male attention, but it was only when he was outside that she allowed herself a little sniffle. "I'll miss him while he's at that training camp." Nick would always be her baby boy.

Jackson put down the paper he'd been reading and came over to hug her from behind. "It'll only be a few days."

She leaned back into his strength. "He's going to be all grown up soon, and then what'll I do?"

Kissing her neck, her sexy man laughed in a way that sent tingles up her spine. "Love our four other children."

"Four?" She laughed. "Let's get this one out first."

"I like to plan ahead."

She bit back a smile. "Speaking of planning ahead—don't forget we have to go to that premiere tomorrow."

"Nick?"

"He wants to visit Mrs. Willis and she adores him, so we'll drop him off at her place on the way to the theater."

Jackson made a sound of agreement. "There's a family film premiering in three months—Nick can come to that with us."

Emotion shot through her at the way her husband never forgot her brother, never tried to push him aside. "He'll love that." Reaching up, she clasped her hands over his arms. "Is this premiere going to be like the last one?" Three weeks ago, she'd attended her first glittering premiere by Jackson's side.

The pre-movie get-together had been interesting. Relaxed because she knew several people from her dinner party, people who'd made it a point to introduce her to others who hadn't yet met her, she'd enjoyed the energy in the air as nervous actors and directors mingled with just as nervous producers. However, the movie itself had left her with a headache—from trying to comprehend the plot.

Jackson chuckled. "I promise this one's not a would-be art film that takes itself way too seriously. It's a chick-flick—sure to be a big hit for us."

Smiling at the resignation in his tone at being obliged to sit through the production, she turned to nuzzle him. "You have good taste, darling. I would've had to kill you if Santorini Studios had backed that other picture."

"*You* are proof of my good taste." He kissed her uptilted lips, the caress an invitation. "Nick's busy. Come upstairs, little wife. I have an intimate matter to discuss concerning our future plans."

Taylor gave Jackson a very female look but let him coax her up to their bedroom. Once there, her generous response soothed his possessive need for her. He was determined to teach her to trust him enough to gift him with her love, but sometimes, patience was difficult. His proprietary instincts demanded her devotion. But, Jackson Santorini was a man of honor and he would never go back on his word, in an attempt to force unnegotiated concessions.

Love had not been part of their agreement.

He would persuade but not demand, fight his instincts to give her the emotional freedom she needed. There was only one catch—he would never let her go. The minute she'd accepted his proposal, she'd become his. Forever.

Almost two weeks after she'd confirmed her pregnancy, Taylor fixed Nick's collar one Friday morning and kissed him on the cheek. "Have fun at soccer boot camp."

He grinned. "I will. Bye." With an excited wave, he jumped in the team minivan and they drove out, followed unobtrusively by a bodyguard posing as a coach. It was a necessity that they were trying to downplay.

"He'll be okay. He's got the cell phone if he needs us." Jackson glanced at his watch. "I'm due at a meeting in forty minutes." He kissed her a soft goodbye. "Think of me, *piccola*." He turned to walk over to his car.

"I'm not going to be so little in a while." She tried to make her words light, but disquiet whispered through her veins. Not for her body, but for her soul. A tiny piece of Jackson was growing inside of her, but an even more dangerous and amorphous thing was taking root in her heart.

Returning, he touched her cheek in a fleeting caress. "You'll always be little to me, *mia moglie*."

For some reason, she wanted to stop him from going to work and ask him to hold her tight. But, putting on a bright smile, she waved him off. Only when he was gone did she drop the mask. What was the matter with her?

Something twisted in her stomach. She made a face. Morning sickness hadn't been a problem yet but maybe that was it; the yucky part of her six-week-old pregnancy was about to start. However, though she stood in the bathroom for a while, feeling nauseous, she didn't throw up.

Instead, tiredness seeped into her bones and barely two hours after she'd woken, she crawled back between the sheets, clad in nothing but Jackson's discarded shirt. The masculine scent of his body lingered in the fibers, tangible and comforting, but it wasn't enough. The nausea had become something worse. She hurt deep inside. Giving up trying to fight the urge, she rang his office.

"He's on a video conference to New York," Naomi, his new secretary, told her. "I can get him…"

A painful cramp brutalized her stomach. "No," she whispered, almost unable to speak. "Just…just ask him to come home after his meeting. Okay?"

"It'll be a couple of hours."

"That's fine." He probably wouldn't appreciate being called home to hold his weepy wife. Hanging up, she tried to slip into sleep.

But, a few minutes later, when she felt a warm wetness creeping between her thighs, she was wide awake. There was no pain, only a shocking emptiness where new life should've existed in nurturing warmth. Instead of confusion, sudden clarity wouldn't allow her to ignore the fatal truth.

"No, no, no." Her voice was a hoarse whisper. "Please, no!" She fought the urge to look down. If she didn't see, it couldn't be true. But it was a futile effort—her gaze was pulled toward the horror.

On the blue sheets, the quickly spreading stain didn't look like blood did in the movies, bright and tomato-red. This was dark, almost black. And she knew her baby was gone. So quickly, so suddenly, so completely. Until that moment, she hadn't realized just how much she'd already come to love their baby, their precious *bambina*.

Clutching her stomach, she keened in grief, unable to stop that sound of utter anguish. How could she do this to Jackson? How could her body betray her this way? Fueled by hormones in disarray, fear and suffering raked her with razor-sharp claws. The baby was gone. *She'd* lost their baby and failed to keep the only part of their bargain that mattered to her husband. Jackson had wanted to create life but she would only give him death…he would hate her like he hated Bonnie. Her heart broke at the realization and her tears became heartrendingly silent.

Jackson had been irritated when Naomi interrupted the video conference barely after it had begun, but upon hearing her message, he decided she deserved a raise. Despite his reputation, she hadn't hesitated to stick her neck out for Taylor. And Taylor was Jackson's life.

Disturbed by her report of his wife's fragile voice on the phone, he immediately called home. No one answered. Worried, he postponed the meeting and got in the car. When he arrived at the house, she didn't respond to his calls. He ran up the stairs to their bedroom, concern laying like a rock on his heart. If anything had happened to his Taylor, he wouldn't be able to bear it. The bed was a jumbled mess. His eyes told him that something was wrong with the dark blue sheets, but hearing movement in the ensuite bathroom, he headed that way.

Taylor was standing propped up in the corner, a white towel tucked haphazardly around her body. Wet hair lay limp and damp around her shoulders. Alarm for her health jackknifed in his gut.

She looked up. "The baby's gone." Her eyes were sunken, her face leached of color.

"Gone?" He couldn't help but remember Bonnie. Anguish at this second loss of a child shot through him like lightning. He was furious with Taylor for a second, incredibly, unjustifiably angry, when he knew that she would've never made such a callous decision.

Her face went even paler and he knew she'd seen the anger. "I'm sorry." Her voice was so forlorn and shivery that it scared him, reaching past the pain and fury to find the tenderness that he felt only for her. Walking over, he put his hands on her shoulders. "What happened?"

"I'm sorry," she whispered again, eyes unfocussed.

He'd seen that expression before, on the faces of shock victims profiled in a recent war documentary. He hissed through his teeth when he touched her bare arms. She was as stiff as wood, cold as ice. Shoving aside his raging need to know what had happened, he took her into his arms. Nothing and no one else mattered. No one. Only Taylor.

It was at that moment that Jackson realized that if he lost his wife, he would simply give up on life. It was a shocking truth but he accepted it. True Santorini men, uncorrupted by the world, never loved with anything less than all their heart and soul. His grandfather Josef had lived only a few days after his grandmother Gia's passing.

"Taylor." Gentleness had no effect. "Taylor!"

She looked up at his harsh tone, but didn't speak. It was almost as if she were waiting for a blow to fall. Frustrated by his inability to reach her, he picked her up and stalked toward the bed, intending to sit on the edge.

"No!" Though weak, she began to struggle. Her tone was horrified and pleading at the same time.

Frowning, he bypassed the bed, and sat down on the window seat instead, holding her in his lap. Because she loved to sit there in the sun and read, there was a soft angora blanket on the seat. He wrapped it around her, scared at her low body temperature. Then he began rubbing her arms under the blanket, clamping her cold feet between his thighs to warm them up.

After a long while, she asked, "Why are you being nice?" Her voice was barely a whisper.

"Is there a reason I shouldn't be?"

"I told you, the baby's gone."

His heart almost broke at the pain in her voice. Even half mad with sorrow, not for a moment did he imagine that she'd deliberately hurt their baby. Not his *piccola*. Not this woman who'd taken every precaution to ensure that her brother grew up loved and protected. "Are you okay?"

She pushed up his chest and looked at him, all dark blue eyes. "What does it matter? The baby's gone!"

He shook her just a little. "It matters. *You* matter. To me and to Nick. What would we do without you?"

She was shaking her head and tears were starting to gather. "No. I didn't keep our baby safe. I couldn't! I couldn't! I couldn't!"

He thought that she was heading toward hysteria but suddenly realized that it was nothing more than pure anger-fueled pain. Taylor was far more like him than he'd ever before guessed. She hated being unable to control her baby's happiness. He let her beat his chest with her clenched fists, let her cry and talk, almost certain that he knew what had happened.

"I couldn't keep our baby safe! I couldn't!" she screamed. "There was just…there was so much blood. Our *b-bambina* got washed away." Wracking sobs infiltrated her body, turning her from a warrior to a grief-ravaged mother.

Fighting his own tears, Jackson held her to him despite her protests, and rocked her. His poor Taylor. So used to protecting those she considered her own, so used to being able to control what hurt them. Memories of her fussing over Nick merged into images of her bristling on his own behalf, taking on those who would dare to hurt him. He couldn't bear her pain. She cried for a long time and each tear felt like acid on his heart.

"Have you called a doctor?" he asked, when her sobs had faded off into silent weeping.

"What for? I'm fine." She was belligerent.

His eye flicked to the bed and suddenly he understood why it had disturbed him. The blue sheets shouldn't have been that almost purplish shade. His heart froze. How much blood had she lost? Shaking, he pulled his cell phone out of his pocket and dialed an ambulance one-handed. Taylor didn't say anything, and when the paramedics came, she went quietly. He held her hand throughout the ride.

At the E.R., he paced like a caged tiger until they pronounced that she'd be fine, though they wanted to keep her overnight for observation. He sat with her as she was hooked up to an IV drip and afterward when she started crying again, he ignored hospital policy and gathered her into his arms, being careful not to dislodge the IV needle. Sitting in a chair beside her bed, he cradled her slender body, so unexpectedly fragile, against his strength. Except tonight, he didn't feel very strong. He could never erase her hurt.

"I don't know how to stop your pain, *cara mia*," he admitted. "Tell me what to do." He was used to doing things, not being a useless observer on the sidelines.

Lifting her head, she framed his face with her gentle hands. "My pain? What about yours, darling?"

He gave her a tight smile. "I didn't go through what you did. I will be fine."

She shook her head, her lips set stubbornly. "Don't shut me out, Jackson. Please don't." The vulnerability beneath the stubbornness was clear. "I need you here with me. More than I've ever needed you before."

He looked at her earnest, tear-streaked face and felt something inside him shatter. "I always thought our *bambina* would have her mother's eyes."

"And her *papa's* heart." Taylor stroked his tears away, and it was only then that he knew he was crying. For the first time since he'd been a mere babe, Jackson Santorini allowed himself to cry, held in his wife's arms. Her honest pain deserved nothing less. The honor of their *bambina* required it.

The next day, Jackson took his wife home. While they'd been away, he'd had the bed replaced, knowing that neither of them would ever want to lie on it again. When they arrived, he made Taylor something to drink and then they sat basking in the sunshine, on the steps leading down from the back verandah. She sat on the step below him, watching the butterflies as steam floated up from her tea. He put his arms gently around her and held her to him.

"The nurse said that if we let ourselves mourn, we'd heal better." Her voice was tentative.

"What do you want to do, *cara?*" He rubbed his face against her soft hair, reminding her that he was at her disposal. He needed to do something for her. Anything.

"I thought we could name her—we don't know if the baby would've been a girl or a boy but we always thought of her…"

"…as our *bambina,*" he completed.

"Yes. Maybe…maybe we could plant something beautiful for her in our garden. It might help Nick, too, when he finds out."

He swallowed the sorrow that choked his throat. Nick was so much like his sensitive sister. Jackson knew that they would have to be very careful with his young heart. "That sounds like a fine idea. What shall we name her?"

"What do you think?" Putting her cup on the step, she tilted her head against his chest and met his gaze.

"Rosa." He quietly admitted to his own dreams.

She nodded. "That's a good name. Rosa Santorini." For the first time since their baby's loss, she smiled a little, his Taylor coming back to him. "I'm glad we're doing this. I don't want to pretend she didn't exist." Despite the smile, there was such deep pain and sadness in her that he wanted to break something in despair.

"We could try again," he suggested, hesitant to do so, but it was all he could think of to alleviate her hurt.

"I'd like that." She smiled slowly. "From what the doctor

said, it happens to first babies sometimes…there's no reason for us not to try again."

He was glad that she no longer blamed herself as she had in those first shocked moments. "But before we do anything, we will get you checked out. We will not do anything if it will hurt you." He refused to lose his wife.

Her face fell. "You don't want me to be the mother of your babies? You said a year…"

His tough little Taylor was still so vulnerable and he knew only one way to change that. What was pride, what was *machismo,* in the face of his wife's pain? Squeezing her tight, he leaned in close to her ear. "If anything happened to you, I would not survive, *mia amore.* Do not ask me to."

Taylor's heart stopped at that powerful statement, made in such a quiet way. "Jackson? But a baby…"

"…would be precious, but only if you were a part of him or her." His legs pressed close against her and it was like being hugged with his whole body. "You are my heart, Taylor Santorini. You. Only you."

Taylor's whole world changed in that instant. She'd always guarded against love because the idea of being emotionally dependent on someone else terrified her. Never had she thought about what it would mean if she was loved in return, never had she imagined that a man with Jackson's passionate heart, a heart which had been hurt as much as her own, would surrender his love into her hands. And never, never had she thought that her proud Italian husband would admit such a great vulnerability to her, not when Bonnie had wounded him so very much.

Nick came home three days later and they held him while he cried. Then together, they planted a red rose bush Nick chose. Roses for Rosa, he'd whispered. Jackson hadn't left Taylor's side for the past four days and now he was right beside her as they held hands and sang a lullaby to the baby they would never get to hold.

It took another week before he was convinced that she'd be okay on her own.

"Will you be all right?" He was cradling her face in his big hands. "*Cara,* if you need me, I'll stay."

She knew that he meant every word. Her husband had shown her that she was the most vital thing in his life. Reaching up, she kissed his cheek. "I'm okay, darling. Promise. I think I'll bake a cake to celebrate Nick's team winning their first game."

Jackson nodded in approval. "He's a strong boy. He's going to be fine."

"We're all going to be okay. We went through the sadness together and we'll go through the joy that comes."

It was time for her to start living again. She was aware that both her husband and her brother had treated her like fragile china for the past week and a half. Though she'd held them in their grief, they were both indisputably male, her husband the most masculine creature she knew. Being who they were, offering her their protection and succor had calmed the rage and sorrow inside them.

She'd let them fuss, aware of their need to do what they could. Now, it was time for her to reclaim her own strength. Her Rosa was in her heart, where she would always dwell, a precious first baby. But she was the only mother Nick had ever known and he needed her. So did her husband.

"I'll be back between five and six." Jackson kissed her once more and then he was gone.

Determined to banish the sadness, she went around the house pulling open every curtain. Light poured in from the windows and skylights while she prepared the cake mix.

As she did so, she thought over the game only two days ago. Nick would've understood if she'd missed it but she would have never forgiven herself for neglecting his emotional needs. Jackson had supported her decision to attend the match with him, though he'd bundled her up in so many layers of clothing, she'd felt like a stuffed goose.

The outing had been a good idea, breaking the spell of sadness that had hung over all of them. Watching Jackson cheer for Nick with as much enthusiasm as any of the other fathers, she'd suddenly realized that somehow, they'd truly become a family.

Smiling at the memory of the stunned look on her brother's face when he'd saved a goal, she put the two cake tins in the oven. Then, when the house was bright with sunshine and redolent with the smell of baking, she sat down with a cup of tea and took the chance to think. At the start of this marriage, she'd made a bargain with Jackson Santorini.

Ostensibly, she'd gained stability and safety for Nick. In reality, she'd gained the rock-solid loyalty and love of a very special man along with Nick's happiness. He'd called her *mia amore*. My love.

You are my heart, Taylor Santorini.

She could barely believe it and yet she knew it was true. Jackson Santorini was a man of honor. He would never lie to his wife. Tears threatened. He loved her. Her husband, the man she'd adored from afar for so long, loved her. She had done well out of their bargain.

What had her husband gained?

A wife who loved his touch and a child who worshipped him. It seemed like a fair trade but it wasn't. Not when she was keeping her feelings locked up behind a wall of practicality and sense, too scared to trust someone with that final piece of her heart in case they abandoned her.

She'd married Jackson because he could keep Nick safe. But, what did she feel for *him*? She knew that she wouldn't be able to function if she lost Nick. Mouth dry, she asked herself the question she'd been avoiding, afraid of the answer—what would happen to her if she lost Jackson? Her mind went black with pain so intense it was unbearable.

And she knew.

If she lost Jackson, a piece of her soul would die and even Nick wouldn't be able to reach her. With his tenderness and protective possessiveness, her husband had become forever a part of her. Now, all she had to do was show him that truth. He wouldn't believe her confession easily, this man who'd been betrayed so publicly. He might think that she felt she had to respond to his declaration, or that she was grateful. Or even that she was emotional after the past week and a half.

And yes, she was emotional, but not in that way. His care of her since they'd lost their baby had opened her eyes to the strength and loyalty inside of her big Italian husband. He would never stop loving her, not even if she failed to keep her part of their bargain. Most importantly, he would *never* abandon her, consigning her to an emotional wasteland. That certainty made her secure enough to tell him that he was the most treasured part of her life.

Convincing Jackson that she loved him without reservation or fear would take determination. But, he was going to believe her because he was hers for life. For the first time since her miscarriage, she felt true joy, knowing that other babies would grow from their precious relationship.

Jackson found himself walking up the steps to their home barely after two that day. Though he'd intended to stay away until at least five, giving Taylor space, his protective instincts had refused to stop clamoring for a look at her. He even had an excuse prepared for why he was home, though it made him feel about ten years old.

The door opened before he could reach it. A softly smiling Taylor stood there, arms folded across her chest. "Now, how did I know you'd be back early?"

Her teasing question released the tension across his shoulders. He'd been afraid that she'd find his protectiveness overbearing, when it was anything but that. She was so important to him that he couldn't bear to see her hurting. "No kiss for your husband, *mia moglie?*" Reaching her, he leaned down.

She met him more than halfway, her lips a whisper against his, a welcome home that he'd been starving for. "Hello, *mio marito*. And yes, I'm okay."

Loving her for understanding his need to care, he hugged her around the waist and nuzzled his face into her neck. "I promise I'll leave you in peace for the rest of the day. I just came to get a kiss."

She chuckled. When he pulled back, to his surprise, she took his hand and tugged him inside the house. He went, more than happy to accommodate her. She led him to the kitchen, where two cakes sat cooling. After sitting him down, she made coffee and then cut him a slice of cake. When he reached to take the saucer it was on, she shook her head and came around to sit on the chair facing him. Then, putting a bite of cake on her fork, she held it out, a smile in her eyes. Grinning, he let her feed him, something taut in his heart soothed by this sign of her healing.

"Jackson?"

"Hmm?" He accepted another mouthful.

"I did some thinking this morning."

He looked up at the sound of her voice. The expression she was wearing made him refuse the next bite she offered. He wanted his mouth free to fight for her if he had to, because there was such purpose in that look that it shook him. "And what did you think about?"

"Loving," she murmured, putting the saucer and fork on the table. "And how it's the greatest trust a woman can give to a man."

His heart jumped. "Why were you thinking of it?"

Her smile rivaled the sunshine. "I was thinking that I love you so much it almost hurts, but that you might not believe me if I just said it, so I was trying to think of some brilliant declaration."

Joy shot through every vein in his body, hot and potent and blinding. Rising to his feet, he hauled her up and crushed her to him. "I believe you."

"Are you sure? I don't want a grumpy husband with doubts about why I'm his wife."

He let the conviction in her wash over him, her sharp words a dare to disbelieve. "I know you're not a woman to say those words lightly. I know you." Lifting her up, he kissed her full on the lips, finding her more than ready, more than willing. When they finally parted, he slid her softly down his body.

Blue, blue eyes met his as she raised her head. "Sometimes, I look at you and my heart feels like it'll explode with the intensity of what you do to me." Her voice shook. "Loving you should terrify me but you know what?"

Touched by her utter honesty and raw from the emotions rioting through him, he could barely speak. "Tell me."

"All I feel is this overwhelming sense of rightness." Her heart was in her eyes. "You were meant to be mine."

A lifetime of loneliness disappeared in the brilliant truth of her claiming. "And you, mine. I will never let you go, *mia moglie e bellissima.*" His beautiful wife. *His.*

"Thank God." Then scowling, she muttered, "Not that you'd get very far if you tried to walk away, Jackson Santorini. I keep what's mine."

Her tart tone made him grin. *"Ti voglio bene."*

"You can't fool me—I know that one." Her kiss was a mix of fire and sweet tenderness. "And, I love you, too."

Epilogue

Jackson hadn't thought that life could get any better but to his delight, it did. Not only was sweet, sexy Taylor his wife, she was now his lover in the most complete sense of the word. He didn't have a single doubt about her feelings—after all, his wife didn't tell lies. And that wife said she loved him so regularly that the Italian in him was coming to expect her adoration as his due.

One night, as she was straddling his back, torturing him with her hands and mouth, as she did on a regular basis, she said, "*Honey,* Nick kind of wants a niece or nephew soon."

He frowned. "I told you, we're waiting until you're perfectly recovered."

"It's been ten months." He could tell she was pouting. She kissed his shoulder. "Please, darling."

"Three more months." He reached back and stroked her calf. She bit him on his bicep. "Bad-tempered little witch."

"One month." She was pressing her naked body along the length of his, knowing full well it drove him crazy. It was only fair, given that his body turned her mindless with lust. He smirked against the pillow.

"Two."

"One and a half." She was stroking his flanks now. "Please. Please, please, please!"

He laughed at her begging because they both knew that she'd get her own way. Turning, he flipped her under him. "One and a half but…" he scowled at her, "only if the doctor gives his okay."

She made a face. "Fine. How many children did you want again? One?" Her gentle laughter at his expense had only become worse after she'd declared her love.

His delight in her grew with every moment. "I always thought five children was a good number." He pressed his arousal into the pool of heat between her legs.

"Five babies? You expect me to give birth five times?" She didn't look too impressed.

"No. Only four. I already have a son."

If Taylor hadn't loved him rather madly by then, that casual acceptance of Nick as his son would have done it. "Let me up, I haven't finished touching your back."

He ground his erection against her body. "Later. I want to take you now."

"You can't just take over. It was my turn!" she protested. He had a tendency to become incredibly dominating if she didn't keep her eye on him.

He started to slide in with an expression of almost painful pleasure. "Are you going to make me leave?"

"Later." There was something to be said for a dominant Italian husband in bed. "Did you get bigger?"

"No. You got tighter, *piccola*. Probably because you exercise those muscles all the time." He was chuckling.

She wrapped her arms and legs firmly around him and squeezed those internal muscles in retaliation. "Like I do it on my own, Mr. Three Times a Day."

"I'll get slower as I get older." He groaned.

"It seems like you're only getting more demanding." She arched up. "Ooooh. Deeper. Deeper!"

Rain splattered against the skylight as Jackson's body started driving into hers. Taylor smiled and thanked the heavens for rainy nights, before her husband demanded her complete attention.

Eleven months later, Nick got his wish. Josef Reid Santorini was a little small to play soccer, but Jackson assured the older boy that that would change. When Nick was scared to hold Josef, it was Jackson who gave him courage, standing by his side. His love for both his boys was apparent in the shining light in his dark eyes.

"I kinda get why Taylor's so protective of me. Do you think I used to be so little?" Nick smiled down at the baby, already showing the same protective tendencies in his careful grasp.

Jackson chuckled. "We'll have to ask her. Don't worry, he's a Santorini like you and we're indestructible."

From the nursery doorway, Taylor watched her men laugh and felt blessed. When Jackson turned to her and said, "*Cara*," she walked over. "You're heavily outnumbered now," he whispered to her, while Nick was occupied with Josef.

She smiled against his chest. "Ha! I'm more than the lot of you can handle. And the other three will be girls."

"Other three?"

"You always wanted five."

Jackson's chuckle was full of surprise, joy and just a touch of smug male approval. But, most of all, it was full of love.

Smiling, Taylor sighed and gave into an embrace she knew
would never break and never hurt. Big, bad Jackson Santorini
knew how to cherish his family.

* * * * *

THE SEDUCTION REQUEST
by
Michelle Celmer

MICHELLE CELMER

lives in southeastern Michigan with her husband, their three children, two dogs and two cats. When she's not writing or busy being a mum, you can find her in the garden weeding or curled up with a romance novel. And if you twist her arm really hard you can usually persuade her into a day of power shopping.

Michelle loves to hear from readers. Visit her website at www.michellecelmer.com, or write to her at PO Box 300, Clawson, MI 48017, USA.

To RDR.
We miss you.

One

"Dress it up however you like, Conway, but behind all your money and fame, you'll always be trailer trash to the people of this town.''

The line went dead and Matt Conway snapped his cell phone shut, fighting off a sense of unease. He should have expected his homecoming would ruffle a few feathers, that some people from his past would never accept him, yet it still stung. Despite everything he'd accomplished, he felt like a vulnerable kid again.

Shaking off the all-too-familiar sensation, he clipped the phone on his belt and gazed around the partially constructed restaurant interior, dragging a bandana across his sweaty brow. He breathed in the scent of freshly cut pine, waiting to feel the satisfaction, the deep sense of accomplishment he'd more than earned. This was to be restaurant number twenty in the Touchdown Bar and Grill chain, yet this one erected in his hometown of Chapel, Michigan, held special meaning. It was a symbol.

The kid who'd grown up on the wrong side of the tracks now owned sprawling homes in three different countries. He'd traded in the beat-up vehicle of his youth for a medley of vintage cars any collector would salivate over. He had achieved nearly every financial goal he'd set for himself.

So why, he wondered, would a man who had accomplished everything he'd set out to do feel this…*dissatisfaction?* Why would he feel deep down that he was still, as his mystery caller had so succinctly put it, trailer trash. He worked longer hours, pushed himself to the absolute limit, yet that gratification, that feeling that he'd finally arrived, eluded him.

He was sure this restaurant would be the key. If he ever finished it, that is. Each day dawned with a new problem to delay construction further. They were set to open on Labor Day, only two months away, and were already three weeks behind schedule. He had too much riding on this. While there was always the possibility a restaurant could fail, the odds were stacked against him this time.

Chapel, Michigan, population ten thousand, wasn't exactly known for its trendy night spots. Touchdown would either bring in patrons from surrounding areas and boost revenue for the city, or it would flop within the first year.

It was a risk he was willing to take. A risk he *had* to take.

Someone called his name, and he turned toward the voice, grinning when he spotted his best friend,

Tyler Douglas, standing in the doorway. Ty cleared the space between them in two long strides and pulled Matt into a bear's embrace, slapping him hard on the back. "Damn it's good to see you. What's it been, almost six months since I visited California?"

"At least that."

"So how does it feel? Your first return home in what, eleven years?"

"Things have changed a lot." But not so much that he didn't get the same feelings of inadequacy. The impression that when people looked at him, they would forever see his parents. In California, people saw a man who had everything he could possibly want.

Honestly, he couldn't decide who was more disillusioned.

"I should have known you couldn't sit around and watch without getting your hands dirty." Ty spun in a slow circle. "They've come a long way since construction started."

"Thanks for keeping an eye on things for me. And I can't thank you and your parents enough for selling me the property. I know it's been in your family for a long time. Sitting right on Main Street, I couldn't ask for a better location."

"Are you kidding? You're part of the family." Ty leaned against a stud that would eventually support the wall separating the dining area from the game room. "As a matter of fact, that's sort of why I'm here. I have an important favor to ask."

"Anything," he said without hesitation. "Just name it."

"I want you to seduce my sister."

Matt's heart skipped a beat—then it felt as though

it had stopped beating altogether. If there was a last woman in the world he wanted to seduce—or more to the point, *should* seduce—it was Ty's sister Emily. "You're kidding. Right?"

Ty's expression was serious. "I know you guys had some kind of falling out before you left for California, but before you say no, hear me out."

"Falling out" was a mild way of describing what had transpired between himself and Emily. More like, he'd broken her heart and deserted her. But to have led her into thinking there was hope of a relationship would have been dishonest. Despite what he'd felt for her, she deserved more than he was willing to give. And though they'd vowed to remain friends, things had never quite been the same after their one night together.

He'd never been the same.

But it wouldn't hurt at least to hear Ty out before he said hell no. He crossed his arms over his chest and took a seat on an unoccupied sawhorse. "I'm listening."

"There's a problem with Emily's boyfriend."

A sensation that felt too much like jealousy soured his stomach. Of course Emily would have a boyfriend. She was a grown woman. Did he really think she'd been in limbo all these years, unable to love anyone but him?

Well, a guy could hope…

No. He shouldn't hope things like that. He didn't. He wanted Emily to be happy. She deserved to be happy. "What kind of problem?" he asked Ty.

"I know she wants to get married and have a family, but this guy is in no hurry to commit. It's a dead-end relationship. I think deep down she's unhappy but isn't ready to admit it to herself. I'm sure it'll only take a nudge and she'll realize the mistake she's making. That's where you come in."

"What am I supposed to do?"

"Spend time with her. Show her how much happier she could be without him. My parents and I have tried to talk to her about it, but you know how stubborn she can be. She'll stay with the guy on principle alone if it proves us wrong."

"Ty, I'm not in the market for a wife and family. If that's what she's looking for, she's not going to find it in me, and I won't lie."

"I'm not asking you to lie. By all means be honest with her."

"I'm a little fuzzy on the seducing concept. How far do you expect me to take this?"

"As far as you have to."

Matt could hardly believe what Ty was suggesting. "We are talking about the same Emily, right? Your twin sister. The same sister guys were afraid to ask out in high school for fear you would break their legs? *That* Emily?"

"You know, you could try just being her friend."

And suppose a friendship wasn't enough? It hadn't been back then. And though hurting Emily in the past had been unavoidable, he didn't want to hurt her again. He hated the idea that she was unhappy, but he wasn't necessarily the man to remedy that.

Ty's tone turned dark. "There is something else. My parents and I have reason to believe this guy might be into something illegal. He and Emily work together. If he's caught, she could be guilty by association."

Apprehension raised the hair on the back of his neck. "Illegal how?"

"He owns a nursery. They have shipments coming in constantly from all over the world and he's always going out of the country on business."

Genuine fear clenched his gut. "Drugs?"

"That was our first thought."

"So tell her you're suspicious."

"What, and you think she would actually believe me? This is Emily we're talking about. The queen of I'm right and you're wrong. She would laugh in my face."

Matt cursed under his breath, and growled, "Let's just beat the guy within an inch of his life and *make* him break up with her."

"And you know exactly what Emily would do."

He did. She was so damned stubborn she would stay with the guy just to spite them.

"Emily doesn't do anything halfway. If she breaks off the relationship, there's no way she'll keep working with him and the problem will be solved." Ty's tone turned pleading. "If you won't do it for me, do it for my parents."

When Ty put it that way it was difficult to say no. Growing up, the Douglases had been Matt's only real family. He'd shared countless dinners with them, slept over a thousand times, had even gone with them on family vacations. When his own parents couldn't pull themselves out of a drunken stupor long enough to buy something as basic as new tennis shoes, Ty and Emily's parents always seemed to find a pair—brand new no less—lying around the house that just happened to be the right size.

Matt owed them. And God knows he owed Emily.

If Ty was right about her boyfriend, it would be worth the sacrifice. No one was going to mess with Emily and live to tell about it as long as he was around.

"I'll do it," he told Ty. "Just tell me when and where."

Emily Douglas pulled the company truck into a parking spot, cut the engine and peered through the windshield at the partially constructed building. Touchdown Bar and Grill was all anyone in town seemed to talk about lately, and honestly, she didn't see what all the fuss was about. And despite her vow to never set foot within its sport-memorabilia-swamped bowels, here she was.

Swell.

If there had been any way to pass this job off to someone else, she'd have done it. But with Alex out of town, and as manager of the nursery, it was her direct responsibility to give his royal highness, the millionaire, the estimate on landscaping. To add to an already miserable situation, this could be the account to pull Marlette Landscape out of its recent financial distress. She would never forgive herself if she blew this. And Alex, her wayward boss, would never live down the failure of driving the family business into bankruptcy. He meant well, he just had no head for business, and frankly, Emily was growing tired of covering his butt.

In another six months it would be out of her hands. She would have the money to buy the property from her father, then she could get a business loan for the building and her dream of owning her own flower shop would become a reality. But she would never raise the money without a job. She *needed* this account. The commission would push her that much closer to her goal. She would sacrifice just about anything, including her pride, to see it through.

And wouldn't Matt—*People*'s sexiest restaurateur—be surprised to see her darkening his doorway? She'd done a fair job of avoiding him the past eleven years. Not difficult, considering Mr. I Only Date Supermodels Now never came back to Michigan to visit the little people. Apparently the phrase, "I'd still like us to be friends," fell from his lips as readily as the sweet words he'd whispered to her that night on the beach. He hadn't meant those either.

But this was business. She had to put aside what had happened all those years ago and act like a professional.

Yet, as she reached for the door handle, a flare of nerves heaved her stomach into turmoil.

What would he be like after all these years? As a teenager he'd been cocky and arrogant. At least, that's what he'd wanted people to think. He'd never come right out and admitted it, but she knew he was ashamed of his family and probably as insecure as she'd been. That common thread had bound them and kept them close. But he wasn't poor anymore. She was sure the vulnerable kid who hid behind the bravado, the Matt she'd been friends with, was long gone. Oddly enough, the thought made her sad.

The sun burned white-hot overhead and sweat trickled down her cheek. No point sitting here melting. The sooner she got in there, the sooner she could leave.

She stuck out her chin, shoved open the truck door and stepped down. Sweaty male construction types in varying degrees of undress gave the site an interesting atmosphere, but she didn't see anyone resembling Matt. Aware that more than a dozen pairs of eyes were suddenly riveted in her direction, she held her head high, prayed she wouldn't stumble over her own feet, and walked through the open door of the restaurant. It took her eyes a minute to adjust in the dim light, then she scanned the interior and—

No one was there.

Any apprehension she'd been feeling was instantly replaced by a ripple of irritation. Granted, her time wasn't as valuable as his, but he could at least have the courtesy to show up when he made an appointment.

"Emily?" someone said from behind her. "Emily Douglas, is that you?"

She froze in place and her heart started doing a crazy dance in her chest. She knew that voice. Its deep baritone rumbled through her, awakening a long-dead awareness.

You're over him, she reminded herself.

She forced herself to turn and face him, confused for a second by the man standing there. Missing was the thousand-dollar suit she'd expected. He was dressed similarly to the other workers, in faded carpenter jeans and a sweat-soaked muscle shirt that clung to his tanned, muscular chest. The nails she'd expected to be manicured were uneven and work-worn and she had the feeling his hands were probably calloused as well. Dirt and sweat streaked down his face, a red bandana covered his hair, and dark sunglasses masked his eyes. But that grin was unmistakable. Riding somewhere in between a smirk and a smile, it was burned permanently into her memory. Matt the millionaire was one of the sweaty construction people.

He slipped the glasses off and staring back at her were eyes the deepest, richest shade of brown. She would never forget those eyes—the way they'd looked at her that night. The tenderness they'd held. And the regret she'd seen there the next morning.

"Emily Douglas." He looked her up and down, as if awed by the sight of her. "I barely recognized you."

And he looked exactly the same. The charming, boyish good looks of his youth had matured right along with the rest of him. In photos and television interviews he always seemed larger than life. An icon. In person, standing here in front of her, he looked like the same old Matt.

A dull ache wrapped itself around her heart and wouldn't let her breathe.

This is business, Emily reminded herself. Just do your job.

"You called for an estimate?" she asked.

An estimate?

Matt stood there, robbed of his voice, completely mesmerized by the woman standing before him. When she'd climbed out of the truck, her legs a mile long, her backside curved under snug khaki shorts, he'd just about forgotten his own name. Oh, man, why hadn't Ty warned him? The rough-and-tumble tomboy was now one-hundred-percent, heart-stopping female.

Unable to do little more than gape, he took it all in, from the pale-blond hair he'd once feathered his fingers through, down the column of her throat to the softly rounded breasts that had fit so perfectly in his palms. His gaze traveled lower, to the toned stomach he'd pressed kisses to, and her legs...*damn.* They were long and trim and looked as smooth as the finest Italian silk. And if memory served, they were. He could still distinctly recall how they'd felt wrapped around him.

When she'd first emerged from the truck, he'd been sure they'd sent the wrong person. It had been Ty's idea to call the nursery where Emily worked, under the guise of needing plants—which Matt really did need. He'd made it clear he would not, under any circumstances, lie to Emily or mislead her in any way.

Emily's expression turned wary. "You did call for an estimate."

"An estimate," he repeated, wondering where his brain had wandered off to. This wasn't going at all as planned. He could barely string a coherent sentence together. He hadn't expected to feel this way. Of course, Emily always did have a way of making him feel things he shouldn't.

"Sorry," he said. "I'm just a little surprised to see you. You look...different."

Her eyebrow quirked slightly. "*Different?* Gosh, Conway. I'm...flattered."

"I didn't mean it like—"

"Look. I realize this is uncomfortable for both of us, but I have a job to do. Let's try to make the best of an inconvenient situation. Okay? I'll get you your estimate and get out of your life."

Damn. This was going to be a little harder than he'd expected. But he had never been one to back down from a challenge. Especially when the stakes were so high. All he needed to do was figure out an angle. Every woman had a weakness. Jewelry, furs, whatever.

Once he determined Emily's, he'd have her eating from his hand.

Two

Matt took a step toward Emily. Close enough to catch a light, flowery scent drifting off her skin. The last time he'd been this close to her, they'd both smelled of the bonfire her father had built on the beach, the fire they sat by long after Ty and Emily's parents had gone to bed.

Back then he'd never imagined Emily wearing perfume. It had always been too girly, too feminine for someone like her. Now it was perfect. *She* was perfect. Just the right height, the ideal combination of lean muscle and female softness. Expressive blue eyes deep enough to drown in.

Or freeze him solid, as they were doing now.

"Well?" Emily tapped her booted foot in the dirt.

"Whatever you want," he said.

"Great." She plucked a pen from her shirt pocket and jotted something down on the form attached to her clipboard. ''What were you thinking about for the interior? Ferns? Philodendrons? Real or silk? Is there a particular theme you follow in all the restaurants?''

''I have a binder with all the specs.'' He gestured to the door and she started toward it, distinctly aware of his presence behind her. *Too* close behind her, she realized as he reached past her to open the door and his sweat-slicked arm brushed hers. No expensive cologne for him today. He smelled like a man who was no stranger to physical labor.

He smelled *good.*

She squinted against the sudden shaft of sunlight slanting across her face as she stepped outside.

''Hey, boss!'' One of the workers waved Matt over. ''The inspector is here. We got a problem.''

''Give me a minute,'' he called and turned to Emily. ''I've got the stuff in my car.''

She followed him to a dusty black SUV parked next to the construction trailer. Honestly, she'd expected something convertible and red with an anorexic blonde permanently fixed in the front seat for that special touch.

He opened the passenger's-side door and grabbed a binder off the front seat. ''This has photos of the other restaurants and all the information you'll need. The inside plants should all be live. No silk or plastic. Does your company handle maintenance?''

''No, but we can recommend someone.'' She flipped through the binder, surprised by what she saw. While a few of the older members of the city council had been openly opposed to building yet another unsightly bar in town—and others had protested out of what she was sure was jealousy—Emily had to admit, Touchdown wasn't a bad-looking place. Classy in fact, but casual enough to stop in for a beer and a bite after work. It might even bring in business when her flower shop went up on the vacant lot next door.

"We like to keep the landscaping consistent," he said.

She flipped past a photo that was obviously Southern-based. "I hate to disappoint you, but you'll be hard-pressed to find a palm tree that will grow in Michigan."

The edge of his mouth quirked up slightly. "As consistent as the climate will allow. Now, if you'll excuse me for a minute?" He nodded in the direction of the men waiting for him.

"Go for it."

"Give me a holler if you need anything."

Emily jotted a few notes on her clipboard, watching Matt in her peripheral vision. He might be dressed like the other men and was unshaven and dirty like them, but he had an air about him that garnered respect—*demanded* it even. The intelligence shining behind his eyes, the way he looked at a person, as if he could see inside their head.

He used to look at her that way. Sometimes she swore he could read her thoughts. How many times had she silently willed him to kiss her, to tell her she was anything but a pal? She would wish so hard for it, her head would hurt and her eyes would sting. But he'd never treated her as anything but a good friend.

Someday he would see, she'd told herself at least a thousand times. But Matt didn't date girls like her. He preferred cheerleaders—the pretty girls. Still, she took it for granted that he would always be around, that someday she would get her chance. Then he'd earned a football scholarship that guaranteed he'd be taken away from her forever.

Every time he talked about leaving Michigan, about getting a new start in California and never looking back, a piece of her heart would die. She'd been in love with him since the third grade when his family had moved to Chapel. She could barely remember a time when he wasn't around. He was like family.

To Emily, he had been her whole world.

But as the end of that final summer drew nearer and his leaving loomed closer, something changed. She would catch him watching her, and the look in his eyes, the longing she saw there, would make her shiver with awareness. It was as if she possessed something he desperately wanted, but knew he couldn't have. For the first time in her life she began to feel feminine and pretty. It had occurred to her that maybe he actually had feelings for her and was afraid to make the first move. Though the thought of any female turning down a man like Matt had been completely out of her realm of imagination, she knew he had a vulnerable side he rarely let show. Maybe he was as afraid of rejection as she was.

It was then that she'd decided to tell him how she felt. She knew it wouldn't stop him from leaving— she would never ask him to give up his dream for her—but she'd thought he could come back and visit, and maybe, eventually, she could relocate to California. Yet every time she tried to tell him, she couldn't make herself say the words. Until that last weekend up at the cottage.

Sitting by the fire, she'd finally worked up the nerve to say it. To say "I love you." And before she'd even gotten all the words out he'd kissed her.

She'd given him everything on that beach, surrendered her innocence to him. She woke the following morning feeling lighter than air, until Matt had said they needed to talk. His somber expression—the regret in his eyes—said more than words ever could. Still she'd listened numbly as he explained that while he cared for her deeply—she was his best friend—he was in no position to start a relationship with anyone. He had dreams to fulfill, a new life to start in California. But he still wanted them to be friends. They would *always* be friends. A few days later he left, and, true to his word, he'd never looked back.

Not to her anyway.

Pain, stark and biting, took hold of Emily. She never should have come here. Tears burned behind her eyes and she turned her attention to the estimate forms. She had a job to do.

She walked the perimeter of the building, taking notes and measurements, then went inside and took down the information she needed there. When she stepped back outside, Matt was still deep in conversation with the building inspector. They were bent over what looked like blueprints spread across the hood of a car.

The silly girl in her longed to talk to him again, to search his face for even a glimpse of the Matt she used to love, while the practical Emily convinced her not to bother.

The practical Emily always won.

Matt watched Emily, head lowered as she scribbled something on her clipboard, wondering what was going on in her head, wondering what he was going to do to get back on her good side. Expensive gifts were a favorite of the women he dated, but somehow he couldn't see Emily impressed by glitter. Short of seeing him strung up by his toes and tortured, he wasn't sure what would impress her.

"Mr. Conway?"

Matt tuned to Eric Dixon, the building inspector. "Eric, I've known you since the third grade. Would you please call me Matt?"

Eyes full of contempt, Dixon said, "As I was saying, *Mr. Conway,* the ratio of square feet to lot space is off."

"By twenty lousy feet."

"Regardless, you're either going to have to reduce the amount of square footage or increase the size of the parking lot."

Matt snapped a tight rein on his anger. There was no way he was going to let this weasel get in his way. The restaurant was going up. He would find an angle. He always did. "What I find interesting is that no one mentioned this when the plans were approved. And only now that the structure is half built do you point out the problem."

Eric's smile was smug and full of satisfaction. "It was a regrettable oversight."

One you'll regret more than I will, Matt thought. If they could play hardball, so could he. He took a step toward Eric, amused to see the man take a nervous step back. "I don't suppose this has anything to do with the fact that in high school I beat you out as starting quarterback and got lucky with your girlfriend in the bed of my truck? Didn't you end up marrying her?''

It was only a rumor; he'd supposedly scored with so many of the girls in high school, but it served its purpose. Eric's face turned an interesting shade of purple and the veins in his temple bulged. At twenty-eight, with a beer gut that hung over his belt and nicotine stains on his teeth and fingers, he looked like a heart attack in the making.

''I'm not shutting down construction,'' Matt said.

''You've got until next week to bring it up to code, then *I'm* shutting you down.'' Eric slammed his briefcase, and flashed Matt a greasy smile. ''Have a nice day.''

Though the majority of the city had been supportive of his restaurant, there were a few people who had given him nothing but grief. The same people who'd had so little tolerance for him when he was a kid. No matter how well he did in school, or how he excelled in sports, thanks to his alcoholic parents he'd been labeled a troublemaker by some—guilty by association. Despite his recent fame, living in L.A. afforded him a certain anonymity. In Chapel, a traffic violation won you a spot in the local paper's ''Police Beat'' column.

He hadn't let them win back then and he wouldn't let them now.

Matt heard an engine start and turned to see Emily's truck pulling out of the lot. She was leaving before he'd had a chance to smooth things over. He felt as if he was being pulled in a dozen different directions at once.

He watched her truck disappear around the corner

and felt more determined than ever to make amends.
The only question was, how?

He was pretty sure there would be groveling involved.

"Look at you," Emily scolded. "If you don't pull
it together, you'll never get out of this place. There's
a sunny window somewhere out there just waiting
for you."

The *Abutilon hybridum,* commonly known as a
Canary Bird Flowering Maple, sat on the isolation
table near the rear of the nursery, looking wilted and
sick, its leaves pale and drooping pathetically. Emily
plucked an errant brown leaf. "It's not aphids and I
don't see a fungus."

She checked the undersides of the leaves for signs
of mites. "Your brothers and sisters are healthy.
What's the deal?"

"Do they ever answer you?"

At the unexpected voice, Emily let out a squeal of
surprise and spun around. She knew who it was even
before she saw Matt standing behind her. Her heart
gave an appropriate flutter at the sight of him.

Damn him for always looking so good, for bringing back memories that were better off forgotten.

"In a manner of speaking, they do," she said.
"It's been scientifically proven that plants respond
positively to verbal stimuli."

He nodded thoughtfully and gestured toward the
sickly plant. "Maybe this one is hard of hearing."

She had to stifle a smile. He always did have a
good sense of humor, and the ability to make her
laugh. He'd been the brightest point in her life. Her
life had grown dim since then, but she was used to

it. She liked it that way. It was tough for people to hurt you, to disappoint you, if you kept them at arms' length.

"What do you want, Conway?" she asked. "I thought we agreed to stay out of each other's way."

"You have my binder with the restaurant specs and I need it for tomorrow. The decorator has my only other copy."

He'd only wanted his folder. Why would she even think he would want to see her for any other reason than business? Why would he be interested in someone like her when he could have a thousand other women? Beautiful, *feminine* women.

And why did she feel disappointment instead of relief?

"I get it for you and you'll leave?" she asked.

"Scout's honor."

"Stay here, I'll be right back." She brushed past him, far too aware of the energy vibrating from his body, and headed toward the front of the building. The man was a walking powerhouse, and even worse, he knew it. Stepping into her miniscule office, she grabbed the binder off her desk, but as she spun around to leave she slammed hard into Matt's chest. The heat radiating from his skin scorched her and she jerked away, bumping the backs of her thighs against her cluttered desk. "What are you doing in here?"

He reached behind him and closed the door. "Giving us some privacy."

"You said you would leave. You did the Scout's honor thing."

He gave her a wide, toothy grin, looking just like the old Matt. "I was never a Scout."

That was exactly the kind of stunt the old Matt would have pulled. He looked like the old Matt, and he was acting like the old Matt—

No. No way she would let herself even consider that. She didn't want to like him. If she started to like him a little, that might grow into liking him a lot. Then he would leave and she would never hear from him again. No thanks. "What do you want from me, Conway?"

"I just want to talk to you. I've…missed you."

"You *missed* me? That would explain why you stopped calling. Never once visited. Yeah, you sure seemed broken up about it."

"Your parents came out to visit me. You could have come with them."

She'd wanted to. It had torn her to pieces to watch her parents leave, knowing they would see Matt. Knowing how badly she'd wanted to see him, too. And knowing it just wasn't an option. Not if her heart was ever going to heal. "I don't remember getting an invitation."

"You were always welcome."

"Oh, was it one of those mind-reading things us women are supposed to be able to do? I probably should have told you, I was absent the day they taught that in home economics."

Matt gave her a scrutinizing look. "I don't remember you being this cynical."

"I'm being realistic." The phone on her desk rang and she turned to snatch it up. Her mood plummeted even lower when she answered the phone and recognized the voice on the other end.

"Emily, dear," Alex's mother said sharply. "I need to speak with my son."

"I'm sorry, Mrs. Marlette, but Alex stepped out for the afternoon." And tomorrow afternoon, and the one after that.

"This is the third time I've called this week. Haven't you been giving him my messages?"

Emily hated this. She hated lying to save Alex's rear end time and time again. "He's been so busy, he probably just forgot to get back to you."

Busy slathering on the suntan oil and sipping exotic fruit drinks, she wanted to add. He hadn't answered his cell phone or responded to the dozens of pages she'd sent the past three days. She was no stranger to the pressures of a demanding, critical family and understood his need to escape. But without his participation, she wouldn't be able to hold his life together for him much longer.

"Could you please let my son know that the accountant will be out next Wednesday at nine sharp for the quarterly audit and I expect him to be there." The woman's tone was so bitterly cold, Emily was sure she could feel icicles forming on her ear.

"I'll pass the message along, Mrs.—"

There was a click, then the line went dead.

"Nice to talk to you, too," she mumbled as she dropped the phone back in the cradle. If she didn't know the woman better, she might have taken the harsh treatment personally. But Alex's mother regarded everyone, including her own family, with equal contempt.

Emily turned to find Matt leaning against the door, hands tucked loosely in his jeans pockets, watching her.

She gave him her best exasperated look. "Are you still here?"

His grin widened until the hint of a dimple dented his left cheek, raising the boyish-charm-level tenfold. "I haven't asked you out to dinner yet."

"Dinner? You've got to be kidding me."

"It's the least I can do."

She handed Matt the binder. "Goodbye, Conway."

He took it, and something warm in his expression, a glint in his eyes, had shivers crawling up her spine.

He opened the door. "When can I expect an estimate?"

"Give me a week." Maybe by then she would have shaken off this nagging attraction.

"I have one more question," he said.

"I won't go out to lunch with you either."

He grinned and her insides flipped. "How certain can I be that Marlette will complete the job if I accept your bid?"

His question threw her for a moment, then she recognized, like any good businessman, he'd done some digging. Not that he'd have to dig very deep. Marlette's financial difficulties were common knowledge among competing nurseries, several of whom had lowballed them out of many a contract this season. She hadn't yet figured out how, but as low as Marlette kept their bids, there was always someone lower. Though she hoped she was wrong, she was beginning to suspect they had a rogue employee on the loose.

One more thing she didn't have time to worry about.

"This could be the account to save our butts," she said. "If we win the bid, we'll come through for you. You have my word."

"That's good enough for me." Emily's honesty impressed Matt. And what he hadn't mentioned was that Marlette was the only company bidding. He didn't often let sentimentality edge its way into his business dealings, especially with his investors so shaky about the venture, but in this case he was making an exception. Emily was obviously working hard to pull the company into the black. He admired her determination.

Not to mention that this was about the only way she'd let him within a hundred yards of her.

"I look forward to doing business with you." He held out a hand for her to shake. She hesitated a second, then gripped his hand firmly.

Nothing fluffy about that handshake. She was all business, and it was over so quickly he barely had time to relish her soft skin against his fingers.

The phone rang again. She turned to pick it up, and after a pause snapped, "Where in the hell have you been, Alex? I've been trying to get a hold of you for days. Mildred has been all over my back."

The mysterious boyfriend, no doubt.

She listened for a minute, and Matt could swear he heard music over the line. Something Caribbean.

"Hold on, Alex." She cupped a hand over the mouthpiece and turned to Matt. "I need to take this."

"Can I give you a bit of advice?" he asked.

She looked to the door, gave an exasperated sigh, then nodded.

"You'll get nowhere in business cleaning up someone else's mess." With an image of her perplexed expression etched into his mind, he walked out, grinning to himself. Tugging his keys from his pocket, he headed out to the parking lot.

He was wearing her down. As hard as she was working to seem irritated, he could sense her relaxing, letting her guard down. He could also sense her conflict. She wanted to like him, but she was afraid to trust him. It wouldn't be much longer before he had her hooked, and in the meantime, he was enjoying the hell out of himself. For the first time in months he was focused on something other than getting the restaurant built and it was a welcome relief. He would even consider leaving the construction company to its own devices for a day if he could spend the time with Emily.

He thought of the lake up at the cottage where they'd spent so many summer afternoons and wondered if she still liked to fish. Or they could drive to Metro Park, rent bikes and ride the trails. Hell, they could sit on the hood of his car and talk all day for all he cared. As long as he was with her. And maybe, if things went well he could invite her back to his hotel room....

The direction of his thoughts startled him. Taking Emily back to his hotel for…well, whatever they might end up doing, was out of the question. For now. Pushing too hard, too fast, would only drive her away. He had to remind himself, he was doing this for Ty and his parents. If this Alex person was really into something shady, it was imperative Matt not screw this up.

He'd already decided to take Ty's advice and concentrate on being her friend.

Three

The air drifting in the front window, thick and sticky and tinged with the scent of summer rain, zapped the last of Emily's energy. She stretched out on her love seat, waiting for the pizza guy, relieved the day was almost over. As badly as it had begun, when she was convinced things couldn't get much worse, they had.

Alex, it would seem, was having so much fun he'd decided to extend his vacation another few days. She'd tried to explain how difficult it had been holding it together at work lately and he came back with his typical, "Don't worry about it, Em. It'll all work itself out."

He didn't have to face twenty-five employees, not to mention the fifteen or so college kids they hired every spring and summer, knowing it might only be a matter of weeks before they were out of a job. Though he was her good friend and she loved him to death, acting as a human shield between him and his mother was getting old.

The doorbell rang and she rose from her seat, grabbing the ten-dollar bill for the pizza from the coffee table on her way to the door. Money in hand, she pulled the door open, but it wasn't the pizza guy standing outside her apartment. It was Matt.

And she'd be damned if her traitorous heart didn't lift a little at the sight of him. That cocky grin he always wore told her he was up to no good.

She leaned on the doorjamb, trying her best to look annoyed while her lips itched to return the smile. His hair was damp, his chin freshly shaved, and the clean scent of soap and shampoo begged "notice me!" Drops of rain spotted his muscle shirt, drawing her attention to the impressive width of his shoulders and the definition in his biceps and arms.

Something hot and feminine stirred deep inside her.

She conjured up her best annoyed voice. "Are you stalking me?"

From behind his back he produced a large pizza. "If you won't come to dinner with me, I bring dinner to you."

"I'm not hungry," she lied, and as if on cue, her stomach gave a hollow moan.

"Your stomach disagrees." Matt lifted the lid and peeked inside. "Pepperoni, sausage, bacon—you sure you don't want a slice?"

"How did you know…wait a minute, that's *my* pizza! You rat! You stole my dinner."

The grin widened, his dimple winking adorably. "I paid for it, so it is technically mine now. But I'd be willing to share it with you."

"Is there *anything* you won't do to get what you want?"

"That depends on what I want." The simmering look in his eyes, his smoldering tone, warmed her all the way through to her bones. He didn't even seem to be doing it on purpose. It was as if oozing sex appeal came naturally. Effortlessly.

She crossed her arms over her chest. "How did you even know where I live?"

"CIA."

"That's very funny."

"It's classified. If I tell you, I'll have to kill you."

She glared at him, tapping her foot.

"All right, I asked your brother." He lifted the box lid. "Hmm, smells delicious."

Her mouth watered as the scent wafted her way. She'd skipped lunch so she was beyond starving and there was next to nothing edible in the refrigerator.

"Another minute and you're going to be drooling, Em."

This was so unfair. He knew how much she loved pizza.

"Fine, you can stay." She stepped back and held the door open. Only then did she realize she was wearing her baggy pajama bottoms and the University of Michigan T-shirt with the paint splatters on the front. Like he would even notice.

Or care.

Matt stepped inside, gazing around her one-room flat.

"It's small, but I like it that way," she automatically explained. She had no idea why she felt the need to justify her living conditions to him. Although it might have had something to do with her mother's constant, "Why don't you get a real apartment, Emily," or "If you can't afford a decent place to live, why don't you move back home with us?" As if that would ever happen. Emily would be hauled away in a straitjacket inside of a week.

"I have closets bigger than this," Matt said, then cringed and added, "I didn't mean that like it sounded. I'm just thinking how ridiculous it is that I have so much stuff I need closets the size of an apartment."

He looked so disturbed by the idea, she had to wonder if maybe he wasn't quite as egotistical as she'd thought. Or maybe he was only pretending to be like the old Matt. The question was, why? What could he possibly want from her? Was it possible that he really did want to be her friend?

"When I signed my first pro deal, I had money for the first time in my life," Matt said. "I swear all I did that first year was buy stuff. I guess I just never throw anything away."

"I feel your pain. It must have been real rough having all that money to spend."

"You'd be surprised." His eyes darkened with some emotion she couldn't identify, and she had the sudden impression she'd dredged up something he didn't want to confront. She couldn't decide if that was a good or a bad thing.

Probably bad.

She grabbed paper plates and napkins from the kitchenette and opened the fridge. "I suppose you'll want something to drink."

"Whatever you've got," he said, looking around as if he wasn't sure where to put the food.

"I usually eat at the coffee table, so I can see the

game.'' And because it happened to be the only table she owned.

"Still a sports fan, huh?" He set the pizza down and sat on the love seat.

She grabbed two beers. "To my parents' dismay. My mother is always trying to drag me to Junior League meetings and Tupperware parties, when I'd rather stay home and watch the game with Ty and my dad."

She set the beers, napkins and plates on the table and sat next to him. Matt served them each a slice of pizza. Somehow the love seat felt a lot smaller with him sitting on it. They were so close, she could feel the heat of his thigh where it almost touched her own.

Though it was eons ago, she still remembered what it felt like to be close to him. To feel those hard planes of muscle in his chest and stomach, his weight pressing her into the cool sand. Being with Matt had been everything she'd ever imagined—more than she'd ever hoped for. It had scared her as much as it thrilled her. And the tenderness he'd shown her had been completely unexpected. Foolishly she'd thought that meant he loved her.

After all they'd been through together, when all was said and done, she'd been nothing but a conquest to him. All those years of friendship had meant nothing. And now, with all that money he couldn't spend fast enough, she was sure he'd also raised his standards. She was the same unfeminine, in-your-face-girl she'd been back in high school. She hadn't been good enough for him before, and she certainly wouldn't be now, even if she wanted to be. Which she absolutely did not.

"Ty mentioned that you have a boyfriend. My being here won't bother him?" Matt asked.

Boyfriend. Now there's a term she used rather loosely. It wasn't as if she'd actually told her parents she and Alex were anything but good friends. They'd assumed, and she'd never set them straight.

"No, he wouldn't mind. He's not the jealous type." Not when it came to women, anyway. Not only was Alex not her significant other, he was very gay. Flaming at times.

Matt looked down, suddenly enthralled by his pizza. "I'd like to meet him. You should bring him around the restaurant some time."

Emily almost laughed. "You still can't lie worth a damn, Conway."

His head shot up, a combination of guilt and surprise on his face.

"My brother can't stand Alex. And he probably told you that. So I seriously doubt you're all that jazzed about meeting him."

"You work with him?"

"His mother owns the nursery."

Matt gazed around the apartment. Considering her living conditions, this guy obviously wasn't paying her enough. What furniture she did have looked hand-me-down, and with the exception of the twenty or so plants hanging throughout the apartment, it was sparsely decorated. No art hanging on the walls. No photos.

Ty hadn't been exaggerating. This boyfriend of Emily's did sound like a jerk. Abandoning Emily and leaving her to run his mother's company while he was out partying was pretty low. And with a girlfriend as attractive as Emily, how could the guy not be jealous when she invited other men into her apartment? If Emily were Matt's girlfriend, she wouldn't be hanging out with other men. And she wouldn't be living in a matchbox. She would have the best of everything—anything her heart desired.

If she were his *girlfriend?*

Where the hell had that come from? As unfit as this Alex guy was for Emily, Matt was no more properly suited. God only knows where he'd squeeze her into his schedule.

His cell phone rang and Matt checked the display, cursing under his breath. His lawyer. He was awaiting information on the code-violation issue. This could be either really good or really bad news.

"I have to take this."

He answered the phone, and, as he'd expected, it wasn't what he wanted to hear. The violation was legitimate, and their only recourse at this time would be to meet the inspector's demands, or file a lawsuit against the city. Suing Chapel would guaranty the restaurant's failure.

Emily made an impatient noise beside him and Matt had the feeling she wasn't thrilled with the interruption. Now was not the time to be getting on her bad side. Though it was against every principle of business he'd learned, he told his lawyer he'd call him back later, shut the phone off and hooked it back on his belt.

"Sorry about that," he said.

"So, Conway." Emily twisted the top off her beer. "You've got me here. What do you want?"

"What do you mean?"

She took a bite of her pizza and washed it down with a swallow of beer. "After eleven years and no word from you, there has to a reason why you've suddenly popped back into my life.''

He'd thought he'd be able to flub his way through this and skirt around the truth. She never had been one to sit back and let life happen around her. He should have known she would come right out and bluntly ask him what he was up to. He should have expected it.

''I'm reconnecting,'' he said, which wasn't completely untrue. ''The relationships I've been finding myself in lately have been…unsatisfying.''

''What's wrong, the California girls aren't putting out? Or have you slept with them all already?''

''No, there are a few I've yet to violate.'' Out of the corner of his eye, he saw the edge of her mouth lift. ''By unsatisfying, I mean shallow.''

''So what, you expected to come back and just pick up where you left off?''

''That was sort of the plan. I'd like us to be friends, Emily.''

She made a huffing sound. ''I'm not crazy about your definition of friendship, Conway.''

''Look, I know I should have kept in touch. You probably won't believe this, but I never wanted to hurt you.''

''But you did.''

The accusation felt like a knife in his gut. He pushed his plate away, his appetite a memory. ''People make mistakes. You could cut me a little slack.'' The second the words were out, when her eyes turned stone-cold, he knew it was a mistake.

She got up and walked to the door, pulled it open and motioned outside. ''Goodbye.''

''You're kicking me out?''

"I said you could stay for dinner. And I don't know about you, but I've lost my appetite."

He rose from the love seat, balling his napkin and tossing it onto the table. "You were never one to play games, Emily."

"I'm not the one playing games, Conway."

He had a lot of nerve, coming here, manipulating her, then accusing *her* of playing games. He wanted her to cut *him* some slack. She wasn't the one who'd stopped writing, stopped calling. She wasn't the one who'd stayed away for eleven years.

She opened the door wider.

"Is this your way of saying you don't want to be friends?"

"I *was* your friend. That's one mistake I won't be making again."

This time her heart might not survive.

Emily rested her head against the lush ivy twining the cedar arbor, inhaling the sweet scents of her mother's flower garden. Amber clouds streaked the sky as the sun dipped below the horizon and a warm breeze caressed her face. Ordinarily, surrounding herself with nature worked like a salve on her frayed nerves, but it was family dinner night at her parents' house.

Her least favorite, and most nerve-racking Friday of the month.

Nothing short of hospitalization or death held up as a legitimate excuse to miss it. Her parents liked to stay actively involved in her life, which equated to two hours of them telling her exactly what she was doing wrong and how to fix it, while Emily smiled, nodded and tried not to scream. Not that she didn't love her family dearly, but she'd given up trying to please them a long time ago.

And, as if spending the evening with her parents wasn't bad enough, they'd excitedly informed her that Matt was joining them tonight. Given their level of enthusiasm and the extravagant meal her mother was preparing, one might have thought the President was coming to dinner.

She hadn't talked to Matt since he'd left her apartment last night. And while she would never admit it aloud—she didn't even like admitting it to herself—she had hoped he would come back.

Shortly after he'd left she'd gone to bed, listening to the rain tap against the front windows and feeling inexplicably lonely. Every time she heard a vehicle approaching, or the slam of a car door, she'd held her breath, waiting to hear footsteps up her walk. But he hadn't come. And though she hated herself for it, she still missed him somewhere deep down.

Back when they were kids, during summer vacations when Matt was practically living at their house, he and Emily would sometimes stay up all night talking. After everyone had gone to bed, they would go out on the back patio, curl up in chaise lounges and talk until the sky turned pink with the first hint of dawn. There wasn't a thing about each other they hadn't known.

She'd never blamed him for what had happened between them that night on the beach. She'd let it happen, with no second thoughts and no regrets. She only regretted that it had ended their friendship. It was too late to get that back. They had both changed too much.

Sure, he looked the same, and sounded the same

and sometimes he even acted like the old Matt. On the inside, where it counted, he was a different person.

When she'd gotten over the initial shock of his leaving, her heart had begun to heal. And after a while she'd even stopped missing him. Now that he was back, that old longing had returned with him. But she was longing for the friendship of a man who no longer existed.

Behind her on the brick path she heard approaching footsteps. Heavy steps that would indicate the person in question was probably male, and most likely large. Six foot three, two hundred and twenty pounds—most of it muscle—if memory served. She closed her eyes and prayed silently, please let it be someone else.

"Dinner is almost ready." Matt's deep voice wrapped around her, raising the hair on her arms and sending a shiver down her spine despite the heat. "Your mom sent me out to get you."

Thanks, Mom. Without even trying she somehow always managed to make Emily's life a little bit more miserable. "Tell her I'll be right there."

There was a brief silence then, "Emily, come on. You could at least look at me."

Apprehension surging up her throat, she slowly turned. Matt stood, hands tucked casually into the pockets of his pants. At the sight of him, her body sighed with satisfaction. Talk about eye candy. The man was far too attractive for his own good. His hair was damp again and the same near-black shade as his eyes. A hint of his aftershave drifted in her direction, drawing her attention to his chiseled jaw and mouth. And oh, the things that mouth had done to her. Intimate things that still made her blush.

All his features combined, Matt looked rugged and dangerous—which was at complete odds with the conservative polo shirt and chinos he wore. Was it possible for a man to look reckless and sexy wearing Ralph Lauren?

His eyes soft and apologetic, he said, ''I screwed up last night.''

It was the last thing she expected to hear, and it sounded far too much like something the old Matt would say. Don't, she wanted to plead. Don't you dare be nice to me. She wanted to hate him for leaving her, for not loving her.

But how could she hate him for being honest?

She hugged herself, feeling naked and vulnerable in a simple tank top and shorts. Which was beyond ridiculous, because she wore similar clothes all the time and she'd never felt underdressed before. Maybe it was the way Matt looked at her, as if he were studying every inch, memorizing her.

His cell phone rang and he reached down—she thought to answer it. Instead he turned it off.

''Emily,'' he said, taking another step toward her. She wanted to turn and run to the house, but she couldn't make her legs move. ''I'm sorry I hurt you. I'd do anything to take it back if I could.''

She looked for a trace of deceit in his eyes, a sign that he was only manipulating her. All she saw was sincerity, and it put the tiniest crack in the ice covering her heart.

''Can you give me another chance? Can we be friends?''

''For how long, Conway? How do I know you're

not going to go back to California and never call me again? What reason do I have to trust you?''

"None," he admitted. "You have no reason to trust me. I'll have to earn it."

She knew she was losing it when the idea of Matt working to gain her trust gave her a giddy, adolescent thrill. The thrill she used to get every time he smiled at her, or bent his head close to help her bait her fishing line. How many times had she intentionally popped her bike chain off the track for the sheer pleasure of watching him fix it, knowing he was doing something nice for her. And he would do it without question every time. What would he have said had he known she could bait a line with more skill than he could, or tear apart a bike and rebuild it blindfolded.

At times her adoration had been so intense she'd ached with it. But Matt had always been, and always would be completely unattainable. Even now, after everything that had happened, the thought made her inexplicably sad.

"So, what do you say? Tentative friends?" He reached for her, and though she opened her mouth to object, the words died on her lips the second he took her hand. He cradled it gently in his enormous palm. She watched, mesmerized as his thumb brushed across her knuckles. Heat pooled deep in her stomach and her eyelids felt weighted down.

She risked a glance up to his face and found herself instantly locked into his dark gaze. Something sparked deep inside his eyes—a flame she thought had died a long time ago. How could she deny him anything when he looked at her that way?

"Emily! Matt!" Her mother's voice cut through the silence like a guillotine, obliterating the moment.

Emily yanked her hand free, and when he reached for her again, she backed away. "Don't. I need some time to think about this."

"Emily—"

"Just give me a little time."

Matt watched Emily walk briskly down the path toward the house. Though he knew he'd hurt her, he hadn't realized just how badly until that very moment. She was so afraid to be hurt again she wouldn't even risk a friendship with him.

If he could only make her see that his leaving had been for her own good. That he'd been protecting her by breaking all ties. And yes, he'd been protecting himself, too. But last night he realized just how much he'd missed her friendship. He wanted that deep connection back in his life. He yearned for it. But she needed time.

Ironically, time was the one thing he didn't have.

Four

Matt leaned back in his chair, draining the last of his coffee, doing his best not to flinch as the bitter sludge slid down his throat and sat like a rock in his stomach next to the overcooked chicken. "That was an amazing meal, Mrs. Douglas. Thanks again for having me over."

"Aren't you sweet." Emily's mother beamed with pride and reached across the table to pat Matt's hand. "You know you're always welcome, dear."

Beside him Emily, who had been quiet throughout the meal, made a "pfft" sound. Matt glanced over at her, eyebrow raised, and she looked back, the picture of innocence. More than once during dinner Matt had found himself watching her out of the corner of his eye, intrigued by the subtle changes since he'd last seen her. And some not so subtle. Her hair was the same pale shade of blond, but instead of the short, boyish cut she used to wear, it now hung half-way down her back in silky waves. Her neck was long and slim, her face thinner, accentuating the high arch of her cheeks and full mouth. Despite her height, which he guessed to be at least five-nine, and the muscle tone that indicated she was no stranger to vigorous exercise, she was distinctly feminine.

And then there were her breasts. Not too big, not too small. Not that he had a right to look, but damn, they were as pretty as the rest of her. He let his gaze wander down to the front of her tank top, where he could barely make out the pattern of a lace cup beneath the white cotton.

At the sudden, intense pull of lust, and a death glare from Emily, he tore his gaze away.

"Hey, Matt, I'll bet you can't get a home-cooked meal like this in California," Mr. Douglas boomed from the opposite end of the long dining table.

And thank God for that, Matt thought wryly. Mrs. Douglas had a heart of gold, but she still couldn't cook worth a damn. "No, sir, not even close."

"Oh, Phil." Emily's mother waved a hand at her husband. "Don't be silly. Matt probably has an entire staff of cooks in that fancy house of his. Don't you, Matt?"

"I eat out most of the time," he admitted. "And when I'm home I like to cook for myself. I only hire kitchen staff when I'm entertaining."

Ty lifted an inquisitive brow. "Entertaining?"

Matt knew exactly the kind of entertaining Ty was referring to. But it was rare that he invited a woman home. Most of his relationships were far too superficial and short-lived. "Dinner parties mostly or holiday meals." He turned to Emily's mother and grinned. "I've yet to find someone who cooks like you do."

"You flatter me," Mrs. Douglas said, her smile radiant. Her face had a taut, stretched look he didn't remember, and he wondered if she'd had some work done.

Emily cleared her throat and Matt could swear she mumbled something that sounded a lot like "brown-noser." He looked over at her but she was sawing at the rock-hard pecan pie.

"Would anyone like a warm-up on their coffee?" Mr. Douglas asked, holding up the carafe.

"There's more pie in the kitchen," his wife added.

"None for me," Ty said. He leaned back and stretched his arms high over his head. "I'm stuffed. I'm gonna go turn on the game."

Emily stood and began gathering the dishes. "My turn to clear and load the dishwasher."

"Don't you even think about it, young lady," her mother scolded. "We *hand*-wash the good china."

"Wonderful," Emily muttered under her breath, shooting Matt a look of contempt, as if it was somehow his fault. Then he realized it probably was. In all the years he'd known the Douglases, they'd used the fine china only on special occasions. He was guessing tonight's special occasion was probably him.

As Emily reached for her mother's plate, Mrs. Douglas grabbed her hand, studying her nails. "For heaven's sake, Emily, look at your fingernails. They're filthy. What happened to the nailbrush I gave you?"

"I was in a rush."

"It's not bad enough you dig around in the dirt

all day, you couldn't have the decency to wash your
hands like a lady?''

"I did wash my hands," Emily said, calmly tugging her hand away and stacking her mother's plate
atop the others. "Why should I spend an hour scrubbing my nails when they'll just get dirty again tomorrow?''

Mrs. Douglas turned to her husband. "Phil?''

"Hope, leave the girl alone." As Emily picked up
her father's plate, he patted her arm. "Honey, if it
makes your mother happy, would it kill you to take
a few extra minutes with the nailbrush?''

"No, Daddy, of course not.''

"That's my girl.''

Matt watched the exchange with mounting irritation. Throughout the meal Emily's mother had
nagged at her incessantly. It amazed him that after
all these years the woman still nitpicked every little
thing she did. "Emily, chew with your mouth
closed." "Emily, sit up straight." "No elbows on
the table, Emily." Emily, Emily, Emily.

It was enough to drive a person crazy, yet Emily
seemed immune.

Matt rose from his chair, seeing this as the perfect
opportunity to spend some quality time with her—
and yes, earn a few brownie points. "I'll help with
the dishes.''

"Emily doesn't need help," Mrs. Douglas said
sternly. "You're our guest. We'd love to hear more
about your restaurants.''

His restaurants and his social contacts were pretty
much all they had talked about during dinner. He was
getting bored with the subject, and having a hard
time finding anything interesting to say. His life

wasn't nearly as exciting as they seemed to think. He worked so many hours lately, he didn't have much of a social life anymore.

He started clearing away the dishes. "I wouldn't mind catching up with Emily."

Emily disappeared into the kitchen and Mr. Douglas shot his wife a look. "Give the kids some time *alone,* Hope."

As if co-conspirators in some secret plot—a plot to lure Emily from her boyfriend, no doubt—Mrs. Douglas gave her husband a wink and smiled at Matt. Though he'd agreed to do exactly that, he felt a jab of resentment on Emily's behalf. They treated her as if she were a child.

He helped Emily clear away the last of the dishes, and when he was sure the rest of the family was tucked away in the other room and out of hearing range, he asked her softly, "Why do you let her do that?"

She turned on the faucet, filling the sink with hot sudsy water while she scraped the plates off into the garbage. "Do what?"

"Nag you like that. It wasn't even me your mother was riding and I wanted to stuff a napkin in her mouth."

"I barely notice anymore." She held up a dishrag and towel. "Wash or dry?"

He took the towel. "How can it not bother you?"

"I suppose it gets annoying sometimes, but I've learned to tune a lot of it out." She submerged the plates in the soapy water, then dumped a pile of silverware in with it and started washing. "Is that why you're hiding in here with me and not out regaling them with tales of your jet-set lifestyle?"

"My life isn't nearly as glamorous as everyone thinks." He plucked a plate from the drain board, rubbed it dry and set it on the counter. "And I am *not* a brownnoser."

She propped her hands on the edge of the sink and looked up at him, her expression pure sass. "'That was an amazing meal, Mrs. Douglas,'" she mimicked. "What's amazing is that we don't all have ulcers. My mother is and always has been a lousy cook."

"Ah, but I was being polite," Matt said. "It's all in the delivery."

She rolled her eyes up. "Oh, please."

"It was the truth. I've never met anyone who cooks like her." And, he hoped, he never would. "I don't know why they're making all this fuss over me."

She slanted him a sideways glance. "I don't suppose it would have anything to do with you being a celebrity."

He grimaced at the label. "I own a couple of restaurants, so what?"

"Last I heard it was closer to twenty. And let's not forget that you're a millionaire."

He shrugged, taking the serving platter after she'd rinsed it. "I made a few smart investments, I have a good business manager."

"Okay, you're an ex-football star."

"I am not a star. I wasn't even the starting quarterback. My pro career was just beginning when I blew out my knee. Nothing impressive about that."

"*People* magazine?" she said and he grimaced again. "You can't deny that was an attention grabber."

Which is why he'd been so against it when his publicist had called to break the good news. "It was a business decision."

She handed him a dripping wineglass and their fingers touched. She felt it like an electric surge, the soapy water acting like a superconductor. It took all her concentration not to snatch her hand away. Don't let him know, she warned herself. As soon as he figures out you want him, you'll be toast.

"And I'll bet you didn't get a single date from the exposure," she said.

"Would you believe me if I said no?"

Jeez, did he think she was completely naive? She'd seen that magazine; Matt decked out in tight, threadbare blue jeans, his white shirt unbuttoned exposing his wide, muscular chest and deeply tanned skin. His hair was a little messy, as if he'd just taken a romp with his favorite Playboy Bunny. And the "come hither" look on his face, the heat in his dark eyes; it gave her shivers just to imagine it.

She sank her hands deeper into the sink to scrub the silverware, the hot water making her feel edgy and overheated. Or it could have been Matt. Actually, it probably *was* Matt.

The adolescent affection she used to feel for him, the giddy, excited sensation she would get in the pit of her stomach every time she saw him had evolved over the years. This new, hot-all-over, weak-kneed desire felt a lot more like lust. Fortunately, lust was superficial and without substance. It could be ignored—if he weren't standing less than a foot away from her oozing sex appeal and smelling like a million bucks.

"I didn't want to do the photo shoot," Matt said,

and it took Emily a second to remember what they had been talking about. Magazine photo. Right.

She rinsed a handful of silverware and dropped it in the drain board. "So why did you?"

"The truth is, the restaurants weren't catching on the way I'd hoped. I could potentially have lost millions. My publicist thought it might boost business."

"Did it?"

"Within the next three years, I'll be opening five more restaurants."

"You should be really happy then," she said, scrubbing a plate with more vigor than necessary. "Being filthy rich is what you've always wanted."

He was silent for a minute, then he laughed. "You're threatened by my money."

"That's ridiculous," she said, the denial coming automatically.

"No, I could see it in your eyes when you walked into the restaurant the other day. You were on the defensive. You think because I have money, I'm a different person."

Though she wanted to, she couldn't deny it. All these years, she'd just assumed money had changed him. Could she have been wrong? Could it be that this was her Matt, the Matt who had once been as integral a part of her life as the air she breathed? Her mind wrapped itself around the possibility, trying it on for size.

He leaned close and cupped her chin in his hand, turning her to face him. "It's still me, Em. I'm still here."

Right then she had the wildest urge to kiss him. She wanted it so bad she even leaned in the tiniest bit, but came to her senses at the last minute and pulled away. "I guess that remains to be seen," she said instead. He might be the old Matt, but that didn't mean he was incapable of hurting her again. In fact, it made the chances even greater that he would.

He cleared his throat. "So, about the friendship thing…"

"I'm still thinking."

"Come on, Em." He gave her shoulder a nudge. "You know you can't resist me."

"You're right, you haven't changed. You're still an incurable egomaniac."

He gave another one of those grins, the kind that softened her tough, outer shell. "See, I told you I haven't changed."

She suppressed the smile that was itching to creep across her face. Grabbing the scrub brush, she started in on the pan her mother had cooked the chicken in, deciding almost immediately that she would need a sandblaster to loosen the blackened goo clinging to the bottom. She put it aside and grabbed a bowl instead.

Realizing that Matt had gotten awfully quiet, she glanced up and caught him staring at the front of her shirt. Again. All through dinner he'd been looking at her, undressing her with his eyes.

"They're breasts, Matt. I'm sure you've seen plenty, so mine shouldn't be all that fascinating."

He had the decency to look apologetic. "Sorry, I just can't get used to the way you look now."

"*Different,* right?"

"Good, Em. You look *really* good."

She narrowed her eyes at him. "Let's be clear on something, Conway. Friendship is one thing but I am not, under any circumstances, going to sleep with you again.''

Something hot and dangerous sparked in his eyes and her knees instantly went mushy. ''That sounds like a challenge, Emily. And you know how much I love a challenge.''

The bowl she'd been washing slipped from her fingers and splooshed down into the sudsy water. She turned away so he wouldn't see the rush of color in her cheeks. ''I'm sorry to disappoint you, but I'm not the least bit attracted to you anymore.''

''Here, let me help you with that.'' He stepped behind her and slid his arms into the water next to hers. The width of his chest spread heat across her back and every feminine nerve ending in her body screamed to life. His hands folded over hers, fingers linked with her own and her temperature shot up what felt like a thousand degrees.

If there had ever been a question that Matt still desired her the evidence was blatantly clear when he leaned in closer, pressing her against the edge of the counter with the lower half of his body. The firm ridge beneath his jeans took her breath away.

''Remember what it was like, Em? Remember what it felt like when I touched you?''

''Vaguely.'' Her hands began to tremble. Oh, how she'd missed this, this utter passion only Matt could make her feel. And it would be so easy to melt into his arms. She wanted it so badly she ached.

He slid his hands up, wetting her arms all the way to her shoulders, and turned her toward him. Dark and intense, his eyes locked on hers and she was helpless to look away. ''Remember the first time I kissed you?''

She gave a wobbly nod. Droplets of warm soapy water slid down her arms and dripped onto the kitchen floor.

"You tasted like chocolate. I wonder what you taste like tonight."

Probably her mother's chicken. And if it tasted as bad the second time around as it had the first, they were both in trouble.

Or they would cancel each other out.

In her mind, she kept telling herself to run. To get away. Unfortunately, her body wasn't responding. She knew he was going to kiss her. She *wanted* him to kiss her. And she didn't.

Where was rational Emily when she needed her?

Matt lowered his head and she held her breath, heart pounding in her chest. She felt hot and cold all at once. Frightened and excited.

In slow motion he moved closer and her head began to spin. She felt dizzy and breathless, then his lips brushed lightly over hers and everything inside her went liquid.

"Hmm, I remember this," he whispered against her lips.

She had to stop this. She had to come to her senses before someone walked in and saw them this way.

"I've been thinking," she said, easing away from him, thankful that he let her go. "I guess maybe we could try being friends again."

Something virile and primitive burned in his eyes. "Maybe that offer isn't on the table any longer. Maybe now I want more."

She backed toward the door. To hell with the dishes. Matt could finish them. She needed to get out of here before she did something monumentally stupid, like dragging him into the broom closet for a quickie. "You and I both know that would be a really bad idea."

"I don't know that, but I know how we can find out."

She stopped, her hand on the knob, her soapy fingers slipping on the brass. She recognized the determined look on Matt's face. Logically she knew this was destined to be a disaster, while her less logical side wanted everything he offered and more.

It was the "more" in that equation, and knowing he would never give it, that gave her the strength to open the door and walk out.

Matt watched Emily leave, knowing he'd won this round. He'd found her weakness—a way in.

She still wanted him.

When he'd touched her, she'd trembled. Actually *trembled.* He couldn't remember ever having that effect on a woman before. Well, not since the last time he'd been with Emily. That night on the beach they had both done their share of trembling. If she wanted him half as much as he wanted her, leaving tonight hadn't been easy. But this was Emily. She wouldn't give in to him without a fight. If he could build a multimillion dollar corporation from nothing, he could manage to seduce a woman. Even one as hardheaded as her.

And while they were busy fighting to see who would win this battle of wills, he would leave her boyfriend in the dust.

Ty had said to take this as far as necessary, and if this was his only angle, his only way in, he was going to take it. And if he was lucky, he and Emily would walk away from this as friends again. And he was going to enjoy himself.

Five

"**Y**ou want the guy," Alex said from his perch on the corner of Emily's desk. "Why won't you just admit it?"

Emily glared up at him, tired of having this identical conversation for two days running. What was it with everyone lately? Her mother had gotten on her case earlier that afternoon about spending time with Matt while he was in town. "We have to make him feel welcome," she'd said. Not an hour later Ty had called with a similar story, but he didn't possess the same air of subtlety as their mother. "He's rich, good-looking—what's not to like?" he'd asked.

It was like a freaking conspiracy.

She dropped her head in her hands, massaging away a killer headache in her temples. "I do not."

"But he's so *hot*. And rich." Alex grabbed a stack of messages off her desk. Messages Matt had left, that she hadn't yet returned because she was a big chicken. "And he's obviously interested."

"And he's leaving. I'm not looking to get my heart stomped on again. If you like him so much why don't *you* go out with him."

He let out a wistful sigh. "In my dreams, honey."

She gave him an eye roll. "Don't you have work to do?"

"You're awfully cranky for someone who claims not to need sex. I'm telling you, you'll feel so much better if you sleep with him then never call. Revenge is good for the soul."

If she thought it would make her feel better, she might just try it. But she didn't want revenge. She wanted to know what it was Matt wanted from her. One minute he said he wanted to be her friend, the next he was like a wolf on the prowl. And knowing she was his intended prey filled her with a sizzling sexual energy. That he could so effortlessly stir that reaction scared the hell out of her.

Her only defense was avoidance. So she wouldn't do something dumb, like fall in love with him again.

"If you insist on being so stubborn, how about dinner and a movie tonight instead? My treat. You've been working too hard."

Well, one of us has to, she wanted to say but held her tongue. Alex didn't mean to be irresponsible. He couldn't help that he was completely unfocused. "Only if we can see an action movie," she said. "No gushy romantic garbage."

He slipped off her desk. "You're on. I'll pick you up at six at your place."

"And no more talking about Matt?"

"Yes, fine. No more talking about Matt."

An evening when she wouldn't have to see Matt or think about Matt. It almost sounded too good to be true.

Matt pulled up in front of Emily's apartment, and parked. He'd had enough of being brushed off. Problems with the restaurant and office responsibilities had kept him tied up the last two days but now things were running relatively smoothly. This was his chance. This would be the night he would seduce Emily.

He walked up to her door and raised his hand to knock when he saw the note taped there inviting him in.

Well, it was inviting *someone* in, although he seriously doubted he was the intended receiver. Still, it did say to come in. And he didn't know for sure that it *wasn't* for him.

Feeling only slightly guilty, he stuffed the note in his pocket and opened the door, peering inside. From the bathroom, he heard the shower running.

Emily in the shower, water and soap sliding down her body. Naked and wet. His favorite combination.

This just kept getting better.

He stepped inside and closed the door, and as an afterthought locked it. For the briefest of moments he considered joining her in the shower, then wrote it off as a bad idea. Tempting, but unwise. When they took a shower together—and they would—it would be her idea.

Considering her reaction to him the other night in her parents' kitchen, finessing Emily into bed wouldn't really be all that difficult. He had decided, because he liked to continually present himself with new challenges, he wasn't going to make love to Emily until she asked for it.

Until then, he was predicting a fair amount of teasing and foreplay.

Her sofa bed was folded out, and since there was nowhere else to sit, he plopped down and stretched out lengthwise, stuffing a pillow under his head. He caught a hint of Emily's scent mingled with fabric softener and imagined her lying there. The sheets were a disheveled mess, as if she moved around a lot in her sleep. Unless her boyfriend was back and the sheets were messed up for an entirely different reason.

The thought stuck in his side like a thorn. He shouldn't feel this possessiveness toward her. Up until today, after repeated attempts to get in touch with her, he'd done a pretty good job of convincing himself he was only doing this for Ty and his parents. Yet with each unreturned call, his level of frustration had risen, until he could think of nothing but seeing her, of touching her again. One taste of her lips and he was like an addict, craving more.

He sighed and closed his eyes, exhausted beyond belief. He hadn't had a decent night's sleep since he'd gotten to Michigan. As hard as he'd tried to convince himself it was stress-related, or due to sleeping in an unfamiliar bed, odds were it had more to do with Emily. And when he *had* managed to catch a few hours of sleep, Emily had invaded his dreams. More often than not he'd woken aroused and restless and craving Emily's touch.

He stretched his arms over his head, sinking deeper into the mattress, feeling himself begin to drift off. And since a couple minutes of shut-eye wouldn't hurt, he didn't fight it. He had no idea how long he lay there and was only vaguely aware of the sound of a door opening, but he was too relaxed to move a muscle. Then something cold and wet hit him square in the chest and his eyes flew open.

Emily hovered over him. She wore a pair of cut-off shorts and a tank top the exact same silvery-blue as her eyes.

And she didn't look very happy to see him. "What the hell are you doing in my apartment?"

Matt grinned up at her. He grabbed the wet towel off his chest and tossed it back. "You invited me in."

She flung the towel onto the bathroom floor. "How? Telepathically?"

His grin widened and he pulled a slip of paper out of his pocket. "You left a note on the door for me."

She snatched it out of his hand and unfolded it. "This wasn't for you."

"It wasn't? Oops."

Oops my foot. He was far too amused for this to be anything but intentional. The man's ego knew no bounds.

She stomped over to the phone and punched in Alex's number, and when he answered said, "It's six-fifteen, why aren't you here?"

"And break up your little party? Not a chance, hon. I take it that note was for me?"

"You are *so* dead."

Emily peered out the front window and saw Alex's car parked across the street. He waggled his fingers at her.

"Trust me, Em, you need this."

There was a click and the line went dead. What

was this, screw-with-Emily's-life week? Was there anyone who *wasn't* trying to set her up with Matt?

"Stood up?" he asked. He was still lying on her bed, propped up on his elbows. And he looked damned good there.

"I don't suppose someone called and told you to come over here."

"Nope. Just my lucky night." He patted the spot next to him.

She spit out a rueful laugh. "You don't really think I'd get into bed with you?"

"I'll keep my hands to myself. Scout's honor."

She folded her arms over her chest. "Like I would be dumb enough to fall for that one again."

His smile widened, showing his dimples, and her resolve weakened the tiniest bit. "We'll call the bed the safe zone. No touching. I promise."

He might have been arrogant and occasionally sneaky, but when Matt made a promise, he didn't break it. She knew that without a doubt.

She crossed the room and dropped down next to him on the bed. He sat up beside her and nudged her with his shoulder. "Bad day?"

"You ever have one of those days when it feels like the entire world is against you?"

"At least once a week. Anything I can do to help?"

"You could go back to California."

He shrugged apologetically. "Sorry. You're stuck with me until the restaurant is finished. Would you settle for a back rub?"

"I can't, we're in the no-touching zone."

"Oh, yeah."

She gestured to his leg. "I keep meaning to ask, how's the knee? Does it ever give you trouble?"

"Occasionally," he said, rubbing a hand across the scars bracketing either side of his knee. "It aches sometimes when it rains, or if I push myself physically. I avoid contact sports and running."

"That must have been awful. To come so far in your career and then have it all snatched away."

"I was devastated," he admitted. "I felt like my life was over."

"I was watching the game when it happened. I saw you take the hit, the way they flipped you over, and I just knew you would be hurt. It was such a shock, seeing you lying there, your leg all twisted up." The memory made her shudder. "I can't imagine how much that must have hurt."

Matt nodded. "I'd taken a lot of hard hits in my years playing ball, had a couple of concussions, broken fingers, but I'd never felt pain like that."

"Right after it happened, my dad was on the phone with the airline. He didn't even know what hospital they were taking you to, but it didn't matter. My parents wanted to be there for you." Emotion stole up her throat. She laid a hand on his arm. "I should have been there, too. I've always felt that I let you down by not coming."

"God, Em, you didn't let me down." He covered her hand with his own, weaving his fingers through hers. "You didn't owe me anything."

She looked down at her their hands clasped together. This was the no-touching zone, but his hand felt too good, too soothing to pull away. "What are we doing here, Matt? Why is it I don't see you for years and now I can't get rid of you?"

He frowned, rubbing his thumb absently across the top of her hand. "I didn't plan any of this. I came back not knowing what would happen. I just knew I had to come."

"To reconnect?"

It was tough to explain something he didn't even understand. "Lately, I feel like something is missing in my life."

"You're rich, successful. To the world, it looks like you've got it all. What more could you possibly want?"

He shrugged. "Sometimes I wake up in the middle of the night in a cold sweat, gripped with this irrational fear that no matter how hard I work, no matter how much money I make, it will *never* be enough. I'll never be happy." He squeezed her hand and smiled. "But this is good—being here with you. I've really missed you, Em. When I leave this time, it will be as your friend. And I'm going to come back to visit. And you can come to visit me."

"I've always wondered, if I had just kept my feelings to myself, if we had never…maybe we would still be friends. I feel like I ruined everything."

"What happened is not your fault. We both wanted it."

"We did?"

A sick, cold feeling of dread slid through him. He'd always assumed what had happened was mutual. She'd sure as hell acted willing at the time. "Are you telling me I forced you?"

"No! Of course not. It was pretty obvious I wanted it. I just didn't know *you* did."

With a well of relief came a dash of confusion. "How could you not know?"

"I didn't hear from you after. I thought…" She pulled her hand from under his and tried to stand. "You know, we probably shouldn't be talking about this."

"Oh, no you don't." Matt grabbed her arm and pulled her back down next to him. "Talk to me, Emily."

She hesitated before she finally admitted, "I thought maybe you did it because you felt sorry for me."

He didn't know whether to feel insulted or dejected. "How could you think I would do that?"

"It was either that, or it was so bad you couldn't face me anymore." His eyebrow spiked and she added, "I'm sure it was obvious it was my first time. I had, like, zero experience. For all I know, I did everything wrong."

He buried his face in his hands and shook his head. Then his shoulders began to shake, and Emily realized he was *laughing*. Her blood heated to boiling, surging like fire through her veins. "You think this is funny?"

Laughing, he fell back against the mattress. "I think it's hilarious."

"You…you big stupid jock!" Did he have even the slightest clue how humiliating this was for her? Out of sheer frustration, she drove her fist into his gut, encountering only solid, rippling muscle. It was like trying to drive a Volkswagen through a Mack truck. He made a slight "oof" sound, but didn't stop laughing.

"I'm glad you think this is so amusing," she said, trying his biceps this time, giving new meaning to this-is-going-to-hurt-me-more-than-it-hurts-you. Pain radiated through her hand and up into her arm.

Remembering what she'd learned in her self-defense class, she pinched him just below his armpit.

Matt grabbed her wrist. "Ow! Damn it, that hurt."

Well, that had worked. He wasn't laughing at her anymore, only, now she couldn't move. She yanked hard against him. "Let go of me you big oaf."

"Hell, no, you're dangerous."

She pried at his fingers with her free hand, and before she had time to blink, he grabbed that wrist, too, flipped her over and pinned her to the bed. She gasped as the weight of his leg over both of hers trapped her against the mattress.

She struggled against his restraining hands. "Get off me, Conway."

Matt looked down at her, humor crinkling the corners of his eyes. "Not until you calm down."

She pushed up hard with her knee, and he countered the move by increasing the pressure of his leg, driving her deeper into the mattress. He was just too strong for her. Too darned big and heavy.

"We're in the no-touching zone," she said, pushing up against his hands.

"Listen to me, Emily. My not calling you had nothing to do with my lack of interest or your lack of experience. What we did that night was by far the single most erotic thing that's ever happened to me."

Emily stopped struggling and her anger leaked away. Her arms went slack against his restraining hands. "If you're just saying that to make me feel less stupid, I'll kill you."

"I wouldn't lie about something like that."

They were practically nose to nose, and the amusement she'd seen in Matt's eyes was gone. Now they
were dark and intense. In response, she began to feel
warm and heavy and boneless. Then that heat turned
into an ache. An ache that settled itself between her
thighs and tightened the peaks of her breasts into
over-sensitized points. Definitely not the way one
friend should be feeling about another friend.

"I'm not mad anymore," she said, thinking it was
about time he let go of her, before they both did
something stupid.

"Good," he replied, his eyes not leaving her face.

She glanced up at the hands still holding her firmly
to the bed. "Maybe you should, um…move."

He shifted his leg between her two. His crisp leg
hair chafed the sensitive skin of her inner thigh and
she gasped at the intimate contact. As he rested his
body firmly against her, she discovered she wasn't
the only one feeling more than friendly.

"Is that what you had in mind?" he asked.

She wanted to arch against him. She wanted to
take everything he was offering, but she knew it
would be a mistake. And she knew if she didn't put
an end to this soon, he would kiss her, and once he
kissed her, she would be toast. "I'm not going to
sleep with you, Matt."

He stared at her for several seconds, then he swore
softly and let go of her hands. He rolled over onto
the bed beside her and threw an arm over his eyes.

She sat up and poked him in the side. "You all
right?"

"I will be in about five minutes. Sooner if you
have a bucket of ice I could stick my head into."

The fact that he needed a bucket of ice after touching her sent a ridiculous little thrill through her. "'Fraid not."

Matt sighed deeply and sat up next to her. "You've changed, Emily. You're not the tough kid I left behind eleven years ago."

"I'm not?"

"Nope." He looked over at her, eyes full of sympathy. "You hit like a girl now."

The competitor in her rose up and crawled under her skin. Now he was really asking for it. "I may hit like a girl, but twenty bucks says I can still whoop your butt shooting hoops."

He gave her a wide grin, the thrill of the challenge clear on his face. "You're on."

Six

Matt leaned forward, resting his hands on his thighs, sucking hot, humid air into his lungs. The muscles in his legs were burning with exhaustion, his knee was on fire and sweat soaked his clothes, but he wasn't ready to give in yet. Not with Emily circling him, dribbling the basketball and looking as if she could go another ten rounds easy.

"Had enough?" she asked with a cocky grin.

He looked up at her, shading his eyes from the sun as it dipped below the trees bordering the park. "You're looking awfully pleased with yourself."

"For a wimpy girl, you mean? Why don't you just admit I'm better than you and give it up?"

"One more game," he said, pulling himself up and peeling his shirt over his head. "Double or nothing."

"You're already down a hundred and fifty dollars. You sure you want to take that kind of risk?"

"Hey, I'm playing with a handicap," he said, disgusted with himself for using his knee as an excuse for losing.

"So am I," she shot back. "I'm female."

Female or not, he'd forgotten how well she played. It probably didn't help that she still played regularly and he hadn't had his hands on a basketball since his injury. But he was determined to win just one more game.

He ducked past her, stealing the ball, and executed a flawless slam dunk. "First to ten points wins."

Twenty minutes later she made the winning shot, bringing the game to a slaughter of an end at ten to two.

Matt limped off the court, his pride mortally wounded, and collapsed on the blanket they'd spread out in the grass.

"Admit it," Emily said, dropping to her knees beside him. "I play pretty good for a girl."

"You play pretty good for a guy," Matt said, propping himself up on his elbows.

She took a long swallow out of her water then offered it to him. After he took a drink, she capped it and set it on the grass. "So, you didn't *let* me win, right?"

"*Let* you win? Emily, you eviscerated me."

"I just have a hard time believing you're that lousy. Not that you were ever that good at it, but at least it was marginally challenging."

He glared up at her. "Are you done gloating?"

She grinned and stretched out next to him on her side, propping her head in her hand, so they were face-to-face. Damn, she was pretty. If it were up to him, they would be lying this way in his bed back at the hotel. They would be naked and her skin would be flushed and moist not from basketball, but from hours of making love.

How she could think he hadn't enjoyed himself that night on the beach was beyond him. She'd been so aggressive, so sure of what she wanted, and so responsive to his every touch, every taste, he had wondered if it wasn't her first time after all. He'd been hurt that she hadn't told him when it happened. He'd thought she told him everything. And he'd wanted to find the guy who had stolen what should have been his and tear him limb from limb.

The thought of someone else's hands on her had burned him with jealousy. They'd been friends for years, and in all that time he'd barely given a physical relationship with her a second thought. That night he could think of nothing else. *He* wanted to be her first.

He still remembered how hot she'd felt as he'd entered her, how impossibly tight. Then he'd felt the barrier of her innocence give against his thrust, heard her sharp intake of breath, and he'd known she was his. It was as if the piece of him that had been missing had somehow slipped into place.

But it could never be more than one night. He had plans, dreams, and she didn't fit into them. In the morning they would go back to the way things had been. Back to being friends. It wasn't fair, and he knew he would probably hurt Emily, but it was just the way things had to be.

Then morning came, and all those feeling he'd experienced the night before, the need to be with Emily, hadn't burned away with the sunrise. In fact, it was worse. Everything he felt for her was still there, taunting him.

She would never know how difficult it had been to leave, or how close he'd been to giving it all up for her. Without the scholarship, he never would have been able to afford college. He *had* to go to UCLA. And without college ball, he never would have made it into the NFL. Had he not finished school and earned his degree, after his injury he would've had nothing to fall back on. He simply never had time for the kind of commitment Emily would have wanted. The one she deserved.

He still didn't.

"You're not what I expected," Emily said, her inquisitive blue eyes tugging Matt out of the past.

"What were you expecting?"

She shrugged. "I thought you would be more serious."

"I guess I am when I'm in California. More focused. I would never take time off to play one on one."

"How come?"

"Too busy. Weekdays I spend in the office, a couple evenings a week I stop in at the restaurant in L.A. to make an appearance. Every Sunday I fly to one of the other Touchdowns and spend a few hours."

"Every Sunday? Why?"

"It's good exposure and it draws the customers in."

"So when do you take a day off? When do you relax?"

He could barely recall the concept. "I don't. I have a condo in Cancun I've never been to. I own a villa in Italy I never have time to visit. If you want the honest truth, outside of work, I have no life.''

Her brow creased, as if the thought was a disturbing one. ''Then what's the point? Why work so hard if you can't enjoy what you've got?''

''When I figure that out I'll let you know.''

''So what about this Sunday? Which one are you going to?''

''This Sunday, I was supposed to fly to New York, but my plane is in for repairs.''

Her eyes widened. ''*Your* plane, as in the one you *own?*''

''It's a little plane,'' he said. ''A Lear.''

''Unless it's a model plane it's completely out of the realm of my comprehension. You can afford to buy a plane and you want even *more* money? When is it enough?''

He shrugged. He wished he knew. Although he had to admit, he'd felt different since he'd been back. He couldn't even put a finger on the exact emotion. Being with Emily again just felt…good. And not necessarily in a sexual way. He was just enjoying her companionship. Sitting here with Emily, he felt relaxed. Comfortable.

Content.

He couldn't remember the last time he'd felt that way. If only there were a way to capture it, to take it back to California with him.

''I always thought there would be this feeling I would get,'' he said. ''Then I would know that I'd made it, I'd succeeded. Then I could slow down and enjoy what I had. Maybe settle down and have a family. But lately, it seems like the harder I work, the further away the feeling gets.''

"What does building a restaurant here have to do with it? Isn't it even more of a risk? Chapel isn't exactly a hoppin' place."

"I've proven myself in the business community, and had a decent, although short-lived career playing ball. I've resolved things with my parents to the point where I can forgive them and move on. The only thing I haven't done is prove I've made it to the people in Chapel."

"You know what I think?"

"Huh?"

"You spend way too much time worrying about what other people think."

She was probably right. In fact, he was sure she *was* right, but he'd run out of other options.

"You mentioned your parents. Do you see them very often?"

"As little as I have to."

"I heard you set them up in a pretty nice place in Florida."

Yeah, nice and far away, where he didn't have to watch them slowly committing suicide. "I used to think money would be the answer to their problems. I tried for a couple years to get them into detox programs, the best money could offer, but they never lasted for more than a week or two. There came a point where I had to back away. You can't save someone who doesn't want to be saved."

"At least you tried."

"I just make sure they're taken care of. If they're going to drink themselves to death, they'll do it in a nice condo on the beach. My mom has money to play bingo five nights a week and my father has his satellite dish and plasma TV to pass out in front of."

She reached over and rested her hand on his forearm. "They don't deserve you, Matt."

Something in the way she said his name and her gesture of comfort made the next words hard to say without emotion messing with his voice. "They weren't great parents, but they did the best they could."

The sympathy in her eyes nearly did him in. This was why he didn't like to talk to people about personal stuff. It did weird things to him, like turn him into a big wuss.

"So," he said, desperately needing a change of subject, "you haven't said much about your boyfriend. I take it it's not very serious."

"What makes you assume that? For all you know, we could be engaged."

"No ring."

She glanced down at the hand resting on his arm and something in her eyes darkened. He thought for sure she'd pull away, but she let it rest there. "I've never been real big into jewelry."

He reached up, rubbing her earlobe between his fingers. The look in her eyes went from dark to simmering. Don't fight it, he thought. You know you can't resist me. "No piercings."

"That's not exactly true," she said. "I do have one."

He examined her face, at all the obvious places, but didn't see any holes. "Let me guess, you had your navel done?"

She shook her head.

"Tongue?"

She made a face. "Yuck. No way."

"Where else is there?"

Her gaze wandered down to the front of her shirt. When he realized what she meant, all the air backed up in his lungs. "Your nipple?"

"It was purely an act of rebellion. In college, a friend of mine got hers pierced. My mom said if I ever did, she would disown me."

"So you did it anyway?"

A defiant grin spread across her face. "The next day."

"I guess she didn't disown you."

"I never told her. I ended up really liking it. Even though I was the only one who knew it was there, it made me feel...sexy. I'm pretty small up top, so it gives me that extra 'umph.'"

I'll bet, he thought, although from what he could see, she wasn't lacking in any particular area. He found his eyes riveted to her chest, curious whether he could see the outline through her clothing. "Doesn't it get caught on things?"

Her eyes lit with mischief, and something more. Something hot and teasing. "Actually, when you tug on it just a little or give it a twist, it's extremely erotic."

Matt swallowed hard to keep the excessive saliva from dribbling down his chin. He knew he wouldn't be satisfied until he was holding that ring in his teeth. "I've seen them in photos, but never in person."

Her eyebrow arched. "Are you asking if you can see mine?"

Hell, yes, he wanted to see it, but it wasn't so dark that the kids on the playground wouldn't notice if she lifted her shirt, or the group of teenagers playing volleyball several yards away wouldn't possibly see.

And he'd be damned if anyone was going to get a look at Emily's breasts. Anyone besides him, that is.

"This probably isn't the place," he said.

"Then maybe you'd like to see my tattoo instead?"

Nipple piercings *and* tattoos? "I'm afraid to ask where that is."

She shifted onto her back and unfastened her shorts and Matt's eyes just about fell out of his head.

"Uh, Emily?"

She rolled onto her stomach and lifted her shirt so that her lower back was exposed. "You'll have to pull my shorts down."

He sat up beside her and Emily watched, gratified by the hungry look in his eyes as he stared at her bare skin—the same look he'd had since she told him about her nipple. It made her feel desirable and powerful—something she hadn't felt in a very long time. Not since she'd given herself to him on the beach.

She was enjoying it far too much.

"Pull your shorts down?" he asked.

"Not all the way down. It's just below my waistline." She was playing with fire, but she couldn't seem to make herself stop.

He darted a glance around, as if he were afraid someone would see. Then he reached down and slipped two fingers under the waist of her shorts. The backs of his fingers caressed her skin as he eased the denim down, and gooseflesh broke out across her arms.

A breath escaped him in the form of a sigh. "What is it?"

She looked back over her shoulder at him. "An orchid. My favorite flower."

"The detail is amazing." He pulled her shorts lower, to see the entire yellow flower blooming across the lowest part of her back and the very top of her buttocks. As if he were touching the living specimen, he brushed a thumb across the delicate petals. That frustrating ache burned to life low and deep inside her.

"No tan line," he said, but it came out sounding more like a growl.

"It shows up best against tanned skin."

"I'm not even going to ask how you managed that." Matt flattened his palm against her, his large hand encompassing her entire lower back. "I think I want to see the nipple ring now."

"I think that would be a bad idea."

He slipped his hand down her side, his fingers just inside the waist of her shorts, which were already several inches lower than they should have been. His hand traveled slowly up her side, lightly tracing each of her ribs, all the way up to the edge of her bra. She closed her eyes and curled her fingers into the blanket. The ache was now a throb as need overwhelmed her and blood raced through her veins.

She rolled onto her side and looked up at him. His eyes were dark with desire. "I'm not going to sle—"

Before she could finish the sentence, Matt lowered his head and pressed his lips to hers. The sizzling reaction was instantaneous. She was lost.

It began slow and sweet, his lips brushing oh-so-gently. She felt herself go weak under the tender pressure of his mouth. Very lightly, he traced her lower lip with the tip of his tongue. When she touched her tongue to his, the grip on her side tightened and his fingers pressed deep into her flesh, sending shocks of sensation through her stomach. He tasted exactly as he had eleven years ago. He smelled the same and his hands felt just as good against her skin. And now that she'd had a taste of him, a sample of what he could give her, she was having a hard time putting on the brakes. Of course, with Matt kissing her senseless, she wasn't using a lot of brain power.

Somewhere in the back of her mind she knew they were in a public park, but she also knew it was growing darker by the minute. Families were packing up and clearing out. Teenagers gathered in packs around picnic tables, others hung out in the wooded areas most likely doing exactly what she and Matt were doing. No one was paying attention to the couple on the blanket.

Just for a few minutes, she promised herself. Then I'll stop him. But those few minutes passed too quickly, so she decided to give it just a few minutes more.

Matt flattened his hand over her stomach, dipping inside her open shorts to the very tops of her bikini underwear, and she froze.

He must have sensed her apprehension because he went very still above her.

"Matt, I—"

"I know," he growled, rolling away and sprawling out flat on the blanket. "You're not going to sleep with me."

Seven

Matt stabbed the off button on his cell phone and repressed the urge to chuck it at the nearest brick wall. Construction on Touchdown was officially shut down.

Apparently, Eric Dixon had a little more clout than Matt had anticipated. His lawyer was pressing for a lawsuit, but the last thing Matt needed was a long drawn-out legal battle. It wouldn't exactly endear the people of the city to the idea of eating at his restaurant.

And every day the building sat there deserted, he lost more money. Not to mention that until it was finished, he would be stuck in this godforsaken city, where more than a few people had made it clear he was no longer welcome.

Late last night someone had spray-painted derogatory comments and a few colorful expletives across the exterior of the restaurant and the construction trailer. The police promised to increase future nightly patrols of the area, but were already making noise like there was little chance of catching the responsible party. And though he'd hired a painter to cover the evidence, he couldn't erase the foul image from his mind.

He watched as the construction crew cleared out their equipment. They had other jobs to occupy their time while he worked something out. Eric had approached Matt earlier in the morning offering a monetary solution. One that would cost Matt in the neighborhood of six figures. If only he'd had a tape recorder handy to nail the sleazy bastard.

Matt already knew what he needed to do. He had a solution. He just had to take that step. Emily's parents had done so much for him already, he didn't know how to ask what would be his final favor.

Then he would win.

He flipped his phone open and dialed Emily's father at his engineering firm. He was told by the secretary that Mr. Douglas would be out of the office all week. Matt tried him at home next, but got the answering machine, so he called Ty.

"They drove up to Saugatuck to stay with friends," Ty told him. "They're due back next Thursday or Friday, I think."

A full week. Damn.

Matt hung up, cursing himself for waiting. If he'd known Mr. and Mrs. Douglas were going out of town he would have approached them before they left. If they had agreed to his terms he could have at least gotten the ball rolling. He'd have lost maybe a week, now he was looking at two or three.

Which meant he had that much more time to sit around and twiddle his thumbs. He could always go back to L.A., but his plane was still awaiting a part and the thought of taking a flight on a commercial airline held about as much appeal as a bikini wax— which he'd never actually had, but they sure as hell didn't look like much fun to him. And oddly enough, he didn't want to go back to L.A. He didn't feel like working, which for him was like saying he didn't feel like breathing.

The thought of sitting in his office, submerged in a mountain of paperwork his staff could just as easily handle without him made Matt feel restless. Anything important that needed going over he could do through e-mail or fax and anything that needed signing would reach him overnight via Fed Ex. Meetings he could handle through conference calls. The office ran just fine without him, and that had him wondering why it was he spent so damned much time there.

On the positive side, time off from work meant more time to seduce Emily. The memory of her skin, her scent, the taste of her lips was driving him nuts. And he hadn't been able to stop thinking about that nipple ring. Though it was a slow process, last night he'd made some serious headway. If he'd been insistent, he probably could have taken it even further, but what was the fun in that? When the time was right, she would be begging for it. Then he would finally get to do everything he hadn't done that night on the beach. Which, come to think of it, wasn't much.

The question now was, what would his next move be? With all this time on his hands, what was he supposed to do with himself?

As the last truck pulled out of the lot, Matt took a final look at the building and smiled, knowing exactly what he needed to do.

"Hey."

Emily looked up from her computer screen, her traitorous heart fluttering at the sight of Matt standing in her office doorway looking tanned and healthy and way too gorgeous for his own good—or hers. "Hey. What's up?"

"I came to talk about work."

"Okay." She tried to keep her tone light when in reality her heart was sinking. He was probably here to tell her that they'd lost the contract to another nursery. Maybe sleeping with him had been a condition of the job.

As the thought formed she knew it was completely unfair. She'd been the aggressor last night, the one to bring up the nipple ring, to take down her pants and show him her tattoo. She still didn't know what had gotten into her. Maybe it was the way Matt looked at her as though she was the only woman on the planet. He made her feel so desirable and, well…feminine. She hadn't realized how much she'd missed that.

She'd pretty much given up on men—at least for now. As far as she could figure, they felt threatened by her independence. Most men seemed to like a woman they could coddle and take care of. Someone gentle and delicate that they could put up on a pedestal. Not one who could run circles around them on the basketball court, or recite from memory the stats from the Detroit Red Wings entire last season. She didn't wear makeup, didn't own a dress—nor did she plan to purchase one—and pantyhose gave her a rash. At five feet nine inches, high-heeled shoes put her at eye level with most men she knew, and several inches above others. Which is why she didn't own any of those either.

Alex loved her for the person inside. He was her best friend, her confidant. He had great taste in clothes and even better taste in men. Unfortunately, being friends with a gay man didn't do much for a girl's ego.

When Matt looked at her—very much the way he was looking at her now—she felt like a woman.

Matt stepped into her office and sank into the chair across from her desk. "I've run into a bit of a snag with the building inspector. Construction has been put on hold. I just wanted to let you know there's no rush getting that bid to me."

Which meant her commission would come later, and her shop was that much further away. Swell. "Thanks for the heads up."

"Instead of flying back to L.A. while my lawyers work this out, I thought I might take a couple of days off. Maybe go fishing."

"What, like a vacation?"

"Yeah, I figure I'm due."

Emily narrowed her eyes at him. "Who are you and what have you done with Matt?"

He grinned. "I want you to come with me. Can you get a couple of days off?"

Before she could say no, Alex appeared in the doorway. "Of course Emily could get a couple days off."

He breezed in, a hand stretched to Matt in greeting. His hair, as always, was perfect, his clothes spotless and his manners impeccable. And he could play the man's man role to a T. "You must be the infamous Matt Conway."

Matt stood and shook Alex's hand, looking to Emily for an explanation.

"Matt, this is Alex Marlette."

"A pleasure," Alex said, pumping Matt's hand. "What's this about Emily needing a few days off?"

"I don't," she told Alex. "I have too much to do here."

Alex dropped Matt's hand and turned to her. "I had my vacation. It's only fair you get some time off, too. Where did you plan to take her, Matt?"

Matt looked hesitant to answer, as if maybe this was some sort of trick question. "Um, fishing?"

"Emily loves to fish. Of course she'll go."

"But the accountant is coming," Emily told Alex. "We need to go over the books."

Alex turned to Matt. "I'm sorry, could you give us a minute alone?"

"I'll wait out front," Matt said, looking back and forth between the two of them as if they were both more than a little weird.

He had no idea.

When he was gone, Alex turned to her, fanning his face, slipping easily back into his typical, flaming self. "Whoa. Talk about steamy."

"I'm not leaving."

"This is your big chance."

"To do what? Screw up my life?"

"Em, honey, this self-imposed celibacy thing you've got going is getting really old. Take a couple of days and have fun."

"There is no self-imposed celibacy. I just haven't

met anyone I've wanted to sleep with." If he only knew how close she'd been to doing exactly that last night.

Emily rubbed her eyes with a thumb and forefinger. She was exhausted after one very long, sleepless night. In just a few days her prudently managed life had been propelled into chaos and Alex was asking her to make it even worse. "I can't just pick up and leave. I have responsibilities."

"It'll all be here when you get back." He grabbed her arm and physically hauled her from the chair. "If you don't go I'm going to fire you. Then you'll never get the money together for your shop. I swear I'll do it."

"You would not. This place would fall apart without me."

"Honey, you give yourself far too much credit. I'm not completely incapable."

"Yes, you are."

The insult slid right off his back. "I'll pay you time and a half for your vacation days."

That one stopped her. She did a mental calculation of how much money that would be. "Seriously? You would actually *pay* me to go on vacation? For the whole weekend?"

"I would, now will you go?"

"Is there something you're not telling me?"

"Yes, you're a major pain in the butt. Just go and have fun."

Honestly, the idea of a couple days away from the nursery sounded like heaven. She couldn't recall the last time she'd taken a vacation. She'd been too focused on raising the money for her shop, on keeping the business running smoothly. How much damage could Alex possibly do?

On second thought, she didn't even want to go there. "What about the accountant? We have to get ready for the audit."

"I can handle it. I'm really not as incompetent as you like to think."

"Maybe I don't want to go with him. Did that ever occur to you?"

"You need closure, hon. As much as you refuse to admit it, after all these years, you still have a thing for the guy."

"Says who?"

"Says you, every time I catch you looking at his picture in a magazine, or watching a clip about him on the news. You get that sappy, sad, faraway look and you swoon all over the place."

She snorted. "I've never swooned in my life."

"When was the last time you were on a date? Or had a relationship? Or *sex?* You do remember what that is?"

Emily gave up the battle and allowed him to shove her out the office door. "I'll get paid time and a half? Even though the nursery is barely hanging on?"

"I'll take it out of my salary."

"For how long?"

He glanced at the calendar on her desk. "Today is Thursday? I don't want to see you back here until Monday morning."

"You promise you're not just saying this to get rid of me?"

"I promise."

She hesitated. "I don't know…"

Alex lowered his voice. "Okay, how about this.

Take some time off or I'll tell your parents we're not really dating.''

She knew exactly what that meant; her parents trying to set her up with every available single man in the city. Anything to get themselves a tribe of grandchildren. She narrowed her eyes at him. "You wouldn't."

"Try me." He slammed and locked the door before she could reply to his threat. It looked as if she would be taking a few vacation days. That didn't mean she would be spending them with Matt.

He was in the parking lot waiting for her, leaning against the back of his SUV, arms folded across his chest. The sun glinted off his dark hair and made his skin look golden. As usual, the sight of him accelerated her heartbeat and punched up her hormone level several notches.

This was not good. After what had almost happened last night in the park, a fishing trip with Matt would be a very bad idea.

"Did your boyfriend really just encourage you to go away on vacation with me?" he asked.

"That doesn't mean I'm going." She pulled out her keys and headed for the company truck.

He fell in step beside her. "He's a nice guy."

"You sound surprised. Did you think I wouldn't be able to attract someone nice?"

"You know that's not what I meant. If you were my girlfriend, no way in hell would you be going away anywhere with anyone but me."

The passion with which he made the statement alarmed and thrilled Emily at the same time. What would it be like to be Matt's girlfriend? To be his wife? To have homes all over the world. To own expensive cars and clothes and have a plane at their disposal.

Lonely.

It would be unbearably lonely. The hours he worked, it would be like living with a ghost. No amount of wealth would be worth that. If he were penniless and worked a nine-to-five job he would be a better catch as far as she was concerned.

Besides, she didn't have the time to invest in a relationship either. Like Matt, she enjoyed the challenge of earning what she wanted. She would feel the pride that shone like a prize in his eyes when he talked of his accomplishments. It's what she had waited her whole life for. True independence.

If she were to marry Matt, on the entirely remote chance that he ever asked, along with the wealth and prestige, she would feel like a sellout. Where would the challenge be?

If the business didn't take off as she hoped, she would be disappointed, but at least she could say she'd tried, she'd given it one hundred percent. On her own.

When they reached the truck Matt stepped ahead of her, blocking the door. "Come with me," he said. "We'll have fun. We can go anywhere in the world you want."

"Alex may be trusting, but I know you too well, Conway. You want to get me away from here so you can get me into bed."

"Not true," he said, and at her look of complete disbelief, added, "Not *entirely* true. I'd just like to spend time with you."

She would love to go away with him. But not if

this was some quest to soften her up. She didn't know if she had the strength to fight it anymore.

God, she was having trouble remembering *why* she was fighting it.

Oh yeah, because she would fall in love with him again, and he would leave, and she would be devastated.

"Can you promise that you will not under any circumstances try to seduce me?" she asked. "Promise that this vacation will be one hundred percent platonic."

When he didn't answer, disappointment burned deep. At least he was honest. He could very easily lie to get what he wanted, but that wasn't Matt's style. If things were different, if they both had very different lives, they might have been good together.

And they both knew it.

He seemed to realize it was a lost cause, and stepped away from the door. It wasn't like him to give up so easily and she felt equal parts relieved and disappointed. She climbed in and started the engine.

He leaned in the open window. "Think about it. If you change your mind, call my cell phone."

Because he looked so hopeful, and completely irresistible, she leaned over and pressed a kiss to his cheek before she drove away.

Emily climbed out of the truck and stretched her stiff limbs, inhaling the earthy scents of pine and moss and feeling an odd mix of emotions—the way she always felt when she came up to her parents' cottage. She relished the peace that came with submersing herself in nature, yet this place held so many memories. Some full of laughter and fun, others bittersweet. She'd experienced the best and worst times of her life here.

The best, when Matt had made love to her on the beach, the worst when she woke the following morning, her heart swelled to capacity, only to have a "talk." She'd been back dozens of times since, and still experienced that sense of loss. Maybe it would never go away.

She grabbed her things from the front seat and let herself into the cottage. Exhausted from the three-hour drive, she tossed her bag in her bedroom to unpack later. Right now she was going to take advantage of the last few hours of afternoon sun and lie out on the beach. Later she would go into town and buy a few supplies.

Alone, a voice echoed in her head.

Yeah, so what. It wouldn't be the first time she'd come here alone, and it probably wouldn't be the last.

And what, that was supposed to make her feel better?

She peeled her clothes off, fighting a wave of loneliness despite her internal pep talk. She couldn't help wondering what Matt was up to. Where had he gone? His villa in Italy? His condo in Cancun? And who was he with? Had he found someone else to keep him company? Someone willing to do what Emily wasn't?

She tried to convince herself she didn't care, but that didn't take away the sick feeling in the pit of her stomach. What an impossible situation. Two people who were hopelessly attracted and completely wrong for each other.

She wrapped herself in a beach blanket, slipped her sandals on, and headed outside. She followed the narrow trail through the trees and down to the lake. As she emerged from the dense foliage onto the sandy cove, sunshine wrapped around her, warming her bare arms and shoulders. With her father semi-retired, her parents came up regularly during the summer months, sometimes for weeks at a time. The boat was parked in the slip next to the dock, and she was sure there were sodas and beer in the fridge. The freezer would be stocked with steaks and burgers ready to barbecue.

Emily kicked off her sandals and dug her toes into the hot sand. Though their own stretch of beach was secluded and private, the lake was alive with activity. Jet Skis and motor boats cut foamy paths through the water. The playful shouts of children swimming and splashing traveled on the breeze.

Emily knelt down in the sand and unfolded herself from the blanket. Boats rarely ventured so close that someone would see she was naked. And if one did, she would hear its engine and have plenty of time to cover herself.

She stretched out on her stomach, her gaze drawn to the fire pit, to the spot where Matt had made love to her. She felt that familiar pull of longing.

Even though it had been her first time, and she'd heard countless horror stories about the pain, she hadn't been the least bit afraid. She'd spent more hours than she could count daydreaming about that moment. Wishing for it with all of her heart. She couldn't have been more ready and Matt had been unbelievably sweet and gentle with her. It might have been her imagination, or maybe just wishful thinking, but at the time she could have sworn he'd been nervous. Matt, who was rumored to have scored with dozens of girls.

The second time had been different. She'd been even bolder and he'd been much more aggressive. Not rough, but not exactly gentle either. He was suddenly the Matt she'd heard rumors about in the girls' locker room. The one who knew exactly what to do to drive a girl crazy. He'd touched her in ways that to this day made her feel that same hot restlessness in her limbs. A deep longing, an ache no one else had been able to relieve.

By the third time, she'd chucked the last of her inhibitions. Her only goal had been to give him the same bone-deep satisfaction he'd made her feel. When the fire died and they'd gone back to the cottage, there had been very little left unexplored. They knew each other more intimately than she thought two people could. She had lain in bed afterward, reliving it all in her head, committing each second to memory.

She thought she'd gotten over him. Now that he was back, she wasn't sure what to feel anymore. He wanted to be friends. He wanted her to visit him in California.

And he wanted sex.

And heaven knows, so did she. Maybe she was being silly telling him no. They were both consenting adults. What was she proving, staying up here at the cottage all by herself? That she could manage on her own? She already knew that. She'd been doing it for years. For *too* long.

As if she'd conjured him up by sheer will alone, Emily heard the low rumble of Matt's voice behind her.

"Now I see why you don't have tan lines."

Eight

Matt watched as Emily shrieked in surprise and yanked the edges of the blanket around herself. She needn't have bothered. He'd been standing there long enough to see everything. And a little longer to commit it all to memory. Now that he'd seen all of that gloriously tanned and flawless skin, his desire for her had multiplied to an aching need. A need not only to lay her out beneath him and bury himself deep inside her, but to feel that closeness, that connection he'd felt only with her.

"What the hell are you doing here, Conway?"

He flashed her a wide grin. "Fishing."

She tucked the blanket tightly around herself and rose to her feet. "You *followed* me?"

"Look me in the eye and tell me you're not happy to see me. That you wanted to stay up here all by yourself."

She shoved her feet into her sandals and stomped past him. "That's not the point."

On the contrary, that was exactly the point.

He followed her through the woods to the cottage, a grin on his face. He'd seen the flash of excitement when she'd first turned around. She was happy to see him, and trying awfully hard to hide it. "I didn't have to follow you. I knew you would come here."

"How could you possibly know that?"

"It was the first place I thought of, too."

There was the slightest hesitation in her step, and he knew his words had hit their mark. He followed her into the cottage and to her bedroom. He leaned in the doorway while she rummaged through a duffel bag for clothes, reminded of one of the things he'd always liked about her. She could throw a couple of days' worth of clothes together in less than ten minutes and didn't need a ten-piece set of luggage to carry it all. He'd never dated a woman who wasn't severely high-maintenance. Even in high school. It had him wondering what it was about him that attracted that kind of woman. And what it was about that kind of woman that he found attractive, because honestly, the luggage thing really annoyed him.

It occurred to him that Emily was the complete opposite of everything he normally looked for in a woman. Which made him wonder if he wasn't deliberately dating women he knew would irritate him.

"If you're only here to get me into bed, you might as well leave right now," she said, her back to him.

"I told you before, I want us to be friends. When I leave Michigan, I want us to continue that friendship." Why was it every time he thought about going back to L.A.—his home—he felt utterly empty?

She turned to him, eyes scrutinizing. "So, you're saying you no longer want to get me into bed?"

"Do I want you, Em? Yeah, I do. But if friendship is all you can give me right now, that will have to be enough." He took a step toward her, but hung back just far enough so the move wouldn't come off as overtly sexual. He wished she'd drop the blanket so he could see that nipple ring. It was all he'd thought about on the way up.

"Let me stay, Em."

"You promise you won't try to get me into bed?"

He could be wrong, but he had the distinct feeling that by saying "bed," she was leaving open a hell of a lot of options. Or was he letting his imagination get the best of him?

"I promise."

For a long moment she only stared at him, and finally she said, "We'll need supplies. We'll have to go into town for groceries and bait."

She was letting him stay. A slow grin spread across his face. She was as good as his.

She just didn't know it yet.

Matt followed Emily down the aisle of the country market in town. Talk about a blast from the past. A typical mom-and-pop establishment, little had changed in here in the last decade. And while it still boasted decor reminiscent of the Brady era, it was clean and the selection surprisingly diverse for its remote location.

And like so many other things pertaining to his past, he'd missed it more than he realized.

"We should get cereal for breakfast," Emily said,

swiping a box of Kangaroo Crunch off the store shelf.

Matt took the box from her and read the nutritional chart. "Do you know how much sugar is in this?"

"Well, yeah, that's kind of the point. How else am I going to wake up at four in the morning?" She grabbed a package of iced pastries and tossed those in the cart as well.

"You mean women actually eat this stuff? I thought all you ate was lettuce and tofu."

Emily shrugged. "I have big hips and no diet in the world is going to change that. I may as well enjoy eating."

"Emily, do you know what I find most appealing about you? The fact that you actually have hips. You have meat on your bones." At the odd look she gave him, he added, "That's a compliment."

"I wasn't sure."

She really didn't have a clue how attractive she was. She had no idea how tough it was to stand within a few feet and not touch her, not undress her with his eyes. He was trying really hard not to do anything blatantly sexual. He didn't want to do anything to scare her off. But, damn, it was hard not to touch her.

Take it slow, he reminded himself.

"Believe it or not," he said, "I'm tired of dating women who look as though a strong breeze could knock them over. The kind who excuse themselves to the rest room to throw up after every meal."

She gave him a "yeah, right" look.

"I'm serious. I've taken women out to dinners in five-star restaurants, where you can drop three or four hundred easy on dinner. Double that if they want champagne. There's a reason they're trotting off to the john between every course. I once dated a model who actually excused herself to throw up after dinner.''

Emily made a face. ''Yuck. You run with an interesting crowd, Conway.''

''I don't exactly run with anyone. They just kind of…attach themselves to me.''

Emily grabbed a loaf of wheat bread from the shelf—the first healthy thing she'd picked up. ''People respect you. They want to be around you.''

''They respect who they think I am.''

''How do you expect them to see you for who you really are unless you let them?''

''And what if, when I let them see the real me, they aren't so impressed anymore?'' He winced at his own words. That didn't come out the way he'd meant it to.

A slow smile spread across Emily's face. ''I'll be damned. He is still in there.''

''Who?''

''The Matt I knew when we were kids. The one who looked self-confident, like he owned the world, but on the inside felt like he never quite measured up.''

Her words stunned him.

She was wrong. He simply valued his privacy and was particular about who he let into his life. He'd left those insecurities behind when he left Michigan.

Hadn't he?

''It's okay,'' she said. ''I liked the old Matt.''

Troubled by her words, Matt followed behind her as she picked out packaged lunch meat and cheese, then onto the register where she added half a dozen chocolate bars to the cart.

"That should about cover it," she said, as the cashier rang it all up.

Matt pulled out his wallet.

"I'll get this," she said.

"The hell you will. It goes against the natural order of the sexes. The man pays for the food."

She rolled her eyes. "Spare me the sexist bull, Conway."

"Sexist bull or not, it's the way I do things."

Emily frowned. "I don't like the idea of you buying me stuff."

"Yeah, well I don't like you buying me stuff either."

The cashier looked back and forth between them as if they were seriously disturbed. "Someone has to pay for it."

"We could share the cost," Emily reasoned.

"Yeah, okay," he agreed, because he was pretty sure arguing would get him nowhere. She was struggling to make ends meet, yet she still wouldn't let him pay for the damned food. She was definitely unlike any woman he'd ever dated. He found himself appreciating that fact more every minute he spent with her.

They split the cost of the groceries, packed it in the truck and headed back to the lake. He steered the truck back down the long, tree-lined dirt lane. He'd been there so many times in his youth he could have driven blindfolded. The log-cabin-style cottage, tucked deep into the woods, looked exactly as it had when they were kids. Beyond the cabin he could see glimpses of shimmering blue lake between the trees.

The scent of pine and earth and the warm breeze rustling the leaves greeted him like a long-lost friend. That it felt so good to be back surprised him. He'd missed so many things about his old life, but hadn't realized it until he'd come home.

"We should load the fishing supplies into the boat today so we can get an early start in the morning," Emily said as they carried the groceries in.

"Is it all still in the shed out back?"

"Should be."

"You put the groceries away, I'll take care of the fishing stuff."

She propped a hand on one hip. "Let me guess. Putting groceries away is women's work?"

He flashed her an easy smile, one that said she'd hit the nail on the head, and headed out the door. His ideas were borderline chauvinist, yet she couldn't muster a bit of anger. Men typically saw her as one of the guys and treated her accordingly. They didn't open doors, or pay for meals. And they sure as hell didn't look at her as though they wanted to rip her clothes off and ravage her—the way Matt had been looking at her on the beach. Of course, she hadn't had any clothes to rip off, had she?

He didn't seem to notice that she was about as far from supermodel material as a girl could get. Yet there was no question, their desire was mutual. But for how long? Should this ever progress past a brief fling, if, say, he asked her to go back to California with him, one day he was going to look at her and realize she was all wrong. He would have some fancy event he would want to take her to and discover she wasn't, and never would be, arm-dressing.

Besides, she thought as she put the last of the groceries away, she didn't want to leave Michigan. She had plans. Her family and friends were here. It was home to her. She wasn't sure she could give that up for anyone. Not even Matt. Not anymore.

She headed outside and down to the beach. Matt was still on the boat, so she waded out calf-deep into the water, feeling inexplicably sad. Why, when a relationship was destined to fail, did she still yearn for it?

"Is the water cold?"

Emily turned to see Matt walking across the sand toward her. "Not too cold."

He kicked his sandals off and waded into the water beside her. "Everything looks the same."

She gazed around. Nothing ever seemed to change up here, yet everything was different this time.

"You okay?" he asked.

"Yeah," she lied. Well, it wasn't a complete lie. She was only slightly not okay. "Why?"

He tucked his hands in his pockets and shrugged. "You had kind of a funny look on your face. You looked…sad, I guess."

Her attention naturally strayed to the fire pit, and he followed with his own eyes.

"Having regrets?" he asked.

"There's nothing about that night I regret, Matt. Do you regret it?"

How could he regret the most amazing experience of his life? How could he regret connecting, bonding so deeply with another person? "Never. I just regret that I hurt you."

She nodded. "Yeah, that part did suck."

"Maybe someday, in a couple of years, when things settle down for me…"

"Be still my heart." She clasped a hand to her breast and adopted a horrible Southern drawl. "I shall wait till the end of time for you to return."

"Too much to ask, huh?" Kind of like having his cake and eating it, too. As he'd reminded himself so many times over the years, she deserved better. "Is it because of Alex?"

"Alex is very special."

The next words were almost impossible for him to squeeze out. "Do you love him?"

Her foot swung like a pendulum through the surf. "He's my best friend. He keeps me sane."

Jealousy twisted him in knots. Even worse than the thought of Emily having an intimate relationship with someone else was the thought that he'd been replaced as her best friend. He wanted to fill that spot. He wanted it so badly it was painful. Maybe she just didn't have room for him in her life anymore.

Well, dammit, she would have to make room, because he wanted back in, and he wasn't taking no for an answer. He *needed* her. He was no longer doing this for Emily's family. Or even for Emily. This was all about him, what *he* wanted.

Now all he had to do was figure out exactly what that was.

"Why don't we put on our suits and go swimming before we make dinner?" she said, obviously ready for a conversation change.

"Who needs suits?" Matt said. He peeled his shirt off and tossed it onto the sand. Emily's eyes widened, as if she thought he might strip down naked right in front of her. He would if that's what she wanted. "We can wear our clothes."

"Our clothes?"

"I remember you used to love jumping off the dock in your clothes."

"Conway, the only time I ever went off the dock in my clothes is when you threw me—" Recognition darkened her eyes and she began to back away from him, onto the sand. "You wouldn't."

With an evil grin, he began to mirror her steps. "What kind of vacation would this be if I didn't throw you off the dock, Emily? It's tradition."

"That's one tradition I can do without, thank you." She turned and started to run, and while she was damned fast, even with a bum knee he was faster. With little effort he caught up to her. He hooked an arm around her waist and swooped her lithe form up and over his shoulder.

She screamed and kicked but was laughing too hard to put up much of a fight, as she had when they were kids. "Let me go, Conway!"

If he'd heard an ounce of conviction in her words he would have put her down. Instead he wrapped an arm across her lush behind and tucked her firmly against him. He'd held her this way half a dozen times a year throughout the better part of his childhood, but he couldn't remember it ever feeling this nice. Or having the urge to slide his hand across her firm rear end, between her silky thighs…

"You big dumb jock, let go of me!" she screamed through another fit of laughter.

Ignoring her pleas, he trudged through the sand and down the length of the dock.

She beat at his back with her fists. "You are so dead, Conway. When you least expect it, I'll get my revenge."

"I'm pretty scared," he said, and his mild tone said he was anything but. He reached the end of the dock and, with beautiful execution and no hesitation, tossed her into the lake. She landed with an enormous splash and disappeared under the water.

He crouched down, waiting for her to surface. When she didn't he felt a sliver of concern and immediately dismissed it. She'd been on the swim team in high school. If he knew Emily, she was hiding under the dock, waiting for just the right moment to reach up and pull him into the water.

He sat back a little, just in case.

"I know what you're up to and I'm not falling for it," he called into the water. The words were barely out of his mouth when a shadow passed across him from behind, and he felt a wet hand planted firmly on his back. He looked up to see two perfectly formed breasts with small, dark, erect peaks under a soaked, transparent tank top. And, *aw hell,* the outline of one enticing nipple ring. Then he crashed headfirst into the water.

Matt picked his cell phone up from the picnic table where he'd set it out to dry, feeling an eerie sense of panic. The cottage had no phone, and without a phone line he had no Internet hookup. And Emily, to his disbelief, didn't have a cellular. He'd thought that in this day and age everyone had a mobile phone, or at least a pager.

He was, in essence, completely cut off from the outside world. It felt unnatural, as if one of his limbs had been amputated.

Talk about a wake-up call. There was something

seriously wrong with him if he couldn't survive three days without a cell phone.

"Is it dry yet?" Emily asked as she cleared away the paper plates and plastic cutlery from their dinner. The distress in her voice was more than clear. She felt pretty bad for what she'd done, regardless of how many times he'd told her it was okay. If anyone was at fault, it was him. If he hadn't tossed her in the lake, she never would have retaliated by pushing him in. And if not for the lake he never would have gotten a glimpse of that nipple ring. It was worth the hours of sexual torture he'd endured while he imagined what it would be like to take that tiny ring between his teeth and give it a tug.

The torture of not being able to get hold of his secretary was far worse.

"Maybe you should try turning it on," she said.

"It's only been a couple of hours." He set it back down, resisting the urge to dial his voice mail. "If I turn it on wet, I'll completely fry the circuits."

"I'm really sorry, Matt. If I had known you were wearing your phone—"

"I told you before, it's not your fault."

"If there's any way I can make it up to you."

Oh, man, how often did a guy get an offer like that? Where should he start? Several ways instantly sprang to mind, but he was pretty sure the things he was thinking weren't exactly what she was thinking. Most involved his mouth on various parts of her anatomy.

Just the thought caused a tightening in his groin.

He gazed at her mouth, his lips tingling in anticipation, not to mention the other parts of him that had begun to tingle as well. He needed to get some blood flowing back to his brain. He had to keep his focus.

"If it's ruined I'll replace it. Just let me know how much."

"The cost isn't important," he said.

"You're worried about work. About your office not being able to get a hold of you."

Not just the office, but he'd left a message with Emily's parents asking them to call as soon as possible. The sooner he talked to them, the sooner he could get construction up and running. He hoped.

"You can go back," she said. "If you leave right now you would make it to Chapel by about 1:00 a.m."

At the mere thought of completely abandoning his business, apprehension gripped his stomach. Sweat beaded his brow and trickled down the side of his face. He was in worse trouble than he'd thought if the idea of a few days away from work triggered a panic attack. Had he chained himself so completely to his company that he'd become obsessed?

It ended here, dammit. Maybe it was time he reevaluated his priorities. Maybe it was time he started to live a little. He'd promised himself a vacation and if that meant cutting himself off from the world, he'd try like hell to relax and have a good time.

"No," he told Emily. "I'm not going anywhere."

"You're an important man, Matt. I understand that you have responsibilities. I'll be okay up here alone."

"I'll try my cell phone in the morning. If it doesn't work, I'll drive into town and call my secretary. She'll take care of it."

Through the last traces of daylight she eyed him doubtfully. "You're sure?"

About as sure as he could be in his present state of mind. "Finish up in the kitchen and meet me down at the beach."

"What are you going to do?"

"Gather wood. We're having a bonfire."

Nine

By the time Emily made her way down the dark path to the beach, equipped with the fixings for s'mores, Matt had the fire blazing. When she saw the blanket he'd brought down with him, she stopped dead in her tracks. It wasn't the presence of the blanket that gave her pause, but its placement. He'd spread it in the sand in the exact spot they'd sat that night. No way it wasn't deliberate.

She should have been damned angry about it, but all she could do was picture herself and Matt lying there, bodies intertwined. This time the boundaries of their relationship were drawn. Friendship, with a little hot sex thrown in to spice things up. There were pros and cons, of course. And honestly, she was beginning to believe the pros greatly outweighed the cons. She'd already mostly decided that if he made another move on her, she might not fight it. She might let nature take its course and see what happened.

She walked to the blanket and sat down. Crickets chirped in the woods and she heard the rush of the waves as they slapped against the shore. The fire crackled and hissed and sent plumes of smoke drifting up into the trees. It felt peaceful, serene—until Matt tossed one more log into the fire, the orange glow accentuating the muscle tone in his arms and thighs, and she was flooded with an overload of female hormones. She felt the same giddy nervousness as she had on the last night they'd spent here. Would he kiss her? Would he touch her? Would she have the courage to make the first move if he didn't?

Matt dropped down on the blanket beside her. Close enough to be friendly, and far enough away to be frustrating. "I think that's enough fire to last awhile."

"I brought stuff for s'mores." She opened the bag of marshmallows, loaded the skewers, and handed one to Matt.

"I haven't done this in years," he said, holding his close to the flame.

Emily held her own beside Matt's. She wasn't really in the mood for sweets—not unless she was licking them off his body. What she was really craving was the taste of his mouth, the saltiness of his skin.

Any time now you can try to seduce me, she thought. Instead he stared into the fire, slowly twirling his skewer, and asked, "I noticed that you never answered my question."

"What question was that?"

"I asked if you're in love with Alex."

"I am," she said. "But not in the way you think. The truth is, we see other people."

She could swear she saw relief in his eyes.

"But you can't tell my parents," she added. "Or my brother."

"Why not?"

"To preserve my sanity." At his quizzical look, she added, "My parents are determined to get me married off. I won't sit through one more dinner with some employee of my father's, or the son of a family friend. Having a boyfriend is the only way to get them off my back."

"Why don't you just tell them to stop?"

"Matt, you of all people should know that would never work. They just don't listen."

"Would it hurt to try?"

"*Try?* I've spent my entire life trying." A familiar rush of resentment swelled to the surface. "I've had to fight for my independence. As long as I can remember, they've been making decisions based on what they think is good for me. When I wanted to play T-ball, my mom signed me up for ballet. Instead of letting me play soccer, my parents put me in gymnastics. In kindergarten, my mom decided wearing jeans like Ty wasn't appropriate for a girl and forced me to wear dresses."

"I don't remember ever seeing you wear a dress, so you must have won that battle."

"Yeah, because I started lifting my dress and showing boys my underpants."

Matt laughed. "You didn't."

"Don't you think it's sad that at six years old I had to go to such an extreme? It was like they just couldn't accept me for the person I was supposed to be. They still don't.''

"They just want what's best for you."

"But who are *they* to decide what's best for me? Suppose I'm not ready to settle down?"

He wondered if he should tell Emily what her family was up to, and immediately decided it would be a bad idea. He didn't want to give her the idea that his feelings for her weren't genuine, that they'd put him up to it. Even though technically they had. And there was no way he could mention any of what she'd just said to her family. He would never betray her trust that way. In other words, he was caught in the middle.

This also meant she wouldn't be quitting her job, which presented him with a entirely new problem— how to find out what Alex was up to. Maybe he should just come right out and tell her his suspicions. Maybe she'd seen something fishy and would put two and two together. If he said nothing, and she found herself in trouble with the law because of it, he would never forgive himself.

"How, um, trustworthy is Alex?"

She mushed a piece of chocolate and a golden brown marshmallow between two crackers. "I would trust him with my life. Why do you ask?"

"It's just that, I've heard things."

"What things?" She took a bite, warm chocolate and marshmallow dripping down her chin. Oh, man, did he want to lick it away for her.

"He goes out of the country a lot?"

She sucked chocolate off her fingers. "A couple of times a year. He travels with friends."

"You get shipments from other countries?"

"Now and then. Most are domestic. Uh, Matt?" She nodded toward the fire, and he realized his marshmallow had gone up in flames.

He shook it off the skewer and it landed with a sizzling splat in the embers.

"Here, take a bite of mine." She held it out for him, chocolate oozing down his chin as he bit off a piece.

"Messy," she said, wiping it off with her thumb and holding it up to his mouth. She wanted him to…*oh, man.* He opened his mouth and she slid her thumb over his tongue. He couldn't speak. He couldn't even breathe.

What had they been talking about?

"Why are you suddenly so interested in Alex?" she asked, reminding him. Only he didn't want to talk about her boyfriend now. He wanted to lick melted chocolate off her entire body.

Focus, Conway. This is important. "Do you know what he does when he leaves the country?"

"I have a pretty good idea."

"Are you sure?"

"Matt, why don't you tell me what you're insinuating?"

"Word is circulating that he might be involved in something…shady."

"Shady?"

"Drugs, Em."

Instead of looking concerned, Emily snorted out a laugh. "*Drugs?* You're kidding, right?"

"You could be putting yourself in trouble just working for him."

"I'm not in danger of anything."

"How can you be sure?"

She tossed what was left of her s'more into the fire. "I see every shipment that goes in or out of that nursery. I track every penny. There's no way he could be running drugs through without me knowing about it. I mean, the guy can't even remember to pay the electric bill on time. Who could possibly have had a harebrained idea like—no wait. Don't tell me. *Ty* told you."

His expression must have said it all.

She shook her head. "He's such an idiot."

"He's genuinely worried about you, Em."

"No, he doesn't like Alex, and he doesn't want anyone else to like him either." She started gathering the food. "It's late. If we're going to get up early to fish we should get to bed."

"Em—"

"I'm angry, Conway. Not at you. Just ticked off in general and I wouldn't be very good company. I'll see you in the morning."

He watched as she disappeared through the woods.

He'd blown it. A minute ago she'd been taking the initiative, letting him suck chocolate off her fingers. She would have been his, if he'd just kept quiet.

She was wrong about Ty. He wasn't an idiot.

Matt was.

Emily lay in bed staring at the wood beams above her, unable to sleep, so angry she could spit nails. The small fan on the dresser across the room just circulated the hot, muggy air. Dressed in only panties and a tank top, her skin was slick with sweat, making the sheets stick to her like fly paper. She grabbed her watch off the night table and checked the time. One-ten in the morning.

It was one thing for Ty to tell people he didn't care for Alex. She'd gotten used to that. But to spread rumors that he was peddling *drugs?* That was over the top even for Ty. And as badly as Emily wanted to throttle him, if she let on that Matt told her, it could drive a wedge between Ty and Matt. She just had to be angry until she wasn't angry anymore.

Too hot and sticky even to consider sleep, she rolled out of bed and tugged on a pair of shorts. Maybe it would be cooler by the water. She shoved her feet into her flip-flops and tiptoed into the hall, stopping outside Matt's room.

The door was open and she could see the outline of his body sprawled across the twin-size mattress. He was so large and the mattress so small it was almost comical. It had to be a major step down from the luxury he was accustomed to. She had offered her parents' room, but he had said he wouldn't feel right sleeping there.

So here he was cramped into a bed he'd dwarfed even in high school. She couldn't hear his breathing over the hum of the fan, but his chest rose and fell in a steady rhythm. His *bare* chest, she noticed with a giddy, light-headed feeling. He was covered to the waist with a sheet and she had to wonder what, if anything, he wore underneath. In high school he'd worn boxers to bed. At least, when he'd spent the night at their house he had. She would sometimes walk by Ty's room in the morning and get a glimpse of Matt on the spare bed, sprawled out much as he was now, wearing boxers.

Back then, considering her pathetic lack of experience with the opposite sex, she'd lived for moments like that. She'd felt naughty for spying on him, but it had thrilled her no end to see him that way. So vulnerable. So peaceful. Once she'd peeked in and had gotten more than she'd bargained for when she'd realized his boxers were fitting tighter than usual. A *lot* tighter.

She'd gone beet red with embarrassment and something else, a breathless feeling that had drained all the energy from her muscles and made them quiver. She hadn't been able to pull herself away. She wanted to know what he was hiding under his shorts. Only when she heard her mother coming up the stairs had she dashed down the hall and closed herself into the bathroom.

The feeling she hadn't recognized back then had become more than clear that night on the beach. It had been pure lust. The same thing she was feeling now.

Matt sighed in his sleep and rolled away from her, dragging the sheet with him. From the looks of it, he didn't wear boxers to bed anymore. Now, he didn't wear *anything*.

Her estrogen production instantly went hyperactive.

She gazed at the smooth contour of his bare muscular behind, wishing she could crawl into bed with him. Things had been moving along so well by the fire. When she'd slipped her thumb in his mouth she'd thought for sure his eyes would bulge right out of his head, and she'd nearly melted into a puddle when she'd run her thumb across his tongue. Licking what was left off his chin would have been her next move, had he not dropped the bomb.

Alex running drugs. Ridiculous.

No, not just ridiculous—laughable.

She backed away from Matt's room and headed to the kitchen. She grabbed a beer from the fridge and a beach blanket from the porch on her way out and headed down to the water, feeling her way through the thick underbrush alongside the path. The stifling heat was only slightly less oppressive outside, and the idea of a midnight swim held even greater appeal. On the beach, the fire had just about burned itself out, so she grabbed a few logs and tossed them on the embers. Instantly the parched wood ignited and flames licked up to encompass them.

Emily spread the blanket out, kicked off her shoes and walked down to the water sipping her beer. Across the lake fires dotted the beach and if she strained hard enough she could hear the faintest sound of music and laughter. That should have been her and Matt. Sitting up half the night, laughing and talking about old times. Then reliving them in vivid detail.

Emotion burned the back of her throat and left a bitter taste in her mouth. Tomorrow night, she promised herself. She'd make it up to him. To herself.

Away from the fire, it was so dark she had to keep a hand stretched out in front of her to feel her way to the dock. She stepped into the cool water, instantly feeling soothed. Maybe a swim would ease the restlessness in her muscles, in her soul.

She set her beer down and slipped her clothes off, leaving them on the dock. It's not as if anyone was going to happen by this time of night, and even if they did it was too dark to see anything. She'd thought the same thing this afternoon on the beach just before Matt had happened by. But he was sound asleep now.

She walked several feet out, then dove in, the cool water working her body loose. She swam out several yards, until her muscles began to burn from the exertion, then rolled over and floated on her back for a while. Her body lifted and swelled with the gentle waves, and above her the sky was a showcase of twinkling lights. She closed her eyes and sighed, letting herself sink down until the water covered her head. She surfaced, disoriented in the dark, then spotted the fire and headed in that direction until the shadowy outline of the dock became clear. She followed it up until she was waist-high, feeling her way, looking for the beer she'd set there. Her hand instead collided with a muscular, hairy leg.

She shrieked and yanked her arm away and heard a rumble of laughter from Matt.

"Are you trying to give me a heart attack!" she admonished.

"Didn't anyone ever teach you not to drink and swim?"

As his shadowy form became clear, she saw him raise something to his lips. Probably her beer. "What are you doing out here?"

"Watching you skinny-dip, I think. These *are* your clothes I'm holding, aren't they?"

Her hands automatically flew up to cover her breasts. "I thought you were sleeping."

"I was faking it." She made a sound of indignation and he laughed again. "You didn't seem to mind so much when you were looking at my butt."

"You did that on purpose?" Embarrassment set her face on fire.

"You didn't have to wait until I was sleeping. All you had to do was ask and I would have shown it to you."

Faint light penetrated the darkness and she could almost make out the smirk she heard so clearly in his voice. On the beach the bonfire crackled and hissed, spitting flames high into the air. She didn't think she'd built it that large, then realized Matt must have added wood.

He set her beer down on the dock and stood, looming high above her as he shoved his shorts down his legs and kicked them away. She could see enough to know that he was as magnificently built as he had been in high school. She stood enraptured, unable to make herself look away as he slipped almost soundlessly down in the water beside her.

"I was getting lonely in bed all by myself," he said. She heard husky desire in his voice and he circled her in the water, like a shark stalking its intended victim.

Her heart hammered in her chest and she closed her eyes, waited to feel his hands on her skin. She shivered in anticipation, but he didn't touch her. Finally she turned to him and realized he was gone. He resurfaced several yards away from her, shaking water from his hair.

"Aren't you going to swim?" he asked, treading water.

Actually I was thinking more along the lines of screaming sex, thank you.

It was time she took the initiative, even if she did have zero experience seducing men. And suppose he'd changed his mind and didn't want her anymore? If she came on to him, and he rejected her, she wasn't sure she could take that. It had taken her years to work up the courage to tell him her feelings the first time. Although, since he'd been back, he'd been pretty relentless in his pursuit. And she'd been pretty relentless in her refusal.

She pushed herself backward into the water, sinking below the surface, then rising up to float on her back.

Matt watched her. Backlit by the fire blazing on the beach, the silhouette of her breasts bobbed temptingly in and out of the water. In and out. He couldn't wait to get a good look at them, to take that nipple ring between his teeth. It had nearly become an obsession.

In his life, he didn't think he'd ever been so mystified by the idea of touching a woman. Of course, in his life, he'd never met another woman quite like Emily. When he'd heard her standing in the hallway, he'd hoped she would climb into his bed, not that they both would have fitted in it. He liked the idea of making love to her on the beach again even more. Their eleven-year reunion. They could make it a tradition. Although he wasn't sure he wanted to wait another eleven years to be with her again. Maybe this should be an annual event. Monthly would work, too. Daily and he would be in heaven.

Maybe after the restaurant was built. Maybe then he could slow down, think seriously about exploring a committed relationship with a woman. With Emily. If she wanted that from him.

He swam closer to her, but stayed far enough away that he wouldn't be tempted to touch, enjoying this heightened anticipation. Each time she drifted toward him, he drifted away.

Finally, she rose in the water, naked from the waist up, her skin glistening, her pert breasts begging to be caressed. Oh, man. Not touching her was going to be hell.

But something wasn't right, something in her body language told him she wasn't having nearly as much fun with this as he was. Then she reached up to shield her breasts and he knew he was losing her.

''I think I'll go back to bed now,'' she said, turning away from him and wading toward the beach.

''Em, wait.'' He followed, grabbing her arm to stop her. ''Why are you leaving?''

''You obviously don't want me out here.'' Her voice quivered and he realized she was genuinely upset. ''Every time I come near you, you move away.''

''I'm sorry, Em.'' He pulled her to him. She was a bundle of warmth and softness against him. And that was what he'd forgotten. Emily had a soft, vulnerable side. Unlike the women he normally came into contact with, the barracudas. The ones who didn't hesitate to let a man know exactly what they wanted, and what they were willing to give in return.

What had made him think Emily would be one of those women?

He felt like a jerk because he'd never stopped to look at it from Emily's point of view. He'd come back after ignoring her for more than a decade, chased her for days, and when she finally made a move toward him, he moved away. What the hell had he been thinking?

''You're confusing me,'' she said softly. ''Do you want me or not?''

''Yes, I do.'' He held her snugly against him. ''I

was acting like an idiot. I'm sorry. I thought it might be fun if I could get you to chase me for a while. I guess my ego needed stroking.''

"You could have any woman in the world, Matt. Why does it matter if I chase you?"

He drew back and cupped her face in his hands. "Because of all the women in the world, the only one I want is you."

Ten

He'd said the words out loud—words he'd denied for more years than he cared to admit—and the world hadn't come crashing down around him. It actually felt good to finally have it out in the open, as if he'd been released somehow.

Emily only smiled, smoothing a hand across his cheek. He couldn't tell if she believed him, or thought he was just humoring her. But then it didn't matter, because she looped her arms around his neck, pulled his face to hers and kissed him.

It started with a bang, hot and deep and full of passion, and it only got hotter. Once she got into her comfort zone, she was an explosion waiting to happen. He was so blown away, for a second he only stood there, barely able to keep up as she ravished him. It was as if she was starving and only the taste of his mouth could satisfy her. The buzz of mosquitoes around his head, the cool water lapping against his waist, all faded into the background. There was only Emily. Her lithe body forming just right against him, her breasts a soft contrast to the hard planes of his chest.

He wrapped his arms around her, smoothing his hands across her shoulders, down her back. Every inch of her skin felt exquisitely soft. Naturally soft. Somehow he couldn't imagine Emily seeking the aid of expensive creams or spa treatments. Everything about her was natural and pure. Which was more than he could say about the thoughts running through his head. They were anything but pure.

He cupped her behind, and she moaned into his mouth, arching against him. "Cottage or beach?" he asked, leaving the decision up to her, though he had a definite preference.

She didn't disappoint him. She smiled up at him and said, "Definitely the beach."

He lifted her up out of the water and she locked her legs around his waist, her arms around his neck. Still, as he started toward the beach she began sliding out of his grip. "It's hard to impress you with my strength and charm when you're this slippery. Hang on tight or I may drop you."

The arms around his neck tightened and she whispered, "Don't worry, I'm already impressed."

When they reached the blanket he dropped to his knees and set her down. They stretched out together, and though he felt he couldn't wait another second to make love to her, he could do nothing but stare. They lay side by side for the longest time simply looking at each other. It had been so long since he'd seen her this way he'd almost forgotten how damned perfect she was, and maybe in his youth he hadn't completely grasped what she'd so eagerly offered him. No supermodel or actress he'd known could hold a candle to her beauty. It shone from both inside and out. What she'd given him that night was a gift. One that he hadn't fully appreciated until now, now that he'd realized just how empty his life had been without her in it.

He hadn't had time for her then. Suppose now he could *make* time. What would she say if he asked her to come back to California with him? The possibility buzzed in his head, making his heart race. Was he ready to make that kind of commitment?

The only thing he knew for sure, was that nothing had ever felt as right as holding Emily in his arms. Not back then, and certainly not now.

Firelight danced across her moist skin. He gazed at her lush mouth as it drew up into a semi-shy smile. There was nothing about her that didn't turn him on. Her body was long and lean yet so soft and feminine. She'd matured, filled out just the right amount in all the right places. His eyes were drawn to the gold ring in her left nipple. It glinted in the firelight, shimmering against her tawny skin.

"Damn, that's pretty." He reached up to skim his finger around it, then closed his eyes and sighed. "My life is complete."

Emily laughed lightly. "You're sure easy to please."

"You have no idea how much I've wanted to see this. And do this…" Holding her gaze, he lowered his head and gently took the ring in his teeth.

Emily's lips parted and her eyelids grew heavy.

He tugged just a little bit and she gasped lightly. "Sensitive, huh?"

"Hmm," she said, a dreamy look on her face.

"I don't suppose you would consider getting the other one done." He tugged again, a bit harder, and the dreamy look became one of pure ecstasy.

"I might."

And if she did, would he be around to enjoy it? Or would he wake in the morning and realize he wasn't ready to commit his life to anyone yet? Could he be happy with Emily, all the while fighting the feeling that something was still missing? Would it be fair to her?

She brushed a finger across his nipple and he shivered. "Maybe you could get yours done, too."

If it would make her happy, he might consider it. There wasn't much she could ask of him right now that he wouldn't do.

Lowering his head, he took the ring and the entire blush peak of her nipple into his mouth, tasting the tang of metal and Emily's own unique flavor. Emily moaned, tunneling her fingers through his hair.

So the other nipple wouldn't feel left out, he leaned over and flicked that one lightly with his tongue. After only a minute the ring called to him like a magnet and he couldn't stay away.

He felt Emily's hands trail downward. Over his chest, across his stomach. His pulse surged and liquid desire saturated his blood. When her hand wrapped around him, it felt so damned wonderful he could have passed out.

She pushed him onto his back and rose up on her elbow as she stroked him. His eyes were glued to the movements of her hand. She lowered her head and swiped the sensitive tip with her tongue and his body coiled with pleasure.

Her eyes never leaving his face, she took him deep into her mouth. If it were anyone but Emily the sight wouldn't have been half as erotic. Her total lack of inhibitions still blew his mind. That first night, she'd taken whatever he was willing to give, and didn't hesitate to give back in return. He could see that hadn't changed.

When it would have been so easy to lie back and enjoy it, he rose up on his elbows, knowing instinctively she needed eye contact. It had been like that before. She never took her eyes off his face, as if she thought that when she looked away he might cease to exist. It had been so intimate, so deeply personal. He'd felt a connection with her he'd yet to experience with another woman.

The pleasure in his groin began to build, radiating out until he felt his control slipping. With his eyes on her every move, it was impossible not to lose it. She was just so…hot, yet there was an innocence to her actions that mystified him. He groaned and let his head fall back. "Em, stop. I'm too close."

"I can keep going," Emily said. He had no idea how long she'd wanted to do that again. To see that look of rapture, of total submission. He had no idea how arousing she found it. "I will if you want me to."

Eyes closed, chest heaving, Matt shook his head.

"It didn't feel good?"

He looked up at her, his eyes so dark with desire they looked jet-black. "It felt *too* good. Ladies first."

"You're sure?" she asked, licking her way across his belly.

He tangled his fingers in her hair and ground out between his teeth, "You're making it really difficult for me to do the right thing."

"Sexist garbage," she said, lowering her head to take him into her mouth again. And the next thing she knew, he'd flipped her over and pinned her to the blanket. Damn, he was quick. "No fair."

"Sue me," he said, a grin on his face. He perused her body in a way that made her skin feel too hot and tight. He took her nipple ring between his teeth again, tugging lightly, and her stomach almost turned itself inside out the pleasure was so deep. He switched to the other side, scraped the nipple lightly with his teeth, then closed his mouth over the entire peak and sucked so deeply she cried out.

He backed off to admire his work. The firm tip glistened with moisture and was tinted deep red from the intense suction. "Perfect."

"Not big enough," she said, so breathless she barely had enough air to get the words out.

"Emily, your breasts are perfect." He kissed each one gently. "Everything about you is perfect."

If he was lying, she didn't even care. She just wanted him to keep touching her.

He kissed his way down to the lowermost edge of her rib cage, stopping to caress, to taste. Then lower, down the center of her belly, around her navel. For every inch he sank, her pulse quickened. Watching her, he slipped between her thighs, pressing them apart. Exactly the way he had that first night. And she was filled with the same restless anticipation. She'd heard girls in school giggle and whisper about oral sex. It sounded so private. So forbidden. So...*wonderful*. But she didn't think people really did it. Adults maybe, with years and years of experience. But not teenagers. Then Matt had slipped down between her legs and she'd known what was coming next, and she'd *wanted* it.

There hadn't been anything she wasn't willing to try. Matt had given her her first orgasm that way. And she hadn't hesitated to return the gesture, finding that the girls at school had been dead wrong. There had been nothing gross about it. The look on Matt's face alone, the blind pleasure, knowing *she* was making him feel that way, had made it worthwhile. She'd had so many firsts that night, each more wondrous than the last.

"You're thinking about that night," Matt said.

"Yeah," she murmured. He always seemed to know just what was going on in her head. Sometimes so keenly it scared her.

"Are you remembering the way I touched you?" Matt's rough chin grazed her sensitive inner thigh and she shuddered.

"Uh-huh."

"Like when I did this?" He lowered his head, touching her lightly with his tongue.

Her body tensed and rocked upward.

"Easy." Flattening his hand against her stomach, he held her down. "Relax."

Relax? Was he kidding? She was on *fire* here.

He did it again, stroking with his tongue. So frustratingly light. She had to fight to keep her body still, not to arch up against his mouth. He stopped altogether to kiss her inner thigh. Then the other thigh. Then he was suddenly fascinated with touching the back of her knee. Then her ankle!

He was moving in the wrong direction. Not that it

wasn't all sheer ecstasy, but a woman could only take so much.

She made an impatient noise to move things along.

He lifted his head and looked at her. "You in a hurry, or something?"

"I don't remember it taking this long last time."

"That's usually the case when you're a teenager," he said, then went back to work on her other ankle. By the time he worked his way to her thigh she was sure the anticipation would do her in.

Finally he was pressing her legs even farther apart, and he was…oh! Biting. So softly it was barely more than a tease. She dug her fingers into his damp hair where it curled at his nape, so he couldn't get away again. He nibbled here, tasted there…completely missing his target. Maybe he'd forgotten how, or needed a refresher course in anatomy.

She cleared her throat.

"Don't rush me," he mumbled.

While she was sure she would go out of her mind, he concentrated on that tender, aching, tangle of nerves—

Emily groaned and pressed up hard but Matt held her firmly in place. Her body tied itself into a million aching little knots and her vision went blurry. Pleasure built inside her slowly, like waves lapping gently against the sand, and just before she reached a crest, before release set her free, Matt sat up.

Still teetering on the edge of complete bliss, her mouth refused to form words. She could only moan her displeasure at his abrupt departure.

"Look at me, Em," he said.

She opened her eyes and found Matt braced over her, lowering himself between her thighs. He was going to make love to her again. She almost couldn't believe it was really happening. For only the briefest of moments did she entertain the notion that it might hurt, then he was inside her. He filled her so completely, she gasped at the sudden invasion.

''Oh, Em,'' he groaned, and she knew he'd felt it, too. One look at his face and she was lost again. Pleasure caused her muscles to clench and flex around him. Every thrust propelled her higher, each level more excruciatingly wonderful than the next, until the pleasure finally peaked and exploded in a brilliant spectrum of color.

She clung to him, awash with sensation as Matt drove hard inside her and she felt him reach his own shuddering release. He stilled and settled against her and for a minute they both lay there, quietly catching their breath, arms and legs intertwined. In her life she'd never been closer to another person. Not physically, not spiritually.

It was official, Matt had completely ruined her for other men.

He lifted his head from where it had been resting on her shoulder. ''You okay?''

She looked up at him with eyelids she couldn't quite keep open all the way. ''You have to ask?''

''Just making sure.'' He kissed the tip of her nose, her jaw, the corner of her mouth. ''If I didn't know any better, I would think…'' He shook his head. ''Never mind.''

''No, tell me,'' she said. ''You would think what?''

''You were just so…'' He paused, as if he couldn't identify the word he sought.

''So…?''

"*Tight.* It's almost like you haven't done this since…" He shook his head again, a rueful smile coaxing out his dimple. "Just wishful thinking on my part, I guess."

Emily bit her lip and looked away. So he had been able to tell. Not that it was something she was trying to hide. But it was a little embarrassing.

Matt frowned. "You're not saying anything. You always have some sort of sassy comeback. What's the deal?" He lifted her chin with his index finger, forcing her to look him in the eye. "Em?"

The truth must have been plastered all over her face. It would explain the look of disbelief plastered all over Matt's.

"Don't you dare think for a minute that I was saving myself for you, or something pathetic like that," she said firmly.

"You mean, you really haven't been with anyone else?"

"What happened between us was just so…special. Everyone says the first time is awful. For me it was perfect. It was everything I'd hoped it would be. I guess I didn't want to ruin that."

"For me, it was never the same as…" His brow furrowed deeply.

"The same as what?"

He shrugged. "I don't know."

The same as being with me? she wanted to ask. It was what she desperately wanted to hear.

A cool breeze kicked off the water and Emily shivered. She gathered herself closer to Matt, sinking into his warmth. Then she had a sudden revelation, and the shiver turned into a shudder of fear. "Tell me we did use birth control."

Matt grinned. "Yeah, we did. I brought a condom with me when I came out and left it under the corner of the blanket."

Her entire being sighed with relief. "I'm glad one of us was thinking ahead."

Matt lifted his head, eyes scanning the tree line.

"What's wrong?"

"I'm hoping no one is out there with night-vision goggles."

"Or a telephoto lens?"

His eyes widened. "Jeez, I never even thought about that. I didn't tell anyone where I was going. I doubt the tabloids would ever think to look for me here."

Apprehension slid down her spine. "I was only kidding. The tabloids actually follow you?"

"Occasionally. It was particularly obnoxious after the *People* article. But my secretary knows not to give out personal information. Like where I'm staying."

"Maybe to be on the safe side we should go back to the cottage. I don't even like looking at my bare behind in the mirror. The last place I want to see it is on the cover of a magazine."

"What about our clothes?"

She looked over in the direction of the dock. It was too dark to find much of anything out there. "We'll get them tomorrow."

"You want to walk through the woods *naked?*"

"What's wrong?" she teased. "Are you afraid of the dark?"

"Actually, I'm afraid of certain protruding parts of my anatomy getting caught on a low-hanging tree branch."

She winced. "Yeah, that would be bad. How about if we wrap up in the blanket?"

"That'll work."

Emily shook out the blanket while Matt tossed sand on the fire to douse it. Since walking through the woods barefoot was a health hazard, they put their sandals on, wrapped themselves in the blanket, and stumbled back to the cottage, laughing at how ridiculous they would look to anyone who might see them that way.

When they reached the cottage it was nearly 3:00 a.m. As soon as they were inside he wrapped his arms around her waist from behind and dropped kisses across her shoulder.

"We're supposed to be up in an hour to fish," Emily reminded him.

"I choose making love all night and sleeping till noon over fishing any day. In fact, I wouldn't be opposed to spending the entire weekend in bed. How about you?"

She slipped her arms over his, lacing their fingers together. Two weeks ago, if someone had told her she would be standing naked in her parents' cottage with Matt, she would have said there wasn't a chance in hell. Yet here they were, Matt leading her to her bedroom. Matt lying down next to her in her bed. Matt making love to her until hints of dawn crept in through the open window. Until they lay sated and limp, yet too awake to sleep.

Unbelievable.

"What are you thinking about?" Matt asked.

"How different my life was a week ago." She gazed up at him through the hazy light, idly traced the line of his stubbled jaw with her index finger. "How unexpected this has been."

"Unexpected good, or unexpected bad?"

"Unexpected good, as in, I'll be really sorry to see it end."

"Maybe it doesn't have to."

"We'll always be friends, but we both know it can't be more than that."

"Maybe it could."

She dashed the tiny kernel of hope that began to grow inside her. "How many serious relationships have you been in since you left Michigan?"

A frown slashed across his face. "None."

"Have you *ever* had a serious relationship?"

"That doesn't mean I'm incapable. California is a nice place to live. You would like it." There was so much hope in his voice, she ached inside.

"What about work? You said before that you had no time for a relationship."

"I can make time."

"How much time, and for how long? Are you talking a month? A year? A lifetime? You're still going to feel like something is missing, and you're going to want to find it. You'll start working crazy hours again. Eventually I'll get tired of being alone all the time, and you'll get tired of me complaining, until our relationship is nothing but a burden."

He looked hurt by what she knew to be reality. Even if he didn't want to admit it. "It doesn't have to be that way."

"I have dreams, too, Matt. Things I want to do with my life. You're asking me to sacrifice it all. To move to a strange place where I know no one, where I have no family."

"Emily, I can take care of you. I can give you anything you want."

"Your time, Matt. Can you give me that?"

He didn't answer. As she'd expected, it was more than he was willing to give.

She lay beside him, resting her cheek against his chest, listening to the steady thrum of his heart. "You're asking me to sacrifice so much, yet you're willing to give practically nothing in return. How long do you think we'll last that way?"

He tightened his arms around her. "You make it sound hopeless."

"It is what it is. We're together now. Let's just enjoy each other's company while you're here and not worry about what we'll be doing a month from now. And who knows, by then, we could be tired of each other."

"You can be a real pain in the behind," he said, humor in his voice. "And incredibly stubborn."

"And you can be sexist and overbearing." And perfect in a million other tiny ways. And she would never get tired of him. But some things simply weren't meant to be.

She lay in his arms drifting off to sleep, realizing she was living out the second half of her fantasy—exactly what she had wished would have happened that night eleven years ago. To fall asleep in Matt's arms. There were no parents to walk in on them, no schedules to follow. No businesses to worry about. For the entire weekend, it was just her and Matt.

Eleven

"Emily! Matt! Where are you?"

Emily bolted up in bed, jolted awake by a nightmare. She looked dazedly around until the room came into focus, grateful to find it empty. She'd dreamed her mother called to her, that she was there at the cottage. If her parents saw her and Matt this way, naked, rumpled and sleeping in her bed, they would freak. Or even worse, they would think this meant something. They would think she and Matt were in love. Heaven knows they would like nothing more than to have Matt for a son-in-law, and half a dozen mini-Matt grandchildren running around.

If her parents had even a hint that something was brewing between Emily and Matt, they would relentlessly hound them to get married. That would *really* be a nightmare, considering their conversation last night.

Beside her, Matt mumbled in his sleep and rolled onto his side. The initial horror of her dream behind her, she yawned and lay back down, curling up behind him.

"Emily! Matt! Are you here?"

At the sound of her mother's voice, she shot up in bed again, clutching the sheets to cover herself. It wasn't a dream. Her mother was really here.

She muttered a curse and jumped out of bed, taking the sheet with her. She slammed the bedroom door shut and flattened her body against it.

This could not possibly be happening.

Matt sat up in bed, bleary-eyed, rumpled and unbelievably sexy. "What happened? Where did the covers go?"

"Shh," she hissed. "Don't say anything."

There was a loud rap on the door, then her mother's worried voice. "Emily, are you okay?"

"Fine, Mom, I'm just not dressed yet."

"What happened to Matt? His vehicle is here but we can't find him."

She cringed and said nonchalantly, "He's probably out jogging or something. Give me a minute to get dressed and I'll help you find him."

"We'll wait in the living room," her mother called, then Emily heard her receding footsteps.

"I guess this rules out morning sex," Matt mumbled from behind her.

She turned to him. He was sitting up in bed, his hair disheveled, his eyes cloudy from sleep. And sexy. Lord, did he look sexy. This was so unfair. She wanted her morning sex. "We have to get rid of them."

He raked a hand through his rumpled hair and yawned. "Okay."

"You'll have to jump out the window," she said.

"*Naked?* All my clothes are in the next room."

"Wear this." She tossed the sheet at him and rummaged through her bag for a pair of shorts and a top. She tugged her shorts on and wrestled the shirt over her head.

Matt cursed under his breath and climbed out of bed, wrapping the sheet around his waist. What a way to end one of the hottest nights of his life. "I am not jumping out a window."

"We can't let them see you."

Didn't he know it. He could just imagine it now. Yes, Mr. and Mrs. Douglas, I did violate your trust, and your daughter, who I don't happen to be in love with. Oh, and by the way, I have this favor to ask…

Talk about slitting your own throat.

"Take them outside and pretend you're looking for me," he said. "Tell them you think I'm down at the beach. While you're gone, I'll get dressed, head through the woods on the other side and circle around to the beach."

"I'm so sorry about this," she said, her eyes apologetic. "I didn't want our night to end this way."

Amen to that. "Just go distract them."

Emily paused by the door, then turned and pressed a quick kiss to his lips. "I'll make it up to you when they leave."

With a smile that promised she would live up to that statement, she slipped out the door. And all Matt could think about was getting rid of her parents. But not before he talked to them about the property. That was too important to put off. He had the entire weekend to lose himself in the wonders of Emily's body.

He pressed his ear to the door and listened, heard the anxious tone in her mother's voice and the disappointed edge to her father's, but he couldn't hear what was being said. A minute later he heard the screen door slam shut and figured the coast was clear. He slipped out of Emily's bedroom and into his own. He threw on some clothes, combed his fingers through his hair, and headed for the door. As he was reaching for the handle he heard voices, then Emily pulled the door open and stepped inside, followed by her parents.

He stood there, mouth hanging open, too surprised to speak.

"See, I told you I heard the door," Emily said to her mother, then turned to Matt. "We've been looking for you. How was your walk?"

"Great," he said, following her lead. "It was good."

"There you are, Matt," Mrs. Douglas said, looking distressed. "We were so worried about you. We got your message and you said it was urgent. We tried to call but you never returned our messages and your office said they couldn't reach you either. Then we couldn't get a hold of Emily. We thought something was wrong."

"Ty said you were coming here," Mr. Douglas said, an identical look of concern on his face. "We thought something had happened to one of you."

"And of course Emily refuses to carry a cellular phone," Emily's mother said, shooting her daughter a stern look, as if Emily not owning a phone was some sort of slight against her mother.

"I'm sorry to have alarmed you and made you drive all this way," Matt said. "The urgent issue I had with you was business-related."

"Oh, I'm so glad." Mrs. Douglas fanned herself dramatically, as if she might pass out with relief.

"What kind of business?" Mr. Douglas asked.

Emily took her parents by the arm and ushered them toward the door. "You've had such a long drive and it's so hot in the cottage. Why don't you two sit on the porch while Matt and I get some cool drinks together, then you can talk business."

When they were settled outside, Emily hooked an arm through Matt's and pulled him toward the kitchen. Her skin was damp and sweat beaded her brow. She said in a hushed tone, "Phew, that was close."

"Why did you bring them back? I barely had time to get dressed."

She opened the fridge and pulled out a pitcher of lemonade. She pressed it to her forehead, closed her eyes, and sighed. "We got halfway through the woods when I realized we'd left all our clothes on the dock. And probably a condom wrapper in the sand. I almost had a coronary."

Matt took four glasses down from the cupboard. He'd never even considered the mess they'd left. Thank goodness for Emily's quick thinking. "Sorry I caused all this trouble. When I called your parents I never imagined they would take my message so out of context."

"That's my mother, the drama queen. To hear her talk when we were walking down to the beach, you would have thought she was disappointed we were both intact and breathing." Emily dropped ice into the glasses and poured the lemonade, curious about the nature of this business Matt needed to discuss, and even more curious to know why he hadn't mentioned it to her. And maybe just a little hurt. "You never said anything to me about business with my parents."

He regarded her with a raised brow. "Would you have wanted me to talk about business this weekend?"

Good point. "You're right. It probably would have annoyed me." She picked up two glasses, and Matt took the remaining two. "Ready?"

"The sooner we get this over with, the sooner we'll be alone," Matt said, and the hungry look in his eyes made her heart lurch with anticipation.

They walked out to the porch and distributed the drinks, then took seats next to her parents.

"So, what kind of business do you need to discuss?" her father said, in his typical, no-nonsense way.

In that instant, Matt's demeanor changed. It was subtle, but unmistakable. He sat a little taller, his back straighter, and his expression was serious. This was the all-business Matt she'd wondered about. The one she'd had only a glimpse of at the restaurant the other day.

"I don't know if you've heard," Matt said. "Construction on the restaurant has been stopped."

Emily's mother let out a gasp. "But why?"

"There are certain people in town who don't want me building this restaurant. People in positions of power who have a grudge against me. They don't like that I've come back to town and they've fought the restaurant every step of the way. And this time they might have won."

Emily could see the passion in his eyes, and the hurt as he explained his dilemma with the square footage. Somehow it didn't surprise her. There were a lot of people who resented Matt's accomplishments.

She was ashamed to admit, she'd been one of those people.

"So you see," he concluded. "If I have to tear the restaurant down and rebuild, we would go way over budget and I could lose backing from my investors. They're already shaky."

"We could invest in the restaurant," Emily's father said, but Matt shook his head.

"I could never ask you to do that. It would be too risky."

"There has to be some way we can help you," Emily's mother said.

The business facade slipped and Emily could see a hint of desperation in Matt's eyes, and she suddenly understood how important this was to him. He needed to do this for the same reason she needed to build her shop.

"There's a simple way to solve this. You could sell me the vacant lot next to the restaurant."

Emily's parents exchanged looks, and she cringed inwardly. Matt was asking for something her parents just couldn't do. They had promised that property to her. And if it weren't the absolute perfect location for a flower shop, she might have sacrificed the property and built elsewhere. But Chapel already had two other flower shops, both on the opposite end of town.

This was the best spot for her. As a businessman, Matt would understand that.

Her mother leaned forward and patted Matt's knee. Here it comes, Emily thought. The big disappointment.

Her mother gave Matt a thousand-watt smile. "Of course we'll sell you the property."

For a full minute, Emily was too dumbfounded to form words. They must have forgotten they were saving the property for her. That was the only explanation. They wouldn't sell it out from under her. Not when she'd worked so hard for so long.

"We'll settle on a price and I'll have my attorney draw up the contracts," Matt was saying, to which her father readily agreed.

She had to put an end to this before it went too far. She cleared her throat and said, "Excuse me."

All eyes were suddenly on her.

"You can't sell the property to Matt. You promised to sell it to me. Remember?"

There was a moment of dead silence. A sick feeling of dread filled Emily's heart. They wouldn't. They wouldn't dare pick Matt over her. Their own daughter.

Her parents exchanged a look, then her mother turned to her and sighed. "Emily, honey, be reasonable. Where are you going to get the money for that property?"

"I've earned it. I've almost got it all. I just need another six months."

"Then how do you plan to pay for the building?"

"A business loan."

"Honey," her father reasoned in the same voice he would use with a temperamental child. "You have no collateral. No bank in their right mind would loan you money.''

A slap in the face couldn't have hurt any more. ''The property *is* the collateral. That's why I have to buy it outright.''

''Emily,'' her mother said in her ''be reasonable'' voice. ''Chapel doesn't need another flower shop. I think we've entertained this silly little idea of yours for long enough. Matt is a *real* businessman. He *needs* the property.''

''You promised,'' Emily said, her voice quivering. ''You said you would sell the property to me.''

''Soon you'll be married and having children. You won't have time to work. Then what will happen to your little shop?''

''Your mother is right, sweetheart. It's just not reasonable. You know nothing about the intricacies of running a business.''

She was almost too stunned to reply. ''I have a business degree. I've been running the nursery for three years now.''

''And isn't the nursery in danger of going bankrupt?'' her mother snapped.

With the accusation, Emily's heart cracked in two. What she should have realized long ago was now painfully clear. Her parents had no faith in her—no respect for her dreams whatsoever. They had never intended to sell her the property. They were only humoring her.

Nothing had changed. It had never been about what she wanted. Her entire life, all they had ever done was try to change her, to mold her into the kind of daughter *they* dreamed of having. And now they saw her as nothing more than a baby machine, put on this earth to give them grandchildren.

She felt completely and utterly defeated.

Tears burned behind her eyes. With trembling hands she set her lemonade down, stood on wobbly legs and walked into the cottage.

"Emily, wait," Matt called.

She continued on to her bedroom and began shoving her clothes into her duffel bag.

Matt appeared in her doorway. "Emily, I had no idea you wanted that property. You never said anything about a flower shop."

"You're right, I didn't."

"I need that property, Em. If I have to tear down the restaurant and rebuild somewhere different, I'll lose my investors. If I put up all of my own money, and it fails...I can't take that chance."

It all boiled down to money, and him not having enough of it. She zipped her bag shut and slung it over her shoulder. "Then you should be very happy. You got exactly what you wanted."

"There are other lots available."

"That's really not the point, is it?"

"I'll match whatever money you have saved. I'll pay the difference. You can have any property you want. I'll even have my attorneys handle the deal."

Even Matt didn't care about what she wanted. It was all about building his restaurant. All about money. The hollow ache in her chest grew larger, until she could barely breathe. "I'm going home."

She tried to walk past him but he stepped in the way. "Emily, you have to understand what this means to me."

It was always about what he wanted. About what everyone else wanted. It was never about her.

She looked down at the hand on her arm, then up to Matt's face. "I do understand, Conway. Some things never change."

"This is all my fault." Emily buried her face against Alex's work shirt. Tears rolled down her cheeks and she shook from the inside out. She thought she'd cried all she could over the weekend, but here she was Monday morning, still a blubbering mess. She'd cried more in the past three days than she had in her entire life.

"It's not your fault," Alex said, rubbing her back soothingly.

"It is," she insisted. "I should have put my foot down years ago. I should have made them take me seriously. Instead I came up with little deceptions to keep them placated. I did this to myself."

Alex plucked a tissue from her desk and pushed it into her hand. "And what does your millionaire have to say about all of this?"

Matt couldn't see the forest for the trees. He had become so obsessed with building this restaurant, nothing, not even her friendship would get in his way. And as much as that hurt her, she understood it in a weird way. She pitied him even. Matt was adrift—a lost soul looking for his place. Much as she was. No restaurant or business deal was going to fill the emptiness in his life.

Emily had spent most of the weekend at Alex's apartment, drowning in her misery. When she finally came home Sunday night, Matt had left a dozen messages on her answering machine. She'd erased them all without listening to a single one. She already knew what he would say, and she didn't want to hear again how much the restaurant meant to him.

"Matt will always be Matt," she told Alex now. "It will always be about making more money. About achieving more success. He'll never change."

"You're in love with him." It wasn't a question. It was a fact—one she couldn't deny.

"Maybe I am. Maybe we could have some sort of relationship, and for a while we might be happy. But eventually he would have to make a choice, and I already know what that choice would be. I'll never compromise myself for anyone again. From now on, it's about what I want."

"Your parents are damned lucky to have a daughter like you. If they can't see that, they're the ones with the problem."

Emily stepped up on her toes and pressed a kiss to Alex's cheek. "If you were straight, I'd ask you to marry me."

"And I'd say no. Because you're in love with someone else."

"Maybe it's a good thing Matt is buying the property," she said. "Without it he won't get his restaurant built, and we'd lose the account. Without the Touchdown account, the nursery would be history."

"You let me worry about the nursery for a while, okay?"

"After all that's happened, he may not want to work with me. He never signed a contract." She felt a rise of panic. She would never forgive herself if she were responsible for the demise of Marlette Landscape. She needed to secure the account. "What if he decided to take a bid from a different nursery?"

"That's not going to happen, Em."

"You don't know that."

"I think I do. From what I understand, Marlette was the only nursery bidding on the job."

Twelve

Matt stared blindly at his computer screen, unable to concentrate on a damned thing. He hadn't slept for days. His meticulously managed life was falling apart, yet the only thing he could think about, the only thing he *cared* about was that he'd hurt Emily deeply. He'd gone to her apartment four times Sunday, called and left messages begging to see her. And she'd ignored them all, making her feelings on the matter abundantly clear.

He'd lost. He hadn't even realized until then that this had been like a game to him. A challenge. Could he win Emily over? Could he make her bend to his will? Only when her parents offered him the property they were supposed to be saving for Emily did he realize the stakes. At first he'd actually thought he could reason with her, make her see that building his restaurant was the important thing. She could build her shop anywhere, couldn't she? But it wasn't about where or when or how much money it would cost. It was about faith and respect and loyalty.

None of which he'd shown her with any consistency.

In his life he'd never seen anyone look so defeated as Emily had when her parents had dismissed her dreams as silly then blamed her for Marlette Landscape's financial difficulties. He knew for a fact she was one hell of businesswoman—the glue that held the nursery together—yet he'd been so self-absorbed, so damned worried about building his restaurant that he hadn't come to her defense. And he hated himself for it.

He'd failed her. His betrayal was no less stinging than her parents'. He didn't deserve her friendship. But he'd give damn near anything to get it back. To get another chance.

There was a loud rap at his hotel-room door, then he heard Emily's voice.

"Matt, open up. I need to talk to you."

He jumped up so fast the chair he was sitting on tumbled over backward and crashed to the floor. He sprinted across the room, threw the deadbolt and swung the door open.

Emily stood in the hallway, dressed in her work clothes. She looked him up and down, frowned and said, "You look like hell."

He could have kissed her.

He dragged a hand across his beard stubble, through his tousled hair. Then he noticed the puffiness around her eyes and the joy at seeing her quickly dissolved. She'd been crying. Emily, who never cried, had been hurt that profoundly. By him.

Could this get any worse?

He held the door open for her. "Come on in."

"I can't stay long," she said, stepping inside and hovering near the door. "I just have to ask you a question."

"Okay."

"Is it true that there were no other nurseries bidding on the job?"

Just when he thought things couldn't get any worse. In her present state of mind, he knew she would misinterpret his motives. "Yes, it's true, but—"

Her eyes impaled him like two ice-blue daggers. "I would like nothing more than to tell you to take the account and shove it, Conway. I don't need your pity. But I have a responsibility to my employees."

"My hiring you has nothing to do with pity and everything to do with your competency. Yes, I knew you were having financial difficulties and the business would help, but I have a responsibility to my investors. If I didn't think you could handle the job, friend or not, I wouldn't even have considered you."

She narrowed her eyes at him. "That better be the truth."

He righted the chair on the floor and collapsed into it. "It's the truth, and it's a moot point now, seeing as how the restaurant may not be getting built."

"What are you talking about?"

"What do you mean, what am I talking about? Didn't you get my messages?"

She folded her arms across her chest. "I erased them all."

He laughed wearily and shook his head. Typical Emily. "The only solution I can find is to tear most of the building down and make it smaller, but my investors aren't real happy about it. It's pretty much a lost cause.''

''But you'll have the extra property. You won't need to tear it down.''

''See, if you'd listened to my messages you would already know, I'm not buying the property.''

Emily couldn't believe what she was hearing. ''What do you mean you're not buying it?''

''It belongs to you.''

''But you heard my parents. They don't want to sell it to me. Just buy it, Matt. Save your restaurant.''

''I can't do that. I don't want to do it. I already told them I'm not buying it. And I told them it was time they got their priorities straight. If they had any brains at all they would sell the property to you, as they promised. You're one hell of a good business-woman and it's time they saw that.''

''You actually *said* that?''

''Yep.''

''What did they say?''

A grin lifted the corner of his mouth and his dimple dented his cheek. ''They were too stunned to say much of anything. Your mom did a fair amount of sputtering though.''

She was feeling like sputtering herself. ''But you *have* to buy it. Marlette can't lose this account. We're barely hanging on as it is.''

Matt looked at her as if she had more than a few screws loose. ''What does it matter? You're going to be leaving. You'll have your shop to run.''

''Don't you see, without a job I'll never have the money to buy the property. I need six more months.''

"I'm sure you can work something out with your parents. Some kind of payment plan."

She felt torn in half. On the one hand, she wanted to build her flower shop, but to deny Matt the property, she would be pounding the final nail in Marlette's coffin. "Why, Matt? Why would you do this for me? Do you feel as if you owe me?"

He shook his head, rubbing his eyes with the heels of his palms. "How does it always come back to that?"

"If that's the case, forget about it. You didn't love me. I got over it."

He leaned forward, his eyes dark and turbulent, and her breath caught in her throat. "Emily, do you want to know why I stopped calling, why I never came home?"

She nodded.

"My whole life, all I wanted was to get away from here. I wanted a fresh start in a place where no one knew me. Where I wasn't the son of two worthless drunks. I would have amounted to nothing here. Then that night on the beach happened and suddenly I had these feelings for you."

"Y-you had feelings for me?"

He stood, shoving his chair back. "Yeah, I had feelings for you, and they scared the hell out of me. I started thinking crazy things, like maybe I didn't want to leave. But I knew if I didn't, I'd be throwing my future away. I knew I wasn't good enough for you."

"Why would you think that?"

"I had nothing. I *was* nothing. You deserved better than that. Better than *me*."

She opened her mouth to speak, but no sound came out. Tears welled in her eyes and her throat squeezed shut. That's when she knew, when it became so completely clear to her. She was in love with Matt. The revelation filled her with equal parts joy and sadness because they had no future.

Even if she could never tell him, never say the words, she could at least show him.

Emily threw her arms around Matt's neck, nearly knocking him off his feet. She pulled his head down, locked her mouth on his and kissed the daylights out of him. He didn't think he'd ever been kissed with more enthusiasm than he had by Emily. She put her heart and soul and, in this case, her whole body into it.

He wrapped his arms around her and hugged her close to him. She felt too good, too perfect there. So good, he could imagine never letting go—even if that meant making sacrifices he'd never thought he would be willing to make.

When she finally broke the kiss, her lips and chin were pink and abraded from three days' growth of beard stubble.

"Is that the bedroom over there?" Emily asked, gesturing toward the bedroom door. When he nodded, she grabbed the front of his shirt and pulled him toward it. "Let's go."

"Emily, I'm a mess. I need a shower, and I need to shave."

"The shower." She made a purring noise deep in her throat. "Even better."

How they'd gone from her wanting to kill him, to her wanting to jump him was a mystery. Not that he was complaining. He wanted to spend the rest of the afternoon losing himself in that wonderful body of hers. Then tonight, after he took her out for a nice dinner, he wanted to do it all over again. He had eleven years of wanting her to make up for. Eleven years of dreaming about touching her. Eleven years of looking at the women in his arms and wishing they were someone else.

Wishing they were Emily.

Emily backed them into the bathroom and switched on the light. She smiled when she saw her choices: an enormous Jacuzzi tub or a two-headed shower stall wide enough to fit four people. "This just keeps getting better."

"Your choice." He peeled his T-shirt over his head.

"Both." She unfastened his pants, shoved them and his boxers down his legs. "Shower first, bath second."

He pulled her shirt up over her head and, after some minor fumbling, unhooked the clasp on her bra. Her breasts were perfectly rounded and deeply tanned, her nipples small and dusty rose. And there it was, that enticing nipple ring. Memories of it, of taking it into his mouth, had tortured him for days. They had invaded his dreams, filling them with erotic images. For two nights running he'd awoken aroused and restless and missing her more than he should have. Plagued by a hunger, a thirst, that only Emily could quench.

He brushed a finger across her nipple ring and Emily sighed and closed her eyes. He unsnapped her shorts and as he slid them down her legs he dropped to his knees. All that was left now was a strappy little thong, but he didn't remove it. Instead he pressed his cheek into the softness of her belly, against her sweetly scented skin. He loved the way she smelled, the way she tasted. The way she looked at him, with so much honesty and admiration, as if he were the center of her universe. That scared the hell out of him. What if he let her down again? Suppose he wasn't good enough?

She wrapped her arms around his head and for a minute they simply held each other. He needed her so deeply, so completely, he felt torn up inside. As if his guts had been ripped out, kicked around, then thrown back in upside down. He wasn't used to feeling this for anyone. Not in a very long time. Not since that first night on the beach. It was awful and wonderful at the same time.

He turned his head and she gasped, and he realized how rough his face must have felt against her tender skin. He pulled away. "I should shave first. I don't want to hurt you."

She cupped his cheeks in her hands. "I like you this way," she said. "It's sexy and dangerous."

"You like things dangerous, huh?" He slid his hands up the tops of her thighs and dipped his thumbs underneath each edge of the thong. Emily watched, eyes glazed with desire, as he hooked his fingers under the elastic band and eased the underwear down her legs. The skin under that barely there strip of fabric was golden, the hair pale and downy and soft to the touch.

Perfect.

"Condoms," she said suddenly. "Tell me you have some."

"In the bedroom." He pulled himself to his feet, wincing a little at the pinch of pain in his knee. "You get the shower ready and I'll go get them."

Emily watched his tight backside as he walked out

of the room, then she opened the shower door and turned on the water. She adjusted the temperature, testing it with the inside of her wrist, then stepped under the steamy spray.

Matt stepped in behind her, carrying several condom packets. He set them on the soap dish. "Mission accomplished. The rest of the box is by the sink just in case."

Emily watched as hot water sluiced down his body, over tanned ripples of muscle. He threw his head back into the spray to wet his hair, looking as if he belonged on the pages of a *Playgirl* magazine. She had to wonder again what a man like him was doing with a woman like her. A woman whose breasts were a touch too small and whose hips were a tad too wide. Yet he looked at her with nothing but appreciation and astonishment.

And hunger.

With a single look he could devour her—like the look he was giving her right now.

She grabbed a bottle of shampoo and poured some into her palm. "Turn around. I'll wash your hair."

He turned and let his head fall back. She rubbed the shampoo into that thick, dark hair and built up a lather, massaging his scalp and scratching lightly with her nails.

"That feels good," he said, his voice low and thick. "No one has ever done this before."

She rubbed the base of his skull and around his ears. "You've never had your hair shampooed when you get a haircut?"

"I go to a barber. The same one for, oh, ten years I think."

"You're a loyal customer."

Matt shrugged. "He does a good job."

She patted his shoulder. "Rinse."

He dipped his head under the water, rinsing the suds from his hair. While he did that, she grabbed a bar of soap, building a thick lather in her hands.

He shook the excess water from his hair and drew a hand across his face. "Do I get to do yours now?"

"Soon. Turn and face the wall."

He lifted an inquisitive brow, but did as she asked, bracing his hands against the tile wall. "You're not going to do anything kinky, are you?"

She propped her chin on his shoulder, smoothing her soapy hands up his chest, and said in a teasing voice, "I'll try anything at least once. What did you have in mind?"

"If I had any blood left in my brain I could answer that question. But if you'll let me turn around, I can show you."

A shiver of anticipation danced up her spine. "Not yet."

She drew his nipples between her slippery fingers, pinching lightly. He sucked in a sharp breath. She lathered the silky hair under his arms and the wide breadth of his shoulders, astonished by the solid muscle there. Women all over the world lusted after this man and right now he was all hers. And in a few weeks they would go their separate ways again. She hoped that this time they could part as friends.

Just maybe, if he could stay in Michigan... If he could put her before his career...

She shook away the thought. If she wasn't careful she would ruin what time they did have together. She was going to be thankful for their limited time. She was going to savor each and every minute and store it in her memory.

And darn it, she thought as a wave of emotion choked her, she was *not* going to cry.

"When do I get to wash you?" Matt asked.

"Soon," she promised, hoping her voice didn't betray her emotions. She lathered his back and rubbed herself against him, grazing his soapy skin with the hardened points of her breasts. She ran both hands down his tight, perfectly formed backside, then lower, and felt him shudder.

"Em—"

"Shh." She slipped her hands around to his firm, flat stomach, then down into the coarse hair at his groin. She reached lower still, carefully cupping him and he groaned.

He let his head drop, his forehead resting against the wall. "You wouldn't believe how amazing that feels."

She explored gently, purposely avoiding the one place she knew he wanted to be touched the most until finally he'd had enough. At least she assumed so when he spun around and pinned her to the adjacent wall. She gasped as her back hit the cold tile and Matt's mouth came down hard on her own. His beard was rough against her face, his mouth hot. She wrapped her arms around his neck, arched up, riding intimately against the hard length of him.

"We need a condom," he groaned against her lips. Breaking the kiss, he grabbed one from the soap dish, tore the package open with his teeth and she watched as he rolled it on. He really was magnificent. Everything about him was so strong and male. And so *large*. He was big all over.

"I love this," he said, reaching up to toy with her nipple ring. Then he lowered his head and took it between his teeth, tugging. Suddenly her legs didn't want to hold her up anymore, but that was okay, because Matt lifted her right up off her feet. She wrapped her legs around his waist and framed his face in her hands, locking her eyes on his as he slowly entered her. Inch by wonderful inch he filled her, the transition smooth and effortless because she was so completely ready for him. And when he'd buried himself as deeply as he could go, he stopped and for a long moment they simply held each other. She knew from the look in his eyes he was thinking the exact same thing she was—they were a perfect fit. And not just physically. Mentally, intellectually, spiritually—they were undeniably compatible. Except for the teensy problem of him being obsessed with his work and living a couple of thousand miles away.

Again she began to feel that deep sadness, that emptiness when she imagined her life without him in it. Then Matt began to move, so tenderly, his eyes still locked on hers. It was so beautiful, so magical, tears filled her eyes. She wanted to stay like this all night, Matt's hard body pressed against her, the hot water sharp on her sensitized skin. Her body was already trembling, screaming for release.

"Oh, Em." He pressed his forehead to hers and she could feel him tensing, feel him fighting to hold back for her and that simple act of selflessness was her undoing. She shuddered in his arms, crying out as sweet ecstasy swept over her. When she thought for sure Matt was only seconds behind her, he didn't stop. He drove deep and steady inside her until she felt the pressure begin to build once more. She hovered on the edge, not quite ready to tumble over, then Matt lowered his head, took her nipple ring in his mouth…

They shattered together, their release fierce and intense. They remained wrapped in each other's arms for several minutes afterward, until Matt's knee began to burn from the extra weight, but damn, he didn't want to let go yet. Each time he made love to Emily it was more special, more out-of-this-world fantastic.

His legs began to shake and Emily lifted her head from his shoulder.

"Your knee hurts," she said, sliding from his arms. "Why don't we go lie down?"

"Uh-uh," he said grabbing a bar of soap. "First I get to wash you. Turn and face the wall."

She assumed the position, then looked back at him over her shoulder. "Are you going to do something kinky?"

"Hell, yeah." He slid his soapy hands all over her back and across her shoulders.

She let out a long contented breath and her head dropped forward. "That's nice."

"I'm just getting started." He slid lower, down the sweet curve of her behind, and when she was soapy enough, he pulled her against him. She let out a little gasp of surprise when she realized he was very ready for her again. He was just as surprised. He had no idea he possessed that level of stamina anymore.

She pressed her backside erotically against the length of him. The slippery heat, the bold gesture, nearly did him in. He covered her breasts with his soapy hands. Their soft fullness fitting perfectly in his palms. He massaged gently, squeezing her nipples as she'd done to him. She moaned and pressed herself even harder against him.

He washed lower, down her hips and stomach, then he slipped a hand between her thighs and she shuddered in his arms. He filled her with one finger and she writhed against him—one more and she moaned. She was slick and hot and so ready for him he knew he had to have her again. And as much as he wanted to make love to her right there in the shower, he knew his knee would never last under the strain.

''I was thinking it might be time to move this into the bedroom,'' he said.

''Yes,'' she agreed breathlessly. ''Let's go.''

Thirteen

— — —

They stepped out of the shower, grabbed the box of protection from the bathroom counter, and fell into bed soaking wet.

For a while they only kissed, which was okay with Matt because no one kissed like Emily. Then their hands began to wander, and soon their mouths joined in on the action. They touched and tasted each other in a manner that would make most women blush. But not Emily. She couldn't seem to get enough— enough of touching him or of being touched. And when just touching wasn't enough, she straddled him and drove him deep inside her body.

He lost track of exactly how many times they made love, but when they finally took a break, when he was too exhausted to do any more than lie there like a lump, she sat up, bright-eyed, her hair adorably messy and said, ''I'm starved. Want to go out and get a bite to eat?''

He looked up at her from his sprawled-out position on the rumpled sheets and thought, thank God for room service. Nothing short of a fire was going to get him out of this bed. ''There's a menu by the phone. Knock yourself out.''

She ordered sandwiches and beer, then sprawled out next to him while they waited for it to arrive. They didn't talk, just lay there quietly being together. He wondered what life would be like without this, and had a disturbing thought.

If the restaurant was no longer being built, he had no reason to stay in Michigan. It would be time to go back home soon.

He thought about returning to his life in L.A., and felt sick inside. What he had there wasn't a life. He'd never felt more alive, more complete, than these last few days with Emily. Where he belonged was in Chapel with her. *This* was home.

What he hadn't recognized before was so obvious to him now. No restaurant he could build, no business deal he could close would ever fill the void. What was missing from his life, what had been missing all these years, was her.

And he loved her. Deep down, he'd always known that, and he'd run from it.

It ended here. Today he stopped running.

''Emily, I—'' He was interrupted by a loud knock, and cursed whoever had the lousy timing to interrupt them at that precise moment. ''It's probably our room service. I'll just be a minute.''

He rolled out of bed and tugged a pair of jeans

on. There was another loud knock and he yelled, "Hold on."

He shut the bedroom door partway behind him and yanked the suite door open, but instead of room service, Ty strutted past him and into the suite.

"I've got it," Ty said, waving a manila envelope.

"Got what?"

"The report from the P.I. All the dirt I need on Emily's boyfriend."

Matt swore silently. "Maybe now's not the time—"

"He's cheating on her." Ty pulled a stack of photos from the envelope and shoved them into Matt's hands. Then added with obvious disgust, "With a *guy*."

Matt glanced down at the pictures in his hands and—*Whoa!*—promptly handed them back. "You can have those back now."

"You're off the hook. You can stop trying to seduce Emily now."

Matt cringed, praying Emily wasn't hearing every word they were saying. "Ty, it wasn't—"

"My parents and I can't thank you enough for helping us. When we show Emily these pictures, she won't have a choice but to leave the guy. I'm taking them to my parents right now."

"You're not taking those pictures anywhere."

They both turned to see Emily standing in the bedroom doorway, fully dressed. She had that look on her face, that barely contained fury that told him he was in worse trouble than he'd thought. Matt cursed under his breath.

Ty paled about four shades. "You might have mentioned my sister was here, Matt."

"If you had shut up for two seconds I would have."

"I have an idea. Why don't you both shut up." Emily walked over to her brother and held out her hand. He actually cringed, as if he thought she might deck him. "Give me the envelope."

"I'm so sorry, Em," Ty said, handing her the photos. "You'll get over him. He wasn't good enough for you. You've got Matt now."

"No, I don't," she said, glancing at Matt, icy venom in her eyes. She dumped the contents of the envelope out on the table. She stuffed the negatives in her pocket and began tearing the photos.

"Hey!" Ty shouted.

"I can't believe you paid a private investigator to follow Alex. You've done some really stupid things in your life, but this definitely tops them all." Emily dumped the shredded photos in a trash can. "Are these all the pictures?"

"That's all of them. But tearing them up isn't going to change the fact that he's cheating on you, Em. You have to break up with him."

"Ty, you are such an idiot. Alex isn't my boyfriend, nor has he ever been."

"But you said—"

"I never said anything. You guys just assumed, and I never denied it."

"But—"

"Go home, Ty. Matt and I need to talk. Then I'm going to go explain everything to Mom and Dad. You *will not* say a word about this until I've talked to them, understand?"

Ty nodded and shrank toward the door, obviously intimidated by her threatening tone. "Okay. But when you're done talking to Mom and Dad, you're going to explain a few things to me."

"Go," Emily said sternly, and her brother grudgingly left, flashing Matt a look of sympathy on his way out.

Matt shut the door and turned to Emily. Oh, man, he'd seen her mad before, but never like this. Her eyes had deepened to the steel-blue of his vintage '65 Mustang and he could swear he saw smoke coming out of her ears. "Give me a chance to explain."

"You know what my family is like, the way they try to control my life. And you were *helping* them? Pretending to be my friend so what, you could keep tabs on me for them?" She shook with anger. "You don't have to *seduce* me anymore? What is he, your pimp?"

"It wasn't like that, Emily." The words sounded lame, even to him. "I would have pursued you whether he put me up to it or not. I wouldn't have been able to stay away from you."

"I'm supposed to believe that?"

"I made a mistake. But your parents and Ty were really worried about you. They asked for my help. What was I supposed to tell them?"

"You could have told them no."

"How could I do that? If it wasn't for them, I wouldn't be where I am today. I owe them so much."

"Did it ever occur to you to *tell* me? Who were you protecting?"

"Your brother and your parents. And myself," he admitted, because to do otherwise would be a lie. "I was afraid you would be angry with me."

"Well, you were right, I'm angry."

"By helping them, I thought I was helping you."

"No, Matt, the only person you were trying to help was *you*. That's the way it's always been. I'm just sorry I didn't see it until now."

She turned to leave. He was losing her.

"Emily, wait! I know what it is. The thing that's missing from my life. I finally figured it out."

She stopped, her hand on the knob.

"It's *you*. You're the thing that makes me feel complete. I'm in love with you, Emily."

She stood very still for a long moment, then she turned to him, tears rolling down her cheeks. "The really sad thing is that I love you, too, Matt."

Then she was gone.

Matt stood in the empty lot next to Touchdown, watching the demolition team assemble.

"She'll cool down," someone said and he turned to see Ty standing behind him. "So this is it? You're just going to give up?"

Matt shrugged. "Not much choice. My investors all backed out and I can't take the risk of putting the money up myself. The weird thing is, all I can feel is relieved it's over. Building a restaurant here would have been a mistake. I knew it all along. I just wouldn't let myself see it."

"Matt, I wasn't talking about the restaurant."

Matt shoved his hands in his pockets. "I know what you were talking about."

"She'll come around."

"I don't think so. And honestly, I can't blame her if she hates me forever. I've done nothing but let her down since I've been back. I've screwed everything up."

"And every time you screw up, she forgives you. This is my fault, really. I shouldn't have stuck my nose in. I should have let nature take its course with you and Em."

"Nature? Do you mean you knew…"

"That something was going on with you two? Who didn't? You guys were attached at the hip since you were eight years old. Do you know how jealous I used to get? It was like you two had some secret club I wasn't invited into."

"We were just good friends," Matt said. Until the beach, anyway.

"When you left for college she was a wreck. I knew something happened between you. You made yourself pretty scarce for a long time and she spent way too much energy trying to pretend she didn't care. I must have asked her to come to California with me a dozen times, and she always said no. Getting you two back together was damn near impossible."

Matt could hardly believe what he was hearing. "Are you telling me you set this whole thing up?"

"More or less."

"What about the boyfriend? Was that just part of the plan?"

"No, that part was real. I didn't know they weren't really together. I just knew something about it wasn't right. She wasn't happy."

"And the part about him being into something illegal?" Matt asked.

Ty grinned. "Nah, I just made that up. You weren't looking like you were going to cooperate. I had to give you a good reason to want to help me."

Matt shook his head. "I fell for it."

"Yeah, you're pretty stupid that way. For all your success and your money, you had absolutely no direction. Those people you hang out with, the women you date—it's just not you. And Emily, man, she's just been a real pain in the rear since you left."

"Don't tell her that."

"Already did."

Matt raised an inquisitive brow. "What did you say exactly?"

"Everything that I'm telling you."

"And you walked away in one piece? How did you manage that? There's nothing she hates more than to have you and your parents messing with her life."

"I told her I did it because I was tired of seeing you both so unhappy. And I loved you both too much not to do something about it."

It wasn't often he and Ty displayed any kind of affection, and Matt found himself more than a little choked up. "What did Emily say?"

"She punched me in the stomach. Then she started crying and hugged me."

In the parking lot of Touchdown Matt heard a commotion and saw that the wrecking ball was in position. "This is it," he said.

"You're really going to let them do it? You're going to let them win?"

"It's not about winning or losing. The truth is, I don't care what anyone in this town thinks of me. I'm tired of trying to prove myself. I know what I've accomplished, and that's all that matters."

"What are you going to do next? Build another one somewhere else?"

He shook his head. "I don't think so. I'm thinking

of selling off the Touchdown chain. I've had a couple
of decent offers. I may take some time off. Decide
what I want to do next. But the thought of doing it
alone…'' He shook his head, unable to speak for all
the emotion backing up in his throat. He didn't want
to do it without Emily by his side.

Ty clasped a hand on Matt's shoulder. ''Give her
time. She'll come around.''

The foreman called out a warning to be sure the
area was secure, and Matt took one last look at the
building as the wrecking ball fell.

''How bad is it?'' Alex asked from his seat on the
corner of Emily's desk.

''Bad,'' Emily said. ''If we stretch it, we can make
it through to the end of the summer.''

Alex took a slug of his diet soda. ''Bummer.''

''Bummer?'' she repeated, barely able to contain
her frustration. If her hand wasn't still sore from
punching her brother, she would have broken Alex's
nose. ''I tell you we're going to have to close our
doors, putting our entire staff out of work, and all
you can say is *bummer?* I've been killing myself
trying to keep us in business.''

''And despite the odds you've done a valiant job.
Give it up, honey.''

''I can't believe you're being so flip about this.''

''And I can't believe you still care. Your parents
are selling you the property, you'll have your flower
shop soon.''

''Yeah,'' she said grudgingly.

''You don't sound too happy about it anymore.''

She should have been ecstatic. Her parents were
putting the property in her name next week on deliv-

ery of the first three-quarters of the money; the remaining amount to be paid in installments over the
next two years. They were *finally* taking her seriously. The bank was considering her application, but
had already said that with her impeccable credit and
sound business plan they didn't think she would have
any problems securing a business loan. She had everything she'd been working for, yet it held no satisfaction.

At first she'd blamed it on Conway. But after her
talk with Ty this morning, she was having a really
hard time holding on to her anger where he was concerned. Put in the identical position as Matt, she
couldn't say she wouldn't have reacted as he had.
The guy was loyal to a fault, though slightly mis-
guided. And while she would have appreciated it if
he'd told her the truth, she understood why he hadn't.
She wanted to hate him for what he'd done. But all
these sappy feelings of love kept mucking things up.

So if Matt wasn't the cause of her trepidation,
what was the problem? That's when she'd realized,
she wasn't unhappy about having a flower shop. She
was unhappy about leaving Marlette. As stressful and
crazy and frustrating as it could be at times, she
loved her job. She worked nutty hours, not just for
the money, but because she took so much pride in
keeping the nursery on its feet. She was happy there,
and even if she wouldn't be the one at the helm, she
didn't want to leave until she knew they would open
their doors for another season.

And Alex didn't seem to give a damn.

"Think big," Alex said, leaning closer. "If you
could have anything in the world, *any* job, what
would it be?"

She said without pause, "I would want a nursery like Marlette."

"Suppose you had a chance to buy Marlette? Would you?"

She could only dream it. It was completely out of her financial realm of comprehension. "I could never afford it. And even if I could, I'd be out of business before I started. We just don't have the clientele we used to."

"Suppose you had enough contracts lined up to keep you in business?"

"Alex, we both know that we've lost practically every bid this year. There are no guarantees."

"What if there were?"

He was leading her somewhere, and she wanted to know what he had up his sleeve. "Okay, what's the deal? What are you getting at? Do you know something about the lost bids?"

Alex grinned down at her. "Think about it, Em. How do you suppose I knew your millionaire didn't go to any other nursery. Who had access to all that information in those bids we lost?"

"It was you?" she asked, feeling as if she'd been poleaxed. "You were the one leaking the information?"

"I can't believe you didn't figure it out before this."

The betrayal she felt was so stark, so deep, she was numb with it. "Why would you do it? I worked so hard—"

"A business is always a better buy when it's about to go under. My mother is fed up and she wants to sell. You'll get it for a steal."

"Me?"

"Yes, *you*. You're going to buy Marlette."

"Are you telling me that you deliberately almost bankrupted the business just so *I* could afford to buy it?"

"I told you, I'm not as incompetent as you think."

"Are you nuts?" Emily could barely comprehend what he was telling her. And she couldn't believe he would do that for her. Marlette was his livelihood. His legacy. "What will you do? Where will you work?"

"Anywhere else. I've hated this God-awful business since the day my mother bought it. The only thing that kept me here this long is you and your passion for keeping it going. But I've had enough. I'm ready to move on."

She didn't know what to say. She couldn't even believe it was real. "But, is that fair to your mother?"

"My father left her a fortune when he died. She's not going to be hurting for money."

"But, what about clients?"

"I've got a dozen new clients contracted for the spring," he said. "So, what do ya' say?"

"Yes," she said, but it came out more like a squeal. She covered her mouth to contain a bubble of laughter. "Yes, I'll buy it."

"I'll let my mother know and get the ball rolling."

She was going to own Marlette Landscape. It could be Douglas Landscape or anything else she wanted to call it. It would be all hers. She could barely suppress her excitement. Her office walls were the only thing keeping her from going in a dozen directions at once. She could hardly wait to tell Matt—

And just like that, her bubble burst. She wouldn't be seeing Matt again. Not even as friends. It would be too hard, hurt too much. She'd already decided it would be best for them both if they cut all ties. Even if she could forgive Matt, which she was sure she could, they would never have any kind of life together. She had a business tying her to Chapel and he had a life—superficial as it was—in California. Business would forever dominate his time, and she would always feel as if she were in second place. She was finished compromising herself. For once in her life, she wanted to be number one.

There was no point in dwelling on it any longer. She had a nursery to run. From this day forward, Matt was out of her life.

"I'll have to call my parents, tell them I won't be needing the property—" She gasped and shoved herself up from her chair. "Oh, no!"

"What?" Alex shouted, nearly falling off the edge of her desk. "What's wrong?"

"I don't need the property. Oh my God, what time is it?"

Alex checked his watch. "Three-fifteen."

She fumbled in the file cabinet for her purse. "I have to hurry. I have to stop them."

"Stop who?"

"The demolition crew! They're going to tear it down today. Matt can buy the property!" She found her purse and rummaged through it. "Oh, where are my keys?"

Alex hopped off her desk and yanked his keys out of his pocket. "I have no idea what you're talking about, but it sounds exciting. I'll drive you there."

Fourteen

———

She was too late.

By the time she got there, Touchdown was gone. The only thing left was an enormous pile of rubble. And even that was fast disappearing as a crew dumped the remains in enormous trucks to be hauled away.

"That's one big heap of garbage," Alex said, shaking his head. "What a waste."

"You missed the show."

Emily turned to see Ty walking up behind them. "When did they do it?"

"Noon."

"How is Matt taking it?"

"Why don't you ask him yourself? He's at his hotel packing."

Emily squelched the sudden rush of panic rising

up in her at the thought of Matt leaving Chapel forever.

It's over, she reminded herself yet again. He couldn't stay and she couldn't go with him. It was hopeless.

Ty nodded to Alex. "How's it going?"

Alex returned the nod, adding a touch of flair. "It's been better, and you?"

"You know," Ty said with a shrug, then added, "So, you're gay?"

Alex's brow quirked up with surprise at the blatant question. "Why, you interested?"

Ty's eyes widened and he took a step away. Emily had to bite her lip not laugh.

Alex rolled his eyes. "A homophobe. Great. Don't worry, fly boy, my heart belongs to another."

"Behave," Emily said, and turned to her brother. "When is he leaving?"

"When is who leaving?"

"*Matt.*"

Ty frowned. "Matt's not leaving."

"But you said he was packing."

"He is packing, to move into his rental house."

Emily suddenly felt dizzy, as if the world had shifted on its axis. "Rental house?"

"I found him a place this afternoon. He's decided to stay in Michigan for a while."

It doesn't mean anything, she told herself. Not a single thing. He would leave eventually. He had a business to run. A life in California.

When she didn't acknowledge him, Ty added, "He's even talking about selling the Touchdown chain and taking some time off."

"Oh." She tried to swallow, but all the moisture in her mouth had evaporated.

"Is that all you can say? *'Oh.'*"

Right now, she couldn't say anything. Her heart was beating way too hard and fast for her to think straight.

"It's been five days," Ty said, draping an arm over her shoulder. "Don't you think you've tortured the guy enough? He wants a reason to stay. He loves you for cripes sake."

"But what if he decides to go back? What then?"

Ty shrugged. "You'll work it out."

"Though it pains me to say it, I'm afraid I have to agree with your brother," Alex said. "At least go talk to him."

Matt might not be going back to Los Angeles. He might be selling his restaurants. He'd told her he loved her, that she was what was missing in his life.

Could the message be any clearer?

"Alex," she said. "I need your keys."

Matt dropped his bags in the doorway and looked around the foyer of his rental house. Rental cars, rental houses—he really needed to get some permanence in his life. Tomorrow he would go out and buy a car. And if anyone gave him a reason to stay in Michigan permanently, he might look into having a house built. Something that *wasn't* a mansion.

But as rental houses went, this one wasn't too bad. When his furniture arrived, it would be downright livable.

"Kind of small, isn't it?"

Matt spun around and almost tripped over his luggage. His heart did an end-to-end flip when he saw

Emily in the doorway, a potted fern hanging from each hand.

"You think it's too small?" he asked, following her gaze up the vaulted ceiling in the great room, over the stone fireplace and slate mantel and beyond to the formal dining room.

She took a few steps in, looking around. "Are you kidding, I have closets bigger than this."

A twenty-two-hundred-square-foot closet? Even he didn't have one *that* big. He nodded to the ferns. "Friends of yours?"

"Oh." She looked down, as if she'd forgotten she was holding them. "These are for you. I heard you might be in town for a while and thought you might like the company. You know, someone to talk to."

She was fishing, big-time. Pumping him for information. Let her sweat a little, he decided. God knows she'd made him sweat his share this past week. "Thanks. They'll look great in the kitchen." He took them from her, his fingers brushing hers in the process. It was all he could do not to drag her into his arms and never let go.

He set the plants on the brick floor leading into the kitchen. "I heard from Ty that you talked with your parents. How did that go?"

"As well as can be expected, I guess. I've promised to be honest with them and they've promised not to nitpick and stick their noses in where they don't belong. It may take some time, but I think they're coming around." She took a few more steps in, wedging her hands into her shorts pockets. "It's really beige in here, huh?"

"Yeah, rentals are funny that way. I figure I won't

be here long enough to paint, though, so I'd better get used to it. I only have a three-month lease.''

That wasn't what she wanted to hear, though she was trying damned hard not to let her disappointment show. She took a step back toward the door. ''So, you'll be going back to California?''

''Maybe, maybe not. It just depends on whether or not I have a good reason to stay.''

''Like…a job?''

''Maybe.''

She nodded, looking thoughtful. ''I hear they're hiring at the Dairy-O on Main Street.''

''Really. Sounds…challenging.''

''Of course, that's only seasonal. They shut down during winter.''

Grinning, Matt took a couple of steps toward her. ''I was thinking of something a little more permanent than that. Something with an emotional attachment.''

She took a few steps in his direction, her brow crinkled in thought, then she brightened. ''I know. You could get a dog. Or a cat.''

''I could do that.'' He closed the last few spaces between them, and gently pulled her to him. She just about melted into his arms. She smelled so good and felt so right, he didn't know how could have missed it before. ''Or, I could get a wife.''

Head against his chest, she nodded. ''You could get one of those.''

''And maybe a couple of kids?''

She looked up at him, eyes narrowed. ''I don't know about that.''

''Not necessarily right away,'' he added.

''So there's no confusion here, you are talking

about us, right? Because I'm going to feel really stupid if some supermodel pops out of the kitchen.''

He couldn't stop the goofy grin from spreading over his face. He'd be damned if this wasn't exactly where he wanted to be. "I'm definitely talking about us.''

"What about L.A.?''

"California just isn't where I want to be anymore. I don't know if it ever was. Everything I could want—have *ever* wanted—is right here, in Chapel.''

"I thought you hated it here.''

"So did I. But it's who I am, and I realized, you can't run from who you are. I'm staying, and if there's anyone who doesn't like that, it's too damned bad.''

She squeezed him harder and sighed. "You should know, I have a career to think about. You're looking at the future owner of Marlette Landscape.''

There was no mistaking the satisfaction in her eyes, or his own feelings of pride. "Congratulations.''

"I'll be really busy, so don't get any ideas about keeping me barefoot and pregnant.''

"If we did—have kids I mean—maybe I could stay at home with them part of the time.''

Her brow crinkled. "You? What about work?''

"In another couple of weeks Touchdown is going to belong to someone else. We're negotiating the contracts right now. I figured it was time I tried something different. Something a little less demanding on my time. I've got all this money, I might as well enjoy it. Right?''

"What would you like to do?''

"I've been thinking about that a lot. I got a degree

in physical education as a fallback, and I hear the coach over at the high school is talking about retiring. I've really missed the game, so I thought, what the heck, I could apply for the position.''

"A high-school football coach?''

He frowned. "You don't think so?''

"No, I think you'd be a great coach. You'll be good at whatever you choose to do because that's the kind of man you are.''

He hoped he was good enough for Emily. Good enough to keep her happy. This was all new to him. He didn't want to screw it up. "I can't promise that I won't say or do something dumb and hurt your feelings every now and then, even if I don't mean to. I'm going to make mistakes, Emily.''

"And I can't promise that I won't lock you out of the bedroom and make you sleep on the couch for a day or two. But I'll forgive you eventually.'' She looked up at him, his entire future shining in the blue of her eyes. "I'll always forgive you, because I love you, Matt.''

"I love you, too, Em.''

He couldn't hold back any longer. He cupped the back of her neck with one hand, nudged her chin up with the other, and proceeded to kiss her socks off.

This is it, he thought as he savored the sweetness of her mouth, the silky softness of her hair in his fingers. This was his for the rest of his life. He'd finally found it, that feeling of utter contentment he'd been searching for.

Hard to believe, it had been waiting for him all this time, right in Emily's arms.

*   *   *   *   *

1205/51a

SILHOUETTE®

Desire™ 2 in 1

Dynasties: The Ashtons

ENTANGLED by Eileen Wilks

Dixie McCord and Cole Ashton's summer affair had ended when he put business before love, but now Dixie was coming back to the Napa Valley and Cole had plans to seduce her again!

A RARE SENSATION by Kathie DeNosky

Abby came to the Louret Vineyards to find the family she'd never known, but Russ Gannon began taking up her time instead. What could a brawny man-of-the-land offer a virgin socialite like her?

❧

THE WEDDING IN WHITE
by Diana Palmer

Handsome owner of a huge ranch, Mack Killian didn't waste words and he and virgin teacher Natalie Brock had something special. He branded her his with a kiss and waited for the sleeping beauty to awaken to her needs...

CIRCLE OF GOLD by Diana Palmer

Sparks flew the minute Kasie Mayfield arrived at Gill Callister's home to take care of his two adorable daughters. Before long the young innocent was in love, but how did the enigmatic widower feel?

On sale from 16th December 2005

Available at most branches of WHSmith, Tesco, ASDA, Borders, Eason, Sainsbury's and most bookshops

Visit our website at www.silhouette.co.uk

SILHOUETTE®
Desire 2 in 1

1205/51b

COWBOY'S MILLION-DOLLAR SECRET
by Emilie Rose

One lucky bachelor was about to become a millionaire. But was hard-muscled, smoulderingly sexy Patrick Lander going to believe Leanna's interest in him was genuine when she told him the news?

LIKE A HURRICANE
by Roxanne St. Claire

Quinn McGrath knew he'd met 'the one', but although she'd literally fallen into his arms, she seemed to view him as 'the enemy', who was out to destroy her dream. Could he persuade her that her dream could become his, too?

Men of Courage

RESCUE ME! by Elda Minger

Jennifer Whitney's luck is in when action hero actor Cody Roberts rescues her from an armed robbery. She's shaken, yet drawn to Cody's warmth and strength—it's little wonder they spend hours making love, reaffirming life. But when morning comes…what next?

THE ELEVENTH HOUR
by Wendy Etherington

Smoke jumper Steve Kimball returns to work after a friend's death with a wildfire threatening a small California town. The last thing he needs is to run into former love Laine Sheehan. He thought they were over, but the sparks are brighter than ever…

On sale from 16th December 2005

Available at most branches of WHSmith, Tesco, ASDA, Borders, Eason, Sainsbury's and most bookshops

Visit our website at www.silhouette.co.uk

0106/SH/LC130

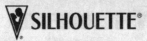

*A family built on lies...Brought together
by dark, passionate secrets.*

January 2006 **Entangled** *by Eileen Wilks*
A Rare Sensation *by Kathie DeNosky*

March 2006 **Society-Page Seduction** *by Maureen Child*
Just a Taste *by Bronwyn Jameson*

May 2006 **Awaken the Senses** *by Nalini Singh*
Estate Affair *by Sara Orwig*

July 2006 **Betrayed Birthright** *by Sheri WhiteFeather*
Mistaken for a Mistress *by Kristi Gold*

September 2006 **Condition of Marriage** *by Emilie Rose*
The Highest Bidder *by Roxanne St. Claire*

November 2006 **Savour the Seduction** *by Laura Wright*
Name Your Price *by Barbara McCauley*

**Visit the Napa Valley in California and
watch the struggle, scandal and seduction.**

*Available at most branches of WHSmith, Tesco,
ASDA, Borders, Eason, Sainsbury's and most bookshops*

Visit our website at www.silhouette.co.uk

0106/SH/LC131

SILHOUETTE®

SPECIAL EDITION™

presents

Summer Affairs

*the latest four-book series from New York Times
bestselling author of over seventy-five books,*

SHERRYL WOODS

**The four D'Angelo sisters find love
when they go back home for the summer.**

THREE DOWN THE AISLE - January 2006

WHAT'S COOKING? - March 2006

THE LAWS OF ATTRACTION - May 2006

FOR THE LOVE OF PETE - July 2006

*Available at most branches of WHSmith, Tesco,
ASDA, Borders, Eason, Sainsbury's and most bookshops*

Visit our website at www.silhouette.co.uk

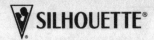

♥ SILHOUETTE®

SPECIAL EDITION™

THREE DOWN THE AISLE
by Sherryl Woods

Summer Affairs

Stunned when a romance blows up in her face, Melanie D'Angelo reluctantly takes refuge in her grandmother's cottage. But when local landscaper Mike Mikelewski arrives with his daughter to fix her grandmother's garden, Melanie's heart is on the mend as well!

HOT AUGUST NIGHTS
by Christine Flynn

The Kendricks

After CEO Matt Callaway and Ashley Kendrick shared a steamy one-night stand, the fear of scandal had separated them. Ashley had never forgotten the way Matt made her feel, but how long could she keep their unborn child a secret…?

IN A TEXAS MINUTE
by Stella Bagwell

Fortune's Heirs: Reunion

When Sierra was left with an abandoned baby, she turned to her closest friend, Alex Calloway. While taking care of the infant, Sierra and Alex's relationship went from platonic to passionate. What prevented them from becoming a family?

On sale from 16th December 2005

Available at most branches of WHSmith, Tesco, ASDA, Borders, Eason, Sainsbury's and most bookshops

· *Visit our website at www.silhouette.co.uk*

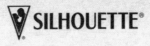

SILHOUETTE®

1205/23b

SPECIAL EDITION™

Where You Least Expect It
by Tori Carrington

No one in Old Orchard knew that teacher Aidan
Kendall was a man on the run. Aidan hadn't intended
to stay in the small town…until he met Penelope Moon.
The mystical beauty made Aidan believe in magic and
miracles. But would their love survive when the danger
on his heels caught up with him?

A KISS IN THE MOONLIGHT
by Laurie Paige

Seven Devils

Lyric Gibson knew she loved blue-eyed rancher
Trevor Dalton and, when she found three orphans in
need, she required Trevor's help—and a marriage of
convenience—to save them. She was determined to win
back his trust…Could his heart be far behind?

A FATHER'S FORTUNE
by Shirley Hailstock

When tough, rugged carpenter Digger Clayton and
nursery school teacher Erin Taylor met, it could have
been happy ever after but for one thing—Erin would love
to have a family of her own and Digger had already lost
one. Was their attraction strong enough to drive the hurt
away?

Don't miss out!
On sale from 16th December 2005

*Available at most branches of WHSmith, Tesco, ASDA,
Borders, Eason, Sainsbury's and most bookshops*

Visit our website at www.silhouette.co.uk

1205/05a

MILLS & BOON

Live the emotion

His Virgin Lover

These powerful men are helpless to resist a virgin mistress.

In January 2006, By Request brings back three favourite romances by our bestselling Mills & Boon authors:

Mistress on Loan by Sara Craven
The Mistress Deal by Sandra Field
A Passionate Proposition by Susan Napier

Make sure you buy these passionate stories!

On sale 6th January 2006

Available at most branches of WHSmith, Tesco, ASDA, Borders, Eason, Sainsbury's and most bookshops

Visit www.millsandboon.co.uk

MILLS & BOON®

Live the emotion

1205/05b

Outback Desire

*It's hot,
passionate and
half the
world away!*

In January 2006, By Request brings back
three favourite romances by our bestselling
Mills & Boon authors:

Outback Heat by Emma Darcy
The Outback Nurse by Carol Marinelli
Outback Fire by Margaret Way

**Make sure you buy these
irresistible stories!**

On sale 6th January 2006

*Available at most branches of WHSmith, Tesco, ASDA,
Borders, Eason, Sainsbury's and most bookshops*

www.millsandboon.co.uk

0106/055/MB004

Indulge yourself with

THE
Passion
COLLECTION

which includes a seductive classic by
top-selling Modern Romance™ author
Miranda Lee and two brand new
Silhouette Desire™ novels.

On sale 16th December 2005

*Available at most branches of WHSmith, Tesco,
ASDA, Borders, Eason, Sainsbury's and most bookshops*

Visit our website at www.millsandboon.co.uk

0106/108/MB001

Reality TV,
real love...and no commercials...

Surviving Sarah *by Vicki Lewis Thompson*
Luke Richards has entered a battle-of-the-brawn reality
TV show for one reason: he wants the "prize" —
Sarah Donovan!

The Great Chase *by Julie Elizabeth Leto*
When rival private investigators Charlotte and Sam partner
for a cross-country reality show, Charlotte can't help
wondering if working together might not be a lot more
fun after all.

The Last Virgin *by Jennifer LaBrecque*
Andrea signs up for a singles show and discovers her
virginity is up for grabs. Contestant Zach is determined to
prove reality TV isn't real at all, but he doesn't count on
wanting to claim the winner's prize so much!

On sale 6th January 2006

*Available at most branches of WHSmith, Tesco,
ASDA, Borders, Eason, Sainsbury's and most bookshops*

Visit our website at www.millsandboon.co.uk

FREE!

2 Books
and a surprise gift!

We would like to take this opportunity to thank you for reading this Silhouette® book by offering you the chance to take TWO more specially selected titles from the Desire™ series absolutely FREE! We're also making this offer to introduce you to the benefits of the Reader Service™—

- ★ **FREE home delivery**
- ★ **FREE gifts and competitions**
- ★ **FREE monthly Newsletter**
- ★ **Exclusive Reader Service offers**
- ★ **Books available before they're in the shops**

Accepting these FREE books and gift places you under no obligation to buy, you may cancel at any time, even after receiving your free shipment. Simply complete your details below and return the entire page to the address below. You don't even need a stamp!

YES! Please send me 2 free Desire books and a surprise gift. I understand that unless you hear from me, I will receive 3 superb new titles every month for just £4.99 each, postage and packing free. I am under no obligation to purchase any books and may cancel my subscription at any time. The free books and gift will be mine to keep in any case.

D5ZEF

Ms/Mrs/Miss/Mr ....Initials ....

BLOCK CAPITALS PLEASE

Surname ....

Address ....

....

....Postcode ....

Send this whole page to:
UK: FREEPOST CN81, Croydon, CR9 3WZ

Offer valid in UK only and is not available to current Reader service subscribers to this series. Overseas and Eire please write for details. We reserve the right to refuse an application and applicants must be aged 18 years or over. Only one application per household. Terms and prices subject to change without notice. Offer expires 31st March 2006. As a result of this application, you may receive offers from Harlequin Mills & Boon and other carefully selected companies. If you would prefer not to share in this opportunity please write to The Data Manager, PO Box 676, Richmond. TW9 IWU.

Silhouette® is a registered trademark owned and used under licence.
Desire™ is being used as a trademark. The Reader Service™ is being used as a trademark.